Nothin' Left To Lose

NOTHIN' LEFT TO LOSE

by Carl T. Smith

For Marge Stallings,
   I hope you enjoy John Ryon
Stone and the music of the book.
         My Best,
         Carl T. Smith
         2/17/2000

SUMMERHOUSE
COLUMBIA, SOUTH CAROLINA

Published in Columbia, South Carolina
by Summerhouse Press

Summerhouse Press
P.O. Box 1492
Columbia, SC 29202
(803) 779-0870
(803) 779-9336 fax

Grateful acknowledgment is made to the following:
"Ring of Fire"
Words and Music by Merle Kilgore and June Carter
Copyright ©1962, 1963 Painted Desert Music Corporation, New York
Copyright Remewed
International Copyright Secured All Rights Reserved
Used by Permission

"AMANDA"
Written by Bob McDill
Copyright © 1972 Songs of Polygram International, Inc.
and Bob McDill Music
Used by Permission. All Rights Reserved.

Library of Congress Cataloging-in-Publication Data

Smith, Carl T., 1937-
    Nothin' left to lose / by Carl T. Smith.
        p.   cm.
    ISBN 1-887714-47-2 (hardcover)
    I. Title.
PS3569.M5127N68   1999
813'.54--dc21   99-30233
                                                                         CIP

Dedication

For Archer Lee

*who nurtured an idea,
but maybe that's not the most important thing.*

Acknowledgments

To Bernard Martin for standing strong over many years with encouragement.

To George Anastasia for an idea and the encouragement to pursue it.

To Daryl Hayden, who was always willing to read and point out the best and the worst.

To Brewster Robertson for mentoring me through the whole process and answering panicked calls.

To Charlotte Hughes for telling me the tricks of the trade and encouraging me.

To Tom Robbins for proving it could be done and being the self-confessed world's worst pen pal.

To Catherine Spencer for support, advice and a wealth of friendship.

To Les Standiford, a mentor who remains a golfing idol of mine.

To Pat Conroy for inspiration and providing an ideal to work toward.

And to Robin Asbury, my publisher, who wasn't sure and gave me the challenge of making her sure.

———•—•———

In Loving Memory

Scott Edward Jones Smith
September 11, 1967–June 14, 1999

The Law of Possibility is always present;
The Law of Probability ain't so certain.
—An American Songwriter

———————

Look in the mirror in total surprise;
at the hair on my shoulders
and the age in my eyes.
—"Amanda" by Bob McGill

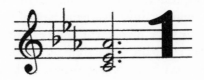

NASHVILLE
1968

"It's gonna be a good day. I can feel it creepin' up in my bones," Don Hendrickson said with his customary smile.

"What makes you say that?" his wife asked.

"Because it's what I say and feel every day. No need to feel any different. Hell, I got a pulse; that's a good sign."

Sylvia Hendrickson smiled. She loved the man deeply, and a good part of that was this attitude. It was present the first time she met him. Working his way up from performer to Nashville vice-president of the music division of Trayhorn International had not been easy, but he had smiled all the way.

They were having breakfast on the patio of their home overlooking the lake in Hendersonville, Tennessee. The patio was laid with fieldstone from an old slave fence that encircled a portion of the property when he purchased it. A small reflecting pool had been put in over the winter, and he started having breakfast outside long before the weather warranted it. Now the weather was more than comfortable; it was exquisite. In another month it would be too hot for Sylvia, but he would continue to take his breakfast in the fresh morning air. It was the only quiet time he had each day, and they reveled in this early morning interlude; it was calm and placid, and it was theirs alone.

At seven o'clock sharp he left for his office on Music Row, as he did every day. Although the business of creating music was his life and he loved it, there was a small regret at leaving Sylvia each morning, even after twenty-three years. She had been his staff of light and hope through all of the travails that success in his profession required.

Every day was busy at the offices of Trayhorn International, but the day he was facing would be a test of endurance. He resented days when the music business interrupted the business of music. Today, he was going to be a tour guide.

Jamie Greshem was coming in from New York at nine-thirty. He could deal with Jamie; that was not in question even though he hardly knew him. It was his daddy, the president of Trayhorn, Bernie Greshem, that concerned him. Bernie could be difficult in the best of times, and these were not the best of times. A huge investment and perhaps some portion of the reputation of the entire company was resting on the debut of a new, offbeat television sitcom based on four singing sisters, each with a different and humorously fractured personality.

In choosing the leads for the series, personality and appearance had been the primary concern. Only after four unknowns were cast was it discovered they couldn't sing. Rumblings of an immense failure permeated the industry, which was ever ready to gloat at someone else's monetary misfortune.

When Bernie called to tell him that his son was coming to Nashville, it was obvious to Hendrickson that he was disturbed. He had been in the business long enough to sense that Bernie was feeling pressured, and he suspected where the pressure was coming from. Greshem, early on and out of necessity, had aligned himself with some tough elements in Philadelphia and New York, the kind of people who concerned themselves only with money. Those same elements existed in Nashville but on a much smaller, almost amateurish scale. Their influence would grow; of that Don Hendrickson was certain. It was only a matter of time before Nashville would lose its innocence. When it happened, it would be a bitter blow.

To him Nashville was the city of adventure. When you woke up in the morning, you never knew what was going to happen by sundown. It was a comfortable and beautiful city built and sustained on music by the less than reliable individuals who made it. There were a lot of good-time places for drinking and working, some for tourists, some for insiders.

Residential neighborhoods awakened each morning with been-theres, wannabes, and even well-established stars having guitar pulls, playing new songs, auditioning for each other, seeing what they could steal and how many pills they could take or how much booze they could drink before the lights went out. Later, they would remember they had written a vague, good song the night before, but no one could recall what it was. That was enough reason alone to start the party all over again.

Downtown Nashville was a carnival, day and night. Linebaugh's was no more than a greasy spoon, but it catered to Nashville's elite with its split hot dogs served on a hamburger bun. Weekends were centered around Ryman

Auditorium, home of The Grand Ole Opry. The sidewalks bulged with crowds circulating from the Ryman to Tootsie's Orchid Lounge or The Wagon Wheel. And, of course, there was always Printer's Alley, two blocks of strip joints and clubs where you could get or hear anything you wanted.

Hendrickson played the whole city in his mind every day as he made the drive in from the lake. Pulling into an open parking space near his office, he thought about Jamie Gresham and decided to play it by ear and let the day run its course wherever it might lead.

John Ryan Stone had just finished his night shift sweeping out the studio adjacent to the Trayhorn offices and was leaving the building when Hendrickson got out of his Lincoln. The two men had seen each other coming and going often enough. Occasionally they engaged in brief conversation but nothing of any consequence.

Stone was tall and lanky, probably from little or no diet. He was a Nashville riddle, one among many—educated, former military officer and teacher and totally unsuccessful as a songwriter. No one had recorded any of his songs, and the slouch in his walk advertised that fact.

As Hendrickson closed the door of his car, he noticed the young man coming toward him, and couldn't help wondering how long he would last; he knew it had been three years already. 'Bout average, he thought. He liked John Ryan though he hardly knew him. Stone had presence and intelligence, though he hid it. Hendrickson had a feeling about Stone—he wasn't sure what it was—but he had learned long ago not to ignore feelings in this business.

"Mornin', John Ryan. Haven't seen you in a month of Sundays. Thought maybe you had packed it in," he said as he approached.

"I been here." Stone smiled, his voice whiskey rough and tired.

"Still writin'?" he asked, appraising the slender songwriter.

"Still tryin'."

"When you gonna let me hear somethin'? I hear a lotta good things about you, but you've never brought any of your stuff in."

"Someday," John Ryan said, "When I get something good."

"Maybe your stuff's too good. Hell, we're drownin' in a world of 'Rascals', Paul Revere's', and Beatles. Maybe you ought to write some crap." He paused. "On second thought, don't ever write crap. I get so frustrated when I see what's out there sellin' today. Half the groups don't even exist until the record's a hit. Then they hire a bunch of kids to front it. It's disgusting."

John Ryan laughed. "If I paid any attention I'd probably be disgusted too."

"You're smart not to pay attention. Hey, Mickey Shackleford says you got some great songs."

13

"Well, there's no accounting for Mickey's taste." Mickey and Howie Newfeldt were part of a triumvirate that gathered regularly at the farmhouse John Ryan and his wife Jenifer had lived in before she left him.

"I wanna hear what you've got. I'm serious, son. I've got to run. Call me," Hendrickson said as he proceeded down the block. "I mean it." He gave a wave of acknowledgment over his shoulder.

John Ryan had a flash of an inclination to turn around but told himself it would be a waste of time. Record companies were like leopards; they seldom changed their spots until the whole industry did. Trayhorn had never done his kind of music. Of course, neither had anyone else. He also needed new demos; the present ones had already been around the whole circuit. The fact that he was on a first-name basis with Hendrickson had no weight; first names didn't mean a lot in Nashville. As he neared his old red Ford station wagon, John Ryan stopped dead in his tracks, and a cold sweat eased its way up his back. He realized he was trying to rationalize himself out of pursuing Hendrickson's offer.

That brought to mind his first days in Nashville and making his first demo. The song wasn't bad, but it sure as hell wasn't good; however, he pushed it proudly to anyone who would give him the time or allow him to leave it at the receptionist's desk. Couldn't wait to get up in the morning to deliver it somewhere, anywhere. Every day was going to be THE DAY. In those days he wasn't aware that virtually none of the records ever got beyond the desk. Now he wasn't even jumping on a request by someone in power to listen to his music.

It took John Ryan thirty minutes to make the drive from Music Row to the ramshackle farm house he rented. It was still early when he pulled the car to a stop in front of the wooden porch where he often sat and worked on his music. The sun was still on the rise, and he was tired. He hadn't slept much lately, never had really adjusted to working nights and sleeping in the daytime.

Looking in the bathroom mirror, there was a mild shock at the face that looked back at him. John Stone, 'Little Jackie' Stone was not aging well. The body was lean—raw-boned lean—and the face thin, which accentuated the lines that ran from his mouth to his chin, made wells of the Paul Newman blue eyes and gave the appearance of more than thirty-two years. Brown, shaggy hair hung raggedly below his shoulders giving him a worn look.

Lying on the bed, he lit a small joint that he had found on the dresser. He had no idea where it had come from. It didn't matter. He wasn't that fond of marijuana—alcohol was his drug of choice—but it was handy and gave him a gentler high. He rested an ashtray on his naked stomach. His eyes were wide open, and he sucked the smoke deep into his lungs.

"You can't stay on vacation forever." It was what Jenifer had said just before she walked out the door. The memory came back sharply. Now, here he was with a job that paid him sixty-five dollars a week. "Good morning, Jean Paul Sartre!" he said to the darkness. That was absurd. How many songwriters in Nashville—even the successful and rich ones—knew who Jean Paul Sartre was? "John Ryan Stone, you are an enigma, an absurd enigma," he said to himself .

His 'career' was a joke. That was the other thing Jenifer had said, and his father agreed with her, had ever since John Ryan left the army. Through it all the music had been inside him even though there were times he wasn't aware of it. He couldn't let go, not just yet.

Hendrickson had asked about his songs, seemed pretty intense about hearing them. The decision whether or not to keep going was at hand; he had known it would come to this, and the call to Hendrickson might very well make it for him. He would do it. There was nothing left to lose.

When he finally turned over to try to sleep, most of Nashville was just attacking the day.

Jamie Greshem was waiting when Hendrickson arrived at his office. He was not his father's son. Bernie was a bottom-line business man; quality garnered little consideration. Bernie liked to play the game, survive shark attacks and come out a financial winner. When Jamie was growing up, there were conversations at the table about the music business, but he was never quite sure what his father did.

It wasn't until he was in ninth grade in Manhattan that he realized knowing music was a catalyst to popularity. With new-found curiosity, he began to listen more closely to table conversations about his father's work and even asked questions now and then. Bernie seemed to like that even though his answers were simple and brief.

Jamie began to listen to all kinds of music. The kaleidoscope of sounds and lyrics all appealed to him on one level or another, but it was the emotional reactions stimulated by the music that really interested him, the compassion he experienced from the lyrics, melodies and harmonies.

He wasn't sure why Bernie sent him to Nashville. He had thrown in some vague rationalization and handed him a plane ticket. Jamie was not in a position to object, and wouldn't have in any case. Although it seemed a momentary decision on his father's part, if it could speed his growth process in the business, so be it.

It was an interesting morning. Don Hendrickson took his young visitor to see the Ryman, which even Jamie Greshem knew still held echoes of Hank Williams lurking in its wings. He had never been taken with country music, but he liked the simplicity of the lyrics and the spartan four chord melodies.

Young Greshem said little during lunch at the King of the Road. He was trying to take it all in and get a feel for everything he was being exposed to. "How did you get started in this business, Don?"

"Well, I'm not braggin' but, to tell the truth, I've done it all. Played a little bit, wrote, sang some gospel, found, produced and promoted a few decent artists along the way, and, above all, I listened. It's history, you know. Music. Some people don't look at it as such, but it is. You ready for me to preach?" he laughed.

"Preach," Jamie said.

"You asked for it. I started as a performer, but never was real comfortable with performin' cause I knew I was limited, and I hate to do anything when I feel limited. I knew there were a hundred keyboard players out there more talented than me. I knew Floyd Cramer wasn't worried. Hell, I couldn't play good 'slip-key' no matter how hard I tried.

"I did enjoy writin'; problem was I could only do it when someone else came up with the idea. I can come up with a melody, but I never felt like it was my own work. Hell, how many melodies are there? Sooner or later everything begins to sound like somethin' else. It got so I'd write a tune and then wonder if I'd heard it on the radio. I guess that's all right for some, but it wasn't for me. You can do a lot with four chords, but there are limits. You tired yet?"

"Not at all," he smiled, "but you haven't told me what you like best."

"I'm gettin' there. Now I know you're lookin' for a niche, and I can understand that. I been there and I know how you feel. I read people pretty well, son, and you'd better, too, if you're gonna survive in this business with your skin still on. Don't let the southern hospitality and slow demeanor down here fool you. There's hustlers here just like in New York. 'Course most of 'em smile. I know people up there think Southerners are slow and kinda dumb, but I never saw one pay to get into a reptile farm.

"I don't think promotion would suit you; you got to be a hustler, and I don't sense that in you. It's sales, pure and simple. You got to sell the program directors at major stations to include a title on their play-list and to do that without payin' 'em, givin' 'em drugs or entertainin' 'em is a feat to be reckoned with."

"I thought payola went out with Alan Freed."

16

"Get serious. It never even slowed down. 'Course we have less of it in country than the rock people do, but it's still there. A fifth of Jack Daniels won't get you much anymore. Some of those guys are real bastards. They ask for the world to program a song for a week, and then if something happens, they want a reward for makin' it a hit. That's the hard part of the business, and it's gettin' harder every day, and I mean hard as in being hard—playing hard and living hard. It all goes together. Can even get dangerous at times. You know Philip Barnessa?"

"I've met him. Promoter from Philadelphia, " Jamie said.

"He's good at promotion, but he's bad people and tough. Be careful of him cause if you come up with something he wants, he'll go to any lengths to get it. Scares people that don't scare. Hell, I'm sure you already know a lot of this stuff."

"I think I've been sheltered, but you're right, selling is not my strong suit. I'm not into cutting throats."

"Now in my book, producin' is where the fun is. It's kind of a high place to start, but it's possible, especially..."

"If your father's the president?" Jamie interrupted. "Let me be honest, Don, I'm not an idealist. I don't want my father to be a major factor in what I do, but if I think I have the ability for whatever I take on." He smiled again.

"Honesty and smarts. That's an unusual combination in this business. Okay, there's all kinds of producers but in my opinion, the best of 'em is Sam Philips. The man has made history. One of the best ears in the business, and, most important, he had the creativity and balls to do something with whatever he discovered. That's the gift. Money was a secondary consideration—not that it wasn't important; it was—but the music was where the excitement was. Sam's an innovator; I'm not. I don't have that kind of genius. I've got the ear. I can find the product and know there's something there, but I can't create like Sam.

"I learned one of the basic lessons from Sam: always keep the door unlocked. He'd listen to anybody, and look who walked through there. Elvis, Jerry Lee, Orbison, Cash. If producin' is what you're interested in, that's a good lesson to learn."

"And do you still keep your door open?"

"You bet. If somebody comes to my door, I'll listen. May not listen long, but I'll listen. I don't think I could handle this job if I didn't have the luxury of doing that once in awhile. There is nothing quite like the excitement of findin' a new song or new artist, or somethin' fresh and good, puttin' all the parts together and seeing it through. You don't get a chance to do that very often. It's funny I was just thinkin' this morning that I haven't really heard anybody in a long time. Too much business; the time just gets away."

Jamie smiled. "I know I'm naive, and that for all the background I grew up around, I hardly know anything about the business, but that's what I want to do," he said without hesitation.

"You got to have an ear and judgment; management today doesn't allow many mistakes even if..."

"You are the president's son. I know again."

"I got an idea that might do us both some good. Let me think on it for awhile, and we'll discuss it after dinner." He looked at his watch. "Right now we'd better hit the road. Sylvia's waiting for us."

In just a few hours Jamie Greshem had come to truly admire the man, was impressed by his knowledge, the way others had reacted to him throughout the day and his apparent peace with himself. There was warmth and trust in every greeting and a comfort factor in the music community he had never seen in New York. They had run into Hank Williams, Jr., whose career was just getting off the ground, and been invited to go boar hunting with him in Crossville, Tennessee. After lunch, a pick-up truck screeched to a halt beside them. Johnny Sea, who had a major hit with a patriotic song, leaned out of the driver's window and laughingly asked them to go to a seance. Jamie began to understand what the term 'good ol' boy' meant.

"I appreciate what you're doing for me, Don, I don't think I could have had a better mentor for a day." Jamie smiled broadly.

"Whatever the hell that is," Hendrickson laughed. "Come on, let's get out of here." He opened the office door and followed Jamie out. Hendrickson could feel the young man's adrenaline beginning to pump. It really had been a long time.

It was one of those days for John Ryan Stone: his mind would not rest and he hadn't been able to sleep at all.

He couldn't concentrate enough to write. He tried to direct his thoughts toward other things, peaceful things, things with no implications. It didn't work. Now there was little time to do anything except go through the ritual of getting ready to leave for work.

The ringing of the phone startled him.

"Hello?" he said quietly when he put the receiver to his ear.

"John Ryan?" There was an enthusiastic, male voice at the other end, one filled with spirit, energy and a suggestion of bourbon or some other emollient. It was vaguely familiar, but he couldn't lock it in.

"You got him," he answered dryly.

"Hope I didn't wake you. It's not your night off, is it? Figured I'd catch you before you left for the studio."

"Well, you did, but I have no idea who the hell it is that I'm talking to." He heard a laugh at the other end.

"It's Don Hendrickson." The smile was evident in the man's voice. "I've had a big dinner, lots of wine, a couple of brandies, not to mention a little bourbon beforehand, so I'm feelin' pretty good, but I do know what I'm doin' and what I'm sayin'."

"Well, Don, I'm proud, pleased and grateful that you decided to call and tell me that." he laughed, "but I think there must be some other enlightening reason for this conversation." John Ryan's glibness belied what he was feeling in his stomach.

"Yes, there is. There surely is." Hendrickson's voice became serious. "I want to see you tomorrow morning. I want you and your guitar to join me for breakfast at my house when you get off work. What time is that? 'Bout seven?"

"Yeah, but hold on a minute. What the hell is this all about? What's goin' on?"

"I'll tell you when you get here, but it could be good. Or it could be nothin' except for breakfast; from what I saw this mornin' you look like you could use a good meal. See you between eight and eight-thirty. Don't disappoint me now." The phone went dead in John Ryan's hand.

He had no idea what the man had in mind. Hendrickson didn't invite an unpublished writer to his house just to listen to songs, not unless there was something special about the songs or the writer. He and Hendrickson were on a first name basis, not a come-out-to-my-house-and-have-breakfast basis.

Although he had questions and doubts, to conclude now that everything he had been doing for three years was a pose or a fantasy would be nothing less than a cruel joke. He was not a man given to playing games or allowing imagination and projection to victimize him. 'Have at it or quit now,' he said to himself.

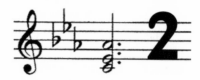

Don Hendrickson and a man John Ryan didn't recognize were seated at a wrought-iron, glass-topped table on the terrace having orange juice and coffee when Sylvia Hendrickson escorted him through the French doors.

"Well, damn! You did show up." Hendrickson rose with a broad smile. "Come on over and meet Jamie Gresham from New York City." He gestured to the young man rising from the table. You want some coffee or juice or something?" Hendrickson asked as the two men shook hands.

"Coffee's fine." He lowered himself into a chair.

His appearance suddenly made him uncomfortable—scruffy jeans, a blue denim shirt, boots that were way beyond the need to be replaced, and his long hair, which had become burdensome since he had no one to cut it.

"What about your guitar? Bring it like I asked you to?"

"It's in the car." John Ryan looked out over the garden. "Beautiful place, Don."

"We like it. Spent too damn much money on it, but what the hell. If you want it and can afford to do it, I say do it. And I can afford to do it." He paused, did a take, and broke into a wry grin. "This month."

Jamie Greshem said nothing but kept his eyes on John Ryan Stone.

"Tradin' New York for Nashville, Jamie? Helluva change," John Ryan said to the young man, his raspy voice giving off a relaxed resonance and reckless attitude that indicated nothing of the turmoil in his stomach.

"Maybe. That wasn't my intention when I came, but from what I've seen, I like it. It caught me by surprise."

"Well, you've got a master salesman talkin' to you."

"I haven't bought any boots yet." The young man smiled.

Hendrickson's eyes danced and his voice bubbled with enthusiasm. "You guys hungry? I'm gonna have me some eggs, grits and country ham. Good ol' killer-cholesterol breakfast. We're just here to have breakfast, talk a little bit and see what happens. Nothin' ventured, nothin' gained. That all right with you, John Ryan? Hell, I don't know what I'm doin' either. Not sure anybody in this business does. I heard a man say once—maybe it was Roy Acuff—that there are only three secrets to being continually successful in the music business. The problem is nobody knows what they are. If there is somebody in Nashville who knows absolutely what he's doin', I ain't met him."

"I'm listenin', but..."

"Just hear me out. Now I don't know if anything's gonna work out here or not, but I'm also not one to believe that the light at the end of the tunnel is always an oncomin' train, and I'm wonderin' if you do. I'm not sayin' that's true; I don't know yet, but we'll find out.

"A lot of people in this town, they get used to wearin' failure, but I don't feel that way about you. I've heard too much good. Let me tell you what I been thinkin'. Jamie's daddy is president of Trayhorn. Thing is, he's convinced me he doesn't want to ride that pony.

"Jamie and I have been talkin' for the best part of the last twenty-four hours about what he wants to do in the business and where he wants to be. I have to tell you from the start, he's not hard country and doesn't care for honky-tonk. Hell, he don't even think much of Hank, and he's not totally sold on Nashville, but he's got some good ideas that I'd like him to follow through on and see what he comes up with."

Jamie Greshem straightened in his chair and hesitated. "John Ryan, I've only been here twenty-four hours, and I don't pretend to know your business or Nashville. But Don has given me what I think is a pretty good education in a very short time. As he said, I've never been a lover of hard country, but I believe there's fertile ground here for new ideas and the kind of music I hear in my mind.

"Everything in L.A. and New York is segmented, designed for a large parcel of the buying public, and I believe they're missing out on a lot. A few try to break barriers, but they've limited themselves to major artists who do the same thing they've always done in a different format, like Dylan going electric. It didn't change Dylan, but it was a good marketing ploy."

"Breakfast," Sylvia announced as she backed through the doors carrying a large tray with a platter of eggs, country ham, biscuits, and a bowl of cheese grits. There was also a bowl of fresh fruit. "Sorry to interrupt, but

21

they'll get cold if I wait, and his honor does not like cold food. I'll just put it down and you can serve yourselves." She put the bowls and platter on the table along with a fresh pot of coffee and left the men alone.

"Thank you, Darlin'," Don said as she went back into the house. "Lord, what that woman does for me. She is truly a wonderment."

"She coulda done worse," John Ryan said as he took the platter and served himself small portions of ham and eggs before passing it on to Jamie Greshem.

"Son, you are gonna starve yourself to death if that's all you're gonna eat. No wonder you look like a summer scarecrow in winter. 'Scuse the interruption, Jamie. Down here we talk between bites. You'll get used to it. Go on with what you were sayin'."

"Anyway, I think country music has a chance to bridge a lot of gaps. I know there have been some crossover hits, Elvis—if you want to call him country. Marty Robbins and Jim Reeves crossed over a couple of times in the fifties, but it's usually a one or two shot deal. Orbison might be the closest thing to what I'm talking about, but even his lyrics are light so far.

"I think there's more, nothing revolutionary as far as the instrumentation goes, but a new and different voice maybe. A different image, different sound—not easy listening, and not the 'Nashville Sound'—one with a new kind of lyric, something people are not used to hearing.

"I want the words to go beyond beer-drinking and divorcing. What causes those two things? What is the aftermath of those two things? What's inside the people who are doing those things and what are they feeling while they're going through it? I want something that will touch the lawyer and loser alike. We're talking about thirty or forty percent of the population here. I want the music to touch them where they feel, provide therapy or justification, whichever they're looking for."

"That's a big order," John Ryan said softly. "I'm not sure what you're describing is country."

"Maybe not and maybe it shouldn't be," Jamie said.

Hendrickson, chewing on a stubborn piece of country ham, interrupted. "I believe what we're thinkin' here is that the foundation, the basic structure, could be country—not hard country—but country. It's the lyrics that have to break the ground. Put some intelligence into it, somethin' universal, make it a little more bold than what's been done. As Jamie said, everybody doesn't spend their time in 'shot-gun' bars drinkin' Lone Star. There are— believe it or not and I can't understand why—martini drinkers out there who are just as sad, just as lonely and feelin' the same things, but they can't relate to the beer-drinkin' atmosphere. So you take a base, a foundation and you build from there." He paused and a mischievous smile came over his face. "You ever see how they grow English walnuts out in California?" Both men looked at the man befuddled.

"English walnuts?" John Ryan asked, wondering where in the world this was leading.

Hendrickson sat back to expound. "The English walnut tree has very weak and shallow roots. Damn trees blow over in a breeze. So what they do is they plant Black walnut trees, which have a strong root system, then they graft the English walnut to the base. If you look at the trees, the bark and everything changes color about two feet off the ground. That's what we're talkin' about. Addin' a new tree to country roots."

John Ryan fought back a laugh. Jamie Greshem had a broad grin.

"Okay, let's get to you." The eyes focused on John Ryan Stone, riveting his attention. In spite of the smiles, the laughter, and good-ol'-boy friendliness, Don Hendrickson let them know he was ready to talk seriously. "John Ryan, it's a very unusual thing for me to invite anyone out here on business; I try to keep this separate, but you interest me. Everything I've heard seems to say the same thing: that it's only a matter of time for you. Based on that, I have a hunch you might be writing what Jamie's lookin' to produce. Whether it's any good or not, I don't know. Won't know that 'til I hear it, but we didn't run into each other yesterday by accident, you know. I don't believe accidents happen."

"Jamie, I don't know what Don's told you, but I'm not a performer. I usually get other people to cut my demos for me..."

"And you haven't sold anything from what Don says. I don't care about that. I want to hear you."

"Nervous?" Don asked. "Now, go get your guitar and play us some songs. Only thing you could do is make money; you can't lose any. The worst that could happen is you got a free breakfast. I know where you are, John Ryan."

"Don, you've got a line that would calm a hungry alligator, but you know damn well it's more than just three guys sittin' around the breakfast table playin' some songs."

"I know, and you're scared to take that on and scared not to. Hell, I know, man. I felt it every time I sat down and auditioned for a road job." He gave John Ryan a focused and sincere look. "Hey, go get your guitar, you got from here to your car to make up your mind." he wheedled good naturedly.

John Ryan looked at him, aware of Jamie Greshem's eyes coming from the other side of the table. Without saying anything, he got up and went through the French doors.

"Think he'll come back?" Jamie asked.

"Oh yeah. He's too smart not to. John Ryan's been around too long with nothin' happenin'; he doesn't have anywhere else to go. I think he knows it's time to fish or settle on cuttin' bait. What do you think of him?"

"I don't know enough to really say. He's got presence. That can't be denied. He's got a good wit, seems to be thoughtful. Listens. I like that. When I saw him walk in and heard him talk, I was afraid he might be too raw for me."

"Don't be fooled. He used to teach English. That kinda talk is somethin' you just fall into if you're down here in this business long enough. Hell, listen to me. But I can change it and speak the King's English when I need to. You'll probably be y'allin' when you've been here awhile." Jamie smiled at the idea. "What else?" Don asked.

"I like his look. It goes with his voice and his speech. Sort of an outsider, sensitive in a strong way. I like the vocal quality, unpolished, something everyone can relate to. Of course that has no relation to what his singing voice might be." He cut short what he was saying as John Ryan, carrying a worn guitar case, came through the French doors.

"You want some more coffee?" Don asked holding the silver pot poised above John Ryan's cup.

"Bourbon would be better," he answered putting the case down.

"I got that too."

"I was only kidding. It's a little too early even for me to start that," he said.

When he had poured the coffee, Hendrickson shifted the conversation to baseball and the Cincinnati Reds chances of winning the pennant. With Pete Rose, it was concluded that the Reds might even win the World Series. From there it went to Jamie talking about living in New York and then back to the music business.

"Did you hear what happened to Randy Crutcher?" Don asked, bringing up the name of Nashville's hottest writer of the moment.

"Nothin' except he can't write anything that somebody doesn't want," John Ryan replied.

Don Hendrickson was laughing. "Well, be that as it may, he sure screwed up on the home front."

"What happened?"

"Seems he had a sweet little thing he wanted to get away with in Atlanta for the weekend. Told his wife he was goin' down to play backup for some friend of his. Problem was he needed money for the trip, so he wrote a check for five hundred dollars to 'Cash'. When the check came through, Marie, his wife asked him what the five hundred dollar check to 'Cash' was for. Ever the quick thinker, he told her it was just to pay off an old debt to Johnny Cash."

Problem was about two weeks later Marie ran into Big John at a party, I think it was at Loretta's house, and thanked him for helpin' Randy out when they were strugglin', and how gratifyin' it was for someone who's established to help someone who's tryin' to make his way in the business, and how glad she was that they were finally able to pay him back. Of course John didn't know what the hell she was talkin' about.

"Now if you knew Marie, you'd know she has the disposition of a fox in heat in a forest fire, so she excused herself to go to the Ladies Room, didn't say anything to anybody, went out the door, got the car, went home, packed, drove to the airport and went back to Arkansas. Randy went nuts. Got drunk, and when he came out of it three days later, she had taken every cent out of the bank and closed all the accounts." They were all laughing by the time Don finished the story.

"Why don't you let us hear something, John Ryan?" Don said.

"You understand..." John Ryan started to say, but Don Hendrickson's expression didn't allow him an introductory apology. John Ryan Stone reached over and pulled the old Martin out of its case.

"We'll want to hear several, so you don't have to play your best first. Pretty guitar," Hendrickson commented.

"My grandmother's. Sat in the attic for years before I started playin' around with it." The husky voice trembled and cracked with nerves when he began. For a minute in the middle of the first song, he thought he might throw up. Halfway through the second song, he lost the lyric and had to stop and start over. It was painful. He tried to stop the shaking in his voice, tried to stop it with volume, tried to lift his shoulders and sit up straight, anything to make the quivering go away, but it was like a drunk trying to steady his hands to get the first drink of the day to his lips. The harder he tried to keep it steady, the worse it got.

It was somewhere in the third song that he moved his focus and emotions into the lyrics, listened to his own words, recreated and concentrated on what he was feeling when he wrote them. It was only then that he forgot what he was doing and relaxed.

"Damn! They're pretty songs," Don said when the third song was over, "but they're not what I been hearin' about. Good as they are—and they are good—any decent writer in Nashville coulda written 'em. You started to relax on the last one. What was it...."

"Crossin' the Border..."

"Yeah, *Crossin' the Border*. It's got a nice melody and the lyrics are nice, but that's the problem. They're nice. Let me hear somethin' with some strength, one you believe really hits what you're tryin' to say on the nose. I wanna hear the one you think Trayhorn will never take."

He started with a basic E-chord and went through a four chord progression several times before he was comfortable enough to begin singing. The voice came out steady, deeper and more husky and raw than it had been on the others. That was appealing, but it was the lyric that caught the two men's attention. It wasn't a sweet song; there were no promises of a happy ending. It was a song about two people trying to relate to each other, to find some common ground to justify their spending the night together, a song of survival, and in one way or another both Don and Jamie understood it. Nashville to New York. That's what made it so good.

"Let me hear that one again," Don said without hesitating. John Ryan looked at him and began again. The voice was strong and tired, disillusioned and uncompromising. It rang of a sadness far deeper than whiskey could cure.

> *Your love is gone,*
> *and you sit all alone;*
> *The worst dream in sight*
> *Is to spend one lonely night*
>
> *So here's my hand,*
> *Won't you please understand*
> *That it's wrong can't be right*
> *Just to spend one lonely night."*

It was the first line of the break that caught both of the men by surprise when he played it the first time. That kind of relationship had never been touched with any depth in country music, and rock and roll isolated it, made it synonymous only with self-serving good times. These lyrics were different; they gave a smooth song a biting edge and defined a loneliness and desperate solitude that people at all levels experience at one time or another.

> *"Our love won't last,"*

John Ryan's voice reached for a depth below any note he had hit before.

> *"Won't go down in time.*
> *Just give me these hours*
> *And be-e-e just mine."*

26

The harsh sound eased on the last stanza and became a comfort zone to the listener.

"So take this night
Love'll make it all right
Don't dream on the sun
For your lonely night is done."

When he was finished, neither of the men said anything. Don Hendrickson looked at Jamie Greshem with a Cheshire-like smile. It was Jamie who broke the silence.

"That's a good song, John Ryan."

Something was happening. The look on Hendrickson's face, the sound of Jamie Greshem's voice and his choice of words. He said *good* not *pretty* or *nice* or *beautiful*. He said *good*. There was a stirring in John Ryan's stomach and an uncomfortable elevation in his chest.

"It's a good song," Jamie repeated. "It's got strength in the melody and the lyric and yet they're both simplistic."

"It's a damned verbal seduction with no promise of tomorrow is what it is," Don added. "I'm not sure how the Bible segment will react to it, but we can't worry about that."

"Have you got any more like that?"

"How many hundred do you want to hear?" The sound of what his own voice was saying shocked him.

"Let's start with what we've got. What's the name of that last one?" Don asked.

"*One Lonely Night.*"

Hendrickson took a pen from his pocket and wrote the title down on a linen napkin he had taken from the table. "She'll kill me," he muttered to himself.

"What's next?" Jamie asked.

John Ryan started a song he had written several years before but Jamie stopped him after one verse. "That's not it. Whether it's love or right and wrong or whatever, when you're alone it usually comes down to skin and heat, your own or somebody else's. That's what I want. That's what the other song has."

Don Hendrickson sat and listened. The charging of the atmosphere around him was invigorating. The pen had been put down after the first line of the second song; he picked it up when he heard the title of the third. It was long for a title, but it worked.

"*What Can I Do To Make You Love Me Tomorrow?*" John Ryan said as he began to play.

It was almost sequential to the first song. When *One Lonely Night* was written, John Ryan began to think about the dangers of that situation. Emotion and desire never progress equally nor do they remain equal between two people, and what happens when one of them begins to care? That's where *What Can I Do To Make You Love Me Tomorrow?* had come from.

When he stopped singing, Hendrickson wrote the title down on the linen napkin.

They liked *Everybody Don't Have To Be A Cowboy*, a raucous tune about the male ego and its penchant for denying sensitivity. There were two others they didn't like, and then he sang the one song he had written since Jenifer left, *I Can't Stand The Silence Anymore*.

"I don't know what to say," Jamie said. "I don't care how much money the lollipop songs out there have made; you have what I want. There's no lack of life in those words."

"Hot damn! That's good. You got me shiverin' in my boots, boy," Don exclaimed.

Jamie Greshem turned to Hendrickson. "I want to do demos on *Silence, One Lonely Night, and What Can I Do To ....*"

"*Make You Love Me Tomorrow.*" Don Hendrickson finished for him.

There was confusion and disbelief in John Ryan's face. The two men's words were disassociated and unintelligible. He tried to put some order into them to make them coherent, but he couldn't. The first word he understood was 'tomorrow'.

"What?"

"Tomorrow," Jamie answered.

"What tomorrow?" John Ryan asked.

"I want to do a demo on those three songs tomorrow. Maybe four. Nothing fancy, straightforward. Keyboards, bass, drums and a guitar or two. Can we get studio time?" he asked Hendrickson.

"I'll get it." The answer came as if there were no question.

"Who's gonna sing 'em?" John Ryan asked. Both men looked at him incredulously, but it was Hendrickson who spoke.

"You're the only one who can," Don said. "I don't think I ever heard a voice with more whiskey and smoke in it than yours. You think I want Whisperin' Bill Anderson or Conway or David Houston recordin' those songs? Other people might do these songs someday, and I'm sure they will, but they are your songs and not just because you wrote 'em. Can you get Mickey and Howie?"

"They're in Shreveport." His head was spinning.

"Get 'em up here."

"They've got a week left on their gig."

"Where are they playin'? I'll send somebody with a bigger name down there to relieve 'em. That'll keep the club owner happy."

"I think it's called Dixie City..."

"I'll take care of it." He wrote again on the linen napkin.

"What about keyboards? Is there anybody really good you can get on this short notice?" Jamie Greshem asked.

"I'll play," said Hendrickson. "We don't have time to go searchin'."

"What do you want me to do?" John Ryan was dazed.

"Go home and get some rest. Call in sick or whatever at work. Hell, quit if you want to. Remember, tomorrow starts at midnight, and that's when we'll record. Right now I'm gonna have to end this party 'cause Jamie and I have a lot of work to do before then. The first things being to get somebody to go play in Shreveport and gettin' plane tickets for Mickey and Howie." He stood up as John Ryan closed the clasps on his guitar case. "And I've got to come up with an engineer. That might be our biggest problem."

"Stringer Edwards could probably do it," John Ryan remarked almost to himself, afraid to wake up truth in what seemed like a fantasy.

"I've heard about him. Mickey and Howie use him a lot, don't they?"

"On just about everything they do."

"You comfortable with him?"

"I'm not comfortable with anybody, Don. But, yeah, I guess." The fear was there like the grits and ham and eggs that were solidifying in his stomach.

"We'll see if we can get him. You rest. Don't get drunk. That happens a lot on these occasions."

John Ryan picked up his guitar and thanked Jamie Greshem even though he was more than anxious about the position in which he found himself.

"It's gonna be good," Hendrickson said as he guided John Ryan around the outside of the house. He had to reach up to put his hand on the tall man's shoulder, but he managed. "We'll take as much time as we need. Jamie made the decision to do this, but I woulda done the same thing, if that makes you feel any better. You've got every chance here, and you've done your work. Hell, this ain't overnight. I know what you been through, and your songs tell it better than you do. I just ask that you trust me. I know that should be a warnin' in this business," he said with a broad smile, "but you can. If it rolls, it could roll so fast that tomorrow will be December and the bullshit around you will be six feet deep."

"I don't know what to say, as ridiculous as that sounds."

"Just say 'Thank you' as ridiculous as that sounds. Now don't go home and practice and come in with your fingers all bloody. And whatever you do, don't even think about improvin' anything. They're not gonna get any better."

"You readin' my mind?"

Don Hendrickson gave him a shrug, a smile and turned back toward the house.

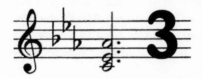

Howie Newfeldt picked up the telephone next to his bed in a shade-darkened room at the Sweet Bay Inn in Shreveport, Louisiana. It had been a long night, and he was in a deep sleep when it began to ring. His first thought was that one or both of the girls he and Mickey had been drinking with until four-thirty had a change of heart. Both men had been less than happy at having spent money they couldn't afford and then being left empty-handed. He had no idea what time it was.

Amid the clearing of the cobwebs he heard a sweet but businesslike voice.

"Mr. Shackleford?"

"No, this is Howie. Who's this?" he asked drowsily.

"My name is Ann Thompson. I'm calling for Don Hendrickson?" There was a pause. "Don Hendrickson of Trayhorn International?" She said making a statement with a question. It took him a minute to place himself and begin to decipher the words he was hearing.

"Trayhorn?"

"Yes. Mr. Hendrickson would like you to be at the airport at twelve forty-five. Tickets will be waiting at the Eastern Airlines counter in the name of Mickey Shackleford. He said to bring your instruments; this is a recording session. Your play dates at Dixie City have been covered, and someone will meet you at the airport in Nashville." Then she was gone.

Mickey would have been more alert, asked some questions, demanded more details, probably taken offense at being told what to do without being asked, Howie thought. All he garnered from the conversation was that they had to be at the airport—in what he now realized was a little less than two hours—that they were flying to Nashville at somebody else's expense for some kind of recording session and that their play dates had been covered.

He woke Mickey and repeated the whole telephone conversation to him word for word. Mickey didn't know what to think. The thought did occur that they should call the Trayhorn offices, that maybe it was a joke. Howie, on the other hand, was having difficulty convincing himself that the whole telephone conversation wasn't a dream. Alcohol was still circling heavily in his brain, but he couldn't admit that to Mickey.

The flight was one of conjecture, confusion and excitement. It wasn't until they were met at International Airport by Son Cochran, a Trayhorn studio regular, that they were told what they were doing. It was also the first time John Ryan Stone had entered their minds. When they heard his name, they couldn't believe it.

Stringer Edwards arrived at his small studio planning to remix some cuts he had recorded the day before. It was eleven-fifteen when the phone rang. The voice on the other end of the line identified himself as Don Hendrickson, which caused the engineer to pause.

"I know this is short notice," the voice said, "but I need to know how much studio time you have booked over the next seventy-two hours."

"I'll have to check, but I doubt it's anything that can't be done later. What can I do for you?"

"I want you to engineer a session for me at Trayhorn. Don't know how long it'll last. We want to cut three or four sides. Mickey Shackleford and Howie Newfeldt will be on the session—I know you've worked with them—and I got Son Cochran to play bass. Jamie Greshem will be producin'. He's a virgin and he's gonna need a lot of patience, so will the artist, but I've heard you're good at handlin' things like that. That's why I'm askin' for seventy-two hours. If we don't need that much time, we'll pay for whatever time you don't re-book."

"Who's the artist?" Stringer asked.

"John Ryan Stone."

"Well, now, then, there." There was a tone of disbelief in the engineer's voice. "How did you manage that?"

"Gave him breakfast and listened to his songs."

"I know it took more than that to get him to sing, but I won't ask. What about keyboards?"

"Me."

"I never recorded a vice-president before," he laughed. "Drums?" He was fighting an urge to explode at the opportunity that was being put before him.

"Bobby Hopwood."

"Well, you sure got the guns. If John Ryan can bring himself to sing, we might just be able to make some music. What time?"

"Session begins tonight at twelve, and we stay 'til we're done. Two sides is an absolute minimum, but I'd like three or four if we can get 'em in. I don't plan a lot of tricky stuff," Hendrickson said.

"His songs don't need it."

"I take it you've heard 'em."

"Recorded most of 'em. Of course he wasn't singing, but he can. With the right turn it could be good."

"I want you to talk with Jamie about exactly what he wants to do, and then I want you to tell him what you think he should do. I told you he's new, but from what I see, I think he's sharp even if he is from New York," Hendrickson added with 'good ol' boy' sarcasm.

"Oh, Lord."

"You won't have any trouble with him. We're having a production meeting at five; I'd like for you to be there early. It'll also give you some break-in time on the equipment."

"I'll be there. I appreciate this, Don."

"Hey, John Ryan wanted you, and if it'll make him sing the way I heard him, I want you too."

"Things sure do change, don't they?" he said, thinking about what had been on his schedule.

"That's what makes life excitin'. I'll see you tonight. Stringer Edwards. I like that name." With those words Don Hendrickson left the line.

It was only after the phone was back in its cradle that the engineer let his emotions come to the surface. A normally quiet and introspective, electronic type, he started the tape rolling on one of his machines and let out a series of whoops and yells into the microphone in front of him. It was recorded. Something to be saved. Sitting back in his chair, his energy exasperated, he wondered if this was the God Almighty break everybody always talked about. It sure sounded like John Ryan Stone was getting his.

Going in, no one—not musicians, producers or writers—knows what will come out of a recording session. It can be a myriad of frazzled emotions running the gamut from panic and frustration to violent temper tantrums and fist fights. At other times it can be a smooth-running, businesslike, and professional experience. Don Hendrickson usually managed the latter although stormy episodes were not outside his experience.

John Ryan Stone's first recording session was neither volatile nor businesslike. It was a long period of hard work that required patience on everyone's part. Jamie Greshem was the producer in name and concept; however, there was no doubt in the mind of any of the participants who was the producer in fact.

Hendrickson was a master of composure. He suggested to Jamie that they work on *Everybody Don't Have To Be A Cowboy* first because of the nature of the music, that even though it is sometimes more difficult to get an upbeat tune exactly the way it should be done, beginning with this type of song can serve to loosen up the musicians and get them into the flow of the session. It can also help relax a new artist. In Hendrickson's experience, nerves always seemed to dissipate in direct correlation to the beat of the music. In the singer's mind, the more complex backup arrangements required by such a song tend to put the pressure on someone else.

By the third rehearsal Stringer Edwards was happy with his sound levels, and after a few additional run-throughs, each musician and the engineer had created their own coded charts from the lead-sheets they had been given. The time had come to put the song on tape.

After eleven attempts, including several false starts, Hendrickson called a 'team meeting'. Everyone sat on the floor and listened as the friendly, smiling man explained precisely where he wanted the session to go, what he expected it to produce, and he did it without usurping Jamie Greshem's position.

Talking was one of Hendrickson's greatest talents. Getting people to react positively to what he said was another. The musicians, the engineer and all of the other people involved who had never worked with him before were surprised that he would spend time talking. Time was money. Those familiar with the man were not surprised at all. It was pure Hendrickson.

After plugging away for an additional two hours during which a lot of changes were made and a lot of ideas thrown back and forth, something began to happen. Perhaps it was the tempering fatigue that all of them were beginning to feel. Perhaps they had been trying too hard or perhaps the hours of going over the same song again and again disassociated them from what they were doing and forced them to relax. Whatever the cause, the magic that all musicians know can happen on rare occasions began to materialize.

The music left John Ryan's head and moved to his gut. It became hard and aggressive. There was no apology in his voice and nothing tentative in the way he sang. He appeared angry with the song and for the first time was telling it what to do rather than the reverse.

Mickey Shackleford and Howie Newfeldt had never experienced that kind of thing before. Son Cochran and Bobby Hopwood recognized it and focused on the keyboard work that was driving them. Each time they replayed the song, the sound was more cutting and vibrant. Hendrickson was conducting without saying anything. The keys of the instrument were dictating what everyone was doing and each time through he shadowed a slight change.

Finally the words, "That's it." came from the control room. Jamie Greshem looked at Stringer Edwards who was smiling.

"It's in there somewhere," the young producer said, referring to the reels of tape they had consumed. "In fact there may be several, but I want just one: the best of the best."

It was seven o'clock in the morning, and one acceptable cut was complete.

After the tedious time required to get what they wanted on *Cowboy*, things ran more smoothly. *One Lonely Night* was done in four hours and it was good. With the fullness of the musicians behind him, John Ryan made it better than either of the producers had perceived when they heard it at breakfast the previous day.

Jamie chose *What Can I Do To Make You Love Me Tomorrow* for the third cut. It was the longest of the four songs they had scheduled, and he hoped that the emotional quotient from the previous song would carry over.

After numerous unsatisfactory attempts, they tried different approaches. None of them seemed to improve the take on the song, It was two o'clock in the afternoon. Hendrickson called a halt and asked everyone to return at midnight.

When they started the second session, Hendrickson brought in some strings, but they still had trouble putting it together and he dismissed them. Finally they went back to the way it had been played the first time—simple, concise, with an emotional level so deep that it was impossible for the listener not to experience the pain that wrote it.

The final cut was much stronger than *One Lonely Night*, and what they achieved with it gave renewed energy to the wearied musicians. There was discussion of another extended rest break before attempting *I Can't Stand The Silence Anymore*, which both Hendrickson and Greshem made known was the signature song for the session, but no one wanted to stop. The adrenaline was rushing. Additional food was brought in to settle the shakes that hours of coffee, other stimulants and no sleep creates. After a brief recess, they settled back into their work. When they were finished, everyone agreed that *I Can't Stand The Silence Anymore* was the best cut of the session.

While Stringer Edwards worked his magic in the control room doing some additional mixing, Jamie and Don had a post-session conference. Jamie made a decision to take the demos back to New York; the vice-president advised against it. It was Nashville music, not New York music, but Jamie was determined. Hendrickson understood, but he wasn't comfortable with it. He reiterated his warnings about Philip Barnessa and others and exacted a promise from the young man to keep him apprised of every move. Two hours later the young producer, carrying a set of rough acetates, left for New York. Stringer Edwards stayed in the studio to clean up two cuts of each song and finish the masters. Hendrickson's uneasiness was growing.

Mickey, Howie and John Ryan went to The Farm, as John Ryan's home had become to be known, planned a nighttime party on Printer's Alley and then collapsed from exhaustion.

Hendrickson walked quietly to his car, tired but not exhausted. The energy of a successful creation still pulsed through his body and mind. When he considered all the factors involved in John Ryan Stone's first recording session, it had gone pretty well, and—based on what was produced—he thought that was an understatement. John Ryan's songs were so personal that only through the music could anyone ever see the emotion that broiled beneath his surface.

Hendrickson's last words to John Ryan after the session were, "be patient." But on the fourth day, when he could wait no longer, he called Hendrickson's office only to be told that he was away in Los Angeles at a sales meeting.

Jamie Greshem was unavailable in New York.

In the beginning it was all so hurried, so exciting, so imminent. As far as he knew, he might have been a dupe. With growing paranoia came the sudden realization that he hadn't even signed a contract. If they had stolen his songs, what could he do about it? Sue Trayhorn? His whole life had changed and remained unchanged all at once.

The first contact John Ryan received came from Jamie's secretary three weeks after the session. It was late in the afternoon on a Thursday.

"Mr. John Ryan?" the voice asked when he answered the telephone.

"I'm calling for Mr. James Greshem. He would like to see you in New York on Wednesday, if that's convenient."

"I have to assume the convenient part is polite?"

"Of course. Well, I guess..." She sounded flustered, and he wasn't sure she had caught his humor.

"That's good because if it wasn't just polite then I'm sure the news wouldn't be good. Of course, he wouldn't call me to New York to give me bad news, would he?" He mumbled the last part more to himself than into the telephone.

"I'm sorry?"

"Nothing. I was just talking to myself. I've been doing that a lot lately."

"I see," she said, still lost in confusion.

No, she didn't see. Didn't have a concept. A little more than three weeks ago he had let the enthusiasm of the moment slip away. There was little sleep. His nights and days ever since were filled with improbable fantasies and fears. If the records were released, what would he do? He didn't have an agent, a lawyer, a manager. Hell, he didn't even have a dentist. No, she didn't see.

"I'm just a secretary, Mr. Ryan..." There was a pause. "Are you still there?"

"Yes, ma'am." He began to calculate his finances and speculate whether or not his car would make it to New York.

"Mr. Greshem will have tickets and a check for expenses sent overnight. He has made reservations for you at the Warwick Hotel. Your flight will be at two o'clock Tuesday afternoon. You will fly into J.F.K. and someone will meet you. Mr. Greshem will have you picked up at the hotel at nine a.m. on Wednesday morning. Is that convenient?"

He almost laughed.

"Yes, ma'am. That is convenient."

"Thank you, Mr. Ryan."

"Thank you, Ms. Secretary," he said to a dial tone.

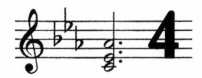

Philip Barnessa sat in his small suite of second-rate offices twelve stories above 13th and Market Streets in Philadelphia looking at his history. The whitewashed walls were covered with pictures of rock and roll stars and framed reproductions of gold records he had promoted over the years, gifts from grateful artists. The names were significant—The Who, Freddie 'Boom-Boom' Cannon, John Sebastian, Rick Nelson, Fabian, The Turtles, side by side with Frank Sinatra, Al Martino and others with whom he had crossed paths. It was a wealthy history. Those were the good years, he thought, as he gazed from one to the other. In those days jocks like a Joe Niagra, Hy Lit or Jerry 'The Geator with the Heater' Blavat could put a thousand kids in a dance on Friday night and sell eight hundred records on Saturday. It was easy. Now it was all turning to shit.

Trayhorn International paid for the office space even though he was not an 'official' employee of the company. As far as anyone knew, he was just an independent promoter. Despite that status, he carried more weight than many company executives. At the moment, however, he was on thin ice and he knew it. Not with Trayhorn, but with Giannini Tedesco, the power that backed him. He could feel the pressure being exerted like a shrinking, wet glove.

It had been almost a year since he had turned any important and ongoing money for the family. Trayhorn had given him nothing to work with from New York and the Philadelphia scene was drying up. He had seen a few 'bar bands'—local notables like Billy Harner, The Young Ideas and Johnny Caswell and the Secrets—with some promise, but nothing had gelled. There were a couple of records he had forced to local hit status with radio-play favors and bought-and-paid-for reviews and advertising, but nothing had happened nationally. The records were quickly relegated to remainder or cut-out lists and forgotten in discount bins at K-Mart.

The family's interest in Trayhorn was significant, but Giannini Tedesco wanted the company. Bernie Greshem was beginning to diversify into television and films and that made the don nervous. Barnessa knew he was the key. He and Greshem had come up through the streets together and in the past he had the power to transform dross into gold for Bernie. Not lately.

It wasn't hard to remember when control was easy to come by, easy to hold on to, and everybody was afraid to question how you got it. Barnessa wanted three things from people: respect, fear and money, but he was never able to decide which he wanted most.

By the time he was five-years-old, Barnessa had already learned that being hard was the only way to survive. He wasn't the biggest kid on Dewey Street, but he became the toughest. He left school in fifth grade—didn't quit, just came home one day and never went back. No one came looking for him. Through his teens he worked in the Italian Market, an area of open stalls and stores selling everything from cheap jewelry to exotic and ethnic foods and drawing a clientele from the Main Line to South Jersey. He was a sausage grinder, but he also ran errands for neighborhood members of the Angelo Bruno crime family, doing everything from running numbers to strong-arm collecting.

He learned a lot during those years, most importantly, that he didn't like jail. He only served a few days for minor offenses, but it was enough to convince him that life as a corner boy wasn't worth the risk. He saw something better for himself and set out to get it.

He got a job as a 'gofer' for a small radio station and began to make contacts in the music business. In those days managers, agents and artists would do almost anything to get a meeting with a disc jockey to push their product. Philip Barnessa became a conduit to the station managers, program directors and the on-air personalities, who, in many cases, were bigger celebrities than the artists.

It wasn't very different from the shakedown scams he had worked in his teens. The difference was that it was clean. No mess, no fuss. A c-note would get you in to see "the man" and get your record played. Fifty went to the jock and fifty went to Phil. It wasn't long before the record companies sought him out to push their product, and the price went up—money, drugs, booze and women, along with the cash. Within five years he was the most powerful independent promoter in Philadelphia and a master at conducting a form of business later known as 'payola'. He knew everybody and everybody knew him.

The telephone on his desk interrupted his 'golden oldie' trip.

"Yeah," he said, trying to put enough hostility in his voice so he could go either way with it depending who was at the other end of the line.

"Good afternoon, Phil. Not a very businesslike way to answer the telephone."

"Depends on what business you're in, Maury. It's the way we do it in Philly." Maury Friedman was an attorney in the legal department at Trayhorn in New York and a close associate of Giannini Tedesco.

"I know Philadelphia, Phil. You forget." His tone was condescending and cold.

"No, I don't forget, Maury. What's on your mind."

"Just checking in." There was a pause. "Are you working?" God! The man sounded like a father questioning a little boy, Barnessa thought. The man would pay; he would see to it.

"Of course I'm workin'. Whaddya think? I'm sittin' on my ass waitin' for a fuckin' pot o' gold to fall in my lap? Are you workin'. Shit." The idea of Friedman and Tedesco sitting in New York deciding how he should do business, how much business he should do and what was enough business made him feel like one of the fish he used to bounce around when he was shylocking.

"I don't know. Are you?" Friedman's calm and superiority infuriated him, but he knew better than to let it get out of control. Some day.

"I asked you before, Maury, what's on your mind?"

"Business or more to the point, the lack of business. Giannini's getting impatient. There's a lot going on at Trayhorn that he doesn't like, and he doesn't want to lose control."

"The whole fuckin' industry is nuts," Barnessa said. "I'm not by myself in this, you know. Nobody knows what's goin' on. You tell me, and I'll make you all the money you want. A few years ago everything was British. Now it's folk, bubble-gum, psychedelic, soul and who the fuck knows what else? Nobody's gettin' anything long term. Mosta these acts are druggin' themselves off the planet before they ever get to make a second record. You know what? I'll tell you what. Guy comes in the other day, a company record promoter, and wants me to give him some help promoting the new Neil Diamond thing. Here's a top artist depending on something called *Brother Love's Traveling Salvation Show* to revive his career. You tell me what's goin' on. I'd like to know."

"Tedesco's tired of excuses, Phil. You're fucking up." Friedman's language was a red flag; it was uncharacteristic of him. Didn't even sound natural coming out of his mouth. He was getting pressure too.

"He puttin' the squeeze on you, Maury?" It was a step across the line, but he thought he was safe.

"I'm trying to help you here. I've got something I think might work for you and it's easy."

"Nothin's easy."

"This will be; let me assure you. Bernie's kid is bringing in a guy from the sticks."

"Jersey?" Friedman laughed.

"Real sticks. Tennessee. Nashville."

"A fuckin' hillbilly?" Barnessa couldn't believe what he was hearing.

"Kid thinks the guy is going to be huge."

"He's a kid."

"That's what makes it easy," Friedman said.

"What are you suggesting?"

"We want you up here. You're usually at all the new artist meetings, but considering the 'artist' I thought you might not bother for this one. His name is John Ryan Stone. He's coming for meetings tomorrow and Giannini wants him. We want some publishing, agency, management, you know the routine. Anything that's not invested in his teeth. It's your shot, Philip. I don't want to see you lose out."

"That's good of you, Maury," he said calmly. He knew the fuck was lying and wondered if everyone in the family was setting him up. "I'll be there."

"See that you are." The telephone clicked on the other end and the line went dead.

Maybe it was time to get out, he thought and then laughed. He walked over to the window and looked down at the street twelve stories below. It would be so easy to open the window, step out and yell, 'Kiss My Ass!' on the way down. The thought made him chuckle and then his face went dead serious.

It had been years since John Ryan was in New York—actually only a week's furlough during a military transfer—and the prospect of finding his way through the mass of humanity that was the Kennedy terminal had been the focus of his thoughts throughout the better part of his flight. Thus, it was a surprise when he came into the gate area to find someone holding a sign and calling his name.

"John Ryan Stone...John Ryan Stone." With both hands stretched as far as they would reach above his head, a man held a sign with the name John Ryan Stone printed on it. "John Ryan Stone..." in a British accent,

"John Ryan Stone," the man repeated the name. John Ryan, in jeans and boots stood for a moment, watching, shook his head in disbelief and approached the immaculately dressed chauffeur.

"Right here," he said. The man looked him up and down, taking in the length of him, making an appraisal.

"Follow me, please. My name is Harry Tipton. Call me Harry, please." The man talked as fast as he walked. "I'll be your driver while you're in the city. On call twenty-four hours. My home number, answering service number and other important numbers that you might need while you're here are next to the phone in your room at the Warwick. I will also give you my card which has my numbers on it. Mr. Greshem made dinner reservations for you at Max's Kansas City."

As they approached the car—a long, black, stretch limousine—another man dressed just like Harry, but quite different in appearance opened the door.

"Mr. Stone?" He extended his hand. "I'm Ivory Black," the man said, pronouncing each of the three syllables of his first name. The name was appropriate. He was the blackest human being John Ryan Stone had ever seen.

"I will be at your service along with Harry. Should he not be available, I will assume his duties." He smiled broadly, flashing the biggest and whitest teeth imaginable. He wasn't exceptionally large, but every feature and aspect of his appearance was so well-defined that he was physically imposing. His voice was deep and resonant. "Welcome to New York."

"It's a long way from Nashville," John Ryan said as he slid into the car.

"It's a long way from anywhere," Ivory Black said, still smiling.

It is not comfortable to ride in a limo by yourself when you're not used to it, John Ryan discovered. It breeds self-consciousness, and there is a sense of isolation that is more clinical than luxurious. He knew he would be more comfortable in a taxicab, jawing with the driver; however, the treatment he was being given was significantly positive.

The hotel was vintage New York, mahogany, leather, burgundy, brass, and chandeliers. Harry had the bellman take John Ryan's luggage and Ivory Black took care of his registration.

He was assigned a small suite on the ninth floor. It came complete with a fully-stocked bar, an hors d'oeuvre tray replete with cheeses, smoked oysters and mussels, and a large bowl of fruit. There were fresh flowers, a view and a note from Jamie Greshem.

Welcome to New York! Hope you enjoy your escorts. Anything you need
or want, feel free to sign for. Harry and Ivory know where the Trayhorn
name is honored, which I have come to realize is most of the city. If you
have any problems, don't hesitate to call me at home, 429-3770. Ivory
also has my service number. ENJOY! Tomorrow will be a busy and exciting day. See you at nine.—Jamie

He thought about taking a shower, but his bags had not yet been delivered. Instead, he went to the bar, poured some bourbon over ice, stood at
the window and looked out over the city. The last time he stayed in New
York his room had afforded him only a view of a brick wall and the alley that
ran between them.

After receiving his bags and taking a quick shower, he put on a plain,
black tee-shirt, jeans, a pair of simple black Acme boots and a jacket. He was
on his third bourbon when the phone rang and a New York voice announced
that his car was waiting.

"This could get to be fun," he said to nobody as he pulled the door to
his room closed behind him.

Eating alone, however, wasn't fun regardless of the quality of the food
or the atmosphere. And despite all that was in the air for him, he didn't look
forward to it as he rode the solitary elevator to the lobby.

Harry Tipton and Ivory Black politely excused themselves from his offer to join him for dinner, and no one appeared to take notice of the long,
black limousine that delivered him to the door of Max's Kansas City.

Throughout the meal he found himself gulping his food, rushing to
get through it, not because there were exciting plans for the evening ahead,
but because of the solitude. In New York that could easily be remedied, but
he didn't need companions; he needed familiarity. It was like catching a big
fish and having no one to show it to or shooting a seventy-three on a golf
course when you're playing alone. The food was good, but dinner was awful.

———•••———

While John Ryan Stone was having dinner at Max's Kansas City, Philip
Barnessa was driving north on the New Jersey Turnpike from Philadelphia.
He was not happy. First, the turnpike was depressing; it passed by the South
Jersey development where he grew up.

Second, he hated New York. For all his confidence and bravado in Philadelphia, New York was intimidating and that thought made him cringe.

43

Those people had no sense of brotherhood; he didn't trust any of them. Third, he didn't like Giannini Tedesco putting the pressure on. The opening would come; it always had. The man was too impatient. He didn't understand and wouldn't listen. Fourth, he didn't like the idea of making this trip to talk to a fucking hillbilly. Fifth, he didn't like doing things when he had no choice or say in the matter. Friedman had called and told him to be there; something hot was in the oven. A fucking hillbilly. What did he know about stump-jumper music?

Finally, he didn't like driving alone. He figured he could probably get to number ten, but then he'd feel worse. "Time to get the fuck out," he mumbled to himself as he approached the Lincoln Tunnel. "John Ryan Stone. Why do all the hillbillies have to have three fuckin' names?" he asked the emptiness of the car as he started down the lighted entranceway to the tunnel.

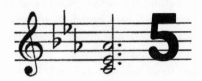

66Big day?" Harry Tipton asked as he guided the limousine through the early morning traffic. Harry was the only smiling face John Ryan saw. The faces of all the other drivers were either dead or seemed to be violently angry.

"Do you know something I don't know, Harry? And how the hell can you be so bright and shiny at this hour of the morning, driving in New York City?"

"It's what I do, sir. Have done for a long time and likely will do until I pack it in. No profit in being unhappy with what one does or one shouldn't be doing it. And no, sir, I don't know anything that you don't know. It just seems logical that this should be a big day for you."

"Logical?"

"Logical." Harry Tipton said. "Neither Mr. Black nor I have ever heard of you; Trayhorn is giving you the red carpet treatment, so it's logical that they consider you something special. Special people coming to New York for the first time on company business at company expense usually have big days. Logical. Here we are," he said as he pulled the car to a stop in front of a soot-smudged, gray, stone building. "Elevators on the right just past the newsstand. You'll want to go to the fourteenth floor. You know how to reach me."

The fourteenth floor—one of three occupied by Trayhorn International—was something else entirely. It glistened, a gleaming City of Oz above the bustling streets. John Ryan Stone felt very out-of-place.

In the reception area, white light reflected off white walls. Glass and chrome provided stark contrasts to the deep green carpet and other luxurious appointments. Large plants were coordinated by color and size with the rest of the design.

Gold and platinum records, framed and labeled with brass plaques, were hung three inches apart covering one entire wall. Other walls displayed company advertisements and charts taken from Billboard, Record World and Cashbox along with pictures of company executives in friendly poses with well-known personalities from the music world, actors, a few politicians and others easily recognizable to the general public. The front office was a monument to Trayhorn's success.

The woman seated behind the desk raised her head and gave John Ryan a dazzling smile. She was blonde and broad shouldered with opulent breasts and a small waist. He guessed she was in her early forties. She smiled at him warmly as she rose and extended her hand.

"You must be John Ryan Stone," she said.

"Yes ma'am," he said taking her hand.

"I'm Barbara Allred, Public Relations Director for our new-artist development program. Mr. Greshem is in his office. The others haven't arrived, including our receptionist, as I'm sure you noticed. If you'll follow me, I'll take you back. You just came in last night?"

"Yes ma'am." She smiled at his reply.

"I hope the ma'am is a courtesy and not a sign of advancing age on my part."

"Yes—" He stopped himself and smiled. "Definitely courtesy."

She was wearing a severely tailored, almost masculine, sand-colored, linen suit. A cascade of white ruffles spilled from her neck down the opening of her jacket. Her legs were long and slender, and she moved with purpose.

She stopped in front of a set of heavy double doors and stepped aside. A brass plaque identified it as James Greshem's office.

"John Ryan. Good to see you," the nattily dressed young man said, rising from his desk as Barbara Allred ushered John Ryan through the doors.

"Well, what have we here? The last time I saw you there were bags under those piercing, brown eyes and your clothes were wrinkled," John Ryan laughed.

"Bags?" Barbara said in mock disbelief. "Wrinkled clothes?"

"Bags and wrinkles," Jamie answered. "I had just spent two nights and two days without sleep listening to him trying to get something down on tape. It was a long session. Have a seat."

"Very long. So what's happened since you've been back in New York. I was beginning to wonder what was going on, everybody so excited and then nothing."

"I'll tell you about it. If all goes well and everything's agreeable, you're going to be a very busy man while you're here."

"If all goes well? Sounds ominous." He smiled. "I didn't come all the way up here to be made sport of." He stretched his legs and tried to relax into his chair. "So do you want to tell me exactly what I'm here for or do I have to guess?" he asked with a mischievous smile.

"There is a reason for what might seem to be our rather silly and secretive behavior. Personally, I thought it wasn't necessary either until I got wised-up—rather forcefully I might add. We did something down there that I got hell about and almost got Don fired. We didn't sign you to a preliminary contract. It's as simple and potentially devastating as that. I didn't believe it myself when I realized what we had done. It's so basic, so elementary, but we were so wrapped up in what we were trying to do and it all happened so fast, that we just plain forgot. Try telling that to the president."

"Why didn't you send me something to sign?"

"I wanted to when I realized it, but Bernie said 'no'."

"It bothered me too. Hell, I practically convinced myself that Trayhorn could probably prove it wasn't even me singin' if they wanted to." There was a cautious smile on his face.

"Probably. Fortunately for you, I don't do business that way. Do you have a lawyer?" John Ryan shook his head. "There's time, but you're going to need one. I won't be able to talk to you on quite the same terms the rest of the day as I can right now. A lot is going to be thrown at you and I may not be able to help you much. I did make sure Don would be in his office, so you can run things by him on the phone if you wish; tell our lawyers you're talking to your lawyer. I've tried to make it as easy and simple as I can."

"I have a feelin' none of it's gonna be simple or easy. I feel kind of like a goose that's gettin' ready to be cooked."

"Nothing in this business is simple or easy anymore," Jamie said. "There are going to be several people through here today, in and out. Some you'll like and some you won't. They're not Nashville people, and they aren't by any stretch of the imagination Don Hendrickson, but they are important to Trayhorn. I know it's a cliché, but they can make you or break you. I don't have the power to do that. All I can do is create an arena for success for you and for me, and, for better or worse, they're a big part of that." There was a tone of warning in Jamie Greshem's voice. John Ryan felt a large knot growing in his stomach.

"Some of these people don't appear very smart, but don't let that fool you. They do their homework. They'll know about your college degree. They'll know you taught school, and they'll know you're presently employed as a janitor, which some may take joy in. They also know that Bernie would not hesitate to take my nameplate off this door if he didn't approve of what I was doing.

"We've got about an hour to prep before the first of them gets here, and I want us prepped." The expression on Jamie's face changed. He became dead serious. "We're going to be talking about a lot of money, a lot of time, and a lot of work. Trayhorn needs a hit, a star, something bigger than anything they have at the moment. The singing sisters on TV are not making it; they'll break even at best this year. They thought Billy Duncan might develop, but after *Dangerous Man,* he hasn't had anything."

"But I'm not a performer. You know how I feel about that..." A cold sweat seeped out beneath his clothing.

"It has to be there; it's part of the package. Don't worry. We can get you ready. These people are not going to beg you. You're good and that's important. You're here; they don't have to look for you. It's the consummate example of being in the right place at the right time. On the other hand, you're not New York and you're not their discovery. With some that's a negative; however, the record will be on a new Trayhorn subsidiary label, Cross Country Records. That's a positive."

John Ryan was quiet.

"I'm going to arrange for coffee and Danish. Barbara can answer any questions that I can," he said as he left the office and closed the door.

John Ryan watched as Barbara Allred got up and took her place behind Jamie Greshem's desk. He wondered if the two of them had 'prepped' for him.

"I know from what Jamie has told me that this is all going to be very new to you. In one respect it's going to be exciting to the point that you might feel you're going to explode, that all of your wildest dreams and imaginings may have come true. In another, you will feel that you have no control over what is happening in your life. Both can be true. One kind of follows the other." Barbara did not mince words.

"If it's at all possible, try not to project. It sounds tough, but in this business things can be over before they get started. I'm not trying to put a damper on anything; I just want you to be prepared. Take care of business one step at a time, one day at a time. It's the only way to live and survive in this atmosphere." She paused. "It's not real, you know. And that's the last piece of personal advice I'll offer you." She showed the smile that was becoming comforting. He wondered if that was real.

"Okay, let's attack reality. At ten o'clock Philip Barnessa—he works out of Philadelphia—will be here. I didn't know he was coming until they told me this morning. He's pushed a bundle of hits over the years, has contacts all over the world, which will surprise you when you meet him, but he can get your records played in garden spots that never heard of Nashville. He's important to you. Treat him civilly regardless of how he reacts to you, but keep your guard up. Enough said. Eager Mills is a Barnessa wannabe who does basically the same thing in Chicago with no power. He will be here along with Joel Dishman from L.A. Joel's young but sharp. He's head of the music division in L.A. but has eyes for the film division." She paused.

"That it?"

"That's everyone who will be at the meeting. Bernie may stop in and there will be Jamie, Kate Belden and myself, of course. Kate will probably have a lot of responsibility in this project, but duties haven't been assigned yet. We're all running without automatic pilot on this. We've never handled a Nashville artist from here, so no one has any idea if we're making mistakes or not. You're an ideal first attempt because you have the background to handle it with less trouble than someone coming out of a more restricted environment." John Ryan Stone laughed.

"Restricted environment? You actually mean hillbilly, mountain man, cotton picker and a number of others I could come up with?" Barbara Allred's face reddened. "I'm sorry," he said.

"I'm the one who should apologize. I also left out talent."

"What do you mean?"

"You're ideal because you have talent."

"Thank you, ma..." They both laughed. "Okay, we've got the cast. You want to tell me a little bit about the play or do I learn as we go along?"

"This morning will be decision time. Barnessa will have reservations, but you've got to keep in mind that Philadelphia is not exactly a hotbed for your kind of music. That city still lives on the glory of Fabian, Frankie Avalon and Bob Marcucci. Something new to them, even though it might be big all over the rest of the country, takes awhile. It's a very eclectic scene there. Big on folk. Still listening and recording some 'doo-wop', but R&B is their main thrust. Barnessa can penetrate despite all of that. He can sell anything if he wants to. He can also destroy most anything, if he wants to.

"Providing the other two are impressed with you, everything will be on go because the company respects their opinion. I might as well tell you that because some money's already been spent, the records will be pressed, which guarantees the company a tax write-off, but that's only the first step. Without promotion no one will ever hear them. Today will determine the money they will risk."

"After lunch," she continued, "you'll meet with Jamie and the legal department. Jamie's done a lot of preliminary work, and I know he's run it by Don Hendrickson. You've got to know, John Ryan, Jamie has as much riding on this as you do. Probably more. Keep that in mind."

"I can appreciate that," he said. "What will we be doing in legal? Exactly."

"Preliminary contract discussions that spell out what the company does for you and what you do for the company. The finals won't be ready for several weeks, but they will want you to sign an agreement giving protection on the money they've already spent. The finals will have to include publishing rights, future options, advances, and penalties among other things. Bernie is the final authority on all contracts. That's about all I know to tell you right now, but I'll be glad to help in any way I can."

"Thanks."

"Good," she said. "After that is completed, whether it is today or tomorrow morning, you will meet with me or someone in my department, so we can put together a bio on you, get some quotes, arrange for pictures and determine if there's anything we have to hide. I have to tell you that even at this stage, they can drop you like the proverbial hot potato if they find out anything they don't want to hear."

"I did French-kiss a ten-year-old once, pure heaven..." he said thoughtfully as if he were trying to remember.

"When?" she asked, changing her demeanor slightly.

"When I was ten," he smiled. Barbara Allred laughed out loud.

"One for you," she said.

"I couldn't resist it. It's my way of dealing with intimidation."

"At least you have a way of handling it. I can't say don't be intimidated, but don't be."

"What's next?"

"Schedule and strategy, but I don't want to overwhelm you even though I know it's overwhelming. Most of that will be decided by Jamie and the others anyway. Do you have any questions?"

"More than I know to ask."

The meeting with the triumvirate from out of town was discomfiting. It was plain from the start that Philip Barnessa didn't like John Ryan Stone or his kind of music. Six feet tall, stocky with silver gray hair, rough Mediterranean features and all the accouterments including gold chains, bracelets and the requisite diamond pinkie ring. He had the polish of a carnival barker. But the man was important in some people's opinion and a joke with connections in the minds of others, John Ryan had learned. What he did seem to have from all of them was respect. It was hard to imagine him a power in the music business, but everyone at Trayhorn seemed to put him in that category, and it was obvious he loved the power.

Eager Mills from Chicago and Joel Dishman from L.A. were more in the mold of what he expected—Mills in his early forties, well-dressed and Midwestern business-like; Joel Dishman, a fireball, New York-sharp and California-casual. Of the three, Dishman appeared to be the most knowledgeable and most in concert with Jamie Greshem's feelings about his music.

When the morning was over, John Ryan wasn't certain what if anything had been decided. Joel Dishman joined Jamie and John Ryan for lunch. Philip Barnessa had an appointment—or so he said—and Eager Mills begged off saying he had calls to make.

Jamie took them to a small Jewish delicatessen not far from the building. It was crowded, but not so noisy that you couldn't hold a conversation. And the food was exceptional: hot pastrami on rye with an abundance of melted cheese, succulent knackwurst, Kosher corned beef shaved, piled two inches high and covered with Swiss, garlicky pickles, a variety of salads and Lowenbrau beer. The only thing that made conversation difficult was the way they attacked the food.

"So how do you feel?" Jamie asked.

"About what?" John Ryan asked. Be smart; let them do the talking, he thought.

"The meeting? The people. What you're seeing?"

"Oh, that." John Ryan feigned surprise and Joel Dishman smiled. "Well, I'm not sure exactly what we were doing. I heard a lot of talk about marketing and a wealth of other things. A lot of ideas were thrown around, but I couldn't tell you in any concrete terms what was achieved."

"You met people," Joel Dishman interjected. "Foreplay. Right now Barnessa's out calling his people, giving them impressions, and discussing what role he can play in the development process. Mills is doing the same thing. They'll put it all together, and then determine how far they think they can go with it. You can bet that Barnessa will make all his suggestions based on money and control."

"What about you?" John Ryan asked.

"I have to be honest; I've got some reservations, but then I thought Jimmy Gabriel was a sure-fire phenom," Dishman said.

"I'm not familiar with him."

"See what I mean?" Joel said with a smile. "At most he sold five hundred records. I think it's there, John Ryan, but you have to remember I have a West Coast mentality. We've got quasi-stars out there no one in the East ever heard of. To be frank, I'm not sure what it is you have. It's not country." John Ryan winced. "And it isn't rock and roll. I can't classify it as blues, but it's got a little bit of all of them. You have a unique quality."

"Barnessa thinks it's hillbilly," John Ryan said.

"Philip Barnessa is a problem and he's not dumb; don't ever underestimate him. We need him," the West Coast representative said with a pointed note of caution in his voice. "He's street-smart and music-business wise. He's also not one to cross. By the next time you see him, he'll know how many times a day you take a piss. He'll ask to run some copies of the acetates and have them played on a variety of small, out-of-the-way stations he or some of his friends have an interest in—for a 'market study'—and see what kind of reaction it gets. He's calling his people right now," Dishman said.

"How can he have it played when I don't even have a contract yet?"

"He can. He knows the risks. He knows it's against all the rules, knows we know what he's doing, but doesn't give a damn. It's the way he operates. He also knows we'll come to some kind of agreement this afternoon even if it's only temporary," Jamie said looking at his watch. "And speaking of that, we'd better get going. We've got lawyers at one."

"How long will it take Barnessa to do all that?"

"Not long," the Californian answered.

On the way back Jamie gave him a thumbnail sketch of what the attorneys might address. There would be discussions regarding sales royalties, publishing, management, agent participation, his physical and financial participation in promotion, and a variety of other things foreign to him. It was big business, and John Ryan felt very small as he passed through the revolving doors.

He was sitting alone in Jamie Greshem's office with his head still spinning from the outline Jamie had given him, when the door opened and a slender and comely young woman entered. She held a clipboard in one hand and closed the door with the other, unaware of his presence. When she turned toward the desk, there was a mixed reaction of surprise, befuddlement and embarrassment on her face.

At first glance she seemed just another of the attractive, polished and self-assured women he had seen passing through the halls of Trayhorn on their way to somewhere with something. Her face was an oval with the barest hint of squareness in the jaw line. There was a shallow dimple in the center of her chin, a pert nose and an easy smile. Her short, brown hair was shot though with golden highlights, but it was her eyes—deep blue with sunbursts of lighter blue and protected by long, dark lashes—that captured John Ryan's attention.

She wore a dark green, silk blouse and black slacks, which complemented an exceptional figure. In the briefest of moments she re-grounded, regained her composure and moved confidently toward him.

"I'm Kate Belden; you must be John Ryan Stone." She extended her hand. He took it and felt a firm, controlled grip.

"Yes ma'am." Kate Belden didn't wear a lot of makeup, and she wasn't New York model beautiful; it was a softer beauty, healthy and clean and unspoiled by working in the miasma that was the city.

"It's nice to finally meet you," she said.

Kate moved to an adjacent chair and sat down with a sigh of relief. John Ryan was immediately likable; she found it easy to relax. "Tough morning?" she asked.

"More than tough. I feel like I've been rode hard and put away wet."

She laughed. "I think I've heard that one before. Is that the standard operational form of Nashville nomenclature when in the big city or is it genuine?"

"I think it's genuine or at least designed to get a smile from city folk. Why?"

"Because I know you're educated, and I've been warned about Southerners. I've heard they can be more devious than big city gangsters."

"You might be right, but I'm still basically in the dark, and the meeting this morning didn't clarify a whole lot other than that a record will be put out and that it's pretty much up to Cassius, Brutus and Casca what's done with it after that." Kate laughed again.

"That's an interesting analogy," she said. "I know Cassius, but I'm not sure who you've cast as Brutus and Casca."

"Dishman and Mills in that order."

"Mills I can see, but I'm not sure about Joel as Brutus. He's pretty much his own man, not easily swayed unless it's in his own interest. Brutus was too noble and idealistic, or so the playwright suggests, to ever act in his own interests. No, if Joel thought something would take him closer to becoming a force in the film division then he might be moved to act. It's where he wants to be and he doesn't make a secret of it."

"'Moved to act,' that's good. I like that. You're quick, Kate Belden. What role will you play?"

"At the moment I'm just an extra, one of the crowd. I guess we'll just have to wait and see." She looked at her watch. "I only gave myself ten minutes to hide; I'd better get back to my office and see if anything has been accomplished." She got up from her chair, straightened her slacks and moved toward the door.

"What are you working on?" he asked.

"You," she answered. "Good to meet you, John Ryan Stone."

If the morning meeting with Barnessa, Mills and Dishman left his head spinning, the afternoon conference with the attorneys left his mind reeling.

Much of what the lawyers proposed was classified in their words as 'standard'. It was an easy word to use, and the more John Ryan heard it expressed in their offhand, smiling way, the more paranoid he became. They discussed everything Jamie had mentioned. Management, with which he was not familiar since he had never been managed, prompted the first call to Don Hendrickson.

Publishing was another major sticking point. The Trayhorn attorneys wanted fifty percent of all publishing rights for the company. This would give Trayhorn half the writer's royalties for sales of the music in any form. On this point John Ryan became wary and had them repeat every article of that section of the contract several times, asking for more specific explanations each time they went through it. That necessitated the second call to Nashville.

There were no standards, he learned, although it was not uncommon for new artists and songwriters to give up half their publishing rights. Yes, it could amount to huge numbers of dollars and long-term earnings if the song became a standard, became a favorite of easy-listening programming, a popular 'golden oldie', sold to Muzak, became a theme song for a television series or any number of other obscure earning niches. Yes, to not give it was a minor risk because the company could still back out of any major promotion, without which—regardless of the music's quality—it could become obscure before it became known. However, without saying anything specific, he gave John Ryan his answer. His last words in the conversation were "You might as well check your balls now; it's as good a time as any."

The Trayhorn attorneys held their own conferences with Bernie Greshem, who had stopped by to check on his son's progress, and others including Philip Barnessa, who seemed to appear at every turn. That in itself was disconcerting and led to a variety of speculations and suspicions.

Jamie invited John Ryan to dinner, but he declined. Barnessa offered to show him the town, which he also refused. The promoter accepted that, shook his hand, smiled and said he looked forward to working with him. The smile gave John Ryan a turn, but he put it aside. All the man could think of was a hot shower and a comfortable bed. He slept for twelve hours.

The second day was less frenetic than the first and perhaps a little easier to handle because most of the day was spent on the life and times and future of John Ryan Stone and his music. In his view it was also more productive because more tangible things were discussed and accomplished.

"Okay," Jamie said in the meeting with Kate Belden, Barbara Allred and the company's advance man, Rance Connelly. "I want to do this by the numbers. I don't want any more mistakes or oversights. I'm going to go through what's been decided and then we'll tackle the unknowns. First, we're going to release the first two sides regionally in small markets." Rance Connelly shook his head and Barbara Allred looked disturbed. "I know. I know. I was against it too, but you know who calls the shots.

"Nobody knows which region is the best barometer, but Barnessa and Mills think that's the safest way to go and Bernie agrees with them." He shrugged his shoulders. "The areas are not definitely decided, but I would guess Tennessee, Mississippi and Georgia in the Deep South, and Delaware, and Pennsylvania in the Northeast. There might also be a couple of small stations around L.A. that Dishman can push. If we don't get any major response, then we'll have to regroup, but let's not think about that.

"John Ryan, Don is arranging rehearsal space for you in Nashville, and we'll have a music director there to work with you if you need him. That's not standard, but you haven't had a lot of experience in front of people, and you're going to need help. Any questions so far?"

"Who am I going to be rehearsing with?" He couldn't help laughing. "I don't think we've quite gotten around to discussing that." The whole situation seemed ludicrous. The idea that he might go out, freeze up and fall flat on his face was prominent in his thoughts.

"I talked to Don," Jamie responded, "and we felt you would probably want to use most of the people we had on the session. There's a lot of good people around, but I want you to be comfortable."

"Would these people be available long-term?" Connelly asked.

"What do you mean by long-term?" John Ryan asked.

"Well, if things start to happen, you can't be changing your backup musicians every two weeks," Jamie said and looked at Barbara.

"We'll try to confirm through Don," she said and wrote something down.

"I think Mickey and Howie are okay, but I don't know about Son Cochran and Hopwood," John Ryan said.

"That leaves us with keyboards," Jamie said, as though Son and Bobby Hopwood were already in the cradle. "And maybe a versatile harmonica man. What do you think?"

"Paul Crockett might be available if you can talk him into leavin' Texas," Rance Connelly commented.

"Paul Crockett?" John Ryan had never heard of him.

"We had a record out last year on a band he played with, but they spent so much time fighting they could never get it together on a regular basis."

"Fighting?" John Ryan remarked with an incredulous look.

"Not him. The two group leaders, but that killed the group. They had a shot, too."

"Sounds wonderful." John Ryan shook his head.

"What about the keyboards?" she asked.

"I'll have to get Don to help me with that one," Jamie said.

"What are we talkin' about time-wise?" John Ryan asked. "I feel like I'm on a roller coaster here. I'm not sure I'm ready for all this." He could feel panic beginning to stir.

"You're not, but you will be. I'd like you to be in rehearsal early next week. We're looking at July or August for release. That gives us some time. We'll wait until you're ready. I've arranged for Stringer to come in and tape your rehearsals a couple of times a week. He'll make copies for you and the music director as well as for Don and me. John Ryan, I'll be honest with you; we're walking on eggshells here. All of us. Barnessa's cold and Bernie's only lukewarm. Mills bends with the wind and Joel is cautiously optimistic."

"I want to have you on the road for a few weeks before the release." Jamie looked to Kate Belden. "Do you have anything scheduled yet?"

"Not scheduled because I haven't heard anything final on an agency agreement, but I've got some ideas that I think will be easy to implement. I'd like to get a few small clubs in Mississippi, Georgia and then use some of Rance's contacts in Florida, but I don't want to schedule him somewhere and then have difficulties. After all this is not the way we usually operate, Jamie." John Ryan thought she sounded a bit annoyed.

"I'll run it by Bernie," Jamie said. "I think we can get the agent and management thing settled this afternoon. What about the Northeast? Any ideas there?"

John Ryan listened, wondering how it was going to be having other people manage his life for him. On one hand it might be easy, like the army, no decisions to make; on the other, he worried about how he could adapt to it. On either hand, it wasn't going be a cakewalk.

"I've got pictures scheduled for later this afternoon," Kate added. Any suggestions for a look?"

"Natural. No change," Jamie said looking to Barbara for confirmation. She nodded.

"Should I put a roll of coins in my pocket?" John Ryan quipped. It was rumored that a lot of rock stars did that to advertise what they didn't have.

"Hey, whatever gives you confidence," Kate smiled.

"Nickels or quarters?"

"Why not silver dollars?" she replied.

"I don't want to be that big a star." They all laughed and everyone relaxed.

The rest of the meeting detailed what they had already discussed. After the women left, John Ryan and Jamie agreed that Trayhorn would provide temporary management until the singer got legal counsel. One person from the company would handle both management and agency to get things rolling. Jamie Greshem suggested it should be Kate Belden and John Ryan agreed.

———·—

When John Ryan Stone arrived at Nashville International Airport two days later, he was not being paged, and no one was there to meet him. As he walked to the ground transportation area, the tightness in his shoulders eased, and he felt the land weakness in his legs. He was home, and for all the excitement and all of the prospects that had been laid before him, he didn't think he would miss New York at all.

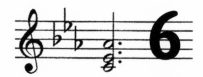

John Ryan poured a bourbon, picked up the old Martin guitar and went out on the porch. There was an old metal sofa-glider that had been there when he and Jenifer moved in. He had done a lot of good work sitting in the glider, moving slowly back and forth, allowing words and music to drift around in his head while he strummed aimlessly on the guitar. *One Lonely Night* had been written there and the rough of *What Can I Do To Make You Love Me Tomorrow* had taken shape in the same spot. It was a good place, and he knew he wouldn't trade it for all of New York.

It was a warm night. Spring had come to Middle Tennessee summer-like and with it a symphony of natural sounds that had been at rest during the cold months. He often amused himself trying to find repetitive melodies and consistent rhythms in the sounds of the cicadas and crickets and frogs whose deep-throated bass sounds emanated from some hidden pond or wash that he had never seen.

Success is strange, he thought. It's much easier to see it from a distance, either coming or gone. He was not a success. Yet. But it did appear that some degree of it was coming. Fast. John Ryan Stone found that difficult to accept. He had worked and there had been a struggle, he guessed, but it was not easy to believe that he had worked hard enough or that the struggle had been long enough—only three years—to have all of this handed to him. None of the days, nights, hours or minutes had ever held any assurance of success. They had been gambled on blind faith if one believed in the possibility at all. Still and all, from his perspective now, it hadn't been that difficult. He wondered if the hard part was over or just beginning.

Rehearsals would begin in the morning at The Warehouse. Howie and Mickey were set, as were Son Cochran, Bobby Hopwood, and a keyboard man Hendrickson had hired known only as Mountain Red. Rance Connelly had brought in Paul Crockett from Texas to play harmonica, and Cade Wilhite, an engineer with Memphis and Nashville credits, had been contracted to create a sound system and act as the band's tech person.

It's all here, John Ryan thought. Everything is in place. It's time to produce. He sipped at his bourbon and idly picked at a small riff he had learned from someone somewhere. He was no lead guitarist, but picking up simple riffs was part of the Nashville learning experience, like playing pinball, guitar pulls, auditions, drinking and drugging, if one chose, and putting everything else in your life one place behind the music, and he had surely done that.

The Warehouse was named appropriately; the name indicative of exactly what it had been. A large corrugated steel building, it had been jury-rigged into a rehearsal hall for minor artists putting shows together for bus tours of one-nighters, artists forming new back-up bands, groups incorporating new players into an existing act or simply for rehearsal periods. None of the amenities had changed from its days as a warehouse except for a few primitive acoustic panels, a stage and one bank of lights. The sanitary facilities were provided by Porta-San, as they had been in its industrial days.

"Well I can't say the accommodations are exactly deluxe," Mickey said as they stood inside the entrance of the building.

"It's big and it's dry," Howie added.

"Made for stars," John Ryan said, looking around.

Son Cochran was moving about the stage following Cade Wilhite as he checked out the equipment. There was nothing they would need and little they could want that was not there. Custom amplifiers and speakers were stacked on either side of the staging area, and a bank of small monitors facing the playing area were lined up across the front of the four foot high platform. Three mikes were stationed up front for John Ryan, Mickey and Howie and booms for Cochran and the keyboard man. It was all just a beginning, and everything would change before anyone ever saw or heard them. For the time being the music was the focus, but the equipment alone took them to an unfamiliar level.

"So, what do you think?" Son asked with a smile. It was obvious he had seen what John Ryan was experiencing before. Raised in Memphis, Cochran joined the musician's union at fourteen and had made his living playing full-time since he was fifteen when he had to lie about his age to get into the bars where he was working. There was little in the music business he hadn't seen.

59

"How the hell should I know what to think?" He looked at Mickey who looked ready to explode. "Do you know what to think?"

"I think I think I don't know what the hell to think." It was vintage Mickey-talk, and they all laughed.

At nine-thirty Mountain Red, a redheaded behemoth, walked through the door. John Ryan wasn't sure he had ever seen a man as big. He stood at least six feet six inches tall and appeared to weigh well over three hundred pounds. A few minutes later Paul Crockett arrived—a dark, sullen man whose attitude said what his words didn't.

At their first rehearsal it was rough. For the first two hours nothing came together. They tried a few familiar songs, but there was no excitement or anything to make them believe that this group of musicians could ever produce anything out-of-the-ordinary. They were like pieces of a jigsaw puzzle, singularly meaning nothing and not yet fitting together.

The emergence began on an old Hank Williams classic, *I'm So Lonesome I Could Cry*. John Ryan's voice was clear and suggested more strength than the remake B. J. Thomas had hit with. John Ryan carried them through it three times, each time refining it, each time beginning conventionally and then moving away from the country take on the song. As they worked it, the band reached deeper into the singer, and Paul Crockett's plaintive harmonica became a second voice, serving as a counterpoint to the words John Ryan was singing. The whole sound began to meld into something they hadn't expected. By the time they were ready to move on to the next song, the old standard had become a country-influenced blues tune.

When it was time to break, no one wanted to stop the flow that was gestating among the seven musicians. They had worked on only three songs. Familiarity with the music eliminated one problem, and even though each had their own interpretation, ideas continued to develop and fused different concepts into a workable whole.

They modified the beat on an old Porter Wagoner song, *Satisfied Mind*, and Paul Crockett, who no one knew could play guitar, showed Mickey how to put a shade of Curtis Mayfield's sound into the break. It was the strangest suggestion Son Cochran had ever heard, but it worked.

Mountain Red suggested a little-known tune called *Midnight Rain*, written by an unsung genius known to Nashville musicians but hardly anyone else. He had died in obscurity on a motorcycle at age thirty-six and then become a Nashville legend.

As they worked, John Ryan's sound changed. It was difficult for those familiar with his voice and demeanor, and most of all John Ryan himself, to understand where the sudden strength and aggressiveness was coming from.

Nothing they accomplished approached performance level, but they saw promise. The blend was raw and coarse by some standards, but they weren't sure that wasn't what it was supposed to be.

At three-thirty in the afternoon Kate Belden, Larry Foster and Connelly walked through the door of The Warehouse. The band was eating lunch. They had been rehearsing for five hours, and weariness had begun to show in their playing and their emotional levels. John Ryan had seldom played so consistently for such a long period, and despite years of chording a guitar, small white blisters were appearing below the calluses on the fingers of his left hand. Mickey had finally called a halt to the work and sent Cade Wilhite out for food. He returned with nine pizzas, two cases of beer and six bottles of Pepsi Cola for Son Cochran who didn't drink. It was a relaxed crew that the threesome from New York walked in on.

"Can I help you?" Howie asked as the group strode toward the stage.

John Ryan smiled when he saw the trio and pulled himself up from the floor. "I don't think you can help them, Howie; I think they're here to help us."

There were assorted greetings, and most of the group returned to their food.

"How's it going?" Kate asked after John Ryan put a pizza box and two Budweisers on the floor. There were several chairs sitting around, but no one used them.

"Thirsty?" he asked.

"Well, I don't normally drink beer, but then I don't normally sit on the floor to eat either." She liked the smile he threw at her and knew it would look even better when she accomplished what she had been assigned to do. He definitely had charisma. "My question?" She returned his smile.

"How's it going? Well, we haven't had any fights. Crockett tried to start one," he said in jest, remembering what Connelly had said about the harmonica player, "but we wouldn't let him."

"My question?"

"Get right to the point, don't you? Now a smart man would try to figure out what you want to hear, but I'm not a smart man. For the first day and the first time together, we're doing as well as can be expected." There was a grin on his face.

"Very informative, Stone. When are you running for President? Seriously. Give me the skinny."

"The skinny? Does the South live in Kate Belden?" She wasn't smiling. "The skinny," he said affirmatively. "Okay. The skinny—in my opinion—is that it's a good group of guys, top pickers. We do seem to be able to work together, but at this point that's all I can say. I think I see some interesting possibilities, but this is a new angle for me. We're gonna run through what we've done after the break and call it a day. Stick around. You be the judge."

"I will," she answered, giving him a false look of skepticism followed by a smile.

When the musicians took the stage, there was a lot of tinkering with sound levels—Cade Wilhite still feeling out the system he had created, trying to fit it to what he had heard during the rehearsal—tuning, some good-natured repartee, and a camaraderie that surprised Kate in a group of men that had been together for only a few hours. It was unlike many of the bands she had worked with in New York who, even after several years of working together, hardly spoke to one another. The butterflies of anticipation were churning in her stomach as the band discussed what song they would begin with and who would do what on the breaks. Connelly was watching Kate and her expressions and smiled to himself as she nervously scribbled meaningless designs on the clipboard she held in her lap.

"Nervous?" he asked.

"I don't know whether I'm nervous or excited. It's strange. I have no idea what to expect, but I do know whatever I report to Jamie before this week is over will have a major effect on the life and times of John Ryan Stone. What about you? Nervous?"

"I guess I'm a realist. Expect little and see what happens; it's a first rehearsal. I've been in this business too long to ever get too excited or too disappointed. Too many sure things have added up to nothing and vice-versa."

Son Cochran counted off the beat for the first song. They began with *I'm Leavin' This Town and Movin' On*, an upbeat standard that was less complicated in its arrangement than any of the other songs they had rehearsed. It was a tension reliever. When it was finished, they went straight into *I'm So Lonesome I Could Cry*. John Ryan had chosen the order, deciding he might as well put himself out front early and bear the brunt of whatever might happen. *Midnight Rain* was next. In the short pause between it and the last song, he could hear Foster, Connelly and Kate Belden talking, but their words were imperceptible.

Satisfied Mind was more unique and offbeat than any of the other songs they had done. When the Curtis Mayfield sounding introduction began, the observers were taken aback. Kate Belden didn't know what to think. She turned to Connelly who shrugged, and they both looked for Larry Foster but couldn't locate him; he had moved to the back of the building. The opening line, sung in harmony by John Ryan, Mickey and Howie turned their attention back toward the stage. John Ryan's voice came in alone on the third line. Mickey played the break, using every intonation Paul Crockett had shown him, and on the final lines Crockett's harmonica formed a duet with the singer that expressed more than the song had to say. It was an uncompromising lyric and John Ryan got all of it. When it was over, there was no reaction from those who were listening.

As the musicians disconnected their instruments and put them away, John Ryan circulated and thanked them. He was subdued as he came off the stage and approached Kate, Connelly and Larry Foster, who had rejoined the group. He didn't know what to expect. There was a smile on Kate's face when he sat down next to them. Foster and Connelly's faces were noncommittal and unreadable.

"Well," Kate said as if she were impressed.

"Well?" he questioned.

"For one day's work, it was impressive. Different, unexpected, but impressive," Connelly said.

"I'm worried about the direction." Larry Foster said with some concern. "I'm not sure how to classify what I just heard. It's country, I guess, but it's different than any country I've ever heard. It's got a little blues, a little soft rock. I like it, but I'm just not sure how to categorize it. I don't want to confuse anybody; it's easier to sell one specific sound. If it gets confused, program directors don't know how to program it, and the P.R. people won't know how to promote it."

"Are you saying that in your opinion what we're doing might not sell?" There was no animosity or resentment in his voice.

"I'm not sure how to answer that," Foster said. "Jamie asked me to help you refine the sound, give it anything I think it needs, determine if the instrumentation needs any modifications, work on harmonies and arrangements if you need it. Of course, selling is a part of all that. The one thing he doesn't want me to do is make any great change in what you do. That's what sold him, and that's what he wants."

"Do we need to change any of those things you mentioned?"

"It's hard to tell yet; I've only heard four songs. What you did today was good. I'm amazed at what you accomplished. I thought it was interesting, and I'm especially intrigued by the mixing of styles, but that's also the thing that concerns me. I'm not sure you have time to spend developing something you can't use immediately. You've only got four weeks and…"

"Whoa, hoss, what's this about four weeks?"

"That's two weeks before the record's released. I was going to tell you," Kate said, looking disappointed, as if it were a surprise she thought would please him. "Jamie wants at least a couple of performances in that week."

"I appreciate your lettin' me know," he said in a mildly sarcastic voice. "I thought we had a couple of months?"

"You did."

"You want to explain that to me?" John Ryan asked.

"Over dinner. You and I have some things to discuss, but I need to go back to the hotel. We'll be spending some time together, so we reserved a room for you, so you don't have to run back and forth. Don said your place was pretty far out..."

"How do you mean that?" He grinned.

"Distance, John Ryan, distance...Is that all right with you?" she asked, suddenly realizing that she hadn't given him any choices.

"I'll have to get some clothes. How long should I plan on?"

"I'm only scheduled here for three days, and we've got a lot to accomplish..."

"Guess I'll bring three days worth. What time do you want me back?"

Kate looked at her watch. "It's a little after five...Seven all right?"

"Seven's fine. I'm not that far out." His blue eyes were bright with amusement.

"Are you sure?'

"I'm sure."

"Room 514. I'll see you then." She gathered Foster and Connelly and was gone.

His room was bathed in dying sunlight when he opened the door. It was comfortable and one floor below Room 514.

John Ryan expected Rance Connelly and Larry Foster to be with them for dinner, but when Kate opened the door, it was apparent that they were dining alone. Looking beyond her into the room, he could see a table set for two and a bottle of wine chilling.

She wore white slacks and a scoop-necked, peach-colored blouse, which accented her breasts without in any way being revealing or obvious. A narrow belt with a small, monogrammed gold buckle encircled her waist. John Ryan was wearing jeans, a blue denim shirt with epaulets and moccasins.

Her smile seemed more casual and less guarded than it was in New York or at The Warehouse earlier in the day. Maybe it was because they were alone. Whatever the reason, relaxation became her. Despite the disparity in their dress, he didn't feel ill-at-ease.

"Reporting at the appointed time and place as ordered, ma'am," he said, his blue eyes complementing a wide smile, "but I didn't know it was formal. I thought you said casual and work."

"It is casual and there will be work. Come on in," she said and stepped aside to allow him to enter the room.

"No Foster and Connelly?"

"Not tonight. I like them and I trust them—Connelly anyway; I really don't know Larry that well—but I want to run some things by you without being concerned about New York knowing your reactions before I get back there."

"Am I dealing with the CIA here?" He laughed. "After all, I'm just a plain, ol' itinerant, country songwriter."

"From what I see and know, you are hardly plain, and you're no longer itinerant, but you do have a lot to learn. The music business can make the CIA pale by comparison."

"Well, I'm here to learn, Teach," he said, seating himself on the expansive couch that graced the sitting room of the suite.

"Dinner before business. Bourbon and water?" she asked as she moved toward the bar. "Isn't that what you drink?"

"Joel Dishman told me Barnessa would know what kind of underwear I wore before I left New York, but I didn't know all of my personal preferences would be common knowledge."

"It pays to know things," Kate replied as she mixed the drinks. "Lemon? Lime? Mint?"

"Just water, thanks."

"I took the liberty of ordering," she said sitting in an easy chair adjacent to the couch.

"You don't mind eating here, do you? I thought it would be more conducive to conversation."

"Depends on what you ordered," he answered, sipping at the amber liquid. It tasted good on his tired throat. He had thought about having a shot of Jack before he left his room, but decided he'd best keep his wits about him.

"A chicken pate with pistachios, asparagus and tomato salad, lamb chops medium rare, Florentine potatoes and glazed carrots. If there's anything you want to change, I can call it in."

"I was hopin' for fried chicken or bar-be-cue, but I guess I can make do."

"You are kidding."

"Yes, I'm kidding," he laughed.

"Drink all right?" He nodded. "So, tell me about you, John Ryan Stone."

"I thought you got all that in New York."

"Hey, we're going to be working together, and with what I have to do for you, I need to know you. More than they know in New York.

"What do you want to know?"

"No secrets?" she asked.

"No secrets."

"Because we can't work together if there are any hidden agendas."

"You a little bit paranoid there, Belden?"

"A little," she smiled.

"Ask away."

"Why are you doing this? I've worked with several artists and it always intrigues me. Each of them had a different answer. At first most of them gave money, fame and sex as reasons, but after I was with them for awhile, I realized that they didn't really know. After all, it isn't the best of all possible worlds despite the trappings." There was intensity in her eyes, but the warm fullness of her smile protected it from being intimidating.

"That's a good question, but I'm not sure I have an answer." His words were relaxed and uncalculated. "I've always loved music, listened to a lot of 'beach music' when I was growin' up back in South Carolina. Never thought about country music until I was in my late teens. That was about the time I started playin' around with a guitar. Guy by the name of Red Hill taught me an E an A and a B seventh. Said I could play most any country song with those three chords, so I started listenin' to country music. Actually I wanted to be able to play what I heard so I could get girls."

Kate laughed. The electricity of her smile was energizing.

"I'd always written little poems that were too romantic and silly, but the girls seemed to like them better than my singing. Problem was they liked guitars better than poems, so I started puttin' 'em to music. Best of both worlds."

"Did you get any girls?" she asked coyly.

"Not many."

"That's just a little too glib for me to swallow, Stone, but sooner or later I'll find out the real reason." There was a challenging curiosity in her voice.

"Tell me something, Kate, from the hip. I know you were treading water in front of Foster, but what did you really think about what you heard this afternoon?" he asked as he filled his glass.

"Honestly?"

"Unless, of course, lying is necessary to make me feel good."

"I have a lot of mixed feelings. First of all, I'm not the world's greatest at choosing what is going to hit and what isn't. I get gut feelings and I have opinions, but they're not always accurate. I manage what's there. I can create an image, sell a persona, run interference, cover up things that need covering up, read a crowd and take care of details. That may be my greatest talent, taking care of details."

"Are you evading the question?" he asked with a wry smile.

"I never evade questions," she said with a smirk. "Sometimes I don't give totally honest answers, but I never evade a question."

"Give me a totally honest answer." It was said in a tone more serious than anything she had heard him say. There was no glibness in these words, no fishing for a compliment.

"I was impressed and surprised. It's hard to believe what you accomplished in such a short time. I know what they say about Nashville musicians—'Hum a few bars, and they'll play it better than anyone you ever heard play it before'—but the sound was tighter than I could have imagined. I guess I expected some major weaknesses, but I didn't really hear any. Don't misunderstand me, there's a long way to go and it was only four songs, but I was truly impressed." Kate looked at him; the intensity in her eyes was still there. "I loved it. From all the tales I'd heard about your reluctance to perform...."

"That's a nice way to put it," he laughed. "Reluctance to perform."

"Your reluctance to perform," she went on, "I wasn't sure you could put it together outside a studio situation; they're two different worlds. I also wasn't sure you could make the transition from writer to performer and ever be able to do anyone's music but your own, but you did that pretty well. The first song—what was it?"

"*I'm Leavin' This Town And Movin' On.*"

"That didn't do much for me. It was okay, but I couldn't have pulled it out of a hundred other country songs I've heard. You got me on the Hank Williams tune. I liked the voice, and I liked the bluesy slant you put on it. Your quality is down and out strong, yet vulnerable at the same time. I've never heard the third one before. It's a great song, and I think you could do a lot with it, but it was *Satisfied Mind* that blew me away. I've heard the Byrds record, but this was something else entirely. Who came up with the sound?"

"Hell, I don't know who came up with any of the sounds. We just played around with all of them. It's kind of the way things are done down here. Paul Crockett gave us the idea. He suggested the Mayfield guitar, and it just went on from there."

Kate smiled, "I said dinner, didn't I? I'll have it here in twenty minutes." John Ryan watched her as she walked to the phone. Somewhere in the past she had been an athlete or a dancer. There was grace and softness in her movement, each step flowing into the next. "Fix yourself another drink, and

I'll tell you about the haircut while we're waiting." She shot him a tongue-in-cheek grin and looked for a reaction, but he just shook his head.

By the time dinner arrived, John Ryan had learned that before rehearsal in the morning, he was going to get a haircut—it would cover his collar but not his ears. It would be thick and long, but it wouldn't touch his shoulders—and that he would be fitted for a new wardrobe, which would consist primarily of jeans, boots and long-sleeved shirts with the epaulets he loved. The look would be neat and strong but unpolished. Barbara Allred, Jamie Greshem and Kate had decided to change their original concept after John Ryan left New York. There was a growing resentment in some segments against long hair on men, and they didn't want visual perception to confuse him with rock and roll, or drugs.

He agreed reluctantly to the haircut because he could see in Kate Belden's face that there was no room for argument. He also agreed to the fittings for the same reason, although, for the sake of not being too agreeable, he wouldn't assure her that he would wear the clothes.

The dinner was lovely: served well, and everything done as ordered. And Kate Belden was lovely.

When they finished eating, John Ryan poured each of them a brandy, warming it in the flame of one of the candles that graced the table, being careful not to get the candle smoke on the glass. Kate relaxed in her chair and took in the whole of the man that sat before her.

"You are one of the most patient human beings I have ever come into contact with," she said as she sipped her brandy.

"You want to explain that?"

"You've been here more than two hours, and you haven't asked one question about the record's release or the fact that you will be performing in four weeks. I expected a million questions—that's the usual reaction—and unbearable excitement."

"Maybe I'm afraid." There was humor in his face, but what he said wasn't entirely inaccurate.

"Somehow I don't think so."

"Well, let's get on with it then," he smiled. "When, where, how and why?"

"Let's start with the 'why'. Barnessa tested the record in a couple of small markets right after you left New York. Jamie said he told you that would happen." John Ryan nodded. "Anyway, the reactions were outstanding..."

"On which one?" he interrupted and leaned forward.

"*What Can I Do To Make You Love Me Tomorrow?*. It was the only one he tested, but it got an eighty-five percent approval mark from the listeners and virtually a hundred percent from the program directors. Now these are small markets, but he thinks—and don't get too excited about Barnessa's opinion—that it could be big."

"Man..." The sound was almost a whisper, uttered as he leaned back in his chair.

"What?"

"I would've picked *One Lonely Night* out of the ones we did. That's amazing."

"These were not country stations. Rural, middle-of-the-road, but not country. That puts a new light on things. It's kind of funny; you don't even have a record out, and your market's already expanding. We'll have a fight with Philip on that one. He thinks you should forget country and go strictly for the middle-of-the-road market."

"I won't do that." His voice was firm.

"I won't let you. I think—and Jamie agrees—that it could get buried in that market. That's why we're releasing in six weeks. We want it into the country market two weeks before Barnessa can get his machine rolling and push you into a niche none of us can get you out of."

"I take it he doesn't know the date."

"Not really. He will, but hopefully by then it will be too late for him to do anything about it."

"I don't want to be around when he finds out."

"Don't worry; you won't be, but that's Jamie's problem anyway. He's doing this all on his own, and there's going to be hell to pay. If he wasn't the president's son, he might not survive." She paused. "I have to be frank with you here, John Ryan, and I'm going out on a limb, but I have to trust you. Barnessa plays rough. There are no allegiances where business is concerned. He has his own people to answer to and he's been a money-maker. That's the name of the game."

Her statement took a lot of the joy out of what was happening in his life. A cold fear had been introduced into the equation. His had always been a simple plan: write songs, sell them to another artist to record and, thus, make a living doing what he loved to do. He was beginning to realize how naïve that was. Now he was the artist; he couldn't say 'good-by' to his songs and let them live on their own.

The continued references to 'Barnessa's people' created a growing concern that an element he had only read about in newspapers and seen portrayed in movies was having an influence on his life. He was beginning to feel threatened by the company that was offering him what he had worked for. Even Kate Belden was suddenly not the pristine and pure guiding light he had cast her as. And what about Jamie Greshem and Don? If they could live and work with these people....

"Sounds sweet," he remarked as he poured another brandy.

"Don't dwell on it; everything's going to work." It sounded like 'trust me' to him.

"Tell me about the 'when', 'where' and 'how'?." His irritation was obvious. There was an inflection of disillusionment or 'I knew it was too good to be true' attitude in his demeanor. She was learning one more thing about John Ryan Stone.

"'When' is four weeks. I've got three dates lined up for you. They won't be advertised, and under no circumstances will you do the new material. There won't be any publicity. This whole thing is just to tighten up the band and give you a chance to feel an audience. It's something only live action can give you, but you know that."

"Where?"

"The Silver Saddle Saloon in Biloxi, Mississippi, The Down-Home Roadhouse in Fort Walton Beach, Florida, and you do a weekend at a place called Doogie's outside of Savannah. Hendrickson has leased a bus for you and the band. Cade Wilhite will bring the equipment on a truck. Jamie and I will probably see you at Doogie's." When she finished, her businesslike posture softened.

"Could I have another, please?" she asked, holding up her glass. Her eyes were focused on him. "Don't let all this scare you, John Ryan. I feel silly saying that to a man with your age and background; I'm used to dealing with twenty-year-old dropouts, but trust me."

There it was. He smiled.

"Isn't that what the guy says to the girl on the third date?"

"You can," she smiled, "and I guess I deserved that."

Looking at her, there was no way to believe he couldn't trust her. She was warm and soft—an enigmatic change from the woman she had been just moments before.

"I'll have to think about that, Kate Belden, but right now I've had enough to eat and drink, and it's time to turn off my brain such as it is, fold my tent and creep off into the night. Tomorrow will come early," he said as he rose from his chair.

"Good song title."

"Write it down."

"I will. Good night, John Ryan Stone."

"Good night, Kate Belden."

He found himself thinking about Kate Belden long after the door had closed behind him.

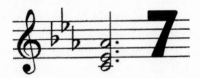

When Philip Barnessa received word that Jamie was releasing John Ryan's record early, he exploded. The pressure from Giannini Tedesco was enough; now the little Jewish fuck was trying to screw him. A lot of things in the business changed, he told himself, but he had no doubts about still being able to scare the hell out of a twenty-five year old punk.

It was three o'clock in the morning when Jamie Greshem awoke in his West End Avenue apartment. He reached for the telephone that was ringing in that fog of space between deep sleep and awareness. The foreboding that usually accompanies a middle-of-the-night phone call was accelerating as he put the receiver to his ear. Intuitively, he knew who was calling.

"Hello?" he answered, trying to clear the sleep from his head and give some impression of lucidity. There were no niceties, no protocol, not even 'hello'. Philip Barnessa's voice was livid.

"Do you want to tell me what the fuck's going on?" He paused. "No, I don't want you to tell me. Not now. I don't want to hear it over the phone; I want to see your face. I'll be in New York day after tomorrow, and I want some fuckin' answers..."

"Phil..." He was cut off.

"No. No, you don't say anything. You're pullin' some shit I'm not gonna deal with, Greshem. You're a baby who don't know his ass from nothin'. I'll be in your office at one o'clock, and don't go runnin' to your daddy; he ain't gonna help you out on this one. Don't do anything between now and then, and I mean nothin'. And don't fuck with me. You got a lot to learn, pal!" The phone was slammed into its cradle, and the dial tone came on immediately as if the connection was dancing to the tune of Philip Barnessa's voice.

Jamie could feel nausea beginning to roll in his stomach. There was little time to create a plan; he had to act and, strangely, that brought a mild relief. Even as he lay staring at the ceiling, his mind began racing toward the day ahead.

Kate Belden and Rance Connelly would be recalled from Nashville. He decided that in addition to Kate and Rance, he would bring in Joel Dishman from L.A. if he was available. He needed support and perhaps they could provide it if Barnessa had questions that he couldn't answer. He would also have to contact Don Hendrickson and make him aware of Barnessa's call and impending visit. Barbara Allred would be present as well. There was brief consideration of talking to his father—not to ask for clout, just advice—but he decided against it. He had to stand up and see how he fared.

Jamie pulled himself up from his bed and went into the bathroom. It didn't occur to him until the steaming, hot water from the shower head was beating down upon his shoulders that he was unconsciously going through the process of getting ready for work, and it was only three-thirty in the morning.

The security guard at the Trayhorn Building knew him well, so he didn't question Jamie Greshem's coming to work before daylight, and Jamie was too lost in thought to acknowledge him. It was too early for any of the 'trades' to have arrived; consequently, there would be nothing to distract him in planning his strategy for what promised to be a tumultuous day.

There was no way to immediately know how Philip Barnessa had discovered his plan for the early release of John Ryan Stone's record, that was something he would have to research. Jamie also suspected that it wasn't the strategy that disturbed the man so much as the fact that the young producer had attempted to circumvent his authority, unofficial though it was. Opposition was not threatening to a man like Barnessa who had survived the neighborhoods, the usurping of control and the challenging of power was. Philip Barnessa would not only lose a lot of money if John Ryan Stone went one hundred per cent country but also, Jamie was sure, a large part of his security.

At eight-fifteen Barbara Allred arrived. She was not surprised to find the coffee made and Jamie Greshem sitting behind his desk. The door was open, so she had no hesitation about entering.

"Good morning," she said from the doorway.

"Barbara. Come in. You're a bit early this morning, aren't you?" He looked at his watch. "Eight-fifteen?"

"I couldn't sleep this morning, so I decided I might as well come in." She was nervous and unsettled.

"I couldn't either. Have a seat. I need to talk to you."

"So tell me, what's been keeping you awake and upsetting your stomach?" He was surprised to find himself wondering if he could trust even Barbara.

"Philip Barnessa called me last night. I think he knows about the early release."

"He knows; he called me too," the young man said leaning back in his chair. "What did he say to you?"

"He started out pleasant enough." She saw the raised eyebrow on Jamie's face. "Well, as pleasant as Philip can ever be, but it didn't take him long to turn. He asked how things were going with the new project. He also wanted to know where Kate is."

"What did you tell him?"

"That she was taking a few days vacation. I assume he had tried to call her."

"I'm sure. What else?"

"Not a lot of specifics. He tried to pick my brain about what was going on in Nashville. When I told him I didn't know, he got nasty. Said he was tired of being kept in the dark, but that he would find out what he wanted to know, and when he did, there would be hell to pay for somebody."

"We don't have any doubt about who he was referring to there, do we?" he smiled.

"I'm afraid not."

"What time did he call?"

"About ten-thirty."

"He must've been busy; he didn't call me until three. I guess he wanted to do his homework, and he must've gotten it done because he didn't have any questions for me."

"What do you mean?" Jamie could see worry in her face. Barbara Allred had been with Trayhorn long enough to have seen the results of the Italian's wrath.

"Just that. No questions, just threats. Nothing that I could repeat to a lady."

"I'm familiar with his language; he doesn't reserve it just for men." There was a tension-relieving smile.

"He put on a ruse that he knew something was going on, but wasn't sure exactly what; however, judging from the temperature at which he was operating, I'm sure he knows every detail." He looked to Barbara Allred's face for a reaction and wondered if he were becoming paranoid. "He's going to be here tomorrow at one o'clock, and I want everyone here."

73

"Bernie?"

"No, not Bernie. Just you, Kate, Rance and Joel. I'm not sure exactly what tack we'll take yet, but I'm working on it. Maybe we'll have strength in numbers," he said, knowing that was an absurd thought. Numbers wouldn't faze the man, but he thought it might change the playing field. Barnessa's type thrived on intimidation, but playing that game was repugnant to Jamie. He wouldn't even know where to start. Phillip was correct on one count: he was a 'baby'. Barbara Allred's voice broke him from the train of thought he was riding.

"I guess I've got some work to do," she said as she got up from her chair.

"Yes. Send the corporate for Kate and Rance, and then call them and tell them what time to be at the airport. Don't tell them any details of our conversation, just that I have something I want them to do back here. Advise them to say nothing to anyone except that. And tell them to stay away from the rehearsal hall. Maybe we can cut one line of communication if there's one there. Check with Joel before you reserve anything."

"Done, done and done."

"Good. Be sure your phone calls are private."

"I will." She looked at him. "Put on your thinking cap, Jamie. You know where to find me."

"Thanks, Barb, and anymore calls from Barnessa, don't put yourself in jeopardy. Give him what you have to."

"Thanks."

He watched her walk out of his office and tried to focus on the explosive situation he was about to face.

Kate Belden was all business the next morning. When John Ryan arrived at her suite, the hair dresser was waiting with style pictures, and after making a choice from among the three styles that Kate found acceptable, he sat back to have his hair reduced by more than eight inches.

As Kate had predicted, he came through it looking ruggedly handsome. He was an extremely good-looking man to begin with, but the 'new do', as he called it, brought his blue eyes forth and added weight to his frame. She asked why he had ever let it grow long, and he didn't have an answer.

When he appeared at The Warehouse for rehearsal, there were comments about his looking too respectable to appear with the band, but after a good laugh and a lot of sarcasm, everyone got down to the task at hand.

The music went well. They put in a Marty Robbins song that Mickey sang, a novelty tune that allowed Mountain Red to show off his keyboard skills as well as his raucous voice and a tough blues take on Johnny Cash's *I Walk the Line* that featured Mickey's guitar.

At the end of two days the band had roughed out nine songs. Larry Foster, who worked with them the entire second day giving them fresh shadings on their own concepts, was amazed at the tenacity of the musicians and John Ryan's growing confidence. The singer plunged ahead willing to try whatever the members of the band or Foster suggested.

Although Kate Belden had said she would be at rehearsal before they finished for the day, only Rance Connelly came by to tell them that he and she had been called back to New York. Foster would stay, and John Ryan's room and expenses would be covered for the next two days. They were also informed that the band's checks and John Ryan's expense advance would be issued by Don Hendrickson's office.

After the previous night's conversation and Kate Belden's cautious warnings, John Ryan wondered what might be going on in New York. More than that, he felt a small disappointment that he would not be having dinner again with her.

When the rehearsal ended, he went back to hotel, nonplussed as to how to spend the evening. He was tired, but the adrenaline was still pumping. Mickey and Howie were out on their own, and he looked forward to the time alone. As he opened the door to his room, the telephone began to ring.

"John Ryan?" He recognized Kate Belden's voice, but it sounded different.

"Kate?"

"Hi."

"Where are you? You sound a million miles away."

"You don't have to shout; I can hear you perfectly. Where am I? I have no idea. Wait a minute; I can see a few lights. Now there's a lot more. I would guess I'm twenty or thirty thousand feet over Baltimore or Washington; I'm not sure which."

"You're on an airplane?" His tone was incredulous.

"I certainly hope so." She laughed.

"I've never had anyone call me from an airplane. This is wild."

"Ah, modern technology. Corporate planes do have their advantages."

"So what's the occasion? From an airplane? Really?" It was a small boy, totally in awe of the moment.

"Well, I felt badly about taking off without a 'Good-by', 'Hi' or 'I'm sorry', so I thought I'd ring you up and apologize."

"Not necessary, but I must admit that it's a thrill to talk to someone so far above me," he laughed at the double entendre.

"Very cute. I don't know what's going on in New York that requires my presence, so I don't know what my schedule will be like, but I don't feel like I accomplished everything I needed to down there. So I thought I'd better call while I had the chance."

"Well you sure know how to make it dramatic and memorable. You do realize that I will never be able to forget that it was Kate Belden who first called me from an airplane at thirty thousand feet."

"Hey, we do what we can to be remembered." She paused. "Seriously, when I find out what the score is in New York, I'll call you. I really hope to get back before you leave for Mississippi, but in the meantime, listen to Larry. We had a long conversation this afternoon and I believe he's good. I gave him some input on what I want the band to wear—just general ideas—and the kind of repartee I want him to help you with. You'll do fine. Just let that facile wit and intelligence you work so hard to keep hidden come out."

"Facile. Good word, Belden."

"You may be the only person I know in this business who knows what it means," she laughed. "I'm serious when I say that the more I think about what I heard down there, the report on the record, and our conversation last night, the more I'm convinced that it's going to be great for you."

"I guess we'll just have to wait and see, won't we?" Despite the hours of rehearsal and all the positive aspects of what had emerged, the thought of a live audience still made him weak in the knees.

"God. The proverbial 'Iceman'."

"It's all a front, but I'm scared to admit to anything else." She could sense the smile on his lips as she listened to him speak. And she could imagine the mischievous look in those ice blue eyes.

"Well, keep up the front until we find out what's underneath. I've got to go fasten my seat belt. Captain's orders."

"I've always wondered if anyone in civilian life ever said that line in truth, and now you have. Kate Belden, you are a wonderment."

"I've never been called one of those before, Stone, but it sounds nice. See ya!"

As he hung up the phone, he was still amused at having been called from an airplane.

Philip Barnessa and Eager Mills walked into Jamie Greshem's office at precisely twelve-thirty. It was a power move that Don Hendrickson had told the young producer to expect. The promoter from Philadelphia was surprised to find a whole team waiting.

"Whadda we got here? A corporate meeting? I thought you and me were gonna talk?"

"We are going to talk, Phil. You didn't mention bringing Eager either," Jamie said, trying to appear calm. Hendrickson had given him a strategy for the meeting, but neither of them was sure it would work.

"So, do we get rid of 'em or do we talk in a crowd?" None of the people sitting in the office moved or reacted to the man's dismissal of them.

"I guess we'll talk in a crowd. You might have some questions I can't answer that they can. Why don't you sit down. You, too, Eager."

Both empty chairs were to Jamie Greshem's right. Someone had once told him that you were always in a stronger position if your adversary was on your right. The theory being that most people are right-handed and that being the 'sword' hand places the person on the side of your protection and strength. He was certain Philip Barnessa had never heard of the theory and, even if he had, could care less from which side he launched his attack.

"I don't give a fuck who's here," he said as he took his chair; however, there was a sense of uncertainty in his attitude. He didn't like to be told to do anything, even to sit down. "Let's have at it."

The graying man's voice softened to a sympathetic, threatening whine. "Why are you trying to hurt me, Greshem? Your father has never done that. What did I ever do to you? I get this hillbilly's record tested—at some legal risk I might add—and the damn thing looks like it might do something. I report back to you, give you the good news, and then you try to shit on me. You're gonna release the record early without even letting me know? Nobody does that to me. Why do you wanna do that, Jamie?"

"I think you're leaving something out, Philip..."

"Whaddya mean?"

"As I understand from sources close to you," Barnessa looked at Mills, and they both shrugged in ignorance. "you received a good response in a couple of small, middle-of-the-road, easy-listening stations," Jamie's voice assumed a veneer of firmness, "and, based on that, you determined—you, nobody else—that it should be broken into that market. You have the power to do that, and I am more than aware of that fact, but once it's set in that niche it's over as far as I'm concerned."

Barnessa looked as though he were going to speak, but Jamie forged ahead.

"Now let me tell you what I'm thinking before you interrupt. You know and I know that some markets allow crossovers—country to pop, pop to easy-listening and so forth—but I have never heard of an easy-listening or mainstream hit crossing over to country." He didn't slow down. "John Ryan Stone is first, country. Now he may crossover, and I believe he will and that will make it better for everybody, but if he breaks in the market you're talking about, they'll be playing his music with Jerry Vale in elevators and dentist's offices. Muzak doesn't pay the company very well, Philip, and when was the last time you saw anybody wearing a Steve Lawrence or an Al Martino tee-shirt?" The young producer looked the man straight in the eye and found himself shaking inside.

There was silence in the room, but he couldn't let it hang; there would be no victory of will in that.

"I'm the producer. I found this man. I recorded him and brought him to New York, and now you decide, on your own, where the hell this product should be marketed."

Barbara and Kate stared with admiration and apprehension at a Jamie Greshem they had not seen before. Rance Connelly watched the man from Philadelphia.

"You either got a lotta guts or you're stupid."

Jamie waited for the word 'kid' at the end of the sentence because Barnessa's words and attitude came right out of Lee J. Cobb in *On the Waterfront* or a number of other movie characters just like that one. The word 'kid' didn't come.

"You tell me."

"I'm not sure yet, but I gotta protect my interests." He flashed a warning look. "Know that, Jamie. If you're smart, know that. Even a guy from South Philly knows that guts with no smarts is stupid. Lemme think about what you said, but remember—and I don't give a fuck who hears or who tells it to who—I gotta have a taste. Know that."

Barnessa rose from his chair and Mills followed suit. "I'll get back to you," he said as they left the office.

No one said anything until they were sure the man was out of earshot, then the sighs of relief and congratulations began.

"It's not over," Jamie said as his body touched the back of his chair for the first time since twelve-thirty p.m. "It's just beginning, and that was round one."

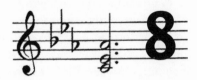

The bus was a cacophony of the odors of long forgotten miles and endless stretches of highway. It was old and musty, not a Greyhound or a Trailways, though it might have been at some juncture in its time. The years of cigarette smoke, spilled whiskey, fried foods and sleeping bodies were pungent evidence of its age. It had been modified to fit the needs of a traveling band, but just barely: seats had been converted into loungers, a booth with a table was put in the back along with a small sink, a miniature refrigerator, a propane stove and a stereo system with a tape recorder. Despite these accouterments, it was still an old bus, not unfamiliar to John Ryan Stone or anyone else who had ever taken a bus trip through the rural local routes in the South.

Rain pelted the Sheraton parking lot, lit only by scattered mercury-vapor lights and the reflections they cast in the black-glass wetness of the macadam. John Ryan Stone sat in the bus alone ingesting the smell of burning diesel fuel emanating from the idling engine. The driver, whose name was Wylie Nate, stood in the step-well with the door open, smoking a cigarette, ready for the mini-tour to begin; he had been through the same scene many times before.

The early morning darkness, prolonged by the aqueous sky, created a smothering cover over the jubilation of the previous night. The excitement and adrenaline of new beginnings and unknown prospects, which always carry with them their own stimulation, seemed a remote memory as the singer waited for the rest of the band to arrive.

There had been a small send-off party at The Warehouse after the final rehearsal ended. Don Hendrickson, noticeably absent during the preparation period, attended, and the contingent from New York called to wish their best.

John Ryan spoke with Jamie, who sounded nervous and anxious, and with Kate Belden, who restated that she would see him in Savannah. They both sounded optimistic if a little cautious. Larry Foster had kept them apprised of the band's progress, and his reports, while guarded, were glowing, but neither he nor anyone else could be certain what might happen in front of a live audience.

At one point during the party, Hendrickson had pulled Son Cochran aside and asked for his evaluation. The bass player confirmed that from everything he could see, they were ready. The band was tight and John Ryan had put muscle in his vocal performance. When the man relaxed, Son told him, he became consumed by the music and generated raw power unlike any of the slick crop of country crooners that were being put out under the guise of the Nashville Sound.

"If he can do it live and handle what follows, I think you've got somethin'," Cochran said. The vice-president's cagey grin returned the smile from the bass player.

"It's his rodeo," Hendrickson said. "We'll just have to see if he can ride."

None of the band was late for the departure, but they waited until the last minute to drag onto the bus. A sense of resignation peculiar only to being 'on the road' was already showing its preemptive symptoms in everyone except Howie and Mickey, who were flying with anticipation, and John Ryan, who watched all of this being played out even though the bus had not yet moved from the parking lot.

When the headlights of the equipment truck appeared, Wylie Nate took his seat, engaged the gears, and the wheels began to roll. It took only a short time on Interstate 65 South toward Birmingham for the snoring to begin. Mountain Red immediately established himself as the most prodigious practitioner of this common song of the road. Mickey and Howie, too high with the moment to think of sleep, sat in the booth playing gin.

John Ryan's stomach was churning as he watched the headlights traveling north on the other side of the unseen meridian. The fear didn't relate to performing. He felt he had overcome that with the help of the band members and the confidence Hendrickson and Jamie Greshem had shown in him. The fear was stimulated by the fact that everything that was happening felt thin, without a firm foundation or justification. There was no systematic plan that guaranteed success. It was a crapshoot.

The day passed with idle conversation and projections on what The Silver Saddle Saloon would be like and Mountain Red and Son Cochran's road stories. There were stops in Huntsville, Alabama, for breakfast, Montgomery for lunch, beer and Jack Daniels—Paul Crockett, being from Texas, felt obligated to buy tequila—and there was a dinner break at a truck stop just south of Mobile. It was a day all too familiar to those who had done it before and a minor disappointment to Mickey and Howie who hadn't.

Thoughts of the next day's opening kept John Ryan from drawing any conclusions about his first day on the road.

It was nine-thirty at night when Wylie Nate rolled the bus to its final stop at the Holiday Inn in Biloxi. The trip had been long and tiresome, and everyone was relieved that they wouldn't be traveling again for three days. The Silver Saddle Saloon couldn't be any worse than fifteen hours on a bus.

Kate Belden paced. Her apartment wasn't small by New York standards, but it didn't have the space of the luxury units on West End, Park or Fifth; consequently, her pacing was limited. She'd found it through a real estate agent she'd been involved with shortly after she began working for Trayhorn. At the time she thought maybe her life plan was finally coming to fruition; however, she soon realized that the man's bravado and superficiality had been worked on her in the same manner he used it on his clients. The one positive lesson learned from the experience was to take northeastern men with northeastern skepticism. The one rewarding thing she gained from the relationship was a decent—better than average—apartment that she would never have found and could never have afforded if it hadn't fallen under the old rent-control guidelines. The apartment was her 'manna from Heaven', her haven, a refuge in alien territory, and within her financial limits. She was certain she would not have lasted in the city if it hadn't come along.

Even though the style of the furnishings was eclectic, the unit was well done, filled with a mixture of quasi-antiques, mid-twentieth century pieces, wildlife prints, a number of family pictures, and some things brought from her parent's home in Indiana. There were two bedrooms—a rarity for affordable housing in the city—a living room, a small semiformal dining area, a kitchen and bath. It was more than enough room for her, except when she was pacing.

Pacing had not been on her schedule for the evening. The itinerary was to have included a quiet dinner alone—Kate always prepared a reasonably full dinner when she was at home; eating Chinese takeout from cardboard containers was not a part of that quiet time for her, her time to feel stabilized—some reading, a slow bath with a glass of white wine and an early departure time to sleep. All of that had changed during the course of the day.

She was anxious. It was silly, she thought, foolish and without justification. John Ryan had sounded calm on the phone, laid-back and seemingly unworried about the performance dates scheduled for him, but she was not. His success had taken on an importance to her that she had not experienced with any of the other performers she had directed. On those occasions it had been simply a matter of economic success, chart position, company image, and making the most of a career moment, which was all too often, all too brief. With John Ryan it was different and Kate Belden was afraid she knew why.

It was a quarter after one in the morning New York time and a quarter after twelve Biloxi time. If the band were on schedule, they should have arrived at the Holiday Inn.

At one-thirty she decided to call.

The voice was dry with fatigue or perhaps sleep or irritation. It didn't sound anxious or depressed. "Hello?"

"Hi," she said softly.

"Who is this?" It was irritation, she decided.

His first thought was that it was a joke. Mickey and Howie had gone down to the bar for a beer, found a girl and persuaded her to call and invite him down to join the party. They had appeared disturbed all day about his quietude in the face of the band's first gig.

"It's Kate Belden," she said.

"Well..." He paused not knowing what to say. "Kate Belden. I guess if I could say one wrong thing in one wrong way at one wrong time, I just did it."

"That's a good answer. Not an apology, not an excuse, just a little humorous skating." She laughed. "I—on the other hand—shouldn't have called you so late after you've had a whole day on a bus."

It was easy to imagine the smile on her face. "I'm sorry I didn't recognize your voice; I should have."

"Not really. We've never talked at any length on the phone, and you didn't expect me to call; in fact, I didn't expect me to call. It was a spur of the moment inspiration."

"I thought it was a joke Mickey and Howie cooked up to get me out and about with them."

"No joke. I just wanted to hear how the trip went, how you're feeling about tomorrow night and to wish you good luck again. I've thought about the John Ryan Stone Traveling Music Show a lot today and wondered how everything went."

"I appreciate that. I really do. I think I needed something. I've been walkin' through my own head all day, and that's a dangerous neighborhood."

"Tell me about it. So, how was the trip?" She sounded relaxed.

"Long in one sense. In another, it actually moved pretty fast. I think I'm excited. The alternative is not too pleasant to think about."

"Tell me."

"It's hard to explain. There's the subdued panic, of course," he said with a laugh, " but I think that's because a few months ago I never would have believed—on a bet—that I'd be where I am, doing what I'm doing. Hell, I used to lose sleep for two days when somebody else was going to cut a demo of one of my songs."

"Well, you are where you are and you're going to do well. I feel it. Right now you just have to move with it. It's going to be fine, you'll see." Her voice was warm and comfortable.

"I wish I were that confident. I thought maybe you called to tell us we'd been canceled."

"Why?"

"Well, that's a pretty ugly bus we rode in on. I was afraid somebody saw us and changed their mind."

"Not a chance. The Silver Saddle, from what I've heard, isn't one of the most exclusive clubs, and if they don't like you, so what? That crowd is not going to make or break you. I'd love to talk more, but I know you've got a huge day ahead of you tomorrow, and I have to go to work. I do hope it goes well. Just remember, at this point one show or one date does not a career make or break. Take it as it comes and go from there."

"I'll try to do that, ma'am, I surely will." He put a broad smile on his face that carried through the line.

"You're too much, but good luck anyway."

"Thanks and you take care."

"I will," she said and put the receiver down.

If appearances stand for anything, Kate Belden was correct in her assessment of the Silver Saddle Saloon. It didn't look as if it had the capacity to make or break anyone's career. The building and its surroundings were typical of Gulf Coast roadhouses where beer and whiskey flowed freely until the fighting started, then it flowed even more freely. It was like the 'shotgun' bars of the Northeast or the 'biker' bars of California, or any other watering holes of the same genre scattered throughout every state from east to west and north to south.

The sandy, gray parking lot had once been graveled, but the white granite had been beaten into pumice and fused with the natural sand by the nightly traffic of cars and trucks. Deep holes created by tropical rains dotted the lot and made finding a level spot large enough to park a bus a challenge.

The building itself was a reflection of the parking lot—cinder block and low, painted governmental green with darker trim. On the roof was a neon display proclaiming its name under a ten foot tall, blue stallion reared up on its hind legs in a 'Trigger-like' pose. The saddle on its back was formed by small, white sequential lights. A red neon cowboy, waving his hat in welcome to the passing traffic, sat astride the horse.

Mickey, Howie and John Ryan stood outside the bus and stared at the building in awe. Paul Crockett, Red, Son Cochran and Bobby Hopwood went about the business of gathering what few items they intended to take in and leave at the club for the duration of their three-day gig.

"Surprised?" Red said with a broad grin as he stepped off the bus. No one responded. "You didn't expect a Las Vegas casino, did you?"

"I don't know what I expected, but I don't think it was this," John Ryan answered. "It looks like the kind of place you either come out of educated or dead."

Mountain Red and Bobby Hopwood laughed.

"Hey, it ain't so bad; remember, this is in the daylight. At night it's gonna look like the Taj Mahal," the drummer said.

"Man," Mickey exclaimed. "that place me and Howie played in Shreveport for two hundred dollars a night looked like Carnegie Hall compared to this."

"It's like knowin' you got a bad bull in the draw," Mountain Red said, "he ain't pretty, but he can be rode by somebody, and it might as well be you."

Howie Newfeldt shook his head. "If the place looks like this, I can't imagine what the people are gonna look like."

"Two arms, two legs, some beer bellies and a head," Paul Crockett, who had just exited the bus, laughed.

"There's not even a damn window in the place," Mickey pointed out.

"Probably keeps people from bein' thrown through 'em," John Ryan muttered under his breath.

"I thought we was travelin' with an up-and-coming, major recording artist," Mickey said with a country flavored W. C. Fields twang. "You sure Hank and Elvis started this way?"

"Worse," Son Cochran threw in. "Hank played for drinks without a band, and E played in junior high talent shows for nothing. We're gettin' paid."

"Well, I guess we'd better go on in and start our glow-ri-us careers," Howie laughed as he started toward the building. "They gotta go up from here."

"Maybe, maybe not," Red guffawed.

The inside might have been as bad as the outside, but entering the building no one would ever know. There was light on the stage or what was designated as the stage, but little else was discernible until the eyes adjusted to the darkness. The natural light of a bar is unnatural light or no light at all. The Silver Saddle Saloon was close to falling into the latter category.

Standing inside the door, afraid to move forward, the musicians could make out two bars—one on either side of the room—fronted with high-backed chairs. Small tables and chairs ran from the end of the bars to where the band stood at the entrance. A small dance floor separated the tables from the bandstand. Mirrors covered the walls behind the bars and reflected the long-necked bottles with chrome spouts that were lined up on glass shelves in front of them. Blue, green, white, yellow and red neons advertised Lone Star, Michelob, Pearl, Budweiser, Jax and a variety of other beers. A large, neon Marlboro man dominated one panel behind the bar to the left and a small reproduction of the outdoor sign waved from behind the bar on the right. A lone bartender was lethargically washing glasses and doing all the necessities of the bartender's perpetual cleanup process.

It was a unique situation for John Ryan, Mickey and Howie. They had never come into a club to play a gig and had a superlative sound system set up for them, instruments uncased, tuned and ready, and two non-band people working to make sure everything was as it should be. Cade Wilhite worked with the sound while Larry Foster played with the minimal lighting the stage offered to see if any effects were possible. There were basically two: bright for upbeat songs and subdued for slower songs. They had been working for two hours by the time the band arrived. All that was left to do was run the songs and set the sound levels. Despite the quality of the room, the acoustics were quite good although it was impossible to determine what effect a large group of bodies might make.

The rehearsal went smoothly. Larry had chosen the order of the songs, and after a few questions from John Ryan, small disagreements and adjustments, everyone immersed themselves in the music.

After an hour Foster told John Ryan to take it easy and save his voice for the night ahead, which stimulated a laugh from him and sharp barbs from the rest of the band. Throughout the morning there was a good deal of laughter at mistakes and cheers when something good happened.

At noon the bartender, whose name was Robert, opened the bar for them and advised that whatever they wanted was compliments of the house. Shortly before one o'clock an elderly black man came in with a platter of Po'boy sandwiches made with oysters or shrimp, tasso ham and andouille sausage with fries and coleslaw on the side.

He smiled and said, "Ya'll must be somebody special cause the boss don't give no band or nobody no nothin' fo' free."

"That we are." Red laughed. "We sure are somebody very special."

"Mus' be," the man said and went back to his kitchen. It didn't take long for the initial shock of the place to be forgotten, and after they had eaten, the bus took them back to the Holiday Inn for a couple of hours rest and dinner before the show.

At six o'clock Mickey and Howie came to John Ryan's room with a bottle of Jack Daniels, a six-pack of Lone Star and a bucket of Kentucky Fried Chicken, but the idea of eating or drinking before the show was not comfortable for John Ryan. He did, however, take one shot and sip on a single beer while Mickey projected on the night ahead.

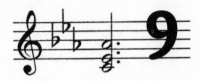

The band was scheduled to start at nine; John Ryan was dressed and physically ready at seven. He wore one of the outfits Kate had sent from New York—jeans, a denim shirt with epaulets, a wide black belt with a buckle big enough to be used as a weapon and black boots that were shined to a gleam. The shade of the denim shirt was carefully calculated to accent his eyes. When he looked at the tall, ruggedly handsome man staring back at him from the mirror, he understood why Kate had been so particular.

It was eight o'clock when the bus worked its way through the half-filled parking lot and rolled to a stop. They entered the club through the back entrance. There was a small room, condescendingly referred to as 'the dressing room', that was fitted with worn-out furniture, exposed rafters and heating ducts, a sink, mirror, and a bathroom that appeared never to have been cleaned. Other bands—lost on the road, living on high hopes or disgusted compromise—had autographed the walls with broad-tipped markers as if to prove their existence or at least leave a record of where they'd been. It was likely that it was the only mark they would ever make.

John Ryan and the band were scheduled for an hour and a half performance; however, on Friday and Saturday nights they were to play two-hour shows. They knew that much of what happened on Friday and Saturday would be determined by what they did on this night. With forty minutes to kill before going on, there was little to do except go to the bar and listen to the local group who were regulars at the club.

It was early and the crowd was sparse. The people who were there were oil field and construction workers, factory employees and a number who probably didn't work at all. A heavy layer of smoke, white from the reflected lights, hovered against the ceiling like a long and flat stratus cloud. The five-piece band on stage was lumbering loudly through their version of Bobby Fuller's *I Fought the Law*. Most of the tables were empty, and no one at the bar appeared to be listening. It was a typical dead opening set—few people and no response.

Although no words were uttered, the six men were aware of questioning glances as they walked to the bar. John Ryan inwardly laughed at the scene, not unlike so many western movies when the bad guys come to town. He and Son Cochran ordered ginger ale, which got a little attention, and the rest of the group ordered beer.

"I thought you might have used a coupla fingers of Jack." Cochran smiled.

"It would probably take four," he answered with a smirk, "but then I might try to sing like I knew what I was doin'. It tends to make me think I'm smarter than I am."

"I know what you're sayin'. Better off if you can keep it that way."

"I guess."

"You boys new around here?" one of the men sitting at the bar asked Mountain Red as the piano player watched the musicians on stage. "I ain't seen you before, and I'm sure I'd remember you."

"Just passin' through," the big man answered without looking at his questioner.

"To where?"

"Florida."

"From where?" Red turned to look at the man.

"Nashville."

"That don't make no sense, goin' through Biloxi on your way to Florida from Nashville." There was a tone of proprietary suspicion in the man's voice.

"Well, there's a lotta reasons for a lotta things," Red said and turned back to the bar.

"Yeah, I guess, but it don't make no sense," the man muttered, miffed at being dismissed.

At eight-fifty the house band, for some reason called The Vaqueros in spite of outfits that consisted of tee-shirts and jeans and looked more East Side New York City than south of the border, closed down their set, and, with Cade Wilhite and Larry Foster helping, moved their modest and well-worn equipment to the back of the stage.

Looks of mistrust and general hostility from the local group pervaded the atmosphere as they watched what seemed an inordinate amount of equipment for a road band that no one had ever heard of uncovered, rolled onto the stage and placed in pre-marked positions. Cade and Larry went about their business oblivious of the bad feelings that were being cast in their direction.

In the short time John Ryan and the band had been there, the crowd at The Silver Saddle had grown. By ten of nine half the tables were occupied and both bars were filled. Although there appeared to be little difference in the class of the new arrivals, they were dressed better than the early birds who had stopped for a beer on their way home from work and hung on through The Vaqueros' first set. Women wore their hair piled high and lacquered with hair spray until it only moved when their whole head did or they wore it straight and blonde. Jeans, short shorts, and minis were as tight as possible regardless of the girth of the person wearing them. A majority of the men wore the uniform: denim, pointed-toe boots, open collar shirts or tees, side burns and an attitude that left no doubt that Mississippi's 'favorite son' from Tupelo lived in their hearts. There was also a smattering of outlaws, wearing their colors and looking sullen, their women glassy-eyed and riding a train nobody else could see.

It was an audience that wasn't going to be easy to please, and no one was more aware of that than John Ryan Stone whose trepidation escalated the closer his partners got to having the stage set for the band's entrance.

"Hit 'em hard, loud and fast from the top," Larry Foster said as John Ryan and the band passed in front of him.

John Ryan Stone wondered if the shaking in his body was obvious to everyone in the club. When he reached for his guitar, there was a momentary fear of dropping it or knocking over someone else's equipment. He couldn't force himself to raise his eyes from the floor or focus on anything until he turned his back to the crowd and looked at Son Cochran and the other members of the band. Cade Wilhite had rechecked the levels, and everything was ready. The noise level of the crowd hadn't quieted which eased the tension a little. There could be no sloppiness; it had to be tight from the opening note, something more intense than these people had ever heard before. The first song had to get them or they would be lost for the night.

Larry and John Ryan had agreed to open with *Ring of Fire*, but the instrumental introduction that Son and Paul Crockett had put together was as unlike Johnny Cash as anything could be.

Mountain nodded his head at John Ryan who took a deep breath as the first clean note blew out of the speakers. It caught the audience off guard. It wasn't as loud as the house band's music, but it struck full with a clean and deep power that was unfamiliar to the people at The Silver Saddle. By the time the opening run was finished and John Ryan stepped in close to the mike, the crowd noise had diminished, and their attention was drawn to the tall, lanky singer with the whiskey voice and the ice-blue eyes. Some few continued to talk, and some, operating within their own self-induced torpor, weren't even aware that anyone was playing.

When Mickey and Howie joined in on the chorus and John Ryan picked up the deep bass notes, the people watching and listening began to take part in what was happening on the stage.

The leader of The Vaqueros continued to stand sullenly at the bar, shaking his head in disgust and anger. He knew even before they started playing—just from looking at their equipment—what this band would do to his group, but there was no way to stop it. What he couldn't understand was why Tony Carbonaro had brought in a group from out of town during their scheduled gig. As he watched, he tried to put all of his vehemence at what was happening on his face, but it didn't help. Finally, he had heard enough, gathered the other members of his band and left the building. It was worse than he expected; there was no hope of getting the audience back on this night or maybe any other night. He had never heard a bar band as good, but he didn't have to stand inside and listen to it. The one thing he couldn't escape was the roar of applause he heard as he walked across the parking lot.

The real test for John Ryan came when the first song ended, and he had to step to the mike and talk. He didn't know whether the dark dampness on his shirt was from the energy he expended on the song or from his fear of talking to a group of people he didn't know. He suggested several alternatives to Larry Foster, but was told he had to face it sometime and no better place than Biloxi, Mississippi.

"My name's John Ryan Stone," he said in a voice so deep and quiet that the words were practically inaudible. "I know that doesn't mean a thing to you, but we just came in to town, and the people here at The Silver Saddle offered to let us do a set for you." There was an awkward pause, and he added, "Hope you enjoy it."

The lights dimmed to half when he stepped back from the mike. The follow-spot picked up Paul Crockett who stepped to one of the forward positions and began blowing the forlorn, wailing opening notes of *I'm So Lonesome I Could Cry* into his harmonica. When John Ryan began to sing, the light moved to him.

He was comfortable in the light, not because of the attention it directed toward him but because in its glare he could no longer distinguish any shapes or faces in the crowd. The light was the ultimate magic; it made the world go away and allowed him inside the music.

With each song the crowd became more involved. They listened to *Satisfied Mind*, surprised by the unusual arrangement and the unique sound of a blues guitar in a country song. Chuck Berry's *Memphis* brought a huge reaction. Mountain Red did a wild rendition of *Drinkin' in the Neon*, and the band did Mickey and Howie's song, *Big Wind*. Son Cochran switched from bass to guitar and did his own arrangement of the Duane Eddy classic, *Forty Miles of Bad Road*.

As the crowd's intensity grew so did the band's. John Ryan was wet with perspiration, but it felt good. It made the whole thing that was happening to him a little less thin. For the first time he felt he was earning something, that what he was doing was tangible.

Before the last song, he introduced the members of the band and announced—to cheers—that they would be back for two shows on each of the following two nights.

Mountain Red hit the first chords of *Midnight Rain*, and everyone else fell in behind. John Ryan literally consumed the emotional content of the song, and it came out in every physical aspect of his body. At some moments the people almost became silent and at others yelled loud encouragement. No one was sitting down. During Mickey's guitar break, Son Cochran eased up behind John Ryan and told him to go straight to the bus at the end of the song and fast.

When *Midnight Rain* ended, the crowd exploded with applause and yells. John Ryan, following the bass man's advice, left the stage as soon as the last note was struck. The rest of the band played some exit music and one by one left the stage until only Mountain Red was left. With his last notes culminating in a fast Jerry Lee Lewis-type run, he, too, wasted no time in getting out of the club.

As he crossed the parking lot, he saw a crowd of people standing in front of the bus door. It wasn't until he got closer that he was able to make out who it was. One of The Vaqueros had Wylie Nate pushed up against the side of the bus, and the other four were blocking the door.

"What's goin' on?" he asked when he reached the group.

"Seems as though these boys have hijacked us or have a notion to," John Ryan said.

"We ain't hijacked nobody," the leader said, trying to sound quietly hostile. It was obvious that now they had gotten into it they had no plan and didn't know what to do next. "We just want you to get in your beat-up kiddie-car here and get the hell out of Biloxi tonight." They were stoked.

Red stepped forward. "Hell, man, we cain't do that; we got gigs here for the next two nights, and if we like it, we might just decide to stay." The leader of The Vaqueros eyed him coldly. The man was big, but he couldn't back down.

"You ain't gonna stay nowhere, Dumbfuck." With those words he began a roundhouse swing with the long-neck he was holding in his right hand. Red had been to this party before and fully anticipated the smaller man's actions. He dipped to his right, blocked the arm halfway between the wrist and the elbow and heard a crack. He wasn't sure until he heard the man scream whether it was bone breaking or the long-neck that sailed over his head.

"Aw, shit, man, you broke my fuckin' arm!" the man screamed.

Another of the house-band members took a run at John Ryan, but the singer was quicker and taller and caught him with a right fist under the chin that straightened him for the left that caught him in the soft part of his midsection. It had been a long time, but as he had been taught, he tried to hit through the body, visualizing his fist coming out the other side. Every ounce of air within the man exited in one explosive grunt, and he fell to the ground, grasping his stomach, his eyes bulging as he struggled to breathe.

Paul Crockett grabbed the man who was holding Wylie Nate, kicked him in the groin and was banging his head against a bus tire until Son Cochran pulled him off. Howie and Mickey took care of the other two with little trouble.

The whole melee was over in minutes, and The Vaqueros, with their leader's arm bending where it wasn't supposed to, beat their retreat, shouting vile epithets and threats of vengeance.

"Damn!" John Ryan said.

"What?" Mickey asked. "You hurt?"

"No," John Ryan said smiling. "I was just gettin' ready to say that was fun. 'Course only because we won." Everybody was laughing as they finally boarded the bus.

"I thought they played bad," Howie said, "but they fight worse."

"I don't think the wagon-master's gonna be saddlin' up his guitar anytime soon." Red said. "I sure do hate when that happens, ruinin' a man's buddin' career and all."

"What career?" somebody in the back of the bus said with a laugh.

"I hope to hell Cade and Larry get out of there alive," Son Cochran said.

"Man, I don't believe what we just did?" Howie said.

"Inside or outside?" John Ryan asked.

"Inside, man. Hell, the fight was nothin', but the music...."

"We did do it." Even John Ryan couldn't hide his enthusiasm. "Damn!"

"Believe it." Hopwood said.

"You did ride the bull, boy," Red shouted and slapped the singer on the back. "Hell, everybody did. Hot Damn!"

"What was the rush to get out of there?" John Ryan asked. "It was the parking lot that was dangerous." Everybody laughed again. They were on a high that no amount of alcohol or drug could produce, only accomplishment.

"Some of those boys were gettin' a little riled about the way their women were actin', not all of 'em but some," Paul Crockett broke in. "You had those gals sweatin' heat sweat, and they don't like strangers—especially musicians— doin' that to their women. Somehow they don't think it's right. So when you see 'em start breakin' into groups, they're probably a little disturbed and plannin' to do something. Maybe not, but it sure as hell ain't worth stayin' around to find out."

"I'll go along with that," Mickey said. "Boys, I don't know what to say. Where in God's name did that music come from?"

"You and me, baby," Red exclaimed. "And everybody else. It happens when it happens, and it don't happen often, so don't get used to it. It ain't gonna happen every time."

"You sound like Mickey," John Ryan laughed. "I didn't think anyone else could use words like that."

"I don't care who I sound like; it was great," Red yelled.

"Enjoy it, but don't forget," Son said, "tomorrow's another day."

When the last patrons had left The Silver Saddle, Tony Carbonaro went to the phone. He spoke to Robert the bartender as he walked. "What's the Philadelphia area code? I can never remember it."

"Two, one, five."

Tony Carbonaro dialed a familiar number and waited.

"Philip? Tony C.," he said quietly.

———

During the ride back to the motel, everyone had an opinion on what had brought it all together at the club. It was so much more polished and professional than they expected at this juncture. It was good—extraordinary. The excitement in the audience didn't compare to the electricity that was circulating among the members of the band on the bus.

It was still early and Mickey, Howie and Paul Crockett made plans to visit a couple of the other clubs in the area that had live music. John Ryan, pleading exhaustion, declined their offer to join them. Mountain Red and

Hopwood were going in search of seafood since they had not eaten before the show, and Son Cochran took off by himself.

When he got to his room, John Ryan collapsed on the king-size bed and stared at the ceiling. It was truly unbelievable. Uncanny, he thought, unreal, unpredictable—he wondered how many adjectives could be prefixed with 'un'. The smile would not stop; he felt giddy, wasn't the same person. This night had changed his whole life, he thought, more than Don Hendrickson, Jamie Greshem, anybody or any thing else. He could feel his heart beating rapidly; his stomach was quivering, and he felt as though he had the power to scream the building off the block. It was the most intense exhilaration he had ever experienced.

He lifted himself from the bed and poured three fingers of Jack Daniels in a motel glass. He deserved it. He went to the phone, but he didn't know who to call. He had to call someone. There was a need to call someone. It was eleven-fifteen in Biloxi, which made it twelve-fifteen in the Eastern Time Zone. He poured another drink and lay back on the bed.

Looking at the ceiling and going over his performance, the enthusiasm began to return along with the desire to tell someone about it, someone who would give him affirmation and join in the joy of what he was feeling. He dialed New York information. Kate Belden's residence number was listed. It was a mild surprise; but when he considered it, maybe it shouldn't have been. The woman appeared to be up front about everything without being hard and driven; that's what made her unique, and that's what he liked about her.

It was one-fifteen a.m. when the ringing of the phone roused her from a fitful sleep. In bed by nine-thirty, hoping that sleep would make the night pass faster so she could find out what had happened in Biloxi, her mind had swirled with visions of great success and devastating disasters on the stage of The Silver Saddle Saloon. At eleven she got angry with herself, got out of bed and had a glass of wine. She refused to 'try to read' knowing full-well that was an unsuccessful panacea reserved for characters in novels. At last with Chopin filtering in softly from the living room, she managed to drift into sleep.

She knew who was calling before she answered. There was no way to surmise what the news would be, but it was John Ryan Stone. She glanced at the clock and picked up the receiver.

"Good morning, John Ryan," she said softly but without hesitation. There was a moment of silence on the other end.

"Am I that predictable or are you that confident?" he asked.

94

"I don't know you well enough to know if you're that predictable, and I'm hardly that confident—anxious maybe and possibly hopeful, but I don't think confident is the right word."

"Knowing I woke you, I will say I apologize for waking you."

"Am I that predictable or are you that confident?"

"Touché, Belden." Now that she was on the phone, he didn't know where to begin.

"I was not truly sleeping; I was sleeping 'fitfully' plagued by the turmoil of anxiety and anticipation."

"Are you writing a novel?" he laughed.

"No, I was just lying here trying to think of how different novelists might describe my condition."

"That was not F. Scott Fitzgerald, I presume."

"No, Harold Robbins, I think."

"What are we doing here?" he asked.

"I have no idea." She laughed. "Let's see. You called to give me the news I've been waiting to hear, and neither of us knows what to say. I don't want to hear bad news, and you don't want to tell me bad news. I want to hear good news, and you want to tell me good news. Now, accepting that, I would assume one of two things: the news is good, which you might call to tell me, or the news is bad, which you wouldn't call to tell me, but if the news is bad and you're calling me, then it must be to announce your swift retirement and exit from the business of music."

He considered a glib response, but couldn't come up with one that good.

"It was good, Kate, better than good. I hardly know how to describe it, and I sure as hell can't explain it. We flew." John Ryan Stone was ebullient.

Kate Belden felt the energy of his excitement in herself. The sensation was not unlike those other moments when peaks arise from all the parts of the body creating a desire to explode with joy. She noticed her arm and saw the chill bumps forming and the soft hairs rising from her skin. There was moisture in her eyes, and she realized how deep her anxiety had been. It was as if his success were her success.

"I want to know it all. Every detail," she said. "Don't leave anything out. I want to hear everything." She arranged her pillows so that she could sit up and then settled in to listen.

"Even about how we had to fight our way out?"

"They liked you that much?"

"No, there were a few of them that didn't like us that much at all."

"You had a fight?"

"A skirmish really."

"Tell."

He talked for forty-five minutes. There were vocal nods of approval, brief comments and questions, but little else. She was enthralled by what he was telling her and her own attempts to visualize everything he described. It was not a John Ryan Stone she had heard before.

"What can I say?" she said when he stopped. "I don't have any words."

"Neither do I. I guess tomorrow night will tell the tale."

"It'll tell a lot, but it won't tell you everything. It may not be as good or it could be better. Either way it's inconsequential at this point. Now you know you can do it. It's possible and that's what's important."

"You always manage to come up with something reassuring, don't you, Kate?"

"I try. It's my job."

"But do you believe it?" he asked.

"I try not to say anything I don't believe."

"Truly?"

"Truly, but you're fishing, Stone." He could imagine the grin on her face, knowing she had caught him. "So what have you been doing since you finished?"

"Smiling," he said. "After the fighting of course."

"I can tell you're still doing that. What else?"

"Getting personal here, Belden?"

"Yep."

"Well, nothing very exciting. I came up to my room, suffering an obvious depletion of adrenaline, and collapsed..."

"My oh my, what happened to the country boy?' He didn't acknowledge her sarcasm.

"I thought about what we did, tried to put myself back there to see if it were real or just imagination or wishful thinking, fantasizing."

"And?"

"Oh, it was real. I could see it all, every nuance, but I couldn't recreate any of the feelings. I couldn't experience them again."

"You never will be able to. That's the problem with live performances, they exist, they're here and then they're gone. You have to do it again to experience it again. The fact that you can't bring it back is what keeps you going, what makes you do it over and over. It's the nature of the lady; that's why so few are able to keep her for very long."

"Tough talk. I guess what surprises me most is that I liked it. I've never experienced anything like that before. Writing a good line for a song, or better yet, finishing a song you know is good is about as good as it gets, but this was something else. Totally different. Not sure I want to do it for a life's work, but it was fun."

"Why didn't you go out and celebrate? I'm sure some of the others did."

"I was invited, but I guess I wanted to hold onto this."

"And you wanted to tell someone who wasn't there."

"I think I accused you of being a mind reader last night."

"No, I'm not a mind reader, but I think I'm beginning to—just beginning, mind you—to know you a little. And I'm glad you chose to call me, maybe not first, but you did." He ignored what he suspected was a veiled question.

"I wanted you to know," he said. "You've got a lot invested in this."

"I couldn't be happier. I'm anxious to see it all myself."

"Well, Savannah's not far away."

"I know and I'm looking forward to it. Have you called anyone else in the company?"

"No, why?"

"Let them call you. It would only be Jamie or Don Hendrickson probably and they're okay; I just don't want too many people knowing everything. 'Let 'em live with concern, and don't give 'em anything to shoot at' is my motto."

"Barnessa and Mills?"

"They don't even know where you are. Don't think about all that stuff; we'll handle it. Enjoy it, John Ryan. Enjoy it all."

"I am," he said.

"I've got to work tomorrow."

"You say that a lot."

"What else can I say? It's the way of the world."

"I'm losin' it, too. That depletion of adrenaline I was talkin' about has returned, so I'll let you get to sleep and see if I can stop shakin'."

"You will...Talk to you soon?"

"Soon. Good night, Kate. And thanks."

"Good night, John Ryan Stone, and you're welcome."

He poured another Jack Daniels and lay back on the bed. The warmth of the whiskey was beginning to take hold. He sat up briefly to smoke a cigarette as the first burst of false energy stimulated by the alcohol began to transform itself into comfortable relaxation and fatigue.

———·•·———

At four o' clock in the morning Philip Barnessa was still replaying his conversation with Tony Carbonaro over and over in his head.

"You got somethin' heavy here, Phil. I ain't heard his songs yet—at least none of those you told me about—but as far as performing goes, ain't nobody got nothin' on this boy. You'd better get some kind of lock on it quick. He ain't gonna sit around and wait. It's gonna happen."

"Thanks, Tony. I won't forget it." The conversation was brief, but it had stolen Philip Barnessa's sleep.

S hortly after one o'clock on Sunday afternoon, John Ryan opened his eyes and watched the sunlight playing through the narrow opening in the drapes that covered the motel room's windows. The windows faced the beach, and the light was deflected, not straight-on as it would be if the sun were just on its rise, so he surmised that it was well into the day.

The two shows on Friday night did not match the band's opening performance. By most standards they were good but lacked the superior edge of spontaneity. It was clear to the musicians that it was not as crisp and tight, but the crowd never knew. Even those who were back for a second time were unaware of any diminishing return in what they heard. To them, it was as exciting as the first, and with a knowledge of what to expect, they reacted with even more enthusiasm—several times breaking into unrestrained applause and cheers for a song whose opening runs struck a familiar note. The Vaqueros had not returned.

Red, Son Cochran, Hopwood and Crockett took the minor dip in stride—even Larry Foster wasn't concerned. For those who had been down the road before, it was to be expected, part of the growth. Mickey and Howie, however, had difficulty with it. Opening night had been a step up, another level for them, and they feared any step backward would leave them there. If anything could describe John Ryan's reaction to the night, it was disappointment. He knew the potential, had seen and experienced it. The words of his keyboard player came back to him: "It ain't gonna happen every time, so enjoy it when it does."

Saturday had been spent in limbo, suspended, hanging fire, waiting for the night. John Ryan didn't see any of the band until late afternoon. He slept until ten, had coffee in his room and turned down an offer from Son Cochran and Paul Crockett to go fishing on a head boat that went out of the local dock. He spent a little time playing with a lyric idea that had been rolling around in his head, but decided he was forcing it, subconsciously trying to write a hit, which he knew was impossible. He finally put it aside and left the motel to walk on the beach.

The beach in Gulfport is not wide like the beaches on some parts of the Atlantic Coast nor as snowy-white and powder-like as those that line the Gulf on the Florida panhandle, but like those other stretches of sand and sea, the sound of the water lapping against the shore has the power to calm.

From where he walked on the Gulf side of Route 90, he could look across the highway at the antebellum mansions that for generations had stood as sentinels over the sea approaches to the port city. It was not difficult to imagine grand lawn parties with women in long dresses, looking down from the white-columned galleries on whatever activities were taking place below.

He saw the final home of Jefferson Davis, the deposed President of the Confederacy, a gentle 'war criminal' who spent his last years in exile without citizenship on the Mississippi Gulf Coast. He wandered off the highway a couple of blocks into a residential neighborhood to see how the less affluent lived and eventually circled back to the main road where he found an unpretentious restaurant and stopped for lunch.

He ate a plate of pasta with shrimp in a thick and rich cream sauce, which he sopped up with crusty bread. As he drained his second bottle of Jax, he wondered what had created such a hunger until he realized that he hadn't had a real meal since he left Nashville.

On the way back to the motel, he walked the beach, his pants rolled up and his moccasins in his hand. The water was Gulf warm as he edged the surf. He did not think about music; instead he cleared his thoughts and tried to take in the serenity of all that he was seeing and feeling. Alone and unconnected.

Back at the motel, he slept until time to go to the club. It had been a good day, and only once had he given any thought to the fact that Kate Belden had not called after the Friday night performances.

The crowd on Saturday night was larger than those on Thursday and Friday. When Tony Carbonaro—for the first time since they had been there—introduced the band saying, 'Ladies and Gentlemen, John Ryan Stone,' there was a resounding ovation punctuated by screams and yells, and the singer, standing just offstage, felt the pleasant chill of cold goose flesh run the length of his arms. When he moved onto the stage, the reaction grew even louder.

The band and John Ryan quickly recouped what they had lost on Friday night. Maybe it was the crowd or maybe the realization that they could fail; whatever it was, they took the people with them.

There were raunchy and suggestive dances when Son Cochran reprised his version of *Forty Miles of Bad Road*, observers yelling for the dancers to take it even further. Bottles were held high and cheers went up for Mountain Red when he sang *Drinkin' in the Neon* and for Paul Crockett's rendition of *The Orange Blossom Special*.

The crowd hushed each time John Ryan stepped to the mike. *Ring of Fire* got clapping and vocal responses while *Satisfied Mind* created a quiet stir among the patrons, and *Midnight Rain* elicited sounds of disappointment and objection from those who had heard the band before and knew the show was over.

It was a party, and it didn't end when the band finished playing. On this last night there was no reason for a hurried escape because everyone loved them and wanted to stand them to drinks. To refuse might have caused the first hostility of the evening. Mickey and Howie quickly hooked up with two sisters who had been there for all five shows, and no one else in the band was left unattended unless they wanted to be.

Son Cochran stayed for a short while and then left. Red, Hopwood and Crockett were surrounded when John Ryan, tired of refusing offers and making excuses not to attend 'parties', went back to the motel.

It was close to three a.m. when he closed his eyes, which might explain why he had slept late on this morning. After rerunning it all in his mind, he still didn't feel like getting out of bed, but there was a knocking at the door that demanded some kind of action.

Howie Newfeldt's eyes were glazed, and Mickey Shackleford looked as though he was running on empty.

"Man, you ain't gonna believe what a night we had," Howie exclaimed as he pushed past John Ryan in an alcoholic-scented swirl of air. "It was unbelievable..."

"It still is," Mickey said as he fell across the bed. "We ain't been to bed yet. At least not to sleep."

"You two look like you been pulled through a lock the hard way. What the hell have you been doin' besides drinkin' and entertainin' the go-go twins?" John Ryan asked.

"They're not twins, just sisters," Howie answered. His motor was running at full steam. "We did everything. Those two had moves I never saw before. Why the hell did you leave? There was plenty of stuff around wonderin' how you got away. You won't believe the party you missed. We wound up in New Orleans. Went to Bourbon Street. Mickey's got to tell you about Bourbon Street," he said and laughed.

"Shut up," Mickey moaned. "Right now my liver needs a crash helmet."

"The way you were carryin' on with Mysterious Mary, I'da thought you needed a seat belt."

"You ain't got no reason to talk. Supersonic Sue had you squealin'."

"I'm glad I left. Mary and Sue? Really? Where are these lovely creatures now?"

"In the room asleep. I'm glad we're leavin' today cause I don't think they want to," Howie snickered. "But you haven't heard the best yet..."

"And he ain't goin' to," Mickey said.

"Aw come on. It was funny, man. You should've seen the look on your face."

"No."

"I've got to tell him, Mick." Mickey Shackleford closed his eyes.

"Well, you gonna tell me or not? Judging from the odor you brought in, I'm surprised you can remember anything to tell."

"I'm gonna tell him, Mick."

"Go ahead; I'm not in any shape to fight."

"Now you've gotta picture this, John Ryan. We're walkin' down Bourbon Street, the four of us, drinkin' Hurricanes from paper cups, the girls are gettin' a few looks, and we're feelin' our oats when this black kid comes up to us and asks if we're gamblin' men. Of course Mickey says 'yes', and the black kid offers to make us a bet. He says, 'I'll bet you five dollars I can tell you where you got your boots.' Mickey says that's a sucker bet cause he got 'em at the Acme Boot Outlet in Cookeville, Tennessee, and there's no way this kid is gonna know that. So he takes him up on it, but the kid asks to see the five dollars, and Mickey obliges. He's got the five in his hand and then says, 'Okay, tell me where I got my boots.' The kid looks at him and smiles and says, 'You got 'em on your feet, man." Grabs the five out of Mickey's hand and he's gone with the wind. You shoulda seen the look on this man's face..." Howie could not contain his laughter, and John Ryan joined in. Mickey just kept his eyes closed and grimaced.

"So what the hell have you been doin'?" Mickey asked.

"Sleepin'. I just woke up."

"You sick?" Howie asked.

"No, tired. First time in a long time I've slept this late, but I'm not sorry I missed your party."

"What time we leavin'?" Mickey asked. "I'm not sure I can face those two again."

"Hey, it might be a long dry spell, man." Howie laughed, still wired.

"Not long enough. Hell, I'm gettin' old. What time are we leavin'?"

"Larry said about four; it's not a long trip. I guess he figured some of you might not be ready for an early morning call. What about Red and the others?"

"We ain't seen nobody."

"Just Mary and Sue," Mickey said. "We better go tell 'em we've got to leave. Immediately."

"Tell 'em immediately or leave immediately?" Howie asked.

"Both."

"Well, maybe not leave immediately," Howie said. "We still got an hour and a half."

"Screw you. I'm leavin' immediately," his compatriot said and rose unsteadily from the bed.

John Ryan laughed as they left the room. They were two little boys having the time of their lives.

Maybe the plane will crash. That thought did occur to Bernie Greshem as he poured a cup of coffee while he awaited the arrival of Philip Barnessa. The message he had received from his secretary said the promoter was taking a commuter out of North Philadelphia Airport and would arrive at nine forty-five. The weather was clear. There was no chance of a flight cancellation, and his musings about the plane crashing were just that: simple mind-crimes not to be taken seriously.

There was a problem, and it wasn't minor; otherwise, Philip Barnessa would never fly to New York when Philadelphia was only ninety minutes away by car. The size of the problem was magnified by the man's white fear of flying and airplanes in general. He even took the train when he went to Las Vegas, which was a frequent sojourn. Of course when there was a problem and Barnessa was involved, it was never simple and it was never pleasant.

It was ten-fifteen before he arrived. Air traffic at North Philadelphia had been so congested that the plane was forced to sit on the runway for thirty minutes before takeoff. A thirty minute delay, sitting on an idling aircraft, was for Philip Barnessa like meeting with a priest before walking the last mile.

"Jesus Christ! Everybody in the fucking world must be flying in and out of North Philadelphia this morning. I should have gone to the Philadelphia Airport except they've been remodeling the son-of-a-bitch for thirty years. I never know where I'm going when I'm there. Who the hell knows where you'll wind up. We gotta talk, Bernie." It was all said as the big man walked into the office, his complexion taking on the tone of his gray hair. "I need a drink."

"Have a seat; I'll get you one. C.C.? Or would you prefer a Librium?" The president decided that humor might be his best suit of armor.

"Both, if you got 'em."

"I don't think that's wise, Philip. Why don't we start with the C.C." The thought of whiskey at ten-thirty in the morning created revulsion in Bernie Greshem's stomach, but better to be an ally or an accessory than an enemy.

He handed the man his drink and set his own on his desk after putting it to his lips without taking any of the liquid into his mouth.

"We gotta settle some things, Bern, and I'd rather we did it between us than bringing anybody else into it."

"If we can settle whatever it is that we have to settle, I'd prefer it that way, too, Philip." The implication in Barnessa's words were not lost.

"We know who's in control here," Barnessa said.

"I hope it's not a matter of 'who's in control'. I hope we can define the problem—whatever it is—and come to a solution that will be mutually satisfactory." Despite what the man said, Bernie Greshem knew who was in control, and it wasn't Philip Barnessa.

"Don't get fancy with me and don't talk down to me. I remember when you were just a little Jew trying to get into the business, and I was pushing—and I mean pushing—cutouts to discount stores. Don't talk down to me." It was a litany that Philip Barnessa went through every time he had a demand to make.

What the man said was true. When Bernie Greshem began working at Trayhorn, it was a small distributorship with a small recording booth. The recording segment of the company's business was little more than a vanity scam. A kid or group of kids' parents came in with what they thought was talent, went through a phony audition, got raves and encouragement from a 'producer,' paid several hundred dollars for a recording session and a pressing of five hundred records. They received two boxes of twenty-five records each, which wound up in the hands of friends and relatives, and a promise that four hundred would be sent to disc jockeys around the country.

In actuality, only a hundred were pressed, and the remaining fifty were kept in storage in case the kid or his parents wanted to buy more to give away. Bernie Greshem hadn't been proud of what he was doing, but it wasn't easy to change the direction of a small company whose owners were making a comfortable living. He finally decided to take a chance and produce a few legitimate records on his own without the company knowing.

Bernie had heard Phil Barnessa's reminders so many times that the only question was when the man would choose to utter them. The president hardened his voice and looked at the Italian from Philadelphia straight-on.

"So tell me what the problem is, Philip."

"Your son—and maybe you, despite all your supposed help—is trying to cut us out of the country boy's action."

"There isn't any action yet," Bernie interrupted.

"Lemme finish! I went along with his cross on the scheduled release date, which he is doing to get it into his market first, but that leaves me out in the cold as far as promotion goes. You know I don't carry any weight with the stump-jumpers, so it's a waste of my time. Now he's got him playin' under cover down in Mississippi, Florida and Georgia. If he's not careful, Stone won't be playin' anywhere."

"You don't need to threaten, Philip. You know and I know that sort of thing is bullshit," he said with no small measure of condescension. "He's doing a couple of days in three dives to get the act together. It's done all the time. You want him to go out and fall on his face? We're going to invest money in this guy, and we've got to know how much. What's the problem?"

"The problem is that from what I hear is goin' on down there, this guy is gonna set the world on fire, and we ain't got a taste. Don't think I'm gonna do a goddamn thing for this hillbilly just for a promotion fee except submarine him. You know you guys are dead without my people. You guys sing serenades. We play by rock and roll rules and those rules make you money." Philip Barnessa softened his voice, made it almost friendly. "You forget, Bernie. You sit up here in your tower and take yourself out of the action, and that's all right; we'll do the work for you, but we ain't gonna work for nothin', and we ain't gonna get cut out. Bernie, you been around long enough; you can deal with me or you can deal with Giannini. I'm your best bet."

"Have I ever let you down?"

"Only because it's not allowed, and you know that."

"What do you want?"

"Whaddya got to give?" For the first time he could remember, Bernie Greshem thought Philip Barnessa might have asked the right question. He smiled to himself. It would be devastating if the man was learning to play the game intelligently.

"I'm not sure. I didn't handle the negotiations; Jamie did. I know that publishing, management and merchandising are totally tied up; there's nothing I can do about that. You were at some of those meetings."

"What about distribution?"

"You know our outlets, Philip; we limit the number of independents we use. That's elementary. What, did you just come into the company?" Bernie Greshem would not be baited.

"Maybe you should add a couple more. What about manufacturing?"

"We do our own; you know that, too. What are you trying to do here? You're asking a bunch of questions you already know the answers to. We do our own manufacturing."

"I know, but I also know you had me help you when you couldn't produce enough Austin Carr product fast enough to feed the market."

"That was a fluke. Nobody in the industry could have predicted that a night club bouncer with no voice would become a rock and roll sensation overnight."

"Maybe you need to have another fluke that no one can predict. I just want a small piece of the distribution and a small piece of the manufacturing if and when it's needed," he said with pointed sarcasm.

"How much distribution?"

"Two or three outlets. Small ones in Philadelphia, Washington, Baltimore, somethin' like that. Just pickin' up what the others can't supply."

"I'm sure you'll leave it at 'just what you can pick up.'"

"Hey, Bern," he said with spread hands and a smile.

"Where would you manufacture if and when it's needed?"

"Jamaica. Same as last time, and I want our concert people used from venue producers to vendors." The man sat back in his chair. It was the first time he seemed relaxed.

"I'm not sure I can give you all that. Jamie..."

"You can give me most of that without the kid ever knowin'. The rest?" He paused. "You'll find a way. And, Bern, if it looks good, we're gonna have to talk more; you know that. Now that that's settled, whaddya wanna do for the rest of the day and don't tell me you gotta work. Let's get some food and some broads. I gotta relax; those damn airplanes take twenty years off me."

"I have to work if you want me to try to arrange all this."

"How did I know you were gonna say that?" The man laughed. "Okay, but make some calls. I need a broad, maybe two." He rose from his chair. "I'll be at the Azalea Club in Brooklyn."

"I'll see what I can do," he said as he got up from his desk to see the man to the door.

"You can do it," Philip Barnessa said with an intimidating grin as he left.

The distribution deal didn't bother Bernie Greshem; there were always skims and cuts involved with that, but the manufacturing and concert management did. It created too many holes and too many opportunities that couldn't be controlled. Jamie was just beginning, and maybe had a winner his first time out. There was no way to know, but he deserved the opportunity. The situation would have to be watched closely, but Bernie Greshem knew where to go if he needed help.

By the time the old Flex bus whispered good-bye to the Mississippi Gulf Coast and moved into the Florida Panhandle, its passengers all had a sense of the bond that had been forged during that first engagement, a thing uncalculated and indefinable, a phenomenon that sometimes happens in such a situation, sometimes doesn't. They were also 'on the road', and despite the brevity of their trip since leaving Nashville, the boredom of the bus, the fatigue of late nights, sleepless days, and the diminishing of their initial excitement had begun to sink in.

There was conversation and conjecture for the first half-hour and then the bus fell silent. Mickey and Howie were semi-comatose, trying to recover from a major overdose of alcohol and too much time spent with 'the go-go twins'; Mountain Red snored, and Son Cochran and Paul Crockett talked quietly.

John Ryan Stone wrote, trying to put on paper the whole experience in Biloxi from a personal perspective. The playing was fine, exciting, but 'the road' itself was tedious. He couldn't imagine doing a hundred and fifty or two hundred dates a year—all one-night stands—as some country artists did. The romance of spending time on a bus, staying in impersonal motel rooms, dieting on grease, fast food and alcohol, being too tired, and not having enough time during the day to spend the money you made at night, was lost on him.

The Down Home Roadhouse was a step up from The Silver Saddle Saloon. It was situated on the water, decorated with more subdued neon and didn't have an after-work crowd. The dressing room was decorated with posters rather than magic-marker graffiti. Hank, Jr. had been there, Mel Tillis, Sonny James, Waylon Jennings and others who spent the greater part of their lives on the road. Most of them had appeared at The Down Home

Roadhouse before their careers took flight or after they had landed. In a small way, John Ryan felt the posters gave some credibility to their efforts.

Florida went smoothly. The crowd appeared to like them as well as the people in Mississippi. Each night their numbers increased even though Mondays, Tuesdays, and Wednesdays were historically slow nights at any club.

John Ryan spoke briefly with Kate after their opening night performance. She was on her way to a meeting and had little time to talk. The conversation was limited to the band's performance. She promised to see him in Savannah, but her businesslike tone made the conversation impersonal and dampened his enthusiasm. He found it hard to put aside.

At the close of each of the first two night's performances, when the club was closed and all the patrons had left, a telephone call connected Fort Walton Beach, Florida, to Philadelphia, Pennsylvania. On the third night a stout but muscular, gray-haired man, wearing a wide gold chain around his neck and a diamond pinkie ring stood unnoticed in the shadows at the back of the club.

The band left Fort Walton Beach, Florida, at two-fifteen a.m. on Thursday morning heading toward Savannah, Georgia. The sour odor of emptiness and idleness that had pervaded the bus's interior when they began the trip in Nashville was gone. It now smelled of food, alcohol, and tobacco and was more the band's home than the motel rooms they slept in on the nights they were playing. No one turned on any seat lights when they left, and only snippets of conversation passed through the darkness.

"All I wanted was a home, a family and a normal life." John Ryan heard Mountain Red say.

"Then why the hell did you get in this business?" Crockett asked.

"So I could afford a home, a family and a normal life," Red answered with a chuckle.

"Good luck," someone said.

"How could anyone do this three hundred days a year?" Mickey asked.

"The music is easy," Son Cochran answered. "It's the life that'll kill you."

"Writers are the ones that got it made," a voice from the front of the bus said.

"Nobody's got it made in this business," Son said. "You always want what you don't have. Sidemen want the security of a studio gig, and studio musicians—some of 'em anyway—want the excitement of an audience, and people leadin' the fast life always want peace and quiet, which would kill 'em."

As the bus moved northeast toward Savannah, Georgia, Philip Barnessa drove north to Philadelphia. He had flown down to Florida but couldn't face the prospect of flying back, so he rented a car. That was bad enough, but his anger was stimulated more by being out of control in a money-making situation. Based on what he had seen in Florida and the reports he had been receiving, handled properly, the hillbilly could be worth millions. Handled the way Jamie Greshem and Don Hendrickson wanted, he would be worth nothing to Philip Barnessa unless he came up with a good curve ball.

At the moment he didn't have any percentage of the representation, none of the publishing, only regional promotion, and a vague promise of a small piece of the manufacturing, but only if the company were in dire straits for product. The only real interest he had was the concert stuff if Bernie pushed that by his son. The take would be peanuts in comparison to the potential. He knew Giannini Tedesco would not settle for 'peanuts'. That was a given. Ownership was the only thing he was interested in.

The second source of his fury was that for a week he hadn't been able to reach either Jamie or Bernie Greshem. Philip Barnessa was not a patient man. Since Jamie was on the coast, he tried to call Joel Dishman, but he was 'out of the office'. Bernie was 'not in the building'. He suspected the next person he called would be 'off the planet'.

He was totally frustrated. What he saw in Florida made him hungry. The stump jumper wouldn't push Elvis or replace the Beatles, but he could hurt a Johnny Rivers and move in with Orbison and Cash. There was a way to make money, big money, off the son-of-a-bitch, and he would find it. Nashville had never dealt with Philip Barnessa. Neither had Bernie Greshem really. He decided to call Maury Friedman as soon as he got back to Philly. The whole situation with John Ryan Stone had been shaky; it was time to look at what the man had signed.

Kate Belden decided to make the trip to Savannah a vacation. It had been more than a year since she had taken any time for herself, and it would be a good time to assess a lot of things that had been roiling in her mind over the last few weeks, not the least of which was John Ryan Stone. The thought was invigorating.

Bernie Greshem had been 'unavailable' to both she and Barbara Allred for more than a week, and with Jamie on the coast until Saturday and no one to approve anything or give any direction, the development of John Ryan Stone was in a holding pattern. She hadn't mentioned her uneasiness to John Ryan; in fact, she had cut their last conversation short, giving some excuse about a meeting, in order to prevent it from showing. Barbara wrote it off to business as usual in the music industry: lots of excitement plus total confusion equals lack of progress. Kate didn't see it that way but was afraid she was being overprotective.

In a moment of decisiveness she had called her travel agent, booked a flight into Savannah for early Thursday morning and reserved a room at The Ballastone Inn, located in the historic district and highly recommended by her agent. She didn't want to stay in the same hotel as the musicians or Jamie Greshem. It was to be a vacation after all.

The thought of seeing the band in performance excited her. It would be interesting to see how the two engagements had changed John Ryan. Although they had spoken on the telephone, she wanted to hear about it again, in detail, face to face, live and in person, to see his expressions and hear the attitude in his voice. The encounter in Nashville had kindled her interest, and the unexpected anxiety over the opening in Mississippi followed by their two-hour telephone conversation, gave her pause. She had been through it all before; there was no room for long-distance fantasies.

Savannah did not have the earmarks of a city. There was no frantic movement. The traffic moved slower, and the faces of the people did not have the agitated, distraught expressions Kate saw on the streets of New York, Chicago or Los Angeles. It was reminiscent of her home in Indiana, which had become less and less memorable the longer she remained away.

As the cab proceeded down Abercorn Street past the failing Victorian houses that formed a buffer zone between the new section of the city and the historic district, a sense of softness, quality and grace enveloped her. None of the cities she had visited before possessed the elegant charm and essence of history that she was seeing.

The Ballastone itself was a wonderful antebellum mansion decorated in Savannah colors and authentic antiques. Not only did the setting take her back in time, but the service itself also reverted to a bygone era when caring and satisfaction were the basis of the guest-hotelier relationship.

It was lovely beyond her imagination. The room included a large Teester bed, a well-lighted bathroom with a sit-down vanity; full-length mirrors, a shower, and a platformed Jacuzzi large enough for two. There was also a fireplace guarded by two wing chairs and other pieces of period furniture. The four days ahead appeared suddenly to be a tranquilizer she hadn't realized she needed.

After unpacking, taking a hot shower, putting on shorts and a loose fitting blouse, she headed down to River Street for lunch. The band would not be arriving until late afternoon, and John Ryan was not expecting her until Saturday. He was in for quite a surprise. That thought made her smile.

John Ryan Stone was overwhelmed at the sight of Doogie's, the nicest of the three clubs they had played. Compared to The Silver Saddle and The Down Home Roadhouse, it was upscale. There were real dressing rooms, bathrooms, furniture, and his name was posted on the roadside marquee in front of the club.

The first set was adequate, but that's the best review he could give it. He was nervous, the early crowd small and quiet. The band slid through the music, doing what they had to do while getting nothing back from the few people sitting at the tables and the bar. It was similar to the second night in Mississippi and in the first set each night in Florida. Relaxing in the dressing room during break, he could hear the noise level build out in the club and knew things would get better.

John Ryan and Son were alone, the others out in the bar 'mingling' as Mickey called it. He wasn't sure Mickey and Howie had spent a night alone in their room since their first night in Biloxi.

111

"Gonna be a big one," Paul Crockett said as he and Red came through the door, drinks in hand.

"We need it. The first set was sloppy," Son remarked without raising his eyes.

"You got a problem?" Crockett asked, paranoid and ever ready for a confrontation. The man seemed to exist on the edge of explosion.

"No. We—I said 'we'—were sloppy. All the records in the world won't make much difference if we can't be consistent live."

"Speak for yourself," the harmonica player said as he slumped in a chair. Everyone had learned quickly that Paul Crockett took every criticism personally.

"What was that old Orbison tune we were playin' around with in Florida?" John Ryan asked, trying to change the subject.

"*Only the Lonely*," Red offered.

"Let's try it tonight."

"Think it's ready?" Son asked.

"No, but let's do it anyway. I think we're gettin' bored. I want to do it the way we did it the last few times we went through it, heavy bass and drums."

"I'm not sure it's wise," Crockett muttered.

"I'm not sure I've ever been wise," John Ryan said. "Someone once said you couldn't go to Nashville if you had a wife; I guess he was right." They all laughed at his line and got up to go back on stage. "Let's blow 'em out."

"Did John Ryan Stone say that?" Red said with a laugh as they passed through the door.

Kate Belden stood in the lounge area and watched Cade Wilhite and Larry Foster making adjustments to the equipment on stage during the band's break. She had entered the club unnoticed just as the band walked off, hadn't heard a note, and hadn't seen John Ryan Stone.

The afternoon had been wonderful. She wandered through the shops along the river, ate a shrimp Po'boy sandwich—something she had read about in a southern novel—walked the Squares, admired the Savannah mansions, took a short nap and a long Jacuzzi. She then dressed for dinner at The Old Pink House, a lovely restaurant suggested by the desk clerk.

The time between dinner and her arrival at Doogie's was filled with what was becoming a familiar anxiety. She felt silly, like a schoolgirl bubbling over with excitement.

She also felt the fear of risk nibbling at her psyche. It had been two years since she allowed any chinks in her emotional armor. It was not the best way to live, but it certainly was easier. This was not a good risk, she told herself. There were possibilities on the one hand and penalties on the other. At least that was a step forward, she thought; in the past there had been little consideration of damage. Yet there was a compulsion to move forward and allow whatever might happen, happen.

Just before the second set was to begin, she took her scotch and sat at a table in the rear of the club, shadowed so she wouldn't be seen. The lights dimmed and Kate settled back to listen.

The stage went dark. Bobby Hopwood began alone, hitting straight-eight's. Son Cochran joined in with the bass, then Howie on rhythm guitar. The solid, unalternating beat on one note continued for what seemed an inordinate period of time although it lasted for little more than a minute. Mountain Red came in simultaneously with the lights, and the whole band hit the first note of *Detour* in an upbeat instrumental version of the old classic, designed to lift the crowd out of the doldrums. Cade Wilhite advanced the volume to its peak and the talking stopped because it was useless. Everyone's attention was riveted to the stage, hypnotized by the incessant beat of the drums and the bass.

When the opening music came to an end, the band went straight into a hard-hitting version of Orbison's *Dream Baby* then slowed down to a heavy blues rendition of *Fever* featuring Paul Crockett. The harmonica began to fade with the lights on stage, but the sensuous sound of the blues anthem continued in the background as Larry Foster, whose voice was surprisingly deep and resonant when it was amplified, said: "Ladies and Gentlemen, John Ryan Stone." The music stopped for a beat as the spotlight picked up John Ryan coming onstage as the introduction to *Ring of Fire* began.

Kate felt a chill as he came into view with a firm and confident stride. The tailored jeans made him look even taller than the man she had been visualizing. The collarless, ivory-colored shirt with the ever-present epaulets set off a tan and healthy look. He wore a conch-shell belt. The overall effect made the ice-blue eyes and white teeth send out a notice that reached beyond the parameters of the stage. Kate let out a small breath of air and wondered what was going through the minds of the rest of the women in the audience. It wasn't hard to guess. The road did not appear to be having any negative effects on the singer.

John Ryan lowered his head to the mike and let the deep, rough voice do its own work. *"Love is a burning thing, and it makes a fiery ring..."* Kate was stunned at the reaction of the crowd, obviously captured by the voice and persona they saw before them. He looked totally comfortable as if it were something he had done every night for a long, long time. He was polished and secure and moved the crowd with him as the music changed.

113

Ain't It Funny How Time Slips Away, by a songwriter named Willie Nelson whose name, though unfamiliar to her, brought a huge response. A country-twisted interpretation of Sam Cooke's *Another Saturday Night* and others she had not heard the band perform stimulated increasingly louder reactions.

When the set was over, when John Ryan Stone had left the stage, when the applause subsided and was replaced by syncopated conversation, Kate sat not knowing quite what to do. She hadn't planned this far ahead. What she had seen changed her whole position in whatever relationship she thought there was with him. He was no longer what she had known him to be. The world didn't know it yet, and she was certain he didn't know it, but John Ryan Stone—if he wanted it—was going to be bigger than anyone ever imagined. What he would need was protection from the industry itself.

As she walked past the bar on her way backstage, Mountain Red was the only band member she recognized. He took no notice of her.

The door to the dressing room was open. Son Cochran was in the room with John Ryan who had his feet propped up on a table, his head back and his eyes closed. It appeared that all the energy she had seen on the stage had been left there, and the man she was familiar with was now sitting in front of her. He wasn't aware that she had entered the room. The bass man looked up, smiled and left them alone. John Ryan didn't move. She stood and watched him for a moment trying to determine what was going through his mind. He wasn't asleep, but he wasn't sitting in the dressing room at Doogie's either.

"Would it seem outrageously corny to say, 'A penny for your thoughts'?" she said quietly. She couldn't be sure whether his feet moved first or his eyes opened, whichever, there was a look of total shock on his face and then he smiled.

"Great God A'mighty! Kate Belden!" He got out of the chair and came toward her, his tallness and the stature of what she had witnessed happening on stage making her feel smaller than she had in his presence before. He didn't know whether to shake her hand, give her a friendly hug or just remain standing there looking like the fool he imagined.

"I didn't think you were coming in until Saturday," he said.

"I wanted to catch you by surprise." She perceived in herself the same uncertainty she sensed in him. He pulled a chair to face where he had been sitting.

"Have a seat."

"So what were you thinking?" she asked as she sat down.

"I have no idea; whatever it was, you surely knocked it out of my head. What are you doing here? Were you serious about catching me by surprise?"

"Well..." she answered coyly, giving him a moment's room for doubt, "actually I did want to catch you by surprise, but not to spy on you. I decided to take a couple of days vacation and thought I could kill two birds with one stone if I vacationed here."

"That's all?"

"No, that's not all. I wanted to see you perform without any pressure. Jamie said things were going well, and I just wanted to see for myself."

"How does he know how things are going? I haven't talked to him. I haven't heard anything from him or Don. I was beginning to wonder if everybody forgot we were out here."

"I don't know how he knows, but he said everything was going better than expected. He's been out on the coast, so I haven't had a chance to talk to him personally. Whatever, you're not forgotten, believe me. The company has its ways of keeping track of things." Kate struck him as being even more beautiful than he remembered. He almost lost her last words with that observation.

"The last set was the best we've ever done," John Ryan said shaking his head and laughing. "And you're right."

"About what?"

"I would have been nervous if I'd known you were out there."

"That's a good sign," she said looking squarely into the blue of his eyes, not knowing exactly what her words meant, but growing more uncomfortable with the confusion of what she was feeling.

"What did you think?" There was momentary embarrassment at the question, as if he were asking for a compliment, but he had no doubt that Kate would be honest. It was business after all, he told himself.

"Do I have to tell you?" Her face turned serious.

"Yes, I want you to."

"I don't know what to say."

"Well, that certainly leaves a lot of room for interpretation." His comment brought a smile. She was quiet for moment and then answered.

"It's difficult to come up with a word that describes what I felt. It was better than anything I could have ever anticipated or guessed. I didn't expect the confidence and assurance or the talent that I saw up there tonight. I thought you were good in Nashville, especially your songs, but everything else was so raw I wasn't sure where it would go from there. Tonight was something different. I've got to think about it before I can give you a more specific evaluation. Is that enough praise and adulation to hold you for a little while, Mr. Stone?"

"Are you making fun of me?"

"No. Just celebrating you with humor. I have a hard time expressing myself when I'm excited. Didn't you once say something about using humor—'glibness' is the way I think you put it—to hide nerves?"

"Why are you nervous?" He was smiling again.

"I'm not...I mean I don't know."

"We've got another set. You gonna stick around? Maybe you can find more praise to heap upon me."

"No. I think I'll go back to the hotel. I don't want to get too overwhelmed."

"Can we have a drink later? It'll be late."

"What time?" She knew whatever he said would be fine.

"It's Thursday. They close at midnight, but it'll probably be one."

"Sure." Kate stood.

"Where?"

"The Ballastone Inn on Oglethorpe."

"Yes, but I have no idea where that is. Hell, I don't even know what it is."

"It's a bed and breakfast, but I don't know where it is either. The Rhett Suite."

"The Rhett Suite?" He smiled. "I'll find it."

"I meant what I said about the music."

"We'll talk about it," he said and put his hand on her back as he led her to the door. "One o'clock?"

"One o'clock," she said.

"And, Kate, I'm glad you're here." She smiled and shrugged her shoulders.

———

The taxi ride from one side of town to the other took no more than twenty-five minutes. Kate rested her head on the back of the seat, closed her eyes and let her mind fall back on what she had just seen at Doogie's and all of the thoughts that had been circling in her mind when she decided to make this trip.

She felt compelled toward John Ryan but held herself back, knowing there was time. There was also their professional relationship to consider. Kate gave up the charade; rational thought was impossible. The man had touched her. Her decision was when or if she would let him know it.

At one thirty-five John Ryan arrived at the inn. As he knocked on her door, he realized that he was charged by more than the impetus of the performances. He worried that she might have lost her enthusiasm for a late night drink and conversation. That concern was allayed when she invited him into the room and mixed him a drink.

They talked long into the early morning hours. They discussed music, books, foods they liked and things they didn't like until the effects of the alcohol having reached a reasonable peak began to subside and the hours slowed and became heavy. After the longest silence of the night, which wasn't very long, Kate decided it was time to end the evening. She hadn't slept well before leaving New York and the day and night had passed with only a brief nap. She had opened herself to him. It felt good, but her thoughts were frazzled. Before she could say anything, as if he had read her thoughts, John Ryan stood and put his glass on the table.

"You're tired," he said.

"Yes."

"I think I've about had my course too. Can I see you later today?"

"Of course," she said as if it were a forgone conclusion.

"I don't mean to be presumptive, but I like you, Kate."

"I like you too, John Ryan. Very much." She stood.

"We'll have to talk about that," he said.

"I'd like to."

John Ryan took her in his arms and held her tightly. "I hope you don't mind; I'm a hugger," he said.

"Me too," she whispered as he broke away. "Call me when you've had some rest."

"I will," he said and opened the door. As Kate closed the door behind him, her hands were shaking.

As John Ryan Stone walked down the stairs to the front desk, his hands were quivering as well.

The commuter flight from New York had delivered Maury Friedman to North Philadelphia Airport three hours before his scheduled meeting with Philip Barnessa. It was the way he did business, always early, always prepared, always with time to review and think.

Friedman looked at the legal documents spread across the desk in his suite. He picked up one and then another. In total they represented the entire legal marriage between Trayhorn International and John Ryan Stone, songwriter/singer. There were few holes. He didn't really expect any. Bernie Greshem was good at protecting the company and himself.

Maury Friedman was a meticulous man, an analyst who would not tolerate any margin for error. Son of middle-class, Jewish parents and raised in Brooklyn, he had through scholastic endeavor and hard work managed to earn a law degree from N.Y.U., pass both the New York and Pennsylvania Bar exams on his first attempt at each, and began representing a few lower-level members of the Catalona Family in minor matters.

After two years of learning the street trade of the legal profession, setting goals, solidifying contacts and tailoring a plan, he moved to Philadelphia where he received his MBA from the Wharton School of Business. It was during that period that he met Philip Barnessa.

From the moment he met the man, Friedman recognized Philip Barnessa as useful—tough, street-smart, emotional, violent and with little ambition beyond money and what or who it could buy. He had never considered the entertainment industry as a crucible for his purposes, but after listening to the promoter from South Philadelphia, he did his research and decided there was no venue as ripe with loose contracts, ever-changing personnel, huge amounts of carelessly handled money, indefensible accounting practices and corrupt to the core. It was ideal.

Philip Barnessa did not know how to knock softly, and if the counselor had not anticipated it, he would have expected the sound to be followed by the word 'Police!' It was only four o'clock; he was thirty minutes early, another trait Friedman was used to. Everything about the man smacked of impatience. Maury Friedman waited until the second knock before going to the door.

"So whadda we got, Maury?" Barnessa said as he strode into the room.

Philip, Philip," Friedman responded. "Calm yourself. You're going to have a stroke. Let's have a drink and we'll discuss it. C.C.?" he asked moving toward the convenience bar.

"Yeah. That's okay. Maury, we gotta do somethin' with this guy. You didn't hear what I heard. This guy—believe me—this guy could be as big as Diamond."

"That good?" Maury said passively.

"That good. We can't be left out on this one. If this guy does what I think he can do and our people don't have a taste, somebody's gonna wind up in a garbage bag."

"You're not in the streets anymore, Philip. Don't sound like it." The man's language was infuriating. It had been hard work raising himself above that level, and he didn't like to be reminded of it. You could take the boy out of the streets, he thought. He knew he was one of the few people who could talk to Philip Barnessa firmly without getting a violent reaction. "I know very little about your kind of music and don't care to, but this guy's a hillbilly. There's never been a hillbilly that did what you're talking about." He took a sip of his drink and looked at one of the papers on his desk. "What makes you think this—what's his name?—John Ryan Stone will be what you say?"

"Jesus Christ, Maury! You're the one who guided me to his guy, told me to get involved." Barnessa paused and looked away. "You know you're right about one thing; you don't know anything about music, but I do. Maury, I'm tellin' you. Me. I know. I'm tellin' you this guy can be a monster."

Maury Friedman looked at the man. He did, in fact, appear on the verge of having a coronary or a stroke. He was panicked. "Why?"

"Why what?"

"Why do you think this guy can be so big?"

Barnessa sat down. "Look, let me explain something to you. Most of the big things that happen in this business are unexpected. Surprises. I mean who the hell could have predicted Tiny Tim or even Bob Dylan for that matter. Sounds like a chicken being choked. It has nothing to do with quality, but this guy is different. I'll give you a list. He doesn't have a pretty voice, but nobody wants pretty voices anymore. They want sex. He has the looks, not polished but the kind that makes women cream. And he writes

119

good songs. And guess what they're about. Sex. Ever heard a country song about sex? The Bible thumpers are gonna have a field day."

"Okay. Let's say you're right. You know I don't personally deal with artist's contracts and these," he gestured to the papers on the desk, "look fairly tight to me. Badly written, but pretty tight. Now, knowing that, tell me how you think I can help you at the corporate level?" Trying to work with Philip Barnessa was like dealing with a child. You have to let them explain even though you are pretty sure of what you're going to do anyway.

"Why the fuck do you think I came to you? If I knew what to do, I wouldn't have called. I've never been in this situation before. I don't know what's goin' on, and Bernie won't say anything because he's suddenly decided to be a father. He's tryin' to look out for his kid, and the kid's in la-la land."

Maury Friedman again paused and scanned the papers on the desk. "There's no opening here for management or agency for at least a year unless they decide to give it, which Jamie won't, so you can forget that. Bernie's added a clause for concert promotion and vending; when the time comes, he assigns the franchise. Since, as president, he controls the contract, we have to live with that unless you can get to Bernie. Beyond that he's inserted an addendum applying to corporate regarding manufacture if it's needed. He gets to choose the company. I don't see anything else."

Barnessa shook his head. "I already got that, but it's not enough," he said sternly.

"I assumed that, so I've been thinking. Maybe we can double-dip, as it were, in other areas. If you're up to it." There was a smile on the lawyer's face.

"Double-dipping. You legal guys are great at that. Speak."

"Do you know Jack Trekorian? Markets all of the overstock and deleted titles?"

"Cut-outs. Yeah, I know him."

"See how this sounds to you. The cut-out market has been in the doldrums, and Jack is not in a healthy position. He's got tons of discontinued product sitting in warehouses, and the company is pushing him to move them, but he can't come up with the buyers. Suppose he designates a separate marketing company to assist in distributing cut-outs. That's you. You get a piece of every unit you move."

"Maury, I am not a cut-out salesman. That has nothing to do with Stone. You're out of your fuckin' mind. I don't know why I called."

"Don't be impatient, Philip; I'm not through. I do my homework. You should know that. I know you have a pressing plant in Jamaica. Nobody knows it's yours, but it is."

"It's not a secret." Barnessa lowered his head.

"Depends on who you're talking to. In any case, we have access to masters and the artwork for whatever the company puts out on Stone. It's golden if this guy does what you say he's going to do. Trayhorn will do a limited pressing and tease the distributors as always, and everybody's going to want product they can't get. You and you alone will be able to provide what they want."

"Bootlegging?"

"Not just bootlegging. You've got the cut-out business. To get your 'home-made' product, the distributors will have to make a cut-out purchase. Say thirty cut-out units for one Stone at whatever price the market will bear. They're buying under-the-table and don't know where the product is coming from, and we don't have to pay anything except manufacturing costs. No royalties, no cut to Trayhorn, and Trekorian gets to move truckloads of unsalable merchandise."

"What about audits?"

"Philip, I'm not an amateur. Don't worry about audits."

"You forgot to mention your piece, but I like it and we can take it further." Philip Barnessa's mind was rolling.

"How?"

"You don't want to know."

"You're right," the lawyer sighed, hoping his friend would not allow greed to ruin what he considered a perfect setup.

"Now all we have to do is make John Ryan Stone a star," Barnessa said.

The scheme was relatively simple by Philip Barnessa's industry standards. There were only two obstacles to overcome as far as he could determine. One was to get Jack Trekorian's cooperation, which Friedman assured. The other ingredient would be more difficult. John Ryan Stone had to become a major star. He had everything it required to be a money-maker, but if it didn't happen as a matter of course, Barnessa thought, what the hell? He'd invented stars before. He couldn't lose and that thought made him smile with relief as he left the Bellevue. He didn't ask Friedman to accompany him for the evening; it was a night for celebration—lots of food, booze and women. He hadn't decided how many, but he would make it a night to remember.

⎯⎯·•·⎯⎯

The anticipation of this night and Jamie Greshem's arrival had dominated Kate Belden's thinking as well as John Ryan's for the past two days. On Friday they had met for drinks in the late afternoon at a small tourist bar on River Street and walked to The Pink House for an early dinner. Kate didn't go to the club. She was wary of being oversaturated with the music and not having the spontaneous enthusiasm that she wanted Jamie to see. John Ryan had come to her room when the night was finished, and they had again talked until the early morning hours, delicately getting to know each other, moving toward familiarity and comfort.

On Saturday John Ryan was busy with rehearsal, putting two new songs on the list and preparing for what everyone in the band knew was a critical performance. Kate took a carriage tour and read. It was a lonely day.

There was an odor of heat in Doogie's by the time the final set was due to begin. A thick odor fomented by cigarette smoke, alcohol and body fever, a dim-lit, sexual heat that generated a breed of excitement stimulated only by risk and promise. It was what the people came for.

Kate, sitting at a table she had 'reserved' at the back of the club, was getting nervous. She had begun to wonder if Jamie was going to show at all when he came through the door accompanied by Joel Dishman and Don Hendrickson. A knot grew in her stomach; she had not expected Hendrickson and Dishman. John Ryan's first two sets had been good, and the capacity crowd had responded in kind, even though in her opinion the performances did not measure up to what she had seen on her first night in Savannah. The three men's reactions would either confirm her judgment or establish her lack of objectivity. When she stood and waved, she caught Joel Dishman's attention and the three men worked their way toward her table.

Jamie leaned forward and gave her a welcome kiss on the cheek. Joel Dishman shook her hand and Don Hendrickson nodded and smiled.

"I didn't think you were going to make it," she said as they all sat down.

"We had some doubts ourselves," Jamie said. "We were late getting out of L.A. which put us into Nashville late. Don had to charter a plane to get us here at all."

"I didn't know you were going to Nashville," Kate said.

"We didn't either. It was a last minute decision. We may have a new strategy, and I wanted everybody here to see what we have to work with. Do we go to the bar for drinks?"

"Depends on how fast you want them. As you can see the place is packed. It's the biggest crowd Doogie's has ever had and they're not quite sure how to handle it."

"John Ryan?" Hendrickson asked.

"John Ryan," she answered. "It's been like this since opening night."

"Damn!" Joel Dishman said. "What the hell have we got here?"

"You'll see in about ten minutes. By the way, if you're going for drinks, you'd better go. Get doubles because once he comes on you won't be able to get to the bar. It gets crazy." The knot of concern was beginning to dissolve into excitement. She had to monitor herself closely to keep her enthusiasm from overtaking her. She prayed John Ryan would show them everything he had and then some. It would be fun to see the looks on their faces.

When Joel and Don Hendrickson went for drinks, Jamie turned to Kate. "I know this sounds ridiculous coming from his producer, but I haven't seen him which is also ridiculous. Is he really this good?" he asked, indicating the crowd.

"I'll let you judge for yourself," she said as the lights began to dim.

Joel and Hendrickson got back to the table just as the lights faded. By the time they were seated, Bobby Hopwood's drums, after being greeted with loud approval, commanded the audience's attention. None of the men said anything as Kate watched their faces. The heavy instrumental warm-up—*Forty Miles of Bad Road,* used for the third set—totally captured the crowd and set them up for the earthy, blues sound of *Fever,* made even more erotic than its content by the dangerous look and sensuous moves made by Paul Crockett as he played.

"Ladies and gentlemen, once again, John Ryan Stone!" Larry Foster's voice boomed through the speaker system. Though the announcer's voice was a surprise in itself to the three visitors, nothing was as astounding as the reaction of the people that surrounded them. It was breathtaking.

Midway through the set Kate quit watching the three men and focused on John Ryan. The music was awesome and the performer electrifying. Nobody on stage was going through the motions. Mickey and Howie were stronger on the harmonies and more decisive with their instruments. Between Crockett and John Ryan's voice and demeanor, *I'm So Lonesome I Could Cry* was plaintive enough to bring on tears. The old Ferlin Huskey hit *Gone* was a surprise; Kate had not heard him sing it before, and Red played the piano break with a tenderness that bordered on candlelight. The now-familiar guitar opening to *Satisfied Mind* brought a frantic response and was followed by the quiet Willie Nelson tune that she had come to like. John Ryan thanked the patrons and the club and ended with *Another Saturday Night* which had been requested each set by the Savannah crowd.

The people didn't want to let go. Women were reaching toward the stage and men were standing on chairs yelling for more. John Ryan came back out, waved to the crowd and was gone. Mickey, Howie, Mountain Red, Crockett and Bobby Hopwood finished the exit music and the stage was empty. It was one o'clock in the morning. The bar was closed and people milled around. No one was ready to leave. Neither Jamie Greshem, Joel Dishman nor Don Hendrickson had spoken during the entire set.

It was Hendrickson who first broke the silence. "If you had bet me a million against a dollar, I never would have believed what I just saw," he said.

"I'm dazed," Jamie said, looking wide-eyed. "Hell, I can't even talk. What in God's name happened?"

"Magic," Hendrickson said.

"I don't know about magic, but it's sure as hell incredible," the young producer said.

"I wasn't in the studio," Joel Dishman said, "but I do know what I just saw, and based on our discussions, I think we need to reconsider our strategy again. Putting a lone single out on this guy is a waste of time. His potential is too big for a single. Nobody takes a single seriously and this is serious. I think we need to break him with an album. That's where the money is and that's where the serious buying public is. An album makes a statement; a single is just a shot in the dark and everybody knows it."

"I'm shaking," Jamie said.

"Me, too," Hendrickson added, "and I'm too damned old and been around too long to shake. God knows what people'll do when they hear his own songs." He broke into a broad grin. "You got a tiger by the tail, boy; you better handle it carefully. You don't get a lot of chances like this; don't screw it up."

"I think we've got to go with an album," Joel repeated.

"You're talking major money," Hendrickson said.

"Hey, it takes money to make money, but this guy is more than money; he's power. I don't think we have a choice."

Kate didn't say anything. She wasn't even sure they knew she was still at the table. She didn't have to say anything; John Ryan had done it all.

"Can we do it?" Jamie asked Hendrickson.

"It's your call."

"What about material?"

"Didn't you hear enough tonight?" Hendrickson asked with a smile. Then he paused. "Let's do it."

"Let's keep it under wraps for awhile," Jamie said.

"Hard to do, but what the hell; we'll give it a try."

As instructed, Kate brought John Ryan to the Sheraton where the three executives were staying. She had been told not to mention anything about an album, just that Jamie was very impressed and wanted to talk with him in a more sane atmosphere than Doogie's afforded. She wasn't to say anything about Hendrickson or Joel Dishman being there.

John Ryan had initially been disturbed when Kate was the only one who came to the dressing room. At first he thought maybe Jamie hadn't made it. Everybody in the room was flying. The fact that Jamie hadn't come back to revel in their success was a disappointment; however, when Kate explained the situation, he thought he understood.

It took her an hour to extricate him from the club and get him into a cab. People were still milling around outside when they pulled away.

"It was good, wasn't it?" he asked as they rode through the early morning streets.

"It was good."

He leaned forward and tilted her face. He looked at her for a moment as if deciding whether or not to go forward. He brushed her lips with feather kisses and saw her eyes close and then they kissed, tasting the sweetness of each other's mouths. When the taxi began to slow, they broke apart.

"Wow," Kate said quietly.

"I think that's becoming our password," he said with a laugh as the taxi pulled to a stop in front of the hotel.

When they reached the designated suite, Jamie Greshem, sporting a Cheshire cat smile, answered the knock at the door. "Kate, John Ryan. Come in. It would be an understatement to say we were just talking about you."

"Good, I hope." John Ryan answered.

"Actually unbelievably good. I've got a little surprise for you. Couple of your old friends dropped by."

As Jamie had promised, he was shocked to see Joel Dishman and Don Hendrickson sitting in the room. They both wore smiles, but Hendrickson's was the broadest.

"Well, boy, you surely did turn out, didn't you?" he said rising to shake John Ryan's hand. "Better'n I ever could have imagined. Renewed my faith in hunches, I'll tell you. Hell, hoss, you're beyond good." He stopped as if waiting for John Ryan to reply.

"As usual, I have no idea how to respond to that, Don," he said. Finding Hendrickson and Joel Dishman there was confusing enough, but lingering thoughts of what had happened in the cab with Kate interfered with logical thinking.

"It was fantastic," Jamie said, adding emphasis to Hendrickson's statement.

125

Joel Dishman rose and extended his hand. "I don't know anything to add to all of the above," the nattily dressed Californian said. "Congratulations."

Jamie gestured toward the sofa. "Have a seat. I got some champagne, and the hotel sent up some food. I do believe it's time to celebrate," he said.

As Kate and John Ryan made themselves comfortable on one of the couches, Jamie went to the bar and began filling crystal flutes with champagne. "I know it's redundant," he said as he poured, "but we didn't expect what we saw tonight." He served the wine and raised his glass. "To the future which appears to be getting brighter by the moment." They touched glasses and drank.

"What happened to the wobblies, John Ryan?" Hendrickson laughed. "I didn't see any up there tonight."

"I quit thinkin'," John Ryan answered, his blue eyes hiding a wariness at the adulation.

"I guess more of us ought to do that. I always thought thinkin' too much hurt a man's common sense."

"How come you and Joel are here? I didn't expect..."

"We didn't either," Jamie interrupted. "We were discussing how to break the record and market it when we suddenly realized that we didn't know what we were marketing or if we even had anything to sell. So Don suggested we charter a plane and all come down and take a look."

Kate Belden listened and took pride in everything the men were saying about John Ryan and his performance. She watched him, trying to discern what was going through his mind as the accolades continued. He appeared impassive or disbelieving except for an occasional smile or shaking of the head. She hoped he would keep that perspective; it could save disillusionment. She felt a stronger connection with him, not proprietary, not a coupling, but heading in that direction.

There was a pause in the conversation and John Ryan spoke.

"You were talking about marketing," he said, "I don't know much about that, but I did ask Kate where we were going from here. I been gettin' a lot of questions I can't answer."

"That's why we wanted you to come over tonight," Jamie replied. "We've got some decisions to make, and I don't want to put things off. Let me explain where we are. The plan was to release a single in about three weeks. Sleeve artwork's done, labels are printed and the pressing could be completed as early as this week. We were going to go with *I Can't Stand the Silence Anymore* and *Everybody Don't Have To Be A Cowboy* on the B side."

"But we've changed our thinking a bit," Joel Dishman cut in. "We don't think, having seen you, that a single by itself is the way to go. It'll be released, but we want to release an album simultaneously. Use one to pro-

126

mote the other. That's the kind of faith we have in what we saw tonight. Manufacturing the product is no problem. Recording it is another matter and that's largely up to you."

"How many songs we talkin' about?"

"We've got four," Hendrickson said. "Probably make it with ten. That'd be six more. I hate to put out a thin product; it'll come back to haunt you."

"All my songs?" John Ryan asked with a doubtful look on his face.

"Don't have to be," Hendrickson answered, "But if we could stick to yours, it would be more impressive. Hadn't been done very often." He looked carefully at the tall, lanky man sitting before him, so different than the man who only months ago sat nervously on his patio in Hendersonville and played his songs. "What do you think? Have you got six more songs that are usable?"

"How the hell should I know? I guess I think all my songs are all right or I wouldn't have written 'em, but I don't know if they're good enough for an album." It was the first pressure he had experienced since the first night in Biloxi. "You're kind of catchin' me by surprise here."

"Tell you what," Jamie said. "You're heading back to Nashville tomorrow, right?"

"That's the plan."

"I know this sounds crazy, but why don't I go with you on the bus. You can play me the songs you think might work, and we can decide if we go with a complete album of your material or not. Maybe the guys in the band can give us some input; they'll be recording them. How does that sound?"

"Crazy," John Ryan laughed, "but what the hell."

"One little note of caution," Hendrickson broke in, "all the guys in the band might not be on the session."

"What do you mean?" John Ryan asked, a cautious tone in his voice.

"Pretty much what I just said. You know there's a problem with road bands goin' in the studio. They take too long, and cost too much studio time. Session men can cut it in a minute." There was a short silence before John Ryan spoke.

"I know this sounds like a line from a movie, but I'll tell you something if the band doesn't go in...You know the rest of the line." His reaction caught Kate off guard.

"I think I do," Hendrickson said, "but all I can say is we'll try it. We got by with Mickey and Howie the first time because I was playin', but I ain't gonna be playin' this gig. If these guys can't cut it in a reasonable time, the way Jamie wants it, I will bring in studio musicians, John Ryan, have no doubt about it."

"Gotcha," the singer said, ending the conversation. "I do appreciate ya'll comin' down, and I am excited about the album. It's just fear that keeps me from showin' it." Kate looked to see if he was smiling. He was.

John Ryan looked at his watch. "Bus leaves at eleven, Jamie. That's only seven hours away, and I got a sneakin' suspicion you don't ride on a bus a whole lot. I think you'd better get some sleep. You got a revelation comin'."

"You're right about the bus, and probably about the revelation. I feel like I haven't slept in three days, but the way my mind is rolling, I'm not sure I'll be able to."

"*Adios,* Don," John Ryan said, shaking the vice-president's hand. He paused. "And thanks. God! Another movie line."

"Hey, maybe you got a second career comin', somethin' to fall back on," Hendrickson laughed. "Or move forward to."

"See you in the morning, John Ryan" Jamie said as they started toward the door. "You'd better get some sleep too."

"Soon as I see this young lady home. Wouldn't want her to come to any harm. Night, Joel."

"Good night, John Ryan. I loved it."

"Thanks."

The bellman called a cab and while they waited neither of them said very much. Neither knowing where the other's mind was.

After a couple of minutes of awkwardness, Kate went back to the bellman. "How far is it to The Ballastone Inn?" she asked.

"If you're talkin' about walkin', it's a fair hike, but you can make it if you're a walker."

She turned to John Ryan. "Are you a walker?"

He smiled. "I can walk."

They got directions, which were not too difficult, and went out into the sticky Savannah night. On some nights in summer in southern Georgia, the air cools once the sun goes down; on others the rising humidity that precedes a storm drives the temperature up. On this night the humidity and the projected thunder squalls were pungent and heavy in the air. They walked in silence for the first block until John Ryan spoke.

"Would it cost more than a penny?" he asked as he took her hand. He was embarrassed with the sense of youthful naiveté he experienced when he realized how nervous he was. She was aware of it. "It's been a long time," he said.

"That's what I was thinking about," she answered.

"Aha! You, too." His blue eyes were laughing with relief. "Kind of silly for people our ages, don't you think?"

"We are human beings. Don't we always quiver a little in the face of danger?"

"Is this dangerous?"

"Could be."

"You want to explain that to me?"

"I feel like I'm traveling in the dark, that maybe my mind is not in the same place as yours. There was a brief hint of light when you kissed me, but it made me tremble."

"My kiss?"

"That. But more the situation. It just isn't simple you know," she said.

"I know. I'm still legally married. I'm in the music business. Not much to base a lot of security on." He said it thoughtfully and, she believed, honestly. There wasn't the usual note of humor in his voice, and he wasn't smiling. Even that was both pleasing and troubling.

"No, it's not really that. The marriage bothers me, I have to admit, but it's a little too early for that to keep me awake nights. I guess it's me more than anything else. I can't allow myself any more hurt; I've been there."

"Me too," he said. "All of the above. And just so you'll know, the marriage also bothers me."

"We've never discussed that."

"There's not a lot to discuss. It's over. If I don't hear something soon, I guess I'll have to get an attorney and get it started myself. Then I guess she'll have to get an attorney, and the two of them will decide how we get divorced."

"How do you feel about that if I may ask?"

"The marriage?" He sighed. "I guess I'm shocked at this point that I don't feel much of anything. Disappointed maybe. A small sense of failure, perhaps, but not really. It's hard to imagine living in a situation for that long and then having so little feeling for it. At first I pined, but I think that was guilt which I guess is normal. Then I got depressed which I suppose is also normal. We always remember things at their best moments and even those as better than they really were.

"Jenifer and I had some good years, but as I look back now, I'm not sure either of us was ever in the marriage. I think we were caretakers rather than man and wife. She was the one who had the courage to recognize it and leave; I admire her for that. And now you know as much about the demise and future dissolution of my marriage as I do. I've gotten over what little guilt I had. Put it behind me."

"Thank you," she said and held his hand a little more firmly.

Kate looked up at the sky. No stars were in sight. "Feels like rain, doesn't it?"

At her door he took her by the shoulders. "It's a beginning, Kate. I'm not any more sure of myself than you are. I feel a lot. I can tell you that."

"Me, too," she said.

"What time do you fly out in the morning?"

"Early, early. Six-thirty I think," she answered looking at him.

"Then I won't see you. Call me tomorrow night at The Farm?"

"I will."

"I really want to kiss you, Kate Belden."

"I really want you to kiss me, John Ryan Stone." She turned her chin up and he took her into his arms.

The newspaper Kate bought before boarding the plane in Savannah lay on the seat next to her. Out of habit, she turned to the entertainment section first. After glancing at the films currently being shown, an announcement of a summer concert, advertisements for a Six Flags theme park and articles about local artists and writers, she was shocked to see a review headlined "NASHVILLE COMES TO DOOGIE'S". She read it with both excitement and concern.

Thursday, Friday and Saturday nights at Doogie's have never been quite as exciting as they were this week. The club, primarily known for its blues and rock artists, hosted a new group of musicians headed by a long and lanky singer named John Ryan Stone.

It is difficult to determine whether this is a group or a singer with a fine backup band. There was no advance promotion and this reviewer had to scratch to find any background whatsoever on this act.

The smooth professionalism and excellent musicianship of the group was evident from the dramatic opening, a stormy and unusual instrumental version of the old Duane Eddy classic 'Forty Miles of Bad Road'. It was, however, the humble charisma of Stone that brought the power of this ensemble to full strength. Mixing his own unique brand of country with rhythm and blues and subtle rock touches, the singer led the band through renditions of such standards as 'Ring of Fire', 'Only the Lonely', the Hank Williams anthem "I'm So Lonesome I Could Cry' and an updated arrangement of the Porter Wagoner classic, 'Satisfied Mind' complete with a Curtis Mayfield influenced guitar played by Mickey Shackleford.

The group includes Paul Crockett whose harmonica solo on Little Willie John's 'Fever' brought the crowd to a fever pitch (Pardon my being a literary bad boy!), Son Cochran, a Nashville regular on bass, Howie Newfeldt on rhythm guitar, Bobby Hopwood on drums and a redheaded keyboard man who looks like a mountain and is aptly named Mountain Red.

Each of the members of the group showed off their own specialty as well as playing together as tightly as any band this reviewer has experienced in a long time. But it was Stone, with his husky deep-throated voice and subtly sensual expressions, who gave definition to the group.

The one thing that was missing was original material, but it is this writer's understanding that Stone is also an excellent songwriter and that original material is being held back pending release of the group's first record for Trayhorn International.

Word has it that it is already in the can and could be on the market most any day. Pay Attention! This is a class act!

Kate was stunned. The review was wonderful, and it was gratifying that someone knowledgeable who was outside the company recognized John Ryan's talent. What surprised her was the fact that the record was mentioned. According to Jamie's orders, any public mention of the release of the record or John Ryan's association with Trayhorn would have to be cleared through her, and she had seen nothing. She liked Jamie, but everything regarding this project was going in a different direction. There was no order. Nothing potentially as big as this should be handled in such a haphazard manner with strategies changing every day. Perhaps it was just a lark to Jamie; he could afford it, but she couldn't and neither could John Ryan.

As the plane began its glide pattern for LaGuardia, she came to the conclusion that it was not turning out to be a great day.

Philip Barnessa awoke in a sweat. The room was not spinning; it was unbalanced. He could feel the dampness in the sheets and the air was oppressive. He stared at the ceiling, trying to find a straight thought and suddenly remembered he wasn't alone. Without looking, he slid his right hand across the sheet and felt for the plump Italian girl he vaguely remembered bringing to the apartment the night before. There was no one there. He yelled out what he thought was her name, but there was no answer.

Recounting the night was difficult. There were blank spots. Spots of darkness that didn't exist. The night had started in The Flower, a small neighborhood bar in South Philadelphia. He had gone there at the request of an agent to hear a group that turned out to be less than exceptional. After that he went to Dick Lee's, a club in South Jersey, to listen to Cook E. Jarr and the Crumbs, a local legend he had heard a number of times before. The man put on a good show and the group was tight, but that was all, nothing original except the name. Barnessa had long ago filed them away as a possible cover group if he ever found a release-ready demo he could steal, press and hand to them to front. They could sound like anything they heard.

It was essentially a wasted night until he stopped at a small go-go bar on Admiral Wilson Boulevard in Camden and found the girl. Angelina. He took her to the apartment he kept in the city. He hadn't been home in days, but his wife wouldn't complain. Why would she? He had made it plain that he was getting ready to dump her. The only question was when. Once a woman knew that, you could treat her anyway you wanted. Six marriages in thirty years. Not a good record, but they had each served their purpose. The downside was they left him forever financially below the water line; however, he had never felt bound by the court's orders, and the wives never tried to enforce them.

Maybe he had been snoring and she had gone into one of the other rooms. He got out of bed and wandered through the two bedroom apartment looking for her. She was gone. His first reaction was anger then suspicion. He felt for the heavy gold chain around his neck and checked to make sure his wallet was still in the pocket of the pants slung carelessly over the chair in the bedroom. It was better that she was gone, but it left him frustrated. He wanted to get laid or better yet have her go down on him; he remembered she was good at that. He needed a power surge for the day ahead.

He was sitting on the edge of the bed, thoughtless, lost in a plain somewhere between indecision and panic when the telephone rang. He felt his body quiver at the first sound and was disgusted at the balloon of fear that spread over him.

When he picked up the phone, he heard a harsh voice, serious, more like a dog's growl than anything human, a sound resulting from too much booze, too many cigarettes, sliced vocal chords or maybe a punch to the esophagus. It sounded like a lot of other voices in South Philadelphia and New York.

"Phil. Lou. Mr. Tedesco's in Philadelphia. He wants to see you. The car will be there in fifteen minutes," the voice said. That was all. It was eight-thirty in the morning. Well before normal business hours in his occupation.

What could he give the man? Giannini Tedesco wanted another Donny Richards and the New Beginnings. That had been beautiful: a bunch of kids from Jersey he signed to Giannini Tedesco's Target Record label, who sold seven million records in their brief career with Target getting ninety-six per-cent and the group four percent of all sales and radio play. Target also got a hundred percent of publishing and paraphernalia. It was truly amazing what a new car could get a kid to sign. Beautiful. When the group's popularity began to dwindle, they questioned studio and promotion charges that left them owing the company money. They never recorded again and within months were playing bowling alleys and supermarket openings. Beautiful.

Maybe it was time to get out. The thought kept recurring to him. Too many fuckin' kids who didn't know priorities ruining the business. Quitting might be the answer. Move to Florida and sit on the beach. Maybe he wouldn't even dump his wife. Take her along to keep house; she wouldn't cramp his style, never had. Who was he kidding? He would need money, a lot of money and that would take a big score. But suppose the money was there? They wouldn't let him quit. There was no retirement plan at his level in the orga-nization. There was only one way out. His hands shook as he slipped on the ostrich skin loafers.

Giannini Tedesco was in the back of his nephew's after-hours social club on Seventh Street in the heart of South Philadelphia. On Saturday mornings the whole area was filled with respectable folks from South Jersey or upper class housewives from the Main Line heading to the Italian Market on Ninth, but before nine o'clock in the morning, it was quiet.

Lights that were never turned on during the 'social' hours shone starkly when Nick Gagliano, Tedesco's chauffeur and bodyguard, escorted Barnessa into the club. It was ratty, worn and dirty. The brightness of the lights revealed the dilapidated state of the tables and chairs, the stained carpet, a small dance floor peppered with cigarette burns. The streamers of shiny, colored foil no longer shone through the dust and cigarette-smoke residue that covered them. One lone custodian was making a vain attempt to clean up. It was a place that belonged in the dark. It was not the place, however, that made Philip Barnessa uncomfortable—he had grown up in 'social' clubs; they were a part of his neighborhood—it was the situation that made him sweat.

The office was better, with clean if modest furnishings and carpet, a small black Formica bar in one corner and some file cabinets in another. There was a couch against one wall and in the center of the room a large round table with six chairs. Giannini Tedesco, Lou Molinaro and Franco Degiovanangelo were sitting at the table.

Tedesco was in his sixties but looked younger. He worked out regularly, dressed immaculately, stood five feet seven inches tall, had Rossano Brazzi gray hair and eyes that held no feeling whatsoever when that was what he wanted. Self-educated, he had 'made his bones' by killing a roofer's union official with a golf club. He was nineteen. When he was forty-three, he was boss. Molinaro and Degiovanangelo wore the scars of a much tougher rise to their positions.

When Philip Barnessa entered the room, Giannini Tedesco rose.

"Phil," he said with a broad smile on his face as if he were greeting a brother he had not seen in a long time. "Phil. It's good to see you. Have a seat." Philip Barnessa did not want to sit down, but when Giannini Tedesco asked you to sit down, it was the thing to do. "You want a drink? Lou, get Phil a drink. C.C. Am I right?" Barnessa nodded. He would have nodded 'yes' even if the man had been wrong. "You see? I'm right. A great memory. That's why I'm successful. A great memory. You want a sandwich? We got Cappicola, mozzarella. You want some sausage with fennel in good gravy? Left over from last night. Makes it better. You want some? What can I get you?"

Lou Molinaro handed him a drink. "Nothing, Gino. I'm good."

Finally Tedesco sat down. The other two men stared.

In the old days Lou Molinaro and Philip Barnessa had been good friends. They drank together, played Bocci ball in Lou's grandfather's backyard, shared women, and escaped to each other's houses when they had a problem with wives. They beat up marks that wouldn't pay up, collected numbers receipts and once Phil had watched while Molinaro beat a guy to death with a sawed-off baseball bat. The punk had tried to skim on the street-corner gambling operation they ran. Then Lou had moved up the ladder and moved to New York. After that they didn't see each other very often.

Barnessa's hand shook as he lifted the glass of whiskey to his lips. He made it a quick move, hoping the others wouldn't see. He wouldn't have tried it, but he needed the drink. He knew they noticed.

"So, Gino, you wanted to see me," trying to sound confident, feeling absolutely stupid and ridiculous playing the charade, but it was their way.

"Yeah, Phil, we need to talk. Can I talk to you, Philip?"

"Of course you can talk to me, Gino. Why couldn't you talk to me? We been...." He felt the moisture from his body dampening his clothes, the feeling a man has when he has been caught in the rain in a wool suit.

"But will you listen?" Tedesco interrupted. "You see, I think I been talking, but I don't think you been listening. For two years you come to me and say you got this deal going and that deal going, but nothing ever happens...."

"But, Gino...."

"Don't interrupt me, Philip. Don't ever interrupt me. You know better than that. I'm talking. You listen." His voice was firm. "You tell me you got deals going, right? Sure things. You got deals, but nothing ever happens. It's all bullshit. There's no vig. This is a business, Philip; maybe you forget that. A business. You know what a business is? A business is to make money. That's all there is. Without making money, you got no business. Without making money, you got nothing. Capisce?" He paused. "You're not bringing in any money. To me that means you're not doing business. What business you bringin' in, Philip? Tell me. I want to hear. I'm not talking about what we already got. What new business?" Giannini Tedesco sat back in his chair and interlaced his fingers over his flat stomach.

Barnessa knew that whatever he said had to be the truth, and truth had never been a precept he lived by. Now he had no choice. Whatever he said would bind him.

"None, Giannini," he said. "None, but I ask for thirty days. You know I've been working on this new singer. His record isn't even out yet, which is good because I have a plan that...." He felt a tightness in his chest. It was difficult to breathe.

"The cut-out business? The plant in Jamaica? Counterfeiting? Philip," he said condescendingly, "we know your plan, and maybe it will work. But that's not enough. We want equity in this young man if he's going to be what you say. Ownership. Like what we had from that bunch of kids from

Jersey. That's what we want. What did we make on them? Ten, twenty million? That's business."

"This ain't a kid, Giannini. This guy's been to college. Was in the army. An officer...."

Tedesco slammed his hand on the table with force enough to shake the room. "I don't care from college, Philip. I don't care from army. I don't care if he was President. If he's that good, we want him. If he's not that good and we invest, you pay. Capisce?" His voice quieted. "We're not greedy, Philip. We been in business a long time. It's like mining gold. Sometimes you strike the mother lode on the first strike of the pick, and sometimes you have to find a small vein and follow it to the mother lode. The cut-out idea is an okay idea, but it's a very thin vein. It's limited. It doesn't show much hope for the future and it's dangerous. But we'll take that as a start."

"Thank you, Gino."

"But we want eighty per cent of the net."

"Giannini..." He felt helpless. His mind was racing, and he was cursing Maury Friedman. His instinct had warned him, but he didn't listen. Now at least one thing was clear: his position had changed again.

"Eighty per cent until the vein gets wider, until there's some hope for the future. I suggest you use all your resources; I know you have some. Who's booking this cowboy?"

"A company broad, Kate Belden, but except for the tryouts they haven't started getting him any dates yet. They probably won't do that until they set the release date on the record."

"That will be awhile. Philip, I worry that you don't know what's going on?"

"I don't know what you mean."

"Your boy is back in Nashville, in the studio I hear. They're making an album I'm told. You don't know about this?"

Barnessa's body sagged with confusion. What was going on? Back in the studio? An album? Jesus Christ, that fucked everything. If Friedman knew, why hadn't he called? Who the hell knew except Tedesco? He couldn't ask. He felt like he was being set up.

"No. I didn't know."

"Now you know. I want you to start unbooking him. Let this Kate Belden hit a brick wall whenever she gets started. Let her have some cancellations and then you offer to help. See Bernie Greshem and get the agency. Then, Philip, then the vein will show some promise. You can't wait. Once the record comes out, it will be too late, and you know I mean that."

"I understand, Giannini."

"Good. Nicky?" The door opened and the bodyguard stepped into the room. "Take Phil home." Tedesco rose from his chair, walked around the table to Barnessa and hugged him, held him at arms length and smiled. "Hey, don't worry. I trust you. You'll do it."

As he and the bodyguard walked through the empty club toward the stairs, Barnessa's heart was pounding. He was afraid to look down at himself for fear that he would see the movement under his coat. He felt like throwing up. His legs were rubbery, and he wanted to kill Maury Friedman. He felt like an outsider, a soldier, nobody of importance. He wanted to kill Friedman, but he couldn't.

In the car his mind was in a panic. He thought of the plump Italian girl and wondered where she might be.

———————

At nine o'clock in the morning when he boarded the bus, Jamie Greshem was fidgety and nervous. He was surprised that everyone else boarding the bus was subdued if not bored. It was silly for a man his age in his position to be excited about a long road trip on a bus, but it was a new experience. He couldn't believe sleep had been difficult as tired as he was, but the idea of being with a band on the road was wild and energizing.

Perhaps it was country music, the people, Nashville, new ideas and aspirations, or the relative honesty, so different from New York and L.A. He had lived in New York his whole life, gone to school and worked there, but it was suddenly becoming stale, old and worn. Coming to Nashville when he did was like visiting a frontier town in the old West. Now he had something of his own, a discovery, four sides completed and an album to be done. Regardless of where the exhilaration came from, he loved it and was determined not to let it go.

By eleven-thirty the young producer's gusto for the trip, though still present, was waning. Only he, John Ryan and Mickey Shackleford were awake. They rode in silence for awhile taking in the scenery as they headed northeast on a route that would take them through Macon, Atlanta and Chattanooga before they arrived in Nashville.

"Not what you expected, huh?" John Ryan asked.

"I don't know what I expected, but I can understand what a grind it must be."

"The bus is the luxury part," Mickey laughed. "Hell, I've been working ten years to become an overnight sensation and I'm not there yet, but this ain't bad. I could be changing tires down at the Tire King or sellin' vacuum cleaners door to door. Now that's a grind. How tough can sittin' on your ass watchin' the countryside roll by be? It's the American Dream."

"The only kicker is," John Ryan said, "the American Dream never ends."

"What the hell do you mean by that?"

"Just what I said. The American Dream never ends. For most people the dream is to be rich and famous, but what do the rich and famous dream about? Being more rich and famous. What other dreams can they have?"

"Have you ever considered writing a song about that?"

"I'm working on a song right now that relates to dreams. Not the American Dream and not happy ones, but I doubt anyone will ever have the guts to record it."

"Are you baiting me or what," Jamie laughed. "I've already broken enough rules and stepped on enough toes to end a career. What's it about? Can we use it on the album?"

"It's called *My Bed Has Echoes*. That tell you anything?" There was a wicked smile on the songwriter's face. His eyes were dancing.

"Why didn't you tell me about this one?" Mickey asked with frustration in his voice. "You never said a damned word about it. That's the damnedest title I ever heard."

"If the song has as much sauce as the title..." Jamie Greshem started.

"We can have every preacher in the South speakin' John Ryan Stone's name in vain," Mickey finished and howled at his own words.

"Can I hear some of it?" Jamie asked.

"When it's ready. I've got two stanzas blocked out, but it needs a lot of work. I'm not sure it's..."

"Let me be the judge of that," the young man said. "Tell me about it."

"I can show you the idea," John Ryan said. He got his guitar case down from the luggage rack, opened it and retrieved a couple of legal pads. He handed one to Jamie who began to read.

"Read 'em out loud," Mickey said. Jamie looked to John Ryan and he nodded.

Lying in darkness hearing soft and tender love sounds in the night,
Telling me the stories that are never out of mind or out of sight,
Bringing back the mem'ries of the thoughts that I have tried so hard to end,
My bed has echoes that I can't hide, break or bend

Thoughts of the touches that brought out the wonder in me,
Unfamiliar sheets and forgotten faces I no longer see,
Calling out my name from the shadows and the corners of my mind,
My bed has echoes that won't let me leave them behind.

"They sure as hell won't play it in Possum Walk," Mickey said.

"I'll have to hear it," Jamie said, "but damn I like it. Little bit of a metre problem depending on how you do it, but the idea's great. It would be hard to push. Could be a trend-setter. Definitely breaks new ground. Can you finish it?"

"Yes," John Ryan said softly.

"Where'd you get the idea?" Jamie asked.

"One of the guys was talkin' about guilt one day, and I started thinkin' about it. Can't imagine why," he said sarcastically.

"Don't we all?"

"I guess, but at the time I had a little more reason than most."

"The marriage?" Jamie asked. "Or is that too personal?"

"You got it. I don't think you ever really know how you feel about a woman until you lose her. Then you believe you shouldn't be able to stand it, but you find out you can. There's inherent guilt at not being terribly affected. You feel totally selfish and that's what you really can't stand. That's the guilt. That's where the echoes come from and, right or wrong, you can't get away from them."

"You are an enigma, John Ryan Stone," Jamie Greshem said. "I hope we can do you justice."

"That's a good word to describe it," John Ryan Stone said and laughed.

Don Hendrickson was good at anticipating problems. Problems were a fact of life in the business, in any business, but to an even greater extent when one dealt with talented and creative people, big money, travel schedules, agents, and the coordination of all these elements. By the time Jamie and John Ryan entered his office, he had anticipated the problems and given himself a few acceptable alternatives.

"Jamie, John Ryan," he said rising from his chair, the always warm expression on his face.

"Have a seat," Don said as he settled back in his chair.

"Don, we've got a problem. Well, not a problem; we just have to make some changes."

"The musicians," Hendrickson offered, not giving Jamie the confidence of surprise. "How'd you know?"

"Mickey heard," John Ryan said.

"Don, we're going to use the band," Jamie said. Don was impressed with the young man's tenacity. It wasn't 'We'd like to use the band.' or 'Could we use the band?' or 'Why can't we use the band?'; simply 'We're going to use the band.' "I know what you said in Savannah," Jamie continued, "but that's just not going to work. John Ryan is confident with the guys. He knows them, and, more than that, they know him. They've built a unique quality together, and there's no way—no matter how good your studio guys are—that a group of musicians who've never heard him before or know what he can do will be able to achieve that. Hell, they'll waste more time getting used to each other than the band will take to cut the whole album."

"Did you work on that speech long?" Hendrickson laughed good-naturedly. John Ryan grinned at the wily approach the vice-president was taking.

"Not long," Jamie said protecting himself from the attempt at humor.

"Well, I'm not sure what we can do about that, Jamie. There are rules and procedures, some written, some unwritten. Our thoughts about keeping this whole thing undercover couldn't work from the beginning. I'm sure New York knew ten minutes after I scheduled the studio time. That means accounting for money spent. Accounting for expenditures means studio time, i.e. studio musicians who can read from a chart or improvise, but either way get it done in less time."

"Did you work on that speech long?" John Ryan asked. It was the first thing he said, and it let the tension out of the meeting as if he had loosened his fingers on a balloon full of air.

"Not long," Hendrickson said with a laugh. "But I'm serious, Jamie. There are unwritten rules down here. Hell, they're everywhere. Road musicians aren't welcome in the studio; it causes problems. Hopwood and Cochran are okay because they've been in the studio, and everybody knows what they can do, but hell, man, nobody knows Red and Crockett."

"I understand what you're saying," Jamie said, " but these guys can cut it. You, of all people, should know that. This 'closed shop' is a nice secure situation that suits a select group of people here in Nashville, but I can't buy it. If necessary I'll rent an independent studio." His voice was calm but firm. Inside Hendrickson was jubilant at the young man's determination and persistence. He was going to need it. "Don. The bottom line is that John Ryan won't do it without them. If it's impossible we'll just go with the single and let it go at that." Jamie's statement caught John Ryan by surprise.

Hendrickson shook his head as if trying to decide whether or not to call the young producer's bluff even though he already knew what he was going to say. The meeting was going just as he had planned.

"Okay, we'll try it." He grinned. "It's what I wanted to do anyway, but you gotta understand, I have to live here and work with these guys long after you're gone. I'll go along with you for now, but if we have a problem and it starts eatin' time and money, then I'm gonna bring people in. Much as I'd like to, Jamie, I can't ignore cost. I've got a house in Hendersonville, and I sure as hell don't want to have to go on the road again to pay for it."

"I don't think there will be a problem. We'll make it simple like the first four cuts. Leave 'The Nashville Sound' to Chet over at RCA."

"Chet ain't doin' so bad. Have you got the songs?"

"I think so."

"All John Ryan's?"

"Seven of his and three others."

Hendrickson sighed. "Damn! All of them bein' by him would give us a good marketing twist."

"I think you'll approve," Jamie said. "So when do we start?"

"Ten o'clock tomorrow night, and I want everybody straight," he said with a wink.

John Ryan had said virtually nothing during a meeting that could determine the course his life would take. He wondered if it was a prophecy of things to come. He would have a hard time if it came to that.

For three days after the meeting with Giannini Tedesco, Philip Barnessa did little else other than make telephone calls designed to call in markers, make threats or whatever else was necessary to subvert Kate Belden's efforts to book John Ryan Stone. Maury Friedman managed to get him a list of clubs and venues that Trayhorn Management frequently used. Those with which he had a connection, he called; others, he had friends in the area contact, and they were not to limit themselves to the Trayhorn list. Anyone who booked country acts was to be contacted. The bottom line was that no one was to book Stone.

Philip Barnessa wanted Kate Belden to have a tough time even getting John Ryan Stone walking around money until she realized that it was he who held the key to her problems. If as the old adage said, 'The agent always gets screwed,' he would be happy to accommodate Miss Belden on any level she wanted. What had begun as a mission stimulated by fear had now become a pleasure. The thought of seeing her on her knees figuratively or literally excited him. Power neutralized anybody, he thought as he poured himself a drink.

The whiskey was not his usual brand and burned his throat. It sent him into a coughing jag that made it difficult to answer the phone which began ringing just as he swallowed. It took several rings for him to get his coughing under control. When he did answer, his voice was so raspy and fearsome that he wished he could maintain it.

"Yeah." He had learned as a youth never to identify himself until he knew who was calling. Never give anybody an advantage.

"Philip Barnessa?" the voice asked. It was firm, angry and southern.

"Depends on who this is?"

"My name is Dana Moultrie. People call me Bubba." Barnessa had to fight off the urge to laugh. "I own a club down here in Myrtle Beach, South Carolina, and we use country acts to kind of offset the Beach Music crowd?" It was phrased like a question that wasn't a question. "I got the only real

143

Country club on the beach. I got a call today about not bookin' a John Ryan Stone. Now I've had a lot of calls wanting to book acts, but this is the first one I ever got not to book an act and I don't like it. First, I never heard of this Stone...."

"Yeah, well, first you will. What's second?"

"Second, if I want to book an act, I book 'em. Now I know you don't know me, but any more calls like the one I got this afternoon, and you will know me, and you won't like it."

Barnessa was speechless. "You threatening me, Bubba?" he asked incredulously. "And stop your voice from shaking for Christ's sake." The voice wasn't shaking, but it was a ploy he often used to intimidate. The voice remained constant.

"No, I'm not threatening you, just tellin' you that your people don't come down here and tell me what to do."

"Listen to me, Bubba—I can't believe that they really call people 'Bubba' down there—listen to me. I don't know what your problem is, but I am not one to cross. You don't know who you're dealing with. We don't want any trouble; we would just like a little cooperation."

"Ain't gonna be no trouble, and I do know who I'm talkin' to. You don't. You people have tried to come in here before and you didn't make it. We don't have no unions down here, so you can't depend on that to give us a problem. Now you people might have a little pull with the politicians up there, but that don't cut no ice on the beach; we pay their salaries. We have our own people, Mr. Barnessa, so you'd better get off the alligator's back before he decides to swim."

"How the hell did you get this number?"

"Maybe you ought to think about that," Moultrie said, and the phone went dead in the promoter's hand. He let out a scream and threw the instrument across the room knocking a hole in the wall. It was as if everything he had ever done in his life had come to nothing. Tedesco was angry and putting him against the wall; nicky numb-nuts, southern retards were telling him what they would and would not do; people he didn't know were getting his phone number, and a damned woman agent was trying to give him grief. It all went back to Jamie Greshem's bringing that country son-of-a-bitch north. It never should have happened. The time had come to put Bernie on notice.

———

At the end of the third day of recording John Ryan and the band were getting tired. It was showing in their work and in their attitudes. Some of the songs had gone smoothly. *Satisfied Mind*, included because of its unique arrangement, was barely more than a run-through. They had done it so many times that the only challenge was to make it fresh. It was done in three hours. A country blues—more blues than country—rendition of *Fever* with John Ryan singing rather than the instrumental version they had been playing caused a few problems, but they were quickly solved.

Don Hendrickson liked *What I've Gone Through For My Heart*, one of the songs John Ryan had written that he hadn't heard, but the instrumentation and backup vocals didn't satisfy him. He wanted a Floyd Cramer sound on piano, but Floyd was out of town. Finally after hours of trial and error, Red came up with a modified slip-note style and sound that Hendrickson found acceptable.

When that song was down, the next three—John Ryan's *It's Over My Head*, *Lay With Me Till the Daylight Comes*, and *Just Findin' Out Where I Am*—went smoothly. The work was never-ending, and that seemed to suit everyone to a point, but things did eventually get ragged. There was no catering. Most of the food consisted of split hot dogs from Linebaugh's—a musician's favorite—fried chicken, pizza, hamburgers or whatever else was quick and easy. Once in awhile when things were going well even Jamie Greshem served as gofer and delivery boy. The time came to halt, take a break, reassess. He gave the band eighteen hours, the longest break they had been given since the sessions began. It was all the time the producer could afford.

Telephone conversations with Kate Belden were the highlights of John Ryan's days. What had begun in Savannah had traversed and survived the distance between them. Distance had been a major subject of discussion. Kate, keeping in mind that John Ryan needed to concentrate on his work, said that at this time it was a blessing in disguise, that it kept them from overloading, gave them time to think, created anticipation, offered the joy of fantasy, and energized what each of them was doing. John Ryan accused her of female rationalization, but allowed her the luxury of feeling she was proceeding cautiously and with adult good sense.

The long distance conversations also created longing, desire and frustration, the experience of having made a decision that would come to fruition in the future but could not be acted upon in the present. It was like refusing to open presents until Christmas morning when you knew that everything you had asked for and wanted was lying under the tree, within reach but untouchable. On occasion there were three or four calls during a twenty-four hour period, some lasting only a minute or two, a brief touch enabling them to get through a difficult moment. The calls were gratifying, but conversation without personal contact was difficult to sustain for an extended period of time. The words got too familiar, the tone of the human voice too easily manipulated to breed security. The honesty of the eyes was necessary to support that.

In Savannah John Ryan had asked her to come to Nashville as soon as work on the album was completed. It seemed like months since that time together. Now there was only one more day of work, two at most and the album would be complete. As John Ryan drove toward The Farm reveling in eighteen hours of totally free time, he worked on the conversation he would have with Kate.

While John Ryan was caught between enthusiasm and anxiety in the cutting of his album, Kate found only frustration in following Jamie Greshem's instructions to book play dates to coincide with the album's release. Venues that were workable in the past were suddenly 'cutting back,' 'unable to afford a headline act,' or 'totally scheduled'. When he was informed, Jamie said not to worry about it; he would speak with his father. He also instructed Kate to say nothing to John Ryan about the difficulties.

The struggle at work combined with her natural doubts made it hard for Kate to maintain her faith and focus on John Ryan without worry. There were holidays in her emotional resolve, sometimes stimulated by an offhand remark or something he said matter-of-factly, without feeling. Nothing important or designed, but enough to make her question whether his intensity was as great as hers.

When the telephone rang on Wednesday morning, Kate had just arrived at her office. There were several refusals to book John Ryan on her desk, messages left during the night to avoid talking to her personally. "Cowards," she muttered to herself as she picked up the receiver expecting yet another.

"Get your ticket. You're needed in Nashville day after tomorrow." The voice brought the sun up in her day.

"Okay," she said, knowing her response would catch him by surprise.

"Okay? That's all? Okay?" he said laughing.

"What did you expect?" she replied coyly, luxuriating in his discomfort.

"Are you playing games with me, Lady?"

"Games?" Her voice sounded nonplussed.

"Pulling my chain? Uh, let's see what else I can think of. Tightening the rope?"

"Games? Ropes? Chains? Sounds kinky. I'm not sure..."

"Hey, whatever works for you." It was the best aspect of their relationship, he thought: they laughed. "Remember I don't know you very well."

"What works for me is coming to Nashville and seeing you, Stone."

"I'm glad. This long-distance stuff is getting old."

"I agree. I checked the daily flight schedules Monday. I had a feeling this might be the week. If I can get the early flight in the morning, I can be there about noon."

"My, my, you sound anxious."

"I am. Nuff said. Now let me get off this phone, so I can see about getting a reservation. Call me later?"

"I will." He paused. "See ya."

When John Ryan returned to Nashville after the Doogie's date, a petition for divorce had been waiting for him. The petition asked for five hundred dollars a month for two years and a policy on John Ryan's life for $100,000. The attorney Hendrickson had recommended chuckled at the policy clause and asked John Ryan if it made him nervous; he also advised him to jump at the agreement, said he couldn't imagine a wife asking for so little, that maybe she believed that was all he would ever be able to afford. They laughed at that, but John Ryan wasn't sure the attorney hadn't hit the mark. He signed the agreement and hoped it was behind him.

John Ryan knew where he was at the moment, but could only surmise where Kate's visit would leave him. She was right about long-distance giving them time to fantasize; he had thought maybe he was too old for that, but had begun to think one was never too old.

The final session took longer than expected. Hendrickson had not heard *My Bed Has Echoes*, and when he did, he was flabbergasted. He had never heard anything quite like it. The song was lyrical and hard. It had a harsh morality that he didn't know how to classify. The one thing he did know was that it could ruin John Ryan Stone's career before it ever got off the ground.

"Jamie, could we talk for a minute," Hendrickson said after a second run-through. "Let's go up to the booth."

"What is it?" Jamie asked as the door closed.

"We're not going to do this song." There was a stern look on Hendrickson's face.

"What do you mean?"

"Just what I said. We're not doing it. You don't understand something, Jamie we're dealing with a generally uneducated audience down here, most of them Fundamentalists if they've had any background at all. Hell, you can take the biggest redneck in the country, insult him, fight him, beat the hell out of him, but if you step on the Confederate flag, insult his woman or family and most of all show any disrespect to his sometimes warped sense of morality, he might just kill you. And the women. They may be abused, half-starved, left to take care of the family by themselves until daddy decides to come home, but they go to church on Sunday and remember what momma

147

taught 'em. They're not gonna accept a song about a guy who feels guilty about all the women he's laid. It ain't gonna happen."

"Don, it's a morality tale," Jamie tried to explain. "He's not saying it's all right. Anything but. If you look at it in the proper way, the song says it's not all right, that if you do it, you're going to regret it."

"There's no admiration there, Jamie. The song is asking for sympathy for the wrong-doer not the wronged. Is the listener gonna admit that he or she can relate in their own life to somebody who's spent his time findin' 'em, foolin' 'em, fuckin' 'em and forgettin' 'em?"

"That's the point. He can't forget them. People will relate to the guilt, to the punishment. I want to include the song, Don." He was adamant.

Hendrickson shrugged. "I admire your balls, but I think you're wrong. It could get the whole album banned."

"Let's wait and see how it comes across when we've got it down. If I think it's wrong, we'll cut it. If not, we'll 'have at it' as you say."

"Did I say that?" They both laughed, and Jamie went back into the studio to start the session.

Echoes was a difficult song. Everyone had their own concept of how it should be arranged. Crockett wanted to do a down and dirty B.B. King take, straight, slow, hip-grinding blues, but that changed the emotional feel of the lyric. Jamie even toyed with the idea of a full orchestra, but quickly canned that idea. It was Hendrickson who came up with what they thought might be the final take on the song. He suggested that to give the song what John Ryan wanted it to have, he do it by himself with only his guitar and then add the backup separately, to let the backup play entirely up to John Ryan instead of the reverse.

After both the solo and the backup portions were done, which took seven hours, the co-producer added some strings to give it the suggestion of an orchestral feel. It gave the ballad depth and fullness. The contrast of the singer's hoarse, gritty and impassioned voice and the quiet elegance of the strings created something unique. The one concern was how they could ever create the same sound in a live performance. Jamie assured them whatever had to be done would be done even if they had to travel with a string section.

When it was over, there was a mixture of exhilaration, fatigue, curiosity about what was next, and fear that all of the cuts except *Echoes* might sound too much alike because in their own minds they were all running together. Now there was nothing left to do except endure the waiting for whatever was to happen.

Before anyone left, Jamie called everyone together to explain what was to come. The letdown that follows any period of intense work and creative

148

energy was obvious. They made themselves comfortable to hear what the young producer had to say.

"Okay, here's the schedule as we know it now, of course, as you know, that may change any minute, but as we see it, the album and the single will be released in four to six weeks. I know that sounds fast, but we have the mechanics to do it. You will go back to The Warehouse with Larry Foster and put a real show together, and—all things willing and the creek don't rise—hit the road the week of the release. These dates won't be in beer bars, but they won't be in stadiums either. I'm not sure at the moment exactly where you'll start. That's up to Kate Belden." John Ryan smiled at the sound of her name. "I have to go back to the city tomorrow, but Don will be able to take care of anything you need.

"I know this is not the way things are usually done down here, but I believe in this. In you, and there's a difference in believing and belief. I want to see it succeed on a bigger than Nashville scale. Don and I both agree that country music is just beginning to happen, and I think your sound is the sound of the future. There will be a lot of changes over the next ten or fifteen years, and we want to set the pace. Rehearsals are scheduled to start next Monday." He paused. "Don, do you have anything?"

"Just for them to get the hell out of here, so you and Stringer and I can finish this thing up."

John Ryan Stone, freshly showered and shaved, dressed in the tailored jeans and ivory-colored, collarless shirt that Kate had liked when she saw him in Savannah, arrived at the airport forty-five minutes before her flight was scheduled to land. He carried a dozen Fire and Ice roses in his hand which seemed a natural and romantic thing to do until he entered the building. Women noticed them and smiled with envy; men just smiled. It made him feel self-conscious until he convinced himself that he didn't give a tinker's damn what anyone else thought. It was a good feeling.

Time passed slowly as it always does when the clock is powered by anticipation. He walked the length of the concourse, started to have a beer but decided against it, checked every few minutes to make sure her plane was on time, and finally, sat down in the waiting area to watch the runways until they announced that her plane was on the ground.

Kate Belden didn't smile until she saw him standing at the gate. She was the picture of softness in a white linen suit and silk blouse. The brightness of her face and her eyes, so full of energy and excitement, made him laugh as she came toward him. He wasn't sure why or how else to respond, but when she put her carry-on bag down, he took her in his arms and held her.

"God, I'm glad you're here," he whispered. Kate pulled back and looked at him.

"I wasn't so sure. You were laughing."

"With joy, Kate Belden. With joy."

"I'm glad." He handed her the flowers.

"These are for you," he said, then laughed and looked at the ceiling. "What a stupid thing to say. Who else would they be for?"

"They're beautiful." She reached up and kissed his cheek. "Thank you. I'm glad to be here too. I've been waiting. Can we get my bags and get out of here? I feel like I've been—what is that phrase you use?"

"Rode hard and put away wet?"

"That's the one."

In the car he looked at her for a moment without saying anything and then leaned forward and lightly kissed her face. He brushed her lips and then pressed them firmly, feeling her mouth open, inviting him inside. The kisses were passionate and grew more intense until there was nothing to do except stop or move forward.

"Wow," John Ryan said as he relaxed the arms that held her.

"Yeah." She held him closer.

John Ryan left Kate at the door to her room in the hotel and went to his own which adjoined hers although he had not made that apparent. As far as she knew, he wasn't staying in the hotel. The newness of the situation required him to use caution. It had been a long time since he had begun a relationship, and he wasn't sure exactly how to proceed. He had merely said he would pick her up in an hour.

With an hour and nothing to do, he poured a Jack over ice and sat down to glance through the paper, but it held no interest for him. He reviewed the plan: a tour of Music Row and the Country Music Hall of Fame, dinner, and then maybe the clubs on Printer's Alley. It was Friday night. Boots Randolph would probably show up at the Carrousel, which he owned, and maybe somebody else of note would sit in at the Black Poodle. Either way Kate would be entertained by the carnival atmosphere of the place. The Alley was like a foreign country located in the middle of small-town Nashville.

"Punctual," Kate said as she opened the door. She looked dazzling.

"Magnificent," John Ryan said and watched her blush.

On the ride to Music Row, John Ryan was the tour guide. He pointed out the Ryman Auditorium, home of the Grand Old Opry, Tootsie's, regaling Kate with tales of Hank Williams' hours spent drinking there making him late for performances and occasionally prompting his not showing up at all, Ernest Tubb's Record Store, Acuff-Rose Publishing and the home of Hickory Records. They finally arrived at Music Row.

"What in the world is that?" Kate asked with a huge smile on her face. When John Ryan looked to see what she was referring to, he laughed. The object was a big, bronze-colored car with longhorn steer horns mounted on the hood where the hood ornament should have been and six-shooters mounted on the fenders.

"That, my New York friend, is Webb Pierce's Cadillac. If you look inside, you'll see that the entire interior is covered with silver dollars."

"You're kidding me,"

"Welcome to Nashville, ya'll," John Ryan said and looked at Kate, who was laughing.

Kate was taken aback by Music Row. She could not have imagined that powerful music publishers and agencies were housed in old dwellings that looked liked somebody's grandmother had just finished shelling peas in a rocker on the front porch. The new RCA studios were more what she expected. She was also surprised when John Ryan pointed out one small but relatively new office building which he told her housed the offices of Screen-Gems Columbia, Merle Kilgore and Johnny Cash. It was apparent there was a far greater distance than a thousand miles between New York and Nashville, Tennessee. She thought she might like Nashville better.

Leaving Music Row, they went to Linebaugh's where John Ryan introduced her to split hot dogs with chili, mustard and onions served on a hamburger bun and then on to the Country Music Hall of Fame. Although she had never been a lover of the music, Kate found herself intrigued by the histories and memorabilia, people like the Carter Family, Hank Williams and Jimmie Rogers, the fringed skirts worn by Patsy Cline, the spangled costumes of Hank Snow whose songs she had never heard, and the story of the unlikely alliance of Roy Acuff and Fred Rose that created a country music publishing giant. The museum was a story of poverty, tenacity, art, success and tragedy all rolled up in one building, small yet too big to take in at one time.

John Ryan enjoyed watching Kate as she went from room to room, reading plaques out loud to him, laughing at some of the outfits and listening to the taped narratives. John Ryan Stone was in awe of Kate Belden.

At a quarter to six they returned to the hotel.

"Can you be ready for dinner by seven?" John Ryan asked as he opened the door to her room.

"Of course," she said.

"Aren't you tired?"

"Am I supposed to be?" she asked lowering her eyelids with amusement.

"You're too much, Belden," he said and took her into his arms. There was a promise in her kiss and in her body.

"Wow," she whispered as his lips left hers.

"You won't be ready if I don't leave," he said.

"Maybe that's the point," she replied.

"I want to take you to dinner."

"Should I be insulted?" She wasn't laughing at him, but she sure as hell was amused with his discomfort. Or so it seemed.

"Nothing I say should ever insult you. If it does, you've misinterpreted what I've said."

"Can I count on that?"

"Count on it."

"Are we going fancy or simple?" she asked.

"Fancy," he said.

"Well. I guess I'd better get busy. Are you going to have time to go home and get back by seven?"

"I have to change, but I'll manage."

"I love the roses," Kate said and hugged him closer resting her head on his chest.

"I'll be on time," John Ryan said and left. He paused in the hall before he went into his room. He could hardly suppress the laughter he felt building inside. He wondered what her reaction would be when she found out he was next door. That would be a revelation worth watching. He could hear her bath water running in the adjoining room and for a brief moment experienced a voyeuristic excitement.

Kate was surprised when she opened the door at precisely seven o'clock to see a John Ryan Stone she had never seen before. There were no jeans. He was wearing the Southern uniform—tan dress slacks, a blue blazer and a blue shirt open at the collar. Despite what appeared to be a total transformation, Kate was certain that beneath the blazer there were epaulets on the shirt. That and the fact that he was wearing polished brown loafers with no socks kept his image intact. She was in a beige silk dress that softened the curves of her body and gave her a look of lithe airiness.

Although he had lived in Nashville for three years, fine restaurants had never found a place on John Ryan's social calendar. Don Hendrickson had suggested Arthur's and offered to make a reservation for them. John Ryan accepted.

"You come here often?" Kate asked as they entered the elegant dining room.

"Every Friday night when the moon is full and I've just finished an album and had a beautiful woman flown in from New York."

"You are absolutely too kind, Mr. Stone," she said in a faux Southern accent.

"Don't mention it, Scarlett," he answered and followed the waiter to their table.

Though the food and the service were exceptional, it was inconsequential. The dinner was a stepping-stone, a prologue, a prefix. An overture. Kate took an occasional taste of her food but spent more time arranging and rearranging it on her plate. The dialogue was starched. Even though they had spent hours on the telephone and a lighthearted, wonderful afternoon together, the reality and uncertainty of the evening was inhibiting.

"What's next?" Kate asked as she sipped her coffee.

"That's up to you," John Ryan answered. "I thought we might go to Printer's Alley and let you see what night life in Music City, U.S.A. is all about. Of course..."

"Sounds exciting."

"Boots Randolph, Mr. Yakety Sax, has a club called The Carrousel, and there's a couple of others that aren't bad. It's not New York, but it's the best we've got." The smile and the blue eyes laughed at the humility he was showing for the city. "Boots usually comes by on weekends and sits in for a set or two, and you never know who else might drop by. Sometimes it's a better show than you can pay for. We will have to brown bag it though."

"Brown bag?"

"Well, since you can't buy a drink in the sovereign State of Tennessee, you have to take your own bottle, buy a club membership for ten dollars and turn the bottle over to the bartender so he can sell you drinks."

"You're kidding me." She looked at him, disbelieving his words.

"Nope, it's a fact, ma'am. They keep talkin' about getting liquor by the drink, but the Christians won't let it pass."

"So you can't change your mind about what you want to drink; you're stuck with whatever you brought, no brandies or Creme d' Menthe to top off the night?"

"You can have whatever you want. They don't just pour from your bottle; and no matter how many or how few drinks you have, your bottle is always empty when you're ready to leave."

"And people in New York think Southerners are dumb. They sell you drinks from a bottle you bought and probably make eight hundred percent on the money you spent."

"Something like that. Are you ready?" he asked.

"Interesting question," Kate laughed and folded her napkin.

Printer's Alley is exactly what its name suggests, an alley filled with old brick buildings that were once print shops. There is no splashy decor, and in the daylight, without the neon signs, it's nondescript. At night, however, when the clubs are open, and the neon strikes out at the darkness like lightning , the Alley becomes a carnival midway with people moving from club to club and milling about the street.

The entrance to The Carrousel appeared more like an entrance to a speakeasy than to the best club on the Alley. It was a simple door in the side of brick building with a medium-sized neon sign that spelled out its name.

The Carrousel was one more source of wonder for Kate. There was little light except on the bandstand and whatever glow emanated from the smoked-glass enclosed candles that burned on each table. She sensed greens and reds, but it was too dark to distinguish colors clearly. Although the room was filled with a plethora of odors, most notably beer, whiskey and cigarette smoke, the atmosphere was not unpleasant.

The thin, middle-aged man holding the tenor saxophone and speaking into the mike looked nothing like a Nashville legend, and yet John Ryan told her as they walked through the door that it was indeed Boots Randolph.

"Now here comes a pretty, young couple," the man said as John Ryan and Kate found a table near the front of the bandstand. Kate felt self-conscious, but John Ryan just laughed. "How Ya'll doin' tonight?" John Ryan nodded a greeting. "Guy is speechless. He must be doin' all right. Anybody seen Roger the last couple of days?"

"Roger?" Kate whispered.

"Roger Miller," John Ryan answered.

"I'm worried about ol' Roger," the man continued. "He stopped by the other night and swallowed the snare drum by mistake. Thought it was an upper." The crowd laughed. "Dang me if I know where he got off to." More laughter. "I guess I'd better quit while I'm ahead and do somethin' I'm more sure of. You've all heard Jimmy Dean's *Big, Bad John* 'bout the mightiest man anybody ever heard tell of; well, we've got another version of that song called," he paused, struck a fey pose and lisped, *"Big, Bad Bruce.* Juicy Brucie, the sweetest hairdresser in Nashville." The crowd erupted as the band began to play the familiar introduction and continued to roar at the lyrics of the parody.

Kate and John Ryan sipped their drinks, laughed and took in the whole of the place. Unlike New York, people here appeared to know each other. There were constant greetings at the tables and from the bandstand. Nashville celebrities she had never heard of in the Northeast were introduced by Randolph. Larry Henley, the lead singer of The Newbeats came by and sat in with the band, singing a ballad uncharacteristic of what he did with the group. Kate decided down-home celebrity was a lot more fun and a lot more inclusive than celebrity in the city ever was.

The time was well-spent. Dinner had exemplified all the discomfort of a first date, but the entertainment at the club was relaxing, and John Ryan's knowledge of Nashville people allowed him to reestablish his territory and share the familiarity of something he knew and was comfortable with. At twelve-thirty Kate reached out and took his hand. John Ryan turned to look at her.

"Let's go home," she said, and the word home by itself removed all the apprehension from both of them.

In the car John Ryan took her in his arms and kissed her deeply. It was a passionate, intimate kiss, a kiss of acceptance.

"Are you scared?" he asked as he laid his cheek next to hers and felt, smelled the freshness of her hair.

"To death," she whispered.

As soon as the door of her room closed behind them, Kate put her purse on the desk and turned to him. She lifted her face and he kissed her. John Ryan could feel the warmth within her growing, a small hesitancy, the push and pull of emotions and then a surrender to it as she folded her body into his. John Ryan's hands moved on the silk of her dress, feeling the smoothness of her back. He felt the softness of her breast, and she responded with a deep, internal sigh. He could feel her nipple hardening under his touch. He separated and held her by the shoulders to look at her.

"Still scared?" he asked.

"No. No, I'm not scared." She paused and lowered her eyelids. "I want you to make love to me."

Kate moved away from him, turned her back and walked to the dresser, removing her earrings as she went. She undid the buttons at the top of her dress and stepped out of it. Underneath she was all lace. The color of her lingerie were the same color as the dress she had been wearing. She removed the slip and unhooked her bra letting the fullness of her breasts free. John Ryan watched her mesmerized.

His eyes ran the length of her, taking in the smooth shoulders, her breasts, the narrow waist, womanly hips and slender legs. She was a woman whose beautiful face matched her naked body.

As she moved toward him, he realized that without conscious thought or effort, he had somehow managed to undress himself. He had never taken his eyes from her. She was smaller and more vulnerable than she had been in her clothes. Her mouth was slightly open, her lips full and sensuous. Kate watched him as she moved, waiting for the first touch of her breasts against his skin. There was an intense hammering in her chest as they touched.

"You are lovely," he whispered as he guided her toward the bed. He leaned her back gently and lay down beside her, looking at her with wonderment. "Just lie still," he said and began kissing her forehead, holding her hair back with one hand and caressing her cheek with the other. He moved down and kissed her eyelids, then her neck. John Ryan raised his head and lowered his lips to hers.

He could sense the anticipation in her, heard her sigh and felt the beginning of movement in her hips, subtle and involuntary, expressing a need long neglected.

"Please," she said. He rose above and entered her. She seemed to enfold him, engulf him, swallow him. They made love without restraint, passionately, their intensity growing as they found a rhythmical pattern. Kate responded to his every move. When she felt him beginning to build, felt the expansion of him within her, she joined him. It didn't take long. She dug her fingers into his back as she moved in concert with him. They held on to each other tightly until their muscles began to relax. He looked deeply into her eyes. "Thank you," he said.

She smiled up at him and realized that for her there would be no turning back.

"Don't say it," he said as he planted small kisses on her face, tasting salt.

She looked at him quizzically. "What?"

"Wow."

I'm trying to help you here, Philip," Maury Friedman was saying, but Philip Barnessa wasn't listening. As he held the phone to his ear, he was running through his memories trying to remember the last time he was afraid. Maybe it was the arrest for attempted murder. He could do time; that wasn't the problem. It was life that scared him, but with Giannini Tedesco's help, he had beaten it. That was one kind of help; Maury Friedman offering 'help' was another matter entirely. He could not be trusted. Philip Barnessa wasn't sure whom he could trust anymore.

Friedman had suggested a plan, and he had listened, but now—minutes later—there was no recollection of what the man had said.

"So what are you tellin' me, Maury?"

"Just that I have thought about it, and I think I have a way for you to get by Jamie Greshem and make the Jamaican project bigger than you anticipated, double or triple the take on the cut-out business and maybe give yourself a wedge into John Ryan Stone's management, which is one step away from ownership, and that is, after all, the objective."

"Yeah." There was a pause. "Run it by me again."

"The single idea is dead. Was from the beginning. There's no money in it. Now with the album, there's money to be made. What's a single? A few cents. And it's likely to be one shot. Tedesco's not dumb. He knows that if Greshem and Hendrickson are willing to let Trayhorn front the money for an album, they've got to make John Ryan Stone succeed. We've got the means to help them if they get in trouble, and the means to assure that they will. Correct?" The threat wasn't even veiled.

"Yeah."

"In the meantime we make money with the original idea, only it's an album, not a single. Dollars not pennies."

"Maury, you don't know the problems. Pressing and delivering a single is no big deal. With an album you gotta have major artwork, labels, sleeves, wrap, not to mention the fact that we don't have a master to press."

"I don't see any of that as a problem." Maury Friedman's voice was cold and uncompromising.

"You don't," Barnessa said matter-of-factly. No matter what he did, he could see it ending badly, yet there was no way to refuse. "You wanna tell me how we're gonna come up with all that, Maury?"

"I will if you'll listen."

"I'm listenin'." Friedman was treating him like a child who'd misbehaved. It was at that moment Philip Barnessa decided that Maury Friedman was a dead man. Not now. Not while he was useful, but the man was as good as dead. It had been a long time since he had felt this way. "Tell me, Maury," he said nicely.

"Promotional copies are to be pressed next week at a pressing plant in South Jersey, right across the river from you. Lou knows a guy who works there, a supervisor. He'll deliver a copy to you at the bar across the street from the plant. He's there every night for his mid-shift meal, so no one will think anything about it. It won't be a master, but you can re-master from it. Trekorian says the artwork is being done here and should be finished in the next day or so. He'll get transparencies—don't ask me how—and get them to you. I have a sleeve manufacturer that will ship blanks directly to Jamaica. I assume you have a printer there."

"I can get one."

"Good. We don't want anything done in the States. You'll have two weeks from the time the promos are pressed to get ready for the market. As far as the cut-out deal goes, we'll prime the pump with Trayhorn copies and then follow up with your product, which the distributors will be happy to take. It's smart, Philip. It's the way it's going to be. Don't fuck it up."

"Yeah," he said.

"The guy at the plant is named Marty Cirone. He'll give you a call Monday night."

"I'll be available." Be nice, be grateful, he told himself.

"Good. I'll stay in touch."

"Yeah, do that, Maury. And thanks." It was all turning to shit, and there was nothing he could do about it. The album was completed three weeks ago. Kate Belden was booking—he was sure of it—but he couldn't get a handle on how she was doing it. He had tried to cover the country, but there were no inroads to the mid-South, and he knew they would go wild over John Ryan Stone. He was scared.

The call from Marty Cirone came on Monday night as scheduled. He gave Barnessa directions and asked him to be at Tucker's Tavern at eight o'clock when the four to twelve shift had its dinner break. The man sounded nervous, which gave Barnessa a little ego boost, but not enough to ease his depression.

Crossing the Ben Franklin Bridge from Philadelphia to South Jersey, Philip Barnessa proceeded down Admiral Wilson Boulevard and the dark carnival that it was. He thought about stopping at one of the go-go bars on the way back. Maybe he'd get lucky or, if not, he could call Angelina. He had found her there and then spent a week looking for her after she had disappeared from his apartment. He went to the Airport Circle, past The Pub Steak House, then south and east through the maze of traffic circles on Route 130 to Brooklawn, past Dick Lee's club and then out into the unfamiliar small towns and farmlands that gave The Garden State its name. As far as Philip Barnessa was concerned it was 'the country', filled with hicks and home-humpers and nobody he wanted to be associated with.

Tucker's Tavern was a low-slung, brick building with a dark bar and package store in front and a restaurant in back. The restaurant was clean and well-kept with the daily specials advertised in iridescent chalk on a blackboard at the entrance. The bar, on the other hand, was a long, dark room with a few tables and booths lined up against the windows. Philip Barnessa sat at the bar, so he could face the front door.

There were only four other people there, and the bartender didn't appear to care if anyone else came in or not. Two men who looked like they had been there for hours—one tall and skinny and one built like a linebacker—talked about track and football at the local high school as they sipped on their beers. There was also a bottle-blonde whose face was beginning to show the warnings of too many hours spent there and an attractive, dark-haired woman sitting at one of the tables by herself. Barnessa watched as she nervously moved the glass in front of her in little circles spreading its sweat into an ever-widening, round puddle. He wondered what the story was there. The place was a tableau of suburbia, he thought. The Twilight Zone.

Marty Cirone, young, tall and dark, came in with several other men at eight-fifteen. He was carrying the identifying athletic bag. Cirone was obviously the leader of the group and led them to a section of the bar a couple of seats away from the man from the city.

Barnessa eavesdropped the men's conversation, but there was nothing of any consequence—talk of the Philadelphia Eagles loss to the Giants, how the 'Iggles' were as bad as ever, not like when they had Sonny Jurgensen, an attempt by the Teamsters to create a shop at the plant, and of a new girl who had just started on the midnight shift.

It took forty minutes for the men to eat their cheese steaks and drink their beers. As they got up to leave, Barnessa followed the scenario he and Cirone had agreed upon.

"You guys work at the plant?" he asked.

"Yeah," Cirone answered.

"If you call it that," one of the others laughed as he moved toward the door.

"Maybe you can help me," Barnessa said. Cirone hesitated as the other men continued their exit.

"You guys go ahead. I'll see you across the street," the young man said. "What can I do for you?" One of the men lifted his hand in acknowledgment as he passed through the door.

"They hiring over there?" Barnessa asked as Cirone sat down next to him.

Their conversation covered nothing except employment, and then the two men left together. Outside, Cirone handed over the bag. There was no mention of what it contained. No piece of conversation except the fact that the man from Philadelphia was looking for a job.

It had gone smoothly, no hitches. On his way back to the city, he decided not to stop on Admiral Wilson Boulevard. He was carrying the means to millions of dollars if all went as planned, and he remembered Maury Friedman's words, 'Don't fuck it up.'

By the time he reached the Ben Franklin Bridge, he was already feeling sick about the flight to Jamaica in the morning.

Three weeks had passed since the album was completed, two weeks since Kate had gone back to New York, and two weeks had passed since John Ryan Stone had slept well. The band was starting its fourth week of rehearsal on Monday morning, and all was not going as well as they thought it would. As happy and relieved as they had been to get off the bus, out of the clubs, and into the studio, boredom was taking its toll. Musicians are a strange breed: on the road, all they can think of is home; at home, all they can think of is the road. Paul Crockett had missed several rehearsals, and Larry Foster had suggested firing him. Mickey and Howie had shown up on one occasion in no condition to accomplish anything. Even John Ryan himself was fighting impatience, thinking the road might be a panacea for Kate's absence.

They had spoken on the telephone every night, long, thoughtful conversations into the early morning hours that left him wondering how she could possibly make it to work. She described her days, and John Ryan gave her daily reports on the mental status of the members of the band. He expressed concerns about the record and the lack of activity, and she explained the difficulties she was having getting the band booked, assured him that between her, Jamie and Don Hendrickson, they would solve the problems.

The days had become an exercise in discomfort, he thought as he lay in bed staring out the window at the browning fields behind The Farmhouse. It was Sunday, a day of rest, and he had nothing to do. It reminded him of the Sunday morning in Gulfport, Mississippi when this whole thing was just beginning. It reminded him of a lot of Sundays, all alike, weighted down with time and remembrance.

As he lay staring into the crispness of the sun-drenched morning, seeing only the broom straw waving in the breeze, looking like faux wheat interspersed with narrow veins of red clay, he tried to reconstruct that Sunday morning they had spent together in Nashville, each small part of that waking, the sound of her voice and the words that made up their conversation.

When he awoke on that morning and blinked open his eyes, Kate was looking down at him, holding her head up with one hand, one breast lying full against the sheet, the other resting against it, the nipples dark and soft. She was smiling at him, and when his eyes opened, she reached over and touched his chest.

"Good morning," she said as she caught his eyes with her own. John Ryan looked at her and ran his fingers through her hair.

"Yes. Yes, it is," he said. "You know, Kate Belden, you are truly beautiful in the morning."

"So are you, John Ryan Stone."

"I appreciate that, but..." Kate pressed her fingers to his lips.

"No 'buts,'" she said softly, whispering the words. "The proper way to accept a Sunday morning compliment is a simple 'Thank you'."

"Thank you."

"You're welcome."

"Since we're both so beautiful in the morning, maybe we ought to limit our time together to morning hours."

"I'm not willing to give up the nights," she said.

"You have a point there. How long have you been watching me?"

"Not long. Why?"

"Makes a body feel kind of vulnerable knowing he's being watched while he's defenseless."

"I can't imagine you ever being vulnerable."

"I am. I can't imagine your imagining I'm not."

"Well I imagine..."

"Okay, okay," he interrupted and laughed.

"All right, I think, better yet, I believe that someone who is very vulnerable would not try to make it in this business, would not come to New York and deal with the people you dealt with and leave them feeling like they'd let things get away from them, would not start singing in front of people when the very thought of doing that made him sick, would go through a broken marriage and ever be willing to take the risk of getting involved again."

"Are we getting involved?" he asked with a look of mock apprehension. Kate looked into the cool blue of his eyes.

"I think so," she said. "If we're not, I'm in deep trouble."

"Me too," he said and pulled her over on top of him.

The memory of that day faded and the field outside came back into focus like a transition shot in a motion picture, a gold fusion from one life to another. It wasn't a dream; it was too real. It bore the weight of remembrance. It was Sunday and tomorrow was Monday. Back to work. If it all happened, so be it. If it didn't, so be that too.

As soon as the album was completed, Jamie Greshem had begun establishing his center of operation in Nashville. It was solely his decision to base himself there. The transition was implemented with a minimum of difficulty, largely due to the efforts of Hendrickson. As far as he knew, rehearsals were going well, although on the few times he stopped by The Warehouse, he did sense a growing restlessness among the musicians. He wasn't sure what to do about it. Kate had been stymied in her efforts to book the band, and he wasn't desperate enough to go to his father. Not yet.

As if the thought that was coursing through his head stimulated action, Mary Louise Wilkes, his newly-hired secretary, buzzed his line.

"Yes?"

"Mr. Greshem, a Mr. Dana Moultrie from Myrtle Beach, South Carolina, would like to speak with you."

"Thank you, Mary Louise. Put him on, please."

"Good mornin', Mr. Greshem....Say, do you mind if I call you Jamie? I always have doubts about confidin' in anyone I have to call 'mister'."

"Of course...Dana, is it?"

"Just call me Bubba, and when you finish laughin', we can have a conversation I think you'll want to hear."

"Okay, Bubba," Jamie said but could not stifle a chuckle.

"That's all right. People from the North think Bubba's a comic strip name or one they only hear on television. Fact is there's probably a whole lot more people legally named Bubba in the South than there are named Barnessa." Dana Moultrie paused waiting for a reaction, waiting to see if he had made the right call to the right person.

"I'm sure of that," Jamie responded. "What's this about, Bubba?"

"Just that I don't like people who try to intimidate me. I didn't like it from the bully in elementary school, I didn't like it when I played football in high school, when I was on Pork Chop Hill in Korea, or in my last divorce. I'm a marginally honest man, relatively speaking. When somebody tells me I need to do something to stay within the boundaries of the law, I'll do it and thank the man for tellin' me because he's right, but I'll be damned if I'll be horse-collared into anythin' out of fear." Dana Moultrie was on a roll.

"You mentioned the name 'Barnessa'."

"You're damned right I did and it was for a reason, but before I tell you what the reason is, I have a question for you."

"I'll try to answer it."

"Do you work for this Philip Barnessa or does he work for you?"

"Well, neither one exactly. He does some promotional work for the company I'm a producer with. Why?"

"'Cause I think he's milkin' across the fence on you, Jamie."

"I'm not sure what you mean."

"I think he's workin' against you more than for you, know what I mean? Bein' unfaithful? Now if you all ain't in the same boat, then I'll tell you what I'm talkin' about."

"I'm listening." Jamie Greshem was getting nervous.

"I'll take that as an affirmative and tell you a little bit about me. I own a 'Country club' down here at the beach. It can handle about five hundred or so drinkers and dancers, no chicken wire in front of the bandstand, gives a little relief from the beach music, all in all a pretty nice place. Anyway a coupla weeks ago, I get this call from one of the local hoods, tells me I'm not to book somebody named John Ryan Stone. Says I may not even get a call on him, but if I do, don't book him. Said I'd regret it..."

"You got a call?"

"Excuse me, Jamie, but let me finish before I get too mad thinkin' about it. I'd never even heard of John Ryan Stone, didn't know who he was, but the call sure made me determined to find out. Nobody—I mean nobody—tells me I cain't do somethin' that's within the boundaries of the law, 'specially if it's good for business. So I told this guy that I'd book who the hell I wanted when the hell I wanted, and that if he wanted to do somethin' about it, he and his army could come on over. Told him they'd better bring their lunches cause it'd be an all-day battle." Jamie Greshem liked Dana 'Bubba' Moultrie and grinned at the thought of him standing up to one of Barnessa's goons.

"Anyway," Bubba continued, "this white-neck thinks he can scare me with name-droppin'. Says, 'You ain't never mixed it up with the likes of Philip Barnessa. I ain't heard of him either, but I do note the name and tell him he better make sure the newspaper knows how to spell it. I also told him I don't go to a gunfight with a switchblade, so he'd better tell the 'eye-talian' to find another garden to play in and then I hung up on him.

"Now—I'm sorry that I'm not finished yet, but I want to show you the whole picture—I got to thinkin' about what he'd said and figured if they were so concerned about this John Ryan Stone and I was gettin' threats, I just better the hell find out who he is and who this Barnessa fella is. I've got some good people here and, beyond that, clubs like mine have a pretty good owner's network when it comes to bookin' artists. Cain't none of us afford a bad act, especially durin' the season. Of course spring, summer and fall is all one big season for us here in Myrtle Beach. Crowd changes from families to kids to golfers, but they all got money.

"So I put out the questions on John Ryan Stone and Philip Barnessa. I won't bore you with the details, but I get a response from a guy in Fort Walton Beach, Florida, tells me Stone is dynamite and has a record comin' out, then I get one from Savannah tells me he's even better than that. Now I wasn't raised in a poke," Jamie smiled at his own recognition of the word—"so I know this is somebody I need to get in my club before he works his way out of the size of my wallet. I also know I need to know how this Barnessa fella fits in. I won't tell you how, but I got Barnessa's personal phone number from the white-neck who has since moved back to New Jersey, which didn't sound smart to me, but then again maybe it was smarter than stayin' here. Anyway, I called the man and told him what I just told you about me.

"I was put onto Don Hendrickson by the network and his secretary referred me to you. I want to book John Ryan Stone, and I assure you there won't be any trouble from Philip Barnessa while he's here. There. That's it.

That's all I know. I thought you ought to know. One more thing, Jamie. I may sound like a wood-hook, but I arezn't one." He laughed at his own joke.

"Bubba, I never thought you were, and you have no idea how glad I am to know what you just told me. You can rest assured that John Ryan Stone will appear at your club. When I switch you back to Mary Louise, I want you to give her the name of your club, your address and your phone numbers. And I want a list of your open dates starting with tomorrow. Don't worry about cost; this one's on me. And if you hear anything else—anything—from Barnessa or about him or any of his people, you get back to me immediately. Mary Louise will give you my home phone number, which I expect you to keep confidential. And, Bubba, if you get a chance, spread the word on your network that club owners don't have to worry about booking John Ryan Stone. You'll be hearing from Kate Belden, who's temporarily in charge of Stone's management and booking. She'll take care of you."

"I'm much obliged, Jamie. We'll have to get you down to the beach." Jamie could imagine the prideful smile on Dana Moultrie's face.

"You can bank on it. I look forward to meeting you."

"Same here. Now if you'll switch me over to your young lady, I'll give her all the necessary information. You can check up on my club and me, by the way. I do some bookings through One-Nighters in Nashville and the Jim Buckram Agency." As if in afterthought he said, "Use the name Bubba Moultrie; they wouldn't know who the hell Dana is. I'll be talkin' to you."

Jamie switched the call back to Mary Louise Wilkes and tried to make up his mind whether to call Don Hendrickson or Kate Belden first. He actually felt relieved by Bubba Moultrie's call. Now he knew why Kate was being stonewalled.

He picked up the phone and punched out the New York City area code.

Jamie's call was not a surprise. The fact that Philip Barnessa was behind the stone wall she was running into didn't shock her. The web of refusals and excuses from the club owners and promoters with whom she had spoken was too organized to be coincidental. Responses too pat and rehearsed to be spontaneous, more like those of criminal cohorts with prepared alibis or prisoners-of-war, brainwashed into programmed repartee when faced with the proper stimulus.

In a conference with Bernie Greshem the week before, the president had given her no help, actually seemed to defend the club owners and promoters, but it was his last comment that really gave her a twist. As she opened the door to leave his office, with his attention on some papers he was shuffling, he had said, "Check with Barnessa. See if he can help." Even though she sensed the statement made him uncomfortable, she didn't question it. Instead she wrote it off to her own fast-developing paranoia.

Jamie advised her to wait two days and then begin re-calling all of the people in the Southeast who had given her what she considered a lame excuse for not booking John Ryan. He also asked her to call someone named Bubba Moultrie who would clear the way for her.

The producer wanted dates for John Ryan as soon as Kate could confirm them. The band was ready, but they would need a few dates to regain the form they displayed in Savannah. He also advised her that he would hold the album's release until she had something concrete on the schedule.

When she arrived at her office, she got out the phone log, in which she noted the responses and results of each call she made. She had learned early-on that assumptions, misquotes and inaccuracies in telephone conversations were standard and deadly in the music business. People could say or promise anything when they weren't looking at you.

From the list of prospecting calls, she marked those clients who seemed most promising. Of course Bubba Moultrie in Myrtle Beach, South Carolina, would be her first call of the day. Kate thought it might work out well since John Ryan was almost a local boy. From there she designed an order of sites that was geographically feasible for the band. Next she listed a couple of co-op agents in Nashville that Jamie had suggested.

It was ten a.m. on Wednesday—late for most people, early for club owners—when she dialed Bubba Moultrie's number. After three rings the phone was picked up.

"Bubba." The word was funny, but the tone of the voice held a determined edge.

"Mr. Moultrie, my name is Kate Belden..."

"Yes ma'am," the voice said enthusiastically. "Jamie said you'd be callin'. Now I already know who you are so we can dispense with history and job descriptions and just get on with what you called me about."

Kate was taken aback. The man sounded as if Jamie Greshem was his best friend. Based on what he said, her sales pitch was unnecessary and unwanted. She was truly at a loss for words—maybe a first—and had no idea how to continue the conversation. Bubba Moultrie must have sensed her predicament and decided to come to the rescue.

"I didn't mean that to sound short," he said. "I'm just not one to beat around the bush, and I'm usually talkin' to men. I hope I didn't offend you."

"No, not at all," she managed to get out.

"Most men have to spend twenty minutes on the telephone tellin' you what you cain't see. Struttin' their stuff like a cock rooster. Buildin' up their image you know. Cain't dare let another man get the notion they're askin' for somethin', which they are."

"Well, I'm not," she said. Bubba Moultrie laughed. From the sound of it, she could imagine him slapping his knee.

"There. You see? Women lay it right up front. Either you buy or you don't. I had two wives did that, and I bought. Big time. Paid for it too. They left, but the alimony goes on till death do us part."

Kate giggled. "Mr. Moultrie...."

"Bubba...Bubba, Bubba. Get used to it. It won't be so funny after the first few times."

"Okay, Bubba. Jamie said you wanted to book John Ryan Stone."

"May I call you Kate?" Bubba Moultrie was a piece of work, she thought, certainly not dumb nor without graces. Might as well play by his rules.

"Sure, Bubba. Kate is fine." The only thing they had settled on was what they were going to call each other and she already liked the man.

"Good. I wrote down all my open dates, which Jamie asked me to do." He paused, and she could hear him flipping pages. "Let's see. We been closed a month for remodeling. Man, I hate that. It's like lettin' dollars blow away in the wind. I don't know who in here would be lookin' at the walls anyway. What I was lookin' for was somebody good I could afford for the grand re-opening next week." He let the words hang. You're a sly one, Bubba Moultrie, she thought.

"Other than John Ryan, may I ask who you had in mind?" It would be interesting to know who he considered 'good'.

"I was thinkin' maybe I could pick up a David Houston or a Waylon Jennings. Sometimes people like that are caught with an open week and are willin' to come. I know that's short-term bookin', and I don't usually do it, but these damned contractors caught me up short. I couldn't get a finish date out of 'em to save my soul, and I didn't want to find myself payin' musicians to drink beer."

"You can really get somebody like that on such short notice?" She was smiling as she asked. The names were familiar, but she wasn't sure why.

"Hell, some of these boys will drive a thousand miles for a one night stand if they've got time on their hands."

"Next week?"

"Yes ma'am. That'd be Thursday through Saturday. Place'll be packed no matter who I get this time of year, but a good act'll keep 'em comin' back after the weather turns and the crowds die down."

"Well, Bubba, if you want John Ryan Stone, I think I could see to it." Damn, she was beginning to talk like him.

"Miss Kate, it is a pure pleasure doin' bidness with you. You got a nice voice, probly pretty too. I'm not sure who was sellin' who, but if you can get him, I want him."

"The pretty part would be up to you to decide, Bubba."

"Well, we'll just have to get you down to the beach, so I can. But you know there is one thing..."

"What's that?"

"You haven't said anything about what it's gonna cost me."

"Jamie said your club was to be booked free of charge."

Bubba Moultrie laughed. "Hell, it's more than a pure pleasure doin' bidness with you, Kate. It's a goddamn joy. Excuse my language; I get carried away sometimes. Tell him I do 'preciate the offer; but I insist on puttin' 'em up and feedin' 'em, unless they're the kind that break up hotel rooms."

"I'll tell 'em to break up some before they come, so it will be out of their systems." Bubba Moultrie hee-hawed on the other end of the line.

"You are somethin' else. I purely do love a feisty woman."

"What I'll need, Bubba, is for you to sign a contract which I will send 'special delivery' today. You should have it tomorrow. Get it back to me right away. I'll list the price at 'accommodations and meals'. They'll need six rooms from Tuesday through Saturday. No flops."

"You're asking so little, I'm beginnin' to wonder if they're as good as I've heard."

"They are, Bubba. You can bet on it. Now that that's settled, can I ask you a question?"

"You just did, but go ahead." Bubba Moultrie loved his own humor.

"Knowing what you know about the group and the record and so forth, under normal conditions what would you have expected to pay for John Ryan?"

"Well, there are never normal conditions in the music bidness, you know that. Doin' a little market research on country music maybe?"

"Not maybe, Bubba, definitely."

"Between eight and ten this week. That record comes out and does anything, you wouldn't be interested in Bubba Moultrie and I couldn't afford him."

"I think, considering what you've done for us, Bubba, We'll always be interested in you, and you'll always be able to afford him."

"I'm much obliged. By the way, I put the word out. You might find some of them closed doors suddenly got oil on their hinges."

"I'm much obliged too. By the way, did you know John Ryan's from South Carolina?"

"You're kiddin' me. No, I certainly sure as hell did not. We'll market the hell out of that. Send me the details. Anything else I can do for you?"

"Not right at the moment, but who can tell? The band will get to town on Thursday. We'll need to get some directions to the club and where they'll be staying."

"I'll get back to you later today with that."

"You're gonna love 'em, Bubba."

"I'm sure I will, Miss Kate," he said.

When the phone was down, Kate let out a resounding whoop. The roller coaster was beginning to roll.

"We got 'em ready, mon. Where you wan' 'em shipped?" Even their goddamned voices sounded arrogant, Barnessa thought. He hated doing business with them, but they worked cheap, and they were too eager for the American dollar to cause trouble.

"How do they look?" Why the hell was he asking the Jamaican? The *mollengen* wouldn't know whether they looked good or not.

"Dey lookin' good, mon. Dat boy he be singin' pretty good too. I like dat. Where you wan' 'em shipped?"

"Write this down. Select Storage. S-e-l-e-c-t." He spelled it out.

The Jamaican, obviously insulted, said, "I can spell."

Yeah, I'll bet, Barnessa thought, between drags on your spliff. "Select Storage. South Jersey Industrial Park." He waited. "Warehouse Number Five. Westville, New Jersey. You got that? Read it back to me." The Jamaican did.

"You got all the units packed?"

"Twenty towsand. I can count too, mon; we not gonna short you." The Jamaican didn't mention the extra eight thousand he had pressed and packaged for his own distribution in the islands.

"Ship 'em tomorrow. I want to start movin' 'em next week. Don't disappoint me. You know what'll happen. You don't want that, Danny."

"You be gettin' 'em." the voice said and the line went dead.

For the first time in weeks Philip Barnessa began to relax. He wasn't at ease, of course, whoever was in this business? The dead ones, he chuckled. Things did seem to be falling into place. The product was ready; the distributors were committed to the cut-out package; Trekorian would see that the cut-outs were delivered and billed, and take care of the Trayhorn product. He would handle the rest. It was golden, and the profits would put a smile on Tedesco's face and take the heat off.

It was only nine-thirty in the morning, but he poured himself a long C.C. over crushed ice, picked up the telephone and dialed a number written on a small piece of paper that lay on the table.

"Angelina?" he said when the voice answered. She sounded like she was still asleep.

"Yeah?"

"Phil."

"I know who it is." She sounded irritated. He wondered if she was alone.

"Why don't you come on over. We can make a day of it?"

"What kinda day?"

"A little exercise." He chuckled. "Some good food, booze. Maybe we go down to Atlantic City. How about that?"

"You want me to dress up?"

"Yeah. Bring some dressy clothes. And start loosinin' up your lips. They got work to do."

"Hey...." Angelina said with false arrogance. "Don't talk to me like that. Whaddaya think I am?"

"I think you're the best, baby. Absolutely the best. Hey, maybe we'll go down to islands in a few weeks. Jamaica. How's that sound?"

"Yeah, I believe that. You gonna pick me up?"

"Get a cab. Riverside Cab Company. They don't charge me."

"An hour," she said. "And don't jump all over me when I walk through the door."

Philip Barnessa felt the anger explode within him, but he held it back. Even the broads were tellin' him what to do and how to act. "I'll treat you like a lady," he said with a smile, picturing what she would be doing in an hour.

"That would be a switch."

"I'll be waiting." He hung up the phone and poured himself another drink. It was gonna be a good day.

John Ryan slouched in a chair in Jamie Greshem's office. It was Friday. Rehearsals ended early on Fridays to allow some of the band to play pick-up gigs on the weekend.

"So where are we? Any problems? Are you ready?" Jamie asked.

"For what?"

"What's coming."

"What the hell is that?" He paused. "Jamie, I gotta be honest, the band is beginnin' to think all the record stuff and the strategy and the big bookin's are just so much bullshit, and I'm beginin' to wonder myself. I mean we rehearse and rehearse and rehearse and we're gettin' paid, but you and I both know musicians want to work. Crockett's goin' insane; Red's gettin' discouraged, and if Mickey and Howie keep improvin' their duo act, we're gonna lose 'em."

"It's about to change," Jamie said.

"Only definites, Jamie."

"Only definites. I've got something for you." He handed John Ryan a package covered in plain, brown wrapping paper.

"Well, it's definitely not my birthday," he said.

"Open it." The young producer leaned back in his desk chair and watched as John Ryan carefully slipped his finger beneath the tape that held the wrapping together.

The first thing he saw was John Ryan Stone. The eyes immediately caught his attention. They were laughing and bluer than he thought. The smile—with teeth whiter than usual—impish and challenging at the same time. His hair glistened with a soft shine. The picture was taken in Kate Belden's hotel room the first time she came to Nashville. It seemed an eternity ago. He felt the weight of the twelve-inch LP in his hands. It seemed heavier than those that were on the shelves at The Farm. The weight and all that it carried with it was his. He was the proprietor of it. There was a surge in his chest—part joy, part anxiety, part pride. It was the most wonderful thing he had ever seen.

"I won't ask you what you think or how you like it because I'm sure you're overwhelmed right now, but I want you to know how I feel about it. I think it's beyond anything I imagined when I heard you on Don Hendrickson's terrace. I had no idea then where it would go or if anything would come out of that conversation or even the first sessions, but I want you to know I am as proud of that as you are. John Ryan, if there is any musical taste in this genre of music, it will be a landmark first album." He punched the intercom. "Mary Louise." That was all he said and the room filled with the sound of *One Lonely Night*. Surrounded by the depth and volume, John Ryan Stone was stunned by his own music.

The sound was incredible. He wondered if he ever really sounded that good. A myriad of thoughts sparking and dying like celestial events were going on in his head. When the music stopped, there were no words because he had no idea what to say or how to react.

"Do you want to hear more?" Jamie asked, a wide smile on his face, expressing the swell of emotion John Ryan was experiencing.

"No...Not now. I've got absorb this. I guess I should say recover."

"I've got more good news."

"Can I take it?"

"I think you can." Jamie punched the intercom again. "Come in, please."

In a moment the door opened. John Ryan was still staring at the picture on the album cover. He was clenching it tightly, as if it might blow away in some nonexistent wind. He hadn't even turned it over to read the liner notes on the back. The door opened, but he didn't look up, couldn't take his eyes from the picture that looked back at him.

"You're booked in Myrtle Beach, South Carolina, on Thursday." John Ryan couldn't bring his thinking into focus. He was still struggling with the shock of the album and the sound of his voice and the music and the sound of that voice speaking to him. He lifted his head. Kate Belden stood just inside the door. She had made no mention of coming to Nashville. He blinked several times, trying to clear his thoughts, and looked at her. She was still standing there.

"Wow!" he whispered.

"I just need you two for a few minutes then I'll leave you to yourselves," Jamie said.

Jamie and Kate told him about Bubba Moultrie and the problems Philip Barnessa had caused. Although Barnessa and his actions were not John Ryan's to deal with, it seemed politic to tell him. The other news was disappointing: the album would be held for an additional three weeks. Hendrickson wanted to coordinate it with a major date, which they didn't have yet, but Jamie assured them both that three weeks was his limit. That didn't leave much time. Hendrickson was trying to place him in an opening spot with an established artist. The man had a lot of favors he could call in.

John Ryan wanted to break the news to the band, but Jamie said they were being notified even as he spoke and excused himself. The treadmill of the last few weeks had escaped its rollers and gone berserk. John Ryan took Kate in his arms and kissed her. She folded into him, soft and warm.

"I want to see The Farm," she said.

"You're not serious," he said. "Is this some kind of audition?"

"Might be." Kate smiled.

"Can I ask you a question? When you go to a party, do you always look in the hosts' medicine cabinet?"

"That's too personal. I'll tell you when I get to know you better."

"Well, I'll tell ya, Missy," he said in a pretty fair John Wayne voice. "There just ain't a whole lot more to know."

"I think you're too modest. I believe there's a whole lot more to know." Kate stood and pulled him up by his hands. "Please?"

John Ryan felt a moment of panic, uncertain about the condition of the house.

"Kate, I'll be happy to..."

"Please?" she said.

"Okay. You pay your money; you take your chances," he answered as he followed her to the door.

"I think we'd better get my luggage; I might decide to spend the weekend." Kate was laughing when she said it, but he knew she was serious.

"Kate...."

"Come on, Duke; it's right out here."

There was a small suitcase, a large oblong box wrapped as a present, a hanging bag and a train case. "What about the box? That go, too?"

"Yes. Get that and the hanging bag. I'll get the rest."

"I'm not even gonna ask," he said, looking at the box.

"I wouldn't tell you anyway."

John Ryan insisted they stop and get some groceries before they left the city. No matter what shape the house was in, he knew there was little food to eat.

It was still daylight as they drove out of Nashville. Kate sat close to him in the old car. He took her on the scenic route, circling Hendersonville Lake, pointing out John D. Laudermilk's house, Don Hendrickson's place, the home of Johnny Cash and June Carter, and others whose success had given the area its fame.

Kate was enthralled with the Tennessee countryside, but most of all she was just happy to be with John Ryan. On the flight down she had worried that things might not be the same as they were on her last trip. She knew that magic first weekends together are hard to top or even equal; succeeding times always carry the baggage and challenge of the first time. She didn't know where it was going or where she wanted it to go. She was 0 for two in relationships and the thought that 'three strikes and you're out' recurred on a regular basis.

The Farm was a surprise. From what he had told her, she pictured an unmade bed, a sink full of dirty dishes, trash cans overflowing and dust-bunnies dancing with each other. In actuality it was neat and orderly— masculine—and held an overpowering sense of John Ryan Stone. He had lived in this place with his wife, which had been her only reservation about coming, but nothing suggesting a woman's presence remained.

"I don't have to stay here," she said as she looked around the large room that was for living and dining and only separated from the cooking area by a bar.

"What do you mean?"

"If it makes you uncomfortable."

"Why should I be uncomfortable? That part was over when you walked in the door. Kinda like takin' your clothes off in front of somebody for the first time."

Kate laughed. "Did that make you uncomfortable? With me, I mean?"

"Truthfully?"

"Truthfully."

"I don't think I thought about it." They kissed, luxuriating in the closeness. It was good.

"I think I'd better get busy with dinner, or we may never get around to it," John Ryan said.

"I think you're right, but I'll help."

"No. I want you to get unpacked, take a warm bath and then tell me what's in that box."

"Got your curiosity up, huh?" Kate lowered her eyelids and smiled suggestively.

"Yep."

"After dinner."

"Okay."

"Damn! I though you'd at least argue. Maybe even beg."

"Never." The look on his face was one of pure joy.

"See ya," she said and walked into the bedroom, closing the door behind her.

Despite his penchant for the convenience of fast food, John Ryan did like to cook. He had decided long ago that half the joy of cooking is the surprised look on people's faces when you put something before them that exceeds their expectations. Cooking for yourself offered no surprises.

He had bought filets, which he put in a mixture of soy sauce, liquid smoke and garlic to marinade while the cast-iron skillet heated on the grill on the front porch. He cut fresh asparagus into small pieces and put them into simmering water on the stove to tenderize while he sliced small potatoes for ranch fries. The salad consisted of Boston lettuce, sliced tomatoes, diced onions and roasted sweet peppers.

When the vegetables were almost done, and the cast iron skillet red hot, he rubbed the steaks with a blend of hot chili seasoning and flour, dipped them back in the marinade and put them in the pan. The heat caramelized the mixture of marinade and seasonings, surrounding the meat with a crusty shell. Before turning them, he knocked on the bedroom door to tell Kate dinner was almost ready.

He opened a bottle of Merlot, poured two glasses, put the salads on the table and wondered if Kate had fallen asleep in the bathtub. Before he could knock on the door a second time, it opened. Fresh and sparkling from a soaking bath and a change of clothes, Kate Belden glowed.

"You are beautiful," he said.

"What? No 'Wow!'"

"That's for later. Come sit, and I shall serve you, milady."

"Is this part of the whole John Ryan Stone package?"

"I guess we'd have to negotiate that," he said.

Dinner was perfect. Kate was duly surprised at what he had done with the food they had purchased and, best of all, they managed the whole meal without once mentioning business. It was the most stable John Ryan Stone had felt in a long time. He was home; he was with a woman he admired, had made love to and would make love to again, yet there was no feeling of urgency.

When they had finished and cleaned up the dishes, she asked him to play his album. He didn't protest. They sat on the couch as the music began and Kate leaned into him resting her head on his chest. The feelings he had experienced in Jamie's office played themselves all over again. At times he felt chill bumps crawling up his arms and at times mild embarrassment when he admitted to himself that something was good. *My Bed Has Echoes* mesmerized Kate. She had never heard it before, and at the final note she turned her face up to his. "That is truly magnificent," she said and kissed him.

"The box," he said when the kiss was over.

"I thought you'd forgotten. Okay, you can open it now. Any ideas?" she asked.

"Well, it's long," he said, sitting on the floor and beginning to unwrap it. When he lifted the top from the box, he lost his breath. Lying in front of him was one of the most famous and sought after guitars ever made, a classic even though it had been produced only a few years before.

"Kate. Where in heaven did you get this?"

"I take it you know what it is." She smiled broadly.

"Know what it is? You've got to be kidding. A '61 Gibson ES-335. It must have cost a fortune. Jerry Kennedy plays one of these. Every side man in the business would give everything but his fingers for one of these. Where did you get it?" He lifted it from the box and looked at it, even smelled it.

"Don found it for me. I asked him what the most extraordinary thing I could get for you was. Of course when he told me, I had no idea what he was talking about."

"But the cost...." John Ryan Stone was stunned for the third time in one day.

"He worked a deal. Don't ask. I wanted to do it."

"You put a lot of pressure on, you know that?" For a moment Kate wasn't sure how to take his statement and wondered if she had overstepped her boundaries. "Now I guess I'm gonna have to really learn to play," he said as he put the guitar back in the box. "Let's turn out the lights and call it a night."

"Let's just turn out the lights," she answered.

When Kate slipped into bed, she was enveloped by John Ryan even though she was alone. The sound of the shower was evidence of him and the sheets the essence of his presence. A small night-light cast a shadowed glow about the room, defining only shapes and passing over detail. The bed was comfortable; it did not intrude on the serenity that surrounded her. She felt secure and privileged to be so happy.

As John Ryan walked toward the bed, Kate felt a shiver of anticipation. The soft light sculptured his body and gave it a lean smoothness, taller and more muscled than she remembered. He moved with the assurance she had seen on the stage in Savannah.

He slid beneath the sheet and pulled her to him. There was shine in her eyes, dim in the quiet light. He looked at every nuance of her—the forehead, lashes, the depth of her eyes, the cheekbones, and her lips, together but in a soft smile.

John Ryan ran his tongue along the silver smoothness of her lips, parting them and reaching in to touch the tip of her own. Their mouths opened, and they explored, tasting remembrance. He heard a soft moan as he moved down her neck to the hollow between her breasts. He kissed each nipple, gently tugging at them, feeling the puckered hardness and texture of each one.

"Please," she whispered. John Ryan slid down her body. He felt the curve of her hips and put his hands under them to lift her up to him. His mouth encompassed her, and her moans were no longer quiet or soft. He entered her in a rush, catching that wave that continued to build within her until she began losing her breath. It was a fierce climax fueled by the sound of her own voice somewhere outside herself, going on until she heard him join her, harsh and guttural.

When it was over, they were silent, trying to hide the sound of their own breathing. They lay quietly and drifted into sleep.

The girl walked around the apartment naked. Barnessa stared as she poured the drink he had ordered. That was the nice thing about her: she could be ordered to do anything, whatever he asked. It was more of a conditioned response than a willingness to please, and that was a negative but who cared. No one had ever done anything for Philip Barnessa because they wanted to.

There had been better-looking women, but they always had reservations of one kind or another; they wanted feelings. Not Angelina. She wasn't a professional, but she knew who she was, what she was and where her value lay. She made it easy. She was willing and able; it was a way of life, and anyone who was in her company for even a brief period of time was aware of it. She didn't advertise; it was just there in her eyes, in the turn of her hip as she walked, in the careless way she strutted naked. He had known other women like her. Their philosophy was simple: If they got through the day, there was a chance for tomorrow.

"Put on some clothes," he said.

"Why?" She turned toward him, the two large, brown nipples forming symmetrical targets.

"Friedman's in town. He's gonna stop by."

"Something to be worried about?" she asked as she brought the drink to him.

"Why should I be worried?"

"I don't know. You just seem nervous. Had a hard time climbing the mountain this morning."

"I was waitin' for you," he said with a smirk.

"Get serious."

"You think every time we fuck I just want to jump on and pop my nuts? Sometimes I'm thoughtful." Angelina DiGirolamo rolled her eyes and walked into the bathroom, closing the door behind her.

He was worried.

Kate Belden was not hollering 'Uncle'. Most of what he had tried had drawn a blank. Short of muscle, he wasn't sure what to do next. Maybe it was time for that. The thought unnerved him; women were off-limits, but desperation could change any rule. There was a churning in his stomach that he knew was out of his control. That had happened a lot lately, sometimes giving him a coppery, bloody taste in his mouth, causing him to gag.

When Angelina came out of the bathroom, she was dressed in black slacks and a red sweater. Her hair was combed and she had put on makeup. She wasn't unattractive. Anybody's receptionist or secretary. She even looked educated. Barnessa had a momentary urge, wondered how soon Friedman would arrive and decided it was foolish to take the chance.

"Where you goin'?" he asked in curiosity, not in anger.

"I don't know. Maybe down to South Street. There's a new consignment shop just opened up. I need something to wear. How long you gonna be with your friend?"

"I dunno. Call before you come back. You need some money?" Angelina stopped in her tracks, turned and looked at him. He had never offered her money before.

"Money?" she asked incredulously.

"Yeah. Money. It's green. You spend it to buy things. I know you're good at buyin' things."

"Yeah, I'm good at buyin' things. For a moment I thought you were gettin' tender."

"Here." He put two hundred dollar bills on the coffee table. She looked at them and then picked them up.

"Thank you, Philip," she said.

"Philip?" he said smiling then frowning. "Philip? Don't get no ideas." She smiled back. "Don't worry."

Maury Friedman saw the girl leave the apartment and passed close enough to smell her perfume as she walked toward the elevator that had just delivered him. He was smiling as he approached the apartment door. His visit to Philadelphia was not expected. When he called to announce he was in town, it put Philip Barnessa on edge; that gave him pleasure.

The knock on the door gave Barnessa a start. His nerves were shot. He had done a lot of talking, made a lot of promises—which he was sure he could fulfill if they gave him a chance—but until money started coming in, Tedesco would be skeptical. There was a second knock. He walked to the door slowly, without energy, his thoughts distracted and confused. He looked through the peephole in the door and opened it.

"Maury, come in. Your call caught me off guard. I didn't know you were gonna be in Philadelphia. I could have arranged something." He didn't know what he might have arranged; Maury Friedman wasn't the type to ever want anything arranged. It was a status statement that he was sure didn't impress the man from New York.

"Not necessary, Philip. I hadn't planned to come here, but I think there are a few things we need to discuss."

"Sure...Drink?" he asked as he went to pour himself another.

"A little Scotch, please. On the rocks."

"So what brings you, Maury?" Barnessa asked, attempting to swagger as he delivered Friedman's drink.

"You, Philip." Barnessa felt the feeling go out of his legs, felt it replaced by the rubbery weakness that for most people would predicate collapse. He sat down quickly to regain physical composure, but his mind remained in a panic, racing. "Giannini's upset." Barnessa took a long swallow of his drink, trying to exhibit bravado and confidence, but the glass betrayed him by tapping against his teeth. Maury was playing a 'cat and mouse' game. Damned if he would allow himself to be the mouse. Set the field and then determine if he should play or run. It was an old credo.

"You're confusing people, Philip, making half-hearted efforts." Another opening. Dismiss it. "We all know about what you have going, but that's marginal at best. We've told you that. We keep repeating ourselves. You're putting all your eggs in that basket. You know what we want, what Giannini said he wanted, and we don't see any progress." We, the pronoun itself held a warning. "The hillbilly is scheduled to work or didn't you know that? You were supposed to prevent that until we had some control. I have to assume that if he's working in Myrtle Beach this week, he'll be working somewhere else next week. The record comes out; he's a star; we're left out. That scenario is highly possible; and if it happens that way, I won't be able to help you, much as I might want to." Poor wax job, Barnessa thought. Concern about his welfare was only relative to his usefulness to Maury Friedman and Giannini Tedesco.

"Talk to me, Maury," Barnessa said trying to look him straight in the eye, but having trouble with the balance. "You were the one brought up the cut-out scheme."

"That was a temporary measure to buy you some time. You have to come up with ownership. Giannini made that clear. Management's a good start." It was an order with no options.

"You wanna give me a fuckin' clue, Maury, or am I just supposed to take it into my own hands? If I do that, things'll get messy. I hope you know that." Violence was the one card he held; Maury Friedman wouldn't dirty his hands or take the chance.

"No. We don't want it that way, Philip, but whatever becomes necessary, becomes necessary."

"Then you tell me. You seem to have all the answers to questions ain't even been asked yet. You tell me. Take out the Belden broad? That's no problem, but they ain't dumb; they'll know where it came from, and Bernie's kid'll blow everything up. He's too dumb to be smart."

"Bernie." Friedman said.

"Bernie," the big man repeated matter-of-factly.

"Bernie controls Stone's contract; there's no reason he can't execute some changes. He could even sell the contract; he has that much authority. Let him convince Jamie that the changes are necessary. You think Stone will complain? It's the chance of a lifetime for him, and without Jamie there isn't any chance at all. There's no protective clause or right-of-refusal for the producer, the writer or the artist. I checked. I told you there had to be a hole somewhere; there always is when things are done in haste. The hole, in this case, is that Bernie's in total control. "

It was simple. Why hadn't Maury told him about the contract before? Why had he been instructed to go to all the trouble to prevent bookings? Why would they even let him go through the counterfeiting and cut-out scam? The answer to that was easy: additional money without risk to them. He was the only one that was vulnerable in that segment, but the contract? That was confusing.

"Why didn't we do this from the fuckin' beginning?"

"Plain and simple."

"Plain and simple?" Barnessa looked at him and laughed. "Yeah, plain and simple. You should know that, Philip." He mimicked the lawyer and then turned back to him with anger. "So tell me how so fuckin' plain and how so fuckin' simple."

"It's a risk. There are two unknowns." He paused, focused on Philip Barnessa. "You and Bernie."

"Me and Bernie?"

"Let me finish." The man's voice was firm. "Bernie Greshem is not easily intimidated; he's been around too long. We've done business on a peripheral basis for a lot of years. We don't want it to be peripheral any longer. We want the company; Stone is the key. The best approach to Bernie is using the kid. Men love their sons. On the other hand, threats have to be carried out, and we're not sure you have the heart for it anymore. Giannini thinks you're getting tired, losing your enthusiasm." Friedman knew the button he was pushing. "Maybe thinking about retiring."

"Fuck you and fuck Giannini if you think that way."

"That'll never happen, Philip." There was silence. Maury Friedman rose from his chair. "I've got a plane to catch. I can't tell you how important it is for you to handle this well."

"Yeah," Barnessa said. "That's all I seem to be hearin' lately."

The lawyer picked up his briefcase, drained the Scotch and put the glass on the table.

"Thanks for the drink," he said and went out the door.

Philip Barnessa sat on the couch staring. His mind was no longer racing; it had come to a dead stop. He couldn't muster a thought. He brought the glass of Canadian to his lips and it was empty. He threw it across the room.

The final strategy was simple. 'Plain and simple', he thought to himself and laughed. He would go to Bernie all right, but Bernie wouldn't be expecting him or what he had to say. Steal a page from Friedman's book. It was simple. Bernie either sold his son on the rules or adjusted the contract on his own and took whatever flack might come or—plain and simple— Jamie was dead. Maybe Kate Belden too. The broad offended him. It had been awhile. The thought energized him.

The effect the booking in Myrtle Beach had on members of the band was immediate and immeasurable. The excitement was back, songs added. There were new takes on the classic *Four Walls* that Jim Reeves had crooned. John Ryan sang it. Mickey and Howie used close harmony on a super-slow, country-flavored version of Wilson Pickett's *In The Midnight Hour*, making it a love song. John Ryan added an old Thomas Wayne ballad, *Tragedy*, to the list. The biggest obstacle that faced them was to produce 'live' a reasonable facsimile of the songs that were on the album. Achieving the quality of the recordings presented a major challenge, but Cade Wilhite assured them that if they could produce the notes, he could produce the sound.

At times John Ryan found his mind wandering back to the previous weekend. What had been a surprise had become a revelation. He and Kate had done nothing that most people would have considered of consequence, nothing that cost money; they had seen no other people, just been together— talking, taking short drives on country roads, stopping for her to buy a handmade quilt, smiling at chenille bedspreads and lacquered cypress knee tables, cooking their meals together, listening to the album and making love. John Ryan felt full and happy. Kate had laughed on Saturday morning when they got in the car and he had put on his sun glasses, started the engine, and said in an exaggerated accent, "I got my shades. I got money and gas in the car. Let's hit them yard sales." It was two days filled with light air.

When Jamie Greshem arrived at The Warehouse, it was almost quitting time. "Hey, Boss," Mickey yelled as the band finished the last song of the day. "What brings you around? 'Fraid we're gonna embarrass you?"

"When you're finished, I've got some news for you," the young producer said.

"If it's good, we're finished," John Ryan said. "If it's not, we'll just keep on playin' till some good comes along."

"Then I guess you're finished," Jamie said.

"That's the first time I ever heard those words that they sounded good." Red laughed as he said it. The band members packed up their instruments, came down off the stage and made themselves as comfortable as possible in the sparse furniture that was available and on the floor.

"So what you got, Boss Man?" Howie asked.

"I have a biggie for you. The North Carolina State Fair in Raleigh in four weeks. The timing's perfect. It's ideal. You're opening for Faron Young."

"The Sheriff?" Hopwood said above the hoots and hollers. "How the hell did you manage that?"

"I didn't. Hendrickson did. The record will come out one week in advance of it. That gives us a weekend and a week to push it before the show. Of course we'll have them available at the performance, and we'll see that some important people are there." Jamie Greshem had to pause for breath.

"Faron Young. Man!" John Ryan said.

"I'm glad we added *Four Walls* instead of *Hello, Walls*," Red said with a loud guffaw. "Faron Young! You runnin' with the big dogs now, boy. Hell, your career may have had the fastest rise in history. From The Silver Saddle in Biloxi to The Faron Young State Fair in three months."

"You're forgettin' the years before Biloxi," John Ryan said, feeling the nerves roiling in the pit of his stomach. "Does Kate know?" he asked.

"I called her as soon as I heard. I didn't want to take the chance of her double-booking you. You're playing the Ranch House in Charlotte and The Thunderbird in Danville, Virginia, in between Myrtle Beach and the fair. They could both up the response to the Raleigh appearance if they go well."

"Well, the man's always the last to know," John Ryan said with a smile. "Any other startling news?"

"That's it for the moment, guys." He turned to John Ryan. "Come on, walk out with me. I've got a lot to do between now and then, a lot of phones to work. Kate's going to be pretty busy too," he added as they moved toward the door. "How's that going, if it's not too personal to ask?"

"It's too personal, but you can ask; you're payin' me. It's a little too soon to call. I'm not sure I'm ready for it."

"Who ever is? John Ryan, if all goes well, and people buy us, the record will do the rest. It's a big engagement, but it's not the only engagement. Faron's going to be in town Wednesday morning, and Don wants you to meet him. He's been in the business a long time. You can learn a lot from him. He's a good star to open for, and he's not worried about you taking anything away from him like a lot of names might be. Your styles are totally different. It couldn't have worked out better."

"I'm beginning to think I owe my life to Don," John Ryan said.

"As far as music is concerned, you probably do." Jamie laughed but with a note of seriousness. "He believes strongly in you, and I think—though he hasn't said so—that you've added some energy to his life. You two are a good match."

"What did Kate have to say when you told her?"

"I heard a loud scream as she hung up the phone." Jamie smiled.

"It looks like a busy four weeks. And thanks."

"Sounds like a movie line to me." Jamie Greshem laughed and left John Ryan standing in the parking lot. As he walked away, he put two thumbs up in the air.

Bernie Greshem did not expect the interruption. He wasn't doing anything particularly important. There had been more and more times lately when there was nothing important to do. The industry was slow, a result of overproduction. Companies had flooded the market with new product, hoping for the one act that would carry them. Small companies were going under, larger companies buying writer's catalogues in order to survive on radio play and performance royalties. Beyond the state of the industry, Bernie Greshem had surrounded himself with exceptional people who were capable of running the company on their own, which limited his job to a few final judgments here and there and signing contracts. It had become dull. He was floating among those thoughts when his office door flew open. He turned quickly, but he did not lose his composure.

"We gotta talk," Philip Barnessa said as he slammed the door behind himself, his voice uncontrolled.

"Phil. This is a surprise," Greshem said.

"I'm sure it is. That's what I wanted it to be." He stood in the center of the office, the anxiety and hostility he had worked on all the way from Philadelphia plainly visible.

"Drink?"

"Yeah, sure. C.C." The Trayhorn executive didn't say anything. He went to the sliding glass doors of the bar, opened them, selected two Waterford Crystal low-ball glasses, filled them halfway with Canadian whiskey, put two ice cubes in each glass and turned back toward Philip Barnessa. He handed the man his drink and went to sit behind his desk. His adversary was dumbfounded.

"Did you hear what I said?"

"You want to talk to me. Has something happened I should know about? Are you in trouble? Can I help? What, Philip?" Bernie Greshem reversed his attitude, his voice now angry. "What is so fucking important that you should walk in here unannounced, slam my door and start acting hysterically? What?"

"Good act," the Philadelphian said when he recovered from the shock of Greshem's words. "You listen to me. You got problems, pal. It ain't me needs help; it's you and your damned kid. Him more than you."

"What in hell are you talking about?"

"Just what I said. You don't talk some sense into him or give him some fatherly advice, he could wind up dead."

"Don't threaten me or my son, Philip. Don't dare."

"We gotta have a piece, Bernie."

"I gave you...."

"I'm not talkin' penny-ante distribution or concert paraphernalia or agency, which it seems we've already been screwed out of thanks to Miss Belden. I may take her to the showers personally on that one. I'm talkin' ownership, Bernie. Fifty-five percent of Stone. Everything."

"You're out of your mind." His eyes were fixed on Philip Barnessa's. "I couldn't give you that if I wanted to, and I assure you even if it were in my power, I would have no inclination to do so."

"Oh, you'll do it all right unless you want him to suffer. If you don't, you got nothin'. You can do anything you want with those contracts you write. You think I'm some kinda street guinea? Give me a break."

"You sound as though you've been talking to Maury."

"Did he talk to you?" Barnessa felt moisture on the back of his neck and down the front of his arms.

"You're walking on thin ice, Philip."

Barnessa turned away from the president. "The record's out next week. It's gotta be done by then. You don't have a choice."

Bernie Greshem had to subdue a smile of superiority. The record wasn't scheduled to be out in a week; he was surprised Barnessa didn't know that. There were obviously struggles going on he wasn't aware of. Bernie had always thought the man's longevity and street-smarts would secure him a retirement in Florida; now that didn't seem so certain.

"So what do you want me to do? Steal the guy from Jamie? Rip off my own son?"

"You know the rules. Do what you gotta do." He smiled. "Hey, forty-five percent is better than no percent, and it guarantees success whether the guy deserves it or not."

"I'll talk to him."

"You do better than that. Deliver. Straight-up and clean. No problems."

"I'll think of something."

"Yeah do that. But do more than think." The big man started toward the door.

"Don't slam it, Philip." Barnessa turned and smiled, walked through the door and slammed it behind him. He felt good. Intimidation was better than the Fountain of Youth.

Once he was alone, Bernie felt like a lame duck. He wasn't sure what he should do or if he should do anything. Just yet. The relationship with Barnessa and 'his people' was necessary to operate; every major entertainment entity accepted that. It was nothing new. It was the price of doing business.

As he stood at the window looking down on the nighttime lights of the city, Bernie made a decision. It would end his tenure at Trayhorn, could even make his son's career in the music industry short-lived, but it was the only way he knew to protect him.

He and Jamie had never gone fishing, spent an afternoon at the ballpark or worked on Boy Scout projects together—the clichés of good fatherhood—but he did love his son, something it takes many fathers a long time to learn. Because of that love, he was going to give Jamie opportunity, even though it would jeopardize his own security and perhaps his life. It was a big price to pay, but less than 'the cost of doing business'. He turned out the lights in his office and walked down the hall to the Legal Department.

———•••———

On the way to Myrtle Beach, John Ryan thought about his meeting with Faron Young on Wednesday morning. It had been brief. The man was a dynamo. Energy exuded from his every word and move. John Ryan had always suspected that the long-term people who were successful in the business would not be shackled by ego, and 'The Sheriff' didn't seem to be. He was pleasant and businesslike; John Ryan liked him immediately. It was obvious why he was found acceptable as an opening act; they couldn't have been more different. Young was easily recognizable as a country entertainer; his dress and turquoise jewelry announced it. John Ryan was unidentifiable. It was the first time he realized what being a star was all about. Where Faron Young was and what he was seemed so far away that John Ryan could never imagine being there himself.

It rained all the way down Route 17; consequently, the traffic on the narrow road had everyone awake long before the bus rolled to a stop in front of the club. It was located at the north end of Myrtle Beach or the south end of North Myrtle Beach, depending on how one viewed the boundary lines between the two communities. The exterior of the place flashed with neon, the largest in-color statement being that it was, indeed, "Bubba Country."

John Ryan, Mickey, Howie and Mountain Red made a run from the bus to the entrance, which was open even though the club was not. "Bubba Country" was unique. Despite the gaudiness of the exterior, the interior was a blend of glass and light and contemporary ranch-house style furnishings. It showed taste and class unusual for a club of its type.

As they stood inside the door feeling the spaciousness of the room, a tall and stocky, red-haired man moved toward them. Looking like an ex-football player gone to seed after years of rigorous training, he appeared to be in his mid to late forties. As he moved, the stockiness was overshadowed by a graceful and challenging muscularity. He seemed old for a bouncer but nonetheless threatening, John Ryan thought. He only hoped Bubba Moultrie had told the man they were coming.

"How ya'll doin'?" the man said sticking out a beefy, freckled hand. "You must be the band. I'm Bubba." The singer was taken aback. From Jamie and Kate's description of Bubba Moultrie's voice, accent and attitude, he had pictured a much older, short and squat man.

"I'm John Ryan Stone. This is Mickey Shackleford, Howie Newfeldt and Mountain Red. The rest of the guys are still on the bus," he said looking around at the new decor. "This is quite a place."

"Glad to meet you. I'm not sure I like the changes. Albamarle—that's my wife, at least my present wife. She was born in Virginia and named after the county she was born in; she designed it. I know Bubba and Albamarle is pretty funny, but we're stuck with it. Anyway, Albamarle thinks it'll bring in a higher class crowd that we can charge more money and have less fights. I'm just not sure. Kinda liked it the way it was." The three musicians were looking at Bubba Moultrie in awe. He had not skipped a beat and spoke faster than any of them could sing.

"She might be right," Red said, breaking out of his stupor.

"I sure as hell hope so. I purely do hate to spend money to make somethin' look good without gettin' a fair return. Daddy taught me that a long time ago. He opened the place back when there wasn't hardly no neon on The Strand. Now it looks like a goddamned carnival out there."

"That must have been awhile back. I used to come here when..." John Ryan started.

"It was. I'd guess thirty-five years ago or so. He hardly ever comes by anymore. Just looked me up and down one day, handed me the keys and said, 'I guess you're big enough to run it now.' and walked out the door. Three months later he bought a big condo down on the beach south of here—'bout sixty units—married a thirty-five-year-old widow and spends his time tendin' the grass and plants around the buildin', fishin' and playin' golf. Said he'd worked enough."

"He bought all sixty units?" Howie asked.

"Yep. It was just finishin' up. Bought the first one, the last one and all of 'em in between. I guess he made a right good profit on 'em, too. They all sold and he ain't workin'. Did buy a bigger boat though. I'll have to tell you about him sometime."

"I thought maybe you just had," Mickey said. Bubba grinned.

"Didn't even get started. Ya'll wanna look around before you start settin' up? I purely am excited about you bein' here. Jamie and Kate say you're somethin' to behold."

"I don't know that I'd say that," John Ryan said.

"I guess we'll see," Bubba Moultrie said. "If you're not, I'll pay you one night and send you on your way, cause it don't make no difference what Jamie and Kate say; it's me that's got to like you." He laughed and moved down toward the dance floor and the bandstand.

"Where'd you play?" Mountain Red asked as he followed the man.

"Position or school?"

"Both."

"Middle linebacker. Alabama."

"I thought so," Red said for lack of anything better. "You collect them little airplane bottles?" he asked, noticing the miniatures lined up in profusion on the shelves behind the bar. John Ryan smiled as Bubba Moultrie answered.

"Nope. That's the way we sell it in South Carolina. It'ud be against the law to sell it any other way. Works out pretty good too. Makes the mixed drinks more expensive and gives the state more taxes. Saves measurin' and it's easier to keep track of what your bartenders are stealin'." John Ryan couldn't imagine anyone stealing from Bubba.

Maybe it was being back in Myrtle Beach, back in South Carolina, a place that held so many youthful memories. Or maybe it was because of the successful turn in his career, which brought with it a sense of victory and accomplishment. Regardless of the reason, John Ryan, lying stretched out on the small couch in the dressing room at Bubba Country, thought of his father. Frazier Stone had never been a likable man, and his disdain for his son had begun when he left the army to become a teacher. According to the retired colonel, the stupidity of the choice should prove that he wasn't qualified to be a teacher. The decision to give up teaching to become a songwriter was even more insane, and the divorce ended all communications between father and son.

John Ryan was relaxed, his mind clear. The internal engine that he had learned would drive him on stage had begun to turn over. It was going to be a good night. When Cade Wilhite opened the door, he was ready.

"The guys are ready as soon as the lights go down. You've got about seven minutes." He turned to leave and then turned back and flashed a mischievous smile. "Oh, don't let anything throw you. Larry got kind of excited by the equipment here and played around with a few new effects." The door closed, leaving the singer with a question on his lips.

When Albemarle Moultrie designed the renovations for the club, she brought in a theatrical designer from Charleston to do the lighting. The board had thirty dimmers controlling more than a hundred lighting instruments including Fresnels. Ellipsoidals, moving lights capable of giving laser effects and a number of other looks. The sound system also incorporated state-of-the-art technology. It was a major step up.

At eight o'clock the lights in the club dimmed to less than half their intensity, and the bandstand went dark. In no longer than it took Bobby Hopwood to get to his position behind the drums, the first rhythmic straight-eight beat captured the crowd's attention.

Conversation among the patrons had centered around the normal things people talk about in a bar interspersed with comments about the new decor, but the electricity of the dim lights, the dark bandstand and the sonorous beat of the drums created an anticipation that was unfamiliar to the regulars. Bubba Country had changed since the doors last closed.

The lights on the stand came up with the opening bass line of *Forty Miles of Bad Road*, washing the stage in a dark blue hue that left the band members barely perceptible, shadowy silhouettes. The arrangement of the music caught the crowd by surprise and conversation subsided.

John Ryan Stone stood in the small area just off stage and watched as the sound became more intense. Son Cochran did a bass run that generated applause. No one was dancing; everyone was fastened to the music and drawn into aura of the lighting. From where he stood, John Ryan could only see Bobby Hopwood, but the whole atmosphere was charged.

The band began to back off as Son did a bass segue into the bottom line of *Fever* and went to silence leaving Cochran's bass line and Mickey's snapping fingers the only sounds to be heard. The stage was in darkness, the bass line hypnotic. John Ryan could not see it from where he was standing, but one pencil-point shaft of intense, white light came up slowly, shinning straight down on the Gibson ES, resting in its stand in the front center of the stage.

"Ladies and Gentlemen, from your own State of South Carolina and the recording studios of Nashville, Tennessee, John Ryan Stone." Larry Foster's voice boomed out the introduction and John Ryan moved into view of the audience to resounding applause, hoops and hollers. The light on the guitar caught him by surprise as he stepped onto the stage. He slipped the guitar strap over his head and felt his rugged and resonant voice bring in the crowd.

The whole set became an intimate exchange between the audience, John Ryan and the band. The singer could feel them pulling him along, trying to eliminate the distance and become a part of the music and the man. John Ryan was comfortable, but moldering in the back of his mind was the anxious anticipation of the final song on the play list that Larry Foster had given him. It would be the first time he had done a song he wrote in front of a live audience. It wasn't only that he had to perform it, but he also had to introduce it. Talking to an audience did not come natural to him. He had put several introductions together but they all sounded stilted or self-serving. Larry said keep it simple, and that's what he decided to do. No planning.

When the time came and the applause from the previous number dissipated, he leaned into the mike, adjusting it slightly with his right hand and began to speak to the audience in the coarse and deep voice they had become accustomed to.

"I'm not sure either one of us is ready for this." He turned to the band. "Are you ready for this?" They grinned, enjoying the discomfort John Ryan was experiencing, letting him know there was no turning back. Facing the audience and smiling, which allowed the lights to pick up the white teeth and his blue eyes, he kept it simple.

"This is a song I lived a few times and finally took time to write down. It's on our first album which will be released..." he paused, shrugged his shoulders, "sometime."

There was a quiet, humorous reaction that faded when they heard the first notes of the intro. As he listened to the opening and played soft rhythm behind the main players, John Ryan ran the pictures that the lyrics summoned up in his mind. By the time the first words came out of his mouth, the bar was a reality, as were the half-filled glasses on the table and the woman sitting across from him.

> *Your love is gone,*
> *and you sit all alone,*
> *The worst thing in sight*
> *is to spend one lonely night.*

After the song ended and the last note had faded, the crowd broke into applause. John Ryan could hear exclamations, but most of them were indiscernible. It continued longer than the responses to any of the other songs he had performed. He bowed his head in appreciation and realized that the women were as enthusiastic as the men. Given the nature of the lyric that was surprising. It had been a concern of Don Hendrickson's. As the band revved up his exit music and he started off stage, the response increased. It threw him into a quandary as to whether he should return to the mike, take another bow or just leave the stage. Larry Foster, standing off stage, signaled him to exit.

Once out of sight, he began to shake; but it was with adrenaline, not fear. He wished Kate had been there, but her schedule made it impossible; she would be coming on Saturday. That thought aside, he reveled in the moment. They liked the song.

Ricky Trocatta liked to think of himself as a loose canon; it made him feel dangerous. As he watched John Ryan Stone leave the stage, he knew that on this occasion he was, indeed, a loose canon, acting on his own with no authority from anyone. That was dangerous. Philip Barnessa had let him know in no uncertain terms that he had fucked up. The call had left him anxious to the point he thought he might throw up. The man had made him feel like a two-bit punk. To Ricky Trocatta that was the worst thing anyone could do.

He hadn't been in Myrtle Beach long; just long enough to extort a number of small beer-bar club owners into booking marginal Top 40 bands he brought down from clubs in New Jersey. He had also built a reputation among those small club owners that he was not to be taken lightly. His business had never before extended into Bubba Moultrie's territory—he didn't even know the man—but now this country boy was trying to destroy everything he had created. It wouldn't happen. He thought maybe just showing up for opening night with a little muscle would be enough. If that didn't work, there wouldn't be a club for very long.

Bubba Moultrie was as thrilled as John Ryan Stone. As far as he was concerned, he had just debuted the future of country music. When the singer sang *One Lonely Night*, and he saw the crowd and Albamarle pick up on the heat in the lyrics, he had no doubt that this man could add a new dimension to country music lyrics.

As the house lights were raised a notch, Bubba noticed two men sitting at a table in the back of the club near the entrance. He recognized Ricky Trocatta, not by name but as the slippery, northeastern, low-life he had often seen on The Strand, the same man, he was sure, who had been foolish enough to try to intimidate him. Bubba Moultrie wasn't one to look for trouble, but when it came to him—particularly in his own place—he handled it. The sleazeball looked like trouble.

Demonde Smalls, black as onyx, six feet five inches tall, two hundred and sixty-eight pounds and former University of South Carolina, all-conference defensive end, had worked for Bubba Moultrie since he left college three years before. He had made a stab at the pros, but after ripping up a knee in pre-training camp drills, had never been given a legitimate shot. With no degree and no pro career in the offing, 'bouncing' on The Strand appeared to be the best of the few options he had left. He had ambitions. Construction work or selling cars were not two of them. Bubba had welcomed him with open arms, sent Demonde to bar-tending school and given him the title of Bar Manager. The two men developed an almost brotherly relationship. In Demonde Smalls' mind, it was a start.

When Demonde saw the look on his boss's face, he began to smile.

"Time to rock and roll?" he asked when Bubba reached him.

"Maybe. Grab a coupla rolls of quarters. Probably won't need 'em, but what the hell." Bubba grinned.

"The two greaseballs at the table in the corner?" Smalls asked as he opened the box under the cash register and removed two coin rolls.

"Don't look like they belong in our place to me. Do they to you?"

"Ain't really dressed for it," Demonde said with a flash of teeth. "And we gotta keep the standards up, don't we? Got a classy club now; gotta live up to it."

"Let's go have a chat." As they approached the two men sitting at the table, Demonde put on the game face that opposing linemen and quarterbacks had feared during his playing days.

Ricky Trocatta and his companion watched as the two men made their way in their direction. It was his guess that Bubba Moultrie had spotted them and sent two bouncers to get rid of them. He wasn't sure how it would go down; he didn't have a plan, but at least Bubba would know he wasn't forgotten.

Bubba put on his best good ol' country boy smile. "How ya'll doin'?" he said as he and Demonde reached the table. "Enjoy the show?"

"We're doing just fine," the wiry, dark-haired man answered. He looked up at the huge black man who wore the coldest expression he had ever seen.

"Ya'll from around here?" Moultrie asked.

"We're just here," the man said. "Why?"

"Just wondered. You don't look like this would be your kind of place. The way you're dressed and all."

"That what your boss said?" The man smiled.

"My boss?" Bubba looked at Demonde.

"The one with the funny name. What is it? Bubba something?" Ricky Trocatta looked at his partner and laughed. "Hell of a name, ain't it, Tony?"

"Now how in hell could I have guessed his name was Tony?" Bubba asked, the smile still on his face.

"You finished your comedy routine, pal?" A fire shown in Ricky Trocatta's eyes. "Just tell that wood hook boss of yours that Ricky Trocatta ain't forgot what he did. I warned him against bookin' this hillbilly he's got playin' here tonight, and he chose not to listen. Then he ran off a friend of mine. Just tell him I can't guarantee what might happen from here on out."

"Well now, I'll tell him, Mr. Terracotta, or whatever the hell your name is, but for right now, I think you might want to let us see you gentlemen to the door. You know, you don't look like you're enjoyin' that hillbilly all that much anyway."

The bruiser sitting next to Trocatta started to get up, but Demonde put his left hand on the man's shoulder and squeezed, not only putting the man named Tony back in his seat, but also sending pain down his arm into his fingers. "Ya'll want to come with us now?" he said.

Trocatta got up staring at Bubba Moultrie, and the four men proceeded out through the door. As soon as they were in the parking lot, as if on a prearranged cue, Bubba and Demonde took the two men by the elbow.

"Where are you parked?" Demonde asked.

"We can find it," the man named Tony answered. The pressure on his elbow didn't lessen. He looked at the black man and made the smart decision. "That red Cadillac over there."

A police car sat with parking lights on near the entrance of the club, but the two cops inside took no notice of the men walking past them.

Three feet from the red Cadillac, Ricky Trocatta made his big mistake. He couldn't let it lie. It was the second time in a week that he had been made to feel like a punk.

"You tell your boss it ain't over. He might wake up some morning to find he ain't got nothin' but a pile of ashes to open up." The words were hardly out of his mouth when he felt himself turned around and smashed against the door of the car so hard that he wondered if his back were broken. On cue, Demonde had picked up Trocatta's partner and slammed him across the hood with such force that his face sent spiderweb cracks across the wind-

195

shield. When he lifted the man to repeat the action, he saw the eyes rolled back, the nose twisted sideways and a large gash above the right eyebrow exposing the bone. Even if his eyes had been functional, he would have been blinded by the blood gushing from the wound.

Bubba pulled Ricky Trocatta to his feet and threw him back against the door. Holding him up against the car, he put his face so close he could smell fear in the breath of the smaller man.

"That's the second and last time you've threatened me." Ricky Trocatta's eyes widened in panicked recognition. "I told you the first time, you don't tell me who I can book. And I'll tell you somethin' else, snake-spit: I don't think that Barnessa fella sent you over here tonight; he's too smart for that. I think you come on your own. That ain't smart. I don't think he knows shit about your bein' over here. It's a bush-league move and those guys don't do that far as I know. I got a mind to call him and tell him what a coupla candy-asses he's got workin' for him down here." Moultrie could feel the tense reaction at his last words and knew he was right. "You ain't got no place down here, boy; and after I get through tomorrow, even them little juke joints you been workin' won't let you in the door. Don't," Bubba yelled, "don't ever come on this property or threaten me again or you'll find yourself neck-deep in alligators. As of this moment your ass don't exist; and if you ever hope to have a pleasant day again, you'd better keep it that way." He loosened his grip and let Trocatta slide down to his knees. He turned to look at the other man lying across the hood of the car, smiled at Demonde and looked back at Trocatta who was trying to get to his feet. "You better get that windshield fixed; you might get a ticket," he said.

Before they went back into the club, they watched the red Cadillac slowly making its way toward the exit. Bubba walked over to the police car and leaned in the open window.

"You boys havin' some fun?" the cop behind the wheel asked with a smile on his face.

"A little. Just cleanin' house. Otey, you might want to check that red Cadillac leavin' the lot. I think its got a broken window, might be unsafe to drive."

The policeman grinned and started the engine. "You got it, Bubba. Anything else?"

"Never can tell what you might find in that car; they was actin' mighty strange."

"No problem. I'm sure we'll find somethin'." The blue lights went on before they exited the parking lot.

"Damn! Them blue lights flashin' is a fearsome sight, ain't it Dee?"

"Fearsome," Demonde said. "Specially when Otey Bivins turns 'em on."

"Let's go listen to some more of that music," Bubba said as they went through the door.

Bubba Moultrie said nothing to anyone about the confrontation; it was over until next time, if there was a next time. If that happened, he would handle it again. For the last time.

On Saturday morning John Ryan awoke before dawn. Bubba Moultrie had provided beach front rooms for the band, and although the accommodations were not as luxurious as some like The Ocean Forest, they were on the beach. Waking to the soft, rhythmical sound of the surf against the sand made him aware of how much he missed living near the ocean. Nashville was another world and far away. The beach had been a great part of his youth, that youth that everyone remembers as better than it was.

By the time the motel coffee-maker had produced its first pot of the day, the sun was casting its peremptory golden glow across the watery horizon. John Ryan filled his cup and went out on the balcony to see the sunrise. Bracing his bare feet against the railing, he leaned back in his chair and watched the ocean performing its never-ending exercise as the gulls swept the shoreline in search of food left behind by the receding breakers. It was, in his mind, about as perfect as it could be.

He was exhilarated with the reception the band had received and even more with the crowd's enthusiasm for *One Lonely Night*. It was the only one of his songs they had done thus far, but they were scheduled to introduce two more: *I Can't Stand the Silence Anymore* and *How Can I Make You Love Me Tomorrow*.

It was going to be a big day in more ways than one, he thought as the sun came fully above the horizon. Kate was to arrive from New York at noon, and there was a slim possibility that his father might come to see him play though he felt the chance of Frank Sinatra coming was better. He had called Frazier Stone the day before and invited him to the beach. There was some reluctance to even discuss it at first; however, after a bit of verbal sparring. Frazier finally conceded that if he could find someone to make the three and a half hour drive with him, he might come, but not to count on it. Even a consideration was more than John Ryan had expected.

There were a lot of concerns that went beyond Kate's arrival. The thought of introducing Kate to his father, should he show up, was not the least of them. In their conversation, neither he nor Frazier had mentioned Jenifer, but John Ryan knew that the breakup of his marriage was still a sore point. He also knew Frazier would be hard-pressed to hide his feelings.

There were other things, things that went beyond personal matters. Son Cochran had spoken to him about Paul Crockett's behavior. It had become more and more erratic. Son attributed it to an increase in his use of pills—Speckled Birds, Bennies, Dexies and Simcos. Pills that lifted him, others to calm him down, and some just to maintain a ragged form of sanity. Everyone in the band was aware he used, so had most of them when the need arose. The problem with Paul was that he needed them to function. Son—more than anyone else—knew that using just to maintain was a dead end road. The harmonica player was so thin that he could almost disappear behind a mike stand, and there was nothing behind his eyes. The thought of making a change in the band at this point was not something the singer even wanted to consider. Life was good; he didn't want to jeopardize that.

Lou Molinaro was vacationing in Jamaica with his wife, compliments of Giannini Tedesco for services rendered. It was also to get him out of New York for a couple of weeks until the heat generated by some of those services cooled down. Molinaro was not a sun-worshipper; consequently, while his wife and youngest daughter, a law student at Temple University, languished on the beach, he spent his time wandering Kingston or driving over to Ocho Rios. He enjoyed the shops, drinking rum in small bars, and listening to those conversations he could understand.

On one of those sojourns into downtown Kingston, he was drawn into a record store by an unfamiliar music blaring from speakers mounted above the rickety shop's doors. The music had a unique rhythm, and though he was not an expert on commercial music, he was struck by the hypnotic quality of the beat. If it was as different as he thought it to be, it might be salable. The clerk in the store told him it was called Reggae, the music of the Rastafarian Movement, a religion that worshipped Haille Selassee, the Emperor of Ethiopia, as the embodiment of The Second Coming, all of which had no meaning or value to Lou Molinaro.

Looking through the bins of albums, he saw covers showing fierce-looking men with long hair worn in what the clerk told him were dreadlocks. There was anger and hatred in their faces. Lou Molinaro could recognize an opportunity when he saw one. He could imagine how the angry *melognena* living back home in Harlem or Watts in L.A. would connect with it. He decided to pick up a few albums and take them back with him; Phil or Maury might be interested. If they were, it might make him some money.

Flipping through one disorganized bin, his eyes widened and his jaw dropped. The picture of the lean, blue-eyed singer on the cover was unfamiliar, but the name had been the primary subject of conversation and planning for months. John Ryan Stone. From everything he had heard in New York, the record was two weeks away from release; there was no logical reason that he should see it in a bin in Kingston, Jamaica. He bought the album and left the store, forgetting all about the new sound and the momentary visions of money that had danced through his imagination.

Out of the store, Molinaro floored the rented Mercedes and headed back to the villa. He had left New York amidst mild celebration that pressure had finally been applied to Bernie Greshem, that the future of the organization's interest in Trayhorn could only grow. Ownership of John Ryan Stone was the first step in that process, he had been told, and unless there was something he wasn't privy to or didn't understand, someone had screwed up. Lou Molinaro could imagine the New York reaction to the news.

He wasn't sure who to call. Giannini would be hard to reach on the weekend, and he didn't want to be the one to break the news to him anyway. Philip was out. They had been friends for years. Their wives had been like sisters when they both lived in Philly. Their kids had spent their childhood's together, but that was all before Philip and his first wife split, and Lou and his family had moved to New York. Unless there had been a change in strategy, Philip was obviously the one who had fucked up. If that were true, Tedesco would not appreciate his being warned. Maury Friedman was the logical choice to call though he, too, would be difficult to reach. Maury could handle either of the others, he thought.

Kate Belden held John Ryan's hand as they walked along the beach. The sun provided a warm welcome to the South, and it was a joy for her to be in shorts instead of the workaday clothing of her life in New York. Flight from the city had become a gift that she looked forward to. John Ryan was certainly a major portion of that gift. It amused her to think that in all of her years in Indiana, Chicago and New York, she had never thought of the South as being anything other than backward, slow and geographically unkempt. *Tobacco Road.* Now she saw it as soft, clean, friendly and warm. It offered most of what the other areas did but at a distance. If one wanted crowds, noise and neon, they were there, but they had to be sought out. It was a choice to be among those things rather than having no alternative. She watched the busy-body sandpipers following the receding foam of the surf, picking up what sustenance they could find then scurrying back to avoid the next mild surge of the sea. Their pace and focus was reminiscent of the streets of New York. Watching the small birds, she didn't miss the city at all.

"A penny?" John Ryan asked.

"Just thinking about how latitude affects the attitude," she said.

"Wow!" He laughed. "Deep thinking, Belden. So how is the latitude affecting you?"

"I think I am falling in love with your part of the country."

"It's a good place." John Ryan believed that. As most young people do, he had looked forward to getting out and seeing the world, but with all the travel he had in college and in the army, he had found nothing better or more appealing than that section of the country in which he had grown up.

"Do you think you'll stay here? In the South, I mean?" she asked.

"I don't see any reason to leave. I guess I'm just a small town boy, and even the cities down here are small towns. At least for the time being."

"That will change."

"I know, but the kicker is all you have to do is move farther out."

"What about your career? I think you know it's going to happen. That could cause some major changes. It might even get bigger than you."

"I sure as hell don't want a career to determine what kind of man I am or am going to be or how I'm going to live the rest of my life."

"That would be a tough one to pull off, if it's even possible."

"It's been done. If it can't be, maybe I'll give it up."

There were few people on their section of the beach. The tide was out and the flat width of sand allowed one to feel unanchored and without restriction, to float without being in the water, to let all semblance of propriety and privacy hang in the balance.

"What else would you do?" Kate asked.

"I don't know. Write books that would shock the water out of people." He grinned. "If I could think of something that would shock the water out of people."

"I think some of your lyrics might do that," she laughed.

"Maybe. I could probably get my old job back."

Kate looked at him askance. "I don't think so."

"What do you think I should do?"

"I don't know what to think. Do you really want this? That question keeps coming back to me."

"For the moment it seems good. It's not uncomfortable. I don't know about the performing part. I'm smart enough to see I could get a little hyper about that, get swept along by it, but I still love the idea of writing songs. I don't think I'll ever stop doing that."

"What about the money? Performing pays better."

"I don't need to be rich; I just need enough."

"Easy to say now; you haven't had it yet. Eventually, someday, you're going to have to decide what you want to be for the rest of your life."

"Maybe. But 'til then, I'll just enjoy walkin' along the beach holdin' your hand and not worryin' about what has been, what is or what can be."

"Sounds good to me," she said and squeezed his hand.

When they returned to their room, the message light on the phone was flashing.

"Uh-oh," he said. "Do we want to be disturbed?"

"How long can it take?"

John Ryan smiled at her. "Not long. You can bet on that."

"Promise?"

"Promise," he said as he dialed the motel operator.

"Yes, Mr. Stone. I have a message for you to call a Mr. Frazier Stone at The Ocean Forest. Would you like me to dial that for you?"

"No ma'am. I'll do it." Frazier's actually being in Myrtle Beach was a shock he hadn't expected. "Can you give me the number there?"

"Surely." As he hung up the phone, he shook his head.

"Wow."

"Wow?" Kate was pouring a glass of Chalk Hill Chardonnay from a bottle John Ryan had iced before he picked her up at the airport.

"Frazier's here." He stood perplexed.

"He came?" There was a broad smile on her face. John Ryan had mentioned the invitation but assured her his father would not come. "That's wonderful."

"I can't believe he actually came."

"Are you going to have dinner with him?"

"He hasn't asked." John Ryan said with a smirk.

"Smart mouth."

"Truthfully? I don't know." And he didn't. He wasn't sure how to handle it. Now that his father was in town, he found himself questioning why he had asked him to come. He had a suspicion that he might have been feeling smug when he made the call. Perhaps he hadn't really changed.

Kate came to him and put her arms around his waist, resting her head on his chest.

"I think you should. I'll be all right."

"If I go, you'll go with me."

"Do you think that's wise? I mean...."

"I've never been wise."

"I don't have any choice?"

He looked down into her face. "No choice at all, but I guess I'd better check the weather," he said as he went to the phone.

"Frazier Stone," the voice on the other end of the line said.

"This is quite a surprise," John Ryan replied.

"You asked me to come. I'm here."

"Who came with you?"

"Hannah."

"Han?" Hannah DeLoache had been Frazier Stone's housekeeper since John Ryan was a child. When his mother left, Hannah filled in admirably.

"I don't feel safe driving that far by myself anymore." It was an admission he had never expected to hear Frazier Stone make. It was said with chagrin, but it was an admission.

"Will she be able to get into the place where you're performing?" his father asked.

"Of course. Why shouldn't she? I'm happy she came."

"I wouldn't want her to be embarrassed."

"Frazier, Hannah is not going to be embarrassed. If she can't go with me wherever I go, then I won't go either. Things have changed over the years, you know."

"I know, but..."

"No 'buts'. She goes. I want to take both of you out to dinner before the show. I have to be at the club at eight, but there's no point in your being there before ten of nine unless you just want to go."

"You'll have to pick the place," he said as if he were giving an order, reestablishing his authority. "It's been a long time since I've been up here."

" I know. I'll pick up at six. And Frazier, I'll have a lady with me." There was silence. "She works for the record company that's putting out my record. You'll like her. She thinks I'm a little crazy, too." It was a weak attempt at humor, but Frazier didn't bite.

"Frazier? I'm pleased you came, and I'm glad you brought Hannah with you." He waited for a reply, but there wasn't one. "I'll pick you up at the door at six sharp."

"Six sharp."

When he hung up the phone, John Ryan turned to Kate.

"Well, that was certainly enlightening. I'm still not sure why he came."

"He came. That's something."

"Do you know what?" he asked, taking her into his arms.

"What?"

"I'm not even going to think about that right now."

"You have something better in mind?"

"Much better." He put his lips to hers and felt the softness of her.

Kate watched John Ryan as he undressed. He moved with grace in even the smallest actions. The smooth texture of his skin was complimented by the coarseness of his hair and magnified the character lines in his face. Just seeing him standing naked before her created an internal heat that she felt was visible. It made her flush even more. He came to her and they made love, faster and more energized than they had in Savannah or Nashville. It seemed a long time since they had experienced the closeness of their bodies even though it had been less than a week.

At six o'clock sharp John Ryan and Kate pulled into the registration parking area at The Ocean Forest. He had done his best to prepare Kate for the meeting; but, in truth, it was impossible. He told her about Frazier's background, the military demeanor, his lack of compassion or compromise, the love of golf, his disapproval of the divorce from Jenifer, the stormy relationships, and Hannah DeLoache's long history with the family. It was a hurried thumbnail sketch that left her wary and unsettled, but she did her best not to let it show, assuring him that everything would go smoothly and that she would follow his lead. John Ryan was on edge.

Frazier Stone, dressed immaculately in sharply-creased pearl-grey slacks, a white shirt, a maroon, paisley tie with a matching handkerchief tucked neatly in the pocket of his blue blazer, was waiting in the lobby. His black shoes were highly polished. Hannah DeLoache, standing with him, was dressed as if she might be his date. Actually, John Ryan thought as he spotted them, they made a handsome couple. Hannah's face broke into a wide smile when she saw John Ryan and Kate come through the door. There was no hesitation in Hannah DeLoache; she opened her arms and took him in.

"John Ryan. Oh, John Ryan," she said happily as she hugged him hard.

"Han," he said squeezing her. "I'm so glad you came."

Frazier Stone had not had a chance to respond to Kate and John Ryan's entrance. When he did, it was not unpleasant.

"John Ryan," he said. And then as if he didn't know what else to say, "You look better than last time."

"Frazier, Hannah, this is Kate Belden. Kate, this is my family, the important part."

"I'm very pleased to meet you both," Kate said.

John Ryan took them to dinner at The Rice Planter's, a native favorite. There was small talk in the car on the way to the restaurant, but nothing of any significance; however, once they were seated, the menu's presented and the drink orders taken, John Ryan felt ill-at-ease. It was no particular surprise that without grousing, criticizing or being hurtfully sarcastic to each other, he and his father had little in common and even less to talk about. He knew Frazier was experiencing the same discomfort.

"How was the trip?" he asked.

"Long," Frazier answered, "There have been a lot of changes since I was up this way."

"I enjoyed it," Hannah DeLoache added. "I did most of the driving, and the Colonel did most of the sight-seeing. Sure is good to get away from Seabrook Island and see something new."

During this exchange John Ryan watched Frazier. He could see his mind working, trying to formulate something to ask.

"Tell me about what you do," Frazier said.

"I pretend to work and they pretend to pay me," John Ryan answered, a humorous tack as a relief from the formal tension they were all experiencing.

"I'd like to know."

"I'd like to hear too," Hannah DeLoache added.

John Ryan began with what he had been doing musically before the meeting with Don Hendrickson and explained everything that had occurred since. He included Kate in the conversation, sometimes asking her questions about details that he could have explained himself, allowing her to establish her position as an integral part to all that had happened. The explanation lasted throughout dinner, with Frazier and Hannah DeLoache asking questions and making comments and John Ryan and Kate doing their best to reply.

"You are getting paid," Frazier said to John Ryan when the questions about his work and the brief history of his success had run out.

"Yes. I am getting paid. And very well."

"It's going to get much better," Kate added. "If all goes as planned, John Ryan could wind up financially secure for life in a very short time."

"Who handles the money?" John Ryan shook his head and smiled at Frazier's bluntness.

"Not me. That ought to relieve you," he said. "Right now Kate does. She's my manager and my agent for the moment."

"As things progress," Kate continued," there will probably be a number of people involved, but I will do everything in my power to assure that those involved are reliable."

"Do you trust her?" Frazier asked John Ryan. He had an impish look on his face.

"Damn, Frazier! You said something funny." John Ryan laughed. Hannah and Kate were laughing too. Frazier joined in with an embarrassed chuckle.

"Kate," John Ryan said, "this might be the first time Frazier and I have laughed together in twenty years."

With that statement the evening entered a comfort zone of sorts. Frazier and Hannah asked about Kate's background, how she got in the business and what her duties were. She told them about her developing admiration for the South and the company's expectations for John Ryan. If anyone was left out of the conversation, it was John Ryan himself. He listened with amusement at the merging of the two sides of his life.

Bubba Moultrie had reserved a table for Kate, Frazier Stone and Hannah DeLoache that allowed an unobstructed view of the stage. The place was already packed when they arrived, and the influx of people didn't stop even when Frazier had decided that there wasn't room for another body. It had been a long time since he had been in a night club, and he had never been in a place like Bubba Country. He was surprised that the crowd was such a diverse mixture of types. His assumption was that it would be young rednecks dressed in jeans, and there were some of those, but the majority appeared to be nice if casually-dressed men and women who ranged in age from their mid-twenties to late forties.

The club itself was another surprise. Although he wasn't knowledgeable about country music or the places it was played, Frazier Stone had expected something quite different. He had read about places with chicken-wire stretched across the bandstand imprisoning the performers while protecting them from flying beer bottles, and a number of other things that on the way up made him wonder why he was making the trip at all. As soon as he saw the interior of the club, his opinions of what his son was doing began to change.

The real revelation came as he sat waiting for the set to begin. He began to focus on the conversations of the people seated and standing around them. If Frazier Stone was surprised at where John Ryan was working and what Kate Belden had to say about his future, he was nothing less than astounded to hear what the patrons of the club were saying about him. They had come specifically to hear John Ryan Stone. The accolades seemed endless; and as the lights dimmed and the band's intro music began, despite his skepticism, Frazier Stone felt his heart beating hard in his chest.

It was a set that validated all of the work, doubts, hopes and dreams that had driven John Ryan Stone since he had made the decision to make music his work. From the opening shaft of light on the Gibson guitar to the closing number, *I Can't Stand the Silence Anymore*, which elicited a deafening response, everything was as perfect as the group could make it. The harmonies from Mickey, Howie and Red were tight, John Ryan's voice strong, his repartee' glib, funny, seductive and on the mark.

After John Ryan had exited the stage, Frazier Stone became aware of Kate Belden and Hannah DeLoache watching him. The two women had shared a few brief comments during the set, but Frazier had said nothing. Now that the lights had come up a few degrees, he was inspired to say something, felt awkward not saying anything, but the words weren't there.

"Well, Colonel, what did you think?" Hannah DeLoache asked, her face split with the widest smile her mouth could make.

"The people seem to like him."

"That's all?"

"Well, I'm not an expert on this kind of music, but..." Frazier Stone paused as if looking for an answer.

"But what?" Hannah would not let him off the hook.

"But he seems to do what he does very well. I'm glad I came."

"Well, then let's go tell him," she said getting our of her chair.

"Good idea," Kate said under her breath.

Lou Molinaro sat up all night trying without success to reach Maury Friedman. In desperation he even tried to call Giannini Tedesco. The whole night was maddeningly frustrating. He was aware that opportunities such as the one that lay before him did not present themselves very often, and every favor was worth its weight in gold. Literally. He didn't intend to let this one slip through his fingers; it might even save his life someday.

After several more attempts early Sunday morning, he got into the Mercedes and drove back to the record shop. Knowing how the Stone album found its way to Kingston, Jamaica, and where it had come from would be invaluable to Tedesco. Lou Molinaro had been made in the family long enough to know every nuance of the business and the personalities of everyone involved. They were not very different; the organization didn't breed individuals.

Although the clerk was initially put off by the American's curiosity, it took only American dollars for Molinaro to get the information he wanted. The albums were purchased from a distributor right there in Kingston. The store had received them a week before, but the American was the only customer who had bought one. It would only begin to sell in Jamaica when it began to sell in the States, he said.

"This I don't understand," Molinaro said. "You stock somethin' you don't know you can sell?"

"Sometimes, mon, you got to buy sometin' to get sometin' else, you know. Dat's de way it work down here." Not only here, Lou thought.

"Who'd you get 'em from?"

The clerk looked at him suspiciously. "Why you need to know all dis?"

"I...uh...I'm in the business, and I never heard of this guy Stone before. That's all. I might want to pick up some myself. He ain't bad."

"Hardtime Danny Steele," the man said sullenly.

"He here in Kingston?"

"Yeah. Right down dere on Duval Street. Blue Mountain Records." He caught himself and stopped talking. Molinaro had seen the look before and knew the reason. The man had let something slip. There was fear in his eyes.

"Thanks," he said as he left the shop.

Out on the street, he paused and wiped the perspiration from his face. Even though it was still morning, the Guyabera he was wearing was soaked through. The heat was intense, but he suspected the situation and lack of sleep was as responsible for his body temperature as the Jamaican sun. He had a street map the car rental agency had given him. It was small, poorly printed and difficult to read. Some of the streets on the route he had chosen to Duval Street were too narrow for the big Mercedes to navigate. After getting lost, becoming frustrated in his attempts to get directions, and passing the building he was looking for twice without recognizing it, he finally pulled to a stop in front of Blue Mountain Records.

The building was actually little more than a wooden, double garage. It was deserted, which was a disappointment; he wanted to ask Hardtime Danny Steele some questions. He considered waiting until someone showed, then remembered it was Sunday. Molinaro got out of the car and went to the lone window in the side of the building. It was difficult to see inside; only dim shadows of machinery and what looked like an office in one corner were visible. One thing was obvious, if the place turned out to be a problem, it could be burned to ground in minutes. He was left with nothing to do except go back to the villa and continue trying to reach New York.

At two-thirty in the afternoon, Maury Friedman finally answered his phone.

"Yes?"

"Maury, it's Lou."

"Lou? Why are you calling me here? This is my home. You know better." His voice was impatient and perturbed, making his caller feel like an unwelcome cousin or a chastised child. "I thought you were in Jamaica."

"I am."

"You're calling me from Jamaica?" The man must be in trouble, he thought, which heightened his anger.

"Maury, listen to me. I think there's a problem. I'm not gonna call you at home for nothin'. You think I'm gonna call you at home for nothin' important? How many times I ever call you at home before, huh?" He sounded insulted.

"No, Lou. I'm sorry. What's the problem?"

"You know what I bought in a record store down here yesterday?" God, the man is playing guessing games, Friedman said under his breath.

"No, Lou, I don't." He had to have these people; he needed them, but he hated dealing with them even if they were a part of his family. Especially at his home. That was a separate life.

"I bought—You listenin', Maury?—I bought a record album by John Ryan Stone. A Trayhorn record album by John Ryan Stone." There was silence on the other end of the line.

"Jesus H. Christ." Friedman was stunned. "You bought it in a record store? It isn't supposed to be out for two weeks." It didn't make any sense. It had to be Barnessa; that's where the counterfeits were being pressed. Hell, he had arranged for the masters himself. The plan was bad and unmanageable to begin with, and now it was all coming apart as he had suspected it would in one way or another, but not this way. "Tell me the whole story, Lou. Everything you know. Don't leave anything out. I've got to relay this to Giannini, and I don't want to make any mistakes."

Lou Molinaro smiled. He had been right. Maury Friedman was indebted. He had cracked the ice and reduced the distance between him and his superior. He told his story beginning with the fact that he didn't like to lie on the beach like his wife and daughter. That was the reason he was wandering around Kingston, how he heard a new sound, and, though he wasn't an expert, thought it was worth checking out. He went on about going into the record store, looking through the bins and seeing the Stone album. He knew it didn't add up, wasn't right; so he started trying to call the day before and just got through. He also told Friedman about going back to the store and questioning the clerk, thought the information might be valuable. When Maury agreed, he told him how the store got the product—about Hardtime Danny Steele and Blue Mountain records—how many copies the store had and that the only one they had sold was the one he bought. When he was finished, there was a quiet pause before Maury Friedman spoke.

"Lou, are you still at the villa?"

"Yeah. We're supposed to leave tomorrow."

"I don't want you to leave until you hear from me. Stay there. I've got to make some calls. I'll get back to you. Give me your number." Friedman wrote down the number and hung up the phone. He didn't thank Lou Molinaro or say 'good-bye'.

Friedman went to the bar and poured two jiggers—he always measured—of Glenfiddich Single Malt Scotch over the two ice cubes he had put in the short crystal glass before Molinaro's call. He took a small sip. He was furious. Business wasn't supposed to be done here, in this place. The lavish Park Avenue apartment was home, and home was not a place for business. This was his refuge, his sanctuary, separated from all the dross and people that provided it. Lou Molinaro's information was welcome; his intrusion on this place was not.

Tedesco had to be informed. There was no decision to be made there, but he also had to be able to answer the questions that he knew would arise. The whole relationship with Trayhorn and the power the family had there rested with him as far as Giannini was concerned. Whatever happened was his responsibility in one way or another, the solution his to handle.

The possible explanations were not numerous, but they each had to be considered. Philip Barnessa might have run extra, unaccounted for copies to distribute on his own, getting a jump on the market and pocketing a hundred percent of that money for himself. Not likely. Philip was not that dumb. He wasn't smart by any means—as far as Friedman was concerned none of them were—but the man had been in the business too long and knew the penalties for trying to pull off something like that. Possible but not likely.

Jamie Greshem had decided on his own to test the market early. But why Jamaica? That choice would be too ironic and had no logic at all. Besides, Jack Trekorian would have known if anything had been shipped and would have told him. That was the least likely scenario.

Hardtime Danny Steele. He had to be the key. He must have done an extra run for himself—albums even Barnessa didn't know about—and distributed them on his own without concern for release dates or being discovered down in his own area. The immediate problem, as Maury saw it, was how far that area extended. He went over the possibilities again, and that was the only one that had any credibility at all.

It was not only a stroke of luck that Lou Molinaro had walked into the record store in Kingston, Jamaica, but it was even more fortunate that he was still there to handle the situation if anything needed to be done. Hardtime Danny Steele was in for a hard time, Maury thought.

He picked up the phone and dialed Giannini Tedesco. The Jamaican situation had to be taken care of first. Friedman always took things one step at a time. Sooner or later, however, Philip Barnessa and ultimately Bernie Greshem would have to be confronted if anything were to be salvaged out of the mess haste, mismanagement and lack of control had created. Now he was left to pick up the pieces.

The band was scheduled to check out of the hotel and leave for Charlotte, North Carolina at four o'clock on Sunday afternoon. John Ryan and Kate had taken Frazier and Hannah DeLoache to breakfast and put them back on the road to Seabrook Island. Like the previous evening, the meal had gone as smoothly as could be expected.

Before he got into the car, Frazier congratulated John Ryan and made the comment that at least now they had something to talk about. The tension between the two men was not resolved, but they both knew that a step toward the resolution of their animosity had been made.

Kate's flight back to New York was scheduled to leave at two forty-five. Since breakfast had stretched until almost noon and since she had anticipated that possibility and put her bag in the car John Ryan had rented, they decided to go directly to the airport and have a drink while they waited for her plane.

As they drove north on Route 17, Kate realized that she was experiencing the same emotional turmoil that had begun when she left Nashville. Her stay in South Carolina had been too brief. Between the hours at the club and Frazier's appearance, there had been little time for talk. Kate found herself fighting the frustration and anxiety of being in a relationship with no definition or parameters. There were too many obstacles for her to move forward on faith alone. She was in New York, and he was in Nashville or on the road. They had never spoken about the future or if there was a future for them. She did know that she couldn't continue with the present uncertainty.

They passed out of the Grand Strand and moved toward the airport. The motels were smaller and less luxurious than those in Myrtle Beach proper, designed more for family weekends, college students and inexpensive holidays. There were cheap and gaudy beach shops that sold T-shirts, shells, plastic buckets and balls and every other kind of seashore paraphernalia that one could imagine. They rode quietly, awkward with the prospect of once again saying good-by.

Kate understood that her worry was stimulated by too much thinking and scolded herself for being presumptive. John Ryan had never promised anything, couldn't. His future was music. It was all ahead of him. How could he be expected to jump into a serious relationship with his marriage so recently over and who knew what in front of him?

Kate was scared. If she wasn't in love with him, she was one step away, and that step loomed before her like uncharted territory into which she could plunge or from which she must turn away. Her thoughts twisted like the reflections of an undulating crystal on a string. She wondered if it showed in her face or her attitude and couldn't believe that it didn't. How could he not know what she was feeling?

She turned and looked at the source of her consternation, holding the wheel with his right hand, the other resting in the open window. John Ryan was handsome and had a presence that could engulf a person as it had done her. He was talented, literate and, to the degree that he could be at this point in their relationship, thoughtful.

She smiled as the next thought went through her mind. He had given life to her body, making it a possession of hers to give and take for herself, something she owned and controlled, not something she was subject to. In her experience no one had opened her body to herself as he had done. Thinking about it aroused her, and she could feel her nipples harden beneath the silk blouse she was wearing.

"Let's stop," she said.

"Stop?" John Ryan looked at her questioningly.

"Yes. There," she answered, pointing to a single-story, white, cinder block motel just ahead of them.

"There?"

"Yes. There. That motel right in front of us."

"I shudder to ask why."

"Because I want you. Right now." And then added, "We have time and I'll be damned if I'm going to let it slip away." He looked at her in total disbelief. It was a Kate Belden he had never imagined.

"Yes, ma'am," he said and lifted his eyebrows in wonderment. The charm of the man was undeniable.

As soon as John Ryan closed the door behind them, Kate turned, her eyes narrowing toward closing as she put her arms around him and parted her lips, kissing him furiously, her tongue forcing its way into his mouth as far as it could go. Her hands worked feverishly at unbuttoning his shirt. He lifted her off the floor and carried her to the bed, literally dropping her on it and pushing her skirt up to her waist. As he undid his jeans, she pulled off her blouse and bra, letting her breasts fall free. He lowered himself and entered her effortlessly.

"Oh, God. John Ryan," she gasped, and with one upward push lifted both of them above the mattress. She moaned as the muscles of her body collapsed in total release.

"I love you," she whispered. "Like it or not, I do love you." She pressed her lips to his mouth.

Despite the fact that he had just gone through one of the most intense climaxes he had ever experienced, he realized that his arousal had not diminished, and he began to move into her again. Their second coupling was not as frenzied or fierce as the first, yet the euphoric relaxation and sense of completion afterwards was even greater.

John Ryan lay on his back, Kate beside him with one leg thrown across his and her head on his chest. They both fought to regain some semblance of regular breathing. Kate's hair was tangled and damp against her forehead. Her face glowed. Her eyes were closed and her left hand caressed his face.

"Did you mean that?" he asked.

"What?" she replied, knowing exactly what he meant and feeling a small discomfort at having said it.

"What you said."

"That I love you?"

"Yes."

"I do," she said. "I know it's a cliché—a movie line as you would say—I didn't want to, and I'm not sure how long I can live with it as it is, but I surely do."

"Why didn't you want to?"

"Because it destroys most of my dreams."

John Ryan looked down at her. "I beg your pardon?"

"My hopes and dreams. Loving you destroys most of them. I have always dreamed and hoped for the same thing that ninety percent of the women in this country hope for and dream about, a home, children, and a husband who comes home for dinner every night."

"Really?" he said. "I wouldn't have guessed. I'm sorry," he said with mild amusement.

She looked up at him, a smile on her face. "Of course that was an Indiana dream. I live in New York now, so maybe that wouldn't make me happy after all. Let's not worry about where it's going to go right now, okay? You've already given me more than I expected."

John Ryan looked at his wide, leather-banded watch. "I guess right now it's gotta go to the airport."

"You come up with the worst ideas," she said. "Kiss me first?"

Giannini Tedesco sat with his hands folded on the table in his office. He suddenly slammed his fist on the table with such sudden and swift ferocity that Maury Friedman was caught by surprise and almost lost his breath.

"How can one man fuck up something so simple?" he screamed. He stood up and turned away to regain his composure. When he turned, he appeared completely calm, almost serene, as if he were entering church for mass. "Get Vincenzo and Phil Carbano on a plane to Kingston in the morning," he said dispassionately. "I want them to find this Hard Steele guy and bleed him. I want to know where every piece he manufactured is, and I want every one we can get our hands on destroyed within forty-eight hours, and I want Lou out of there tonight. When you talk to him, get all the details, Maury. Most of all I want to know if Philip knew anything about this."

"Does that make any difference? He allowed it to happen." Friedman's voice was cold, and his face showed no more emotion than the man he was facing. Two mannequins might have enacted the scene with as much human concern.

"I also want the warehouse in Jersey and everything in it taken care of. Get Miraglia to handle it. This 'idea'," he said the word with sarcastic vehemence, "has to be cleaned up. Do you know what this could do if even one of those albums falls into the wrong hands? Of course you do; you're a lawyer. Everything, every fucking thing we have done for years to get control of this company could go in the toilet and bring in the Feds in the process. I want it all swept clean, Maury. That's your job. I don't want another fuck-up." Giannini Tedesco jiggled a pointed finger toward the man. "You know..." and left the statement hanging in the air, but there was no doubt as to its import.

"We can salvage this thing, Giannini," he said looking up at the immaculately dressed, silver-haired man. When Tedesco was standing up, everyone else remained seated or found a seat.

"Tell me and don't forget the risks. Always consider the risks. We're in a long-term business. Sometimes a bird gets away, and it's better to let it fly. You tell me, Maury."

"We've still got Bernie, and Bernie's got his son, and his son has the bird. It's not that I disagree with you, sometimes you do have to let the bird fly, but from everything I hear Stone is a very special bird."

"You can handle this thing?"

"I can handle it." As he said the words, Maury Friedman felt uneasiness come over him. He had just taken a major risk. Now there was no alternative. He could have let the bird fly, but with the scenario he had in mind, Bernie Greshem's tenure as President of Trayhorn International was coming to the end of its run, and he, Maury Friedman, would be there to take over.

"Good," Tedesco said.

"What about Philip?"

"What about Philip." It wasn't a question; it was a statement. "I think I need to go to Atlantic City."

"When?"

"Tomorrow. Philip will be sent for once we get there and get settled. That give you enough time?"

"I'll take care of it. Who do you want to go with you?"

"Franco and Lou if he's back."

"I'll get him back. Anything else?"

Giannini Tedesco held out his arms. Maury Friedman rose and went to the man for his salute. Holding him in his arms, the don said softly: "You're a good man, Maury. Do it right and don't disappoint me. I've had enough disappointments lately."

"It's done."

———•———

Rolling north toward Charlotte was the same as rolling east toward Myrtle Beach. Some slept, Mickey and Howie talked quietly about their amorous adventures in Myrtle Beach, which on Saturday night had consisted of double-headers for both of them. Paul Crockett sat by himself, his mind far away from the bus and the people that surrounded him. John Ryan settled back in his seat and closed his eyes. The weekend had been a revelation. There were no longer any doubts about the band's or his own ability to capture an audience. Frazier's appearance was a total surprise, and the small step they had taken to resolve fifteen years of hostility lifted a portion of the burden of having a family that wasn't a family. And then there was Kate.

'I love you.' The words rang in his ears. They weren't expected. He wasn't that far in his thinking. There was a lot about Kate Belden to admire. He looked up to her in regard to business and that had given her the dominant role in their relationship in the beginning. Time and familiarity had changed that. He no longer felt the innocent wickedness of a student having a crush on his teacher. He had always thought women had the upper hand in any relationship until they had sex. Women were aware of that; it was the reason they were reluctant to make that physical commitment, because they knew that act was the relinquishing of a certain amount of power. On the other hand, men had the same feelings and reluctance about saying 'I love you.'

He would not see Kate again until Raleigh. There was a lot of thinking to be done in those three weeks. She said she couldn't live with it as it was. At the time he had felt some resentment at being put on the spot. Now, sitting on the bus, he wasn't sure how he felt. He couldn't help considering how his response might affect his position in the business, and then chastised himself for even letting that thought in. He did know, however, it was a thought that would have to be reckoned with.

As the plane rose up and through the clouds over Charlotte, North Carolina, Kate sat alone and thought about the fact that in a few hours John Ryan would be in the very same city she was flying over. What would be on his mind? He had appeared distracted on the trip from the motel to the airport. Perhaps she had overstepped the parameters of their relationship, but then they had never discussed any parameters.

She loved him, and although the sex was beyond any physical thing she had ever experienced, she could not live on just that. That could not happen again. There had to be a connection, one on which to build something secure. Or was she just being an Indiana girl? She had said so often that type of life wasn't for her; she had left home for something bigger. Certainly a little house with shutters, and a flower garden and two point whatever children didn't appear to be any part of a life with John Ryan Stone; but she was no longer sure that scenario was what she wanted either.

Kate breathed a sigh of frustration and confusion closed her eyes. How does anyone know what to think about a relationship? she asked herself. Anything can be rationalized if one wants to justify it badly enough. She couldn't even define what she wanted. Once again she was glad there was no one sitting next to her; she had no need for conversation.

Her mind wandered back to the motel room, at the impulse to stop and make love. The thought made her flush, and the pictures that generated themselves through her mind caused a wave of erotic stimulation to pass through her body. She felt self-conscious, as if everyone on the plane knew exactly what she was thinking, as if everyone were seeing the pictures with her. That idea heightened what she was feeling. The flow of heat through her increased, and she knew it would take very little effort to cross that precipice she was approaching. No one seemed to be aware, but her discretion wouldn't allow her to continue. She let her shoes fall off and curled her feet under her in the seat, feeling warm and comfortable.

Jamie Greshem spent a solitary Sunday in his office studying finances and realized that he was fast coming to the end of the revenue that had been allotted for the John Ryan Stone project. Up to this point a lot of money had gone out, but nothing of any consequence had come in. Neither his father nor the accounting department had pulled in the reins—a fact that Don Hendrickson had laughingly written off to family ties—but he knew there were limits. At four-thirty he had determined exactly how much cash they had to operate with for the next month and went back to his apartment. It was midnight when his phone began ringing.

"Hello?"

"Did I wake you?" Don Hendrickson's voice was always energetic no matter what the circumstances.

"No, I was reading Friday's trades. What's wrong?

"Nothing we can't handle. I'm already workin' on it."

"What happened?" Jamie asked uneasily.

"Paul Crockett," Hendrickson said. "He's in the hospital. They don't know if he's gonna make it or not."

"Good Lord, tell me." Jamie was at full attention.

Hendrickson told him the whole story. The band stopped for dinner in Rockingham, North Carolina. Everybody got off the bus except Paul. Son Cochran noticed he hadn't come into the restaurant and went back to the bus to check on him. He found him unconscious with almost no pulse at all. Son had been down that road with booze and pills, Hendrickson said, so he knew what to do. They rushed him to the hospital, but the doctor's couldn't assess his condition accurately because they didn't know what drugs he had used.

"I've already been on the phone tryin' to get somebody to Charlotte tomorrow, but Sunday's a tough day, and we don't want to send just any-body. Charley McCoy would be best, but he's busy for a month of Sundays.

I talked to Norbert Putnam. He said he might be able to come up with somebody; he'll get back to me first thing in the morning."

"I don't know what to say," Jamie said and he didn't.

"It happens, son. The only thing to do is roll with it. It's a terrible thing to say, but better now than after Raleigh. By then the record'll be out. We're not in the news now; later on it could be a killer."

Even Don Hendrickson, Jamie thought, a good man, put business first. He recalled what his father had said to him when he first approached him for a job. 'The music business is not place for sissies or bleeding hearts.' He was learning the truth of that statement.

"Jamie, we'll get somebody, somebody good. I'm not gonna let them start the game with only eight players in the dugout. I'll get back to you as soon as I know something, and then you can let 'em know who's comin'."

"I have to rely on you for this, Don."

"Hey, it's part of the Hendrickson magic. It made me what I am today, too fat, too gray and too old before my time. Ain't we havin' fun yet? Talk to you." The line went dead. Strangely enough and for no logical reason, Jamie Greshem wasn't worried.

The machine monitoring Paul Crockett's heart rate and vital signs went flat at 3:37 a.m. John Ryan and Son Cochran were in the waiting room. It had been a long night, and what had begun with general optimism in Myrtle Beach less than twelve hours before had deteriorated into dire conjecture on the band's future. After the first two hours, John Ryan convinced the others to go to a motel; they would continue on to Charlotte in the morning. Son declined and stayed with him. At 4:03 a.m. a tired-looking doctor came into the waiting room.

"He didn't make it. I'm sorry," he said with no expression.

"You sound like it," John Ryan said. The remark was uncalled for. He was angry. Angry at the doctor, angry at Paul Crockett, and angry at himself although he wasn't sure why. Maybe because he had believed the dream and let it take him.

"We did everything we could, but the heart can only take so much." Now the doctor was angry. "You people bounce it up and down like a yo-yo. Push on the accelerator; step on the gas. And then you come in here and expect to get a tune-up that will give you another hundred thousand miles. You do what he did," he said in a warning tone, "and you'll end up the same way. And when you do, don't blame the doctors." He turned and went back through the door from which he'd come.

"He's right," Cochran said quietly. "Let it go. There's nothin' you or I or anyone else except Paul himself could have done to stop what happened here. He chose it. Don't ever forget that."

John Ryan didn't respond; he just stood looking at nothing. Of all the members of the band, Paul Crockett was the least a part of the family. He couldn't be called a friend because he wasn't friendly; yet it was impossible for John Ryan to discard him on the side of the road like a piece of broken equipment to be replaced. He couldn't grieve for the man because he didn't really know him that well, but he could mourn the loss of his music, which was sweet and true. That caused a deep sadness within him. He felt his chest fill with a tired sigh and his eyes blur with moisture as Son Cochran turned him toward the exit.

"One man didn't make this band, and one man can't take away what we have. Except you maybe."

The singer was not sure that wasn't what he wanted to do.

———————

At the motel John Ryan's first call was to Jamie Greshem, who was shaken deeply by the news. He advised John Ryan of what was being done in Nashville, and that Don had said someone would be arriving the following day. He also informed him that he would contact the family and arrange for the harmonica player to be sent back to Texas.

The second call was to Kate. "Hello?" There was no sleep in Kate Belden's voice. She had not been to sleep. John Ryan should have arrived in Charlotte by midnight. When three o'clock rolled around and she hadn't heard anything, she had begun to worry that she had been too aggressive, had given him a gentle ultimatum. It was uncharacteristic of her, but she had tried the other way and that hadn't worked either. By the time the telephone rang, she had gone through all the steps of fear and anger and not caring.

"Hi." His voice sounded tired and more raspy than usual and turned what might have been anger or irritation into concern.

"Are you all right? Where are you? I tried to call the hotel in Charlotte, but they said you hadn't arrived. I've been frantic."

"Paul Crockett died." He said, too exhausted and depressed to be gentle. "What?"

John Ryan explained all he could remember of the day and the night spent waiting at the hospital.

"Oh my God," she said when he was finished.

"Jamie's taking care of the arrangements, and Hendrickson's sending someone from Nashville tomorrow. I trust him; it'll be all right. God. Did I really say that?" he said with a note of disgust.

"I was so worried when you didn't call. I didn't know whether you'd had an accident or whether you were disturbed with me."

"I'm sorry." He paused. "I would have called to tell you if I was disturbed with you. I don't play mind games. I thought a lot today before everything started happening, and then I guess Crockett was kind of a wake-up call. I don't know where it's gonna go from here, Kate; but for what it's worth, I love you." It sounded tired, but despite that, Kate Belden's eyes filled with the sound of his words. She had difficulty finding her voice. "Are you there?" he said.

"Yes, I'm here. After today, I wasn't sure I'd ever hear you say that."

"Don't ever try to figure out what I'm gonna do. A lot of people have and it's a bad bet."

"I love you, too, John Ryan Stone."

"Where do we go from here?" he asked, the weight of events still pressing down upon him.

"We take things one step at a time," she said.

"You wanna tell me about the first step?" He was too weary to talk, but he didn't want to let go.

"You get some rest, which you desperately need; and you wake up in the morning and see if you feel the same way."

"I...."

"No," she interrupted . "Please do that for me. And for you. I know what you're feeling right now, this moment, but I don't know what you'll be feeling tomorrow. Neither do you. I'm not pushing in spite of what I said in Myrtle Beach. I can be patient; I don't want any more false hopes. When you're not as tired and emotional as you are right now and you've had time to think, then you tell me."

"And then?"

"And then I'll start making plans," she said with a hint of humor.

"You're not giving me much of a choice, you know."

"I hope not."

The rest of the their conversation was about the day ahead. The band would be going on to Charlotte to await whomever Don Hendrickson sent and then put in as much rehearsal time as possible before Thursday night. Kate also told him about arriving home to find a message from Bernie Greshem asking to see her in the morning. Finally, when there was no energy and nothing left to say, John Ryan asked her to call him in Charlotte and tell him what the meeting was all about. With that they said good-night.

———

Adjoining the luxurious office in which Bernie Greshem conducted business, was a set of rooms that few people ever entered other than the president himself. A door that most would have assumed opened a closet, actually led into a space that housed a private study, which consisted of a small but well-equipped kitchen, a bedroom and an elaborate bath. In the old days when he spent late-night hours planning strategies, it had seen a lot of use. At this stage in his life, it was used primarily for mid-afternoon and before-dinner freshening up. It was private and secure, however; and when there were things to think about and important decisions to be made, it became his retreat. He had arrived at the office early for just those purposes.

Bernie Greshem did not take Philip Barnessa's threats lightly. He knew what the man was capable of and that pressure was being applied from above . If Barnessa didn't come through, other people would get hurt in the fallout. Bernie didn't intend to let his family or himself to be among them.

The present situation was not unexpected. He had used Barnessa and his people, and they had used him. That had been a fair exchange, but things were changing; Barnessa and the people behind him had not built their reputation on fairness.

When he began his association with the family, it was at such a low level that he wasn't certain who he was dealing with. He suspected, but for purposes of business, he kept his eyes closed and didn't ask questions. His youth and ambition didn't allow him to recognize the danger and obstacles such an association might entail. As long as he remained outside and not of them, he was willing to take the risks.

Greshem had often wondered how his values and priorities might change as time went on. In the beginning it had been the excitement of the business—starting from nothing, creating and building a major company, and using whatever means were available to get where he wanted to be. However, when the company and his reputation were on a firm foundation, he found that he had to use those same means to sustain them. The key—he had thought back then—was how long he could use them and how long he could keep them at bay while he was doing it. It had been a long run, but it was coming to an end, and the lever they planned to use was his son.

It was time to 'pay the piper', make amends or escape. Only one of those terms could describe what he had in mind. It appeared to him that his plan was foolproof, but he knew that the man who believes that is the fool.

Sitting in a leather club chair and looking out over the city, Bernie Greshem sipped a cup of coffee and reviewed his priorities. First and foremost was to protect Jamie. His son had become more important to him when the boy reached manhood or maybe it was because the father had grown older. Up until that time, Bernie—like most fathers who are young and ambitious—believed that providing for the family and coming home at night was being a good father. The rationalizations were easy to invent. The day Philip Barnessa charged into his office and threatened both him and his son was an epiphany for him.

The time had come to exercise his options. Regardless of the fact that what he had in mind required perfect timing, Bernie Greshem felt a great sense of victory and that brought satisfaction. Philip Barnessa had no idea what events his threats had put into motion.

He opened the small safe secreted under a corner of the carpet and removed a series of documents he had prepared several days before. Sitting at his desk, he began the first of the letters he had mapped out over the past week. When he finished, he inserted the letter and two documents in a large envelope and sealed it. The remaining letter he put inside the pocket of his suit jacket. That completed, he took a deep breath. It was going to be a busy morning.

Angelina DiGirolamo watched the light getting brighter through the blinds in Philip Barnessa's apartment. There was no light when she awoke. She had no idea what time that had been or how much time had passed. The gold watch he had given her was on the dresser, and she wasn't willing to leave the warmth of the bed to check. He had given her the watch one day for no reason. He did things like that, usually just when she was getting tired of the situation and was ready to move on. She never could understand how he knew, some sixth sense, she guessed, because she never said anything. He said the watch was gold, but she knew it probably wasn't. It didn't make any difference; he had given her a gift when he didn't have to. Nobody had ever done that before.

Philip was a contradiction, she thought, as sun-shadows played on the walls and ceiling. He was gruff, ill-tempered on occasion, a little frightening when he was taken with anger and frustration, yet considerate when he chose to be. As considerate as he knew how to be. There were even moments of softness in him, but as soon as he recognized it, he switched gears and assumed a less than gentle manner. He worked hard not to let anyone see those things in him.

Angelina had not moved into the apartment. He never asked her to and she wouldn't have in any case. She had learned the hard way that a single woman in the city always needed a place to run to, a refuge, but she was spending more and more time there and, in the process, learned a lot about him she hadn't suspected.

Philip appeared to be growing more insecure. For several weeks—ever since that Jew had come down from New York—he hadn't been able to sleep. His drinking had accelerated and she had to work to get him interested in having sex. Lying there, she recognized with some surprise that she was actually worried about him. It was something she never anticipated.

As these thoughts brought a cautious smile to her face, she felt him stir. At the same time, the telephone began to ring. Angelina never answered the phone in his apartment. Philip made that very clear the first time he brought her there. He lifted himself up on one elbow and reached for the phone.

"Yeah."

"Philip?" The voice sounded confused, as if the caller had reached the wrong number.

"Who's this?"

"You all right, Philip?" Lou Molinaro's voice came into focus.

"Yeah, I'm all right. Just overslept. What the fuck time is it anyway?"

"Seven-thirty."

"Jesus Christ, it's the middle of the night. What's up, you callin' me this early?"

"Giannini's in A.C. Thought you'd like to come down and join him, have some dinner."

"Giannini's in Atlantic City?"

"Yeah. He came down on some of that casino business that's gonna be comin' up soon. That's gonna be somethin', Philip. Money flowin' like water. Make everything we're doin' now look like penny-ante poker. So he asked me to call and ask you to come down."

Philip Barnessa felt the sweat beginning to form on his upper lip. "Can I say 'no', Lou?"

"Hey," Molinaro said condescendingly, "he just wants to have some drinks and some dinner."

"That's all?"

"What's the problem?" He couldn't help wondering if Barnessa had in some way learned about Jamaica.

"Nothing, Lou, nothing." He was trying to think, but his mind wouldn't function. "Does he want me to bring some broads?"

"There's plenty of those in A.C. No, just you. I'll pick you up about six."

"No need..."

"It's no problem. I got the car, and I'm gonna be in Philly anyway. Giannini suggested it. I'll see you at six. It'll be good."

"Yeah," Philip Barnessa said, but it was to an empty phone. He leaned back and rested his head on the pillow. There was no air in his lungs, and he was having difficulty breathing. Something had brought Tedesco to Atlantic City and it wasn't casino business, which was a long time off if it ever came at all. He worried that he was 'being sent for'. If that was it, it was all over. It couldn't be; Lou would have told him. They had been together since Dewey Street.

"Are you all right?" Angelina asked, looking at him with alarm. She was lying next to him, naked, touching him, and he wasn't even aware of her presence. "Philip, you look gray."

Kate Belden noticed the difference in Bernie Greshem the minute she entered his office. He came from behind his desk to greet her as she came through the door. His eyes had a brightness and energy that she had not seen before. Long-term employees—and there were few—had seen it, but only from the building days when new challenges presented themselves on a daily basis. Bernie was a whirlwind of creativity and business acuity in those days. Kate, however, had only known him as the distinguished executive who had made his mark, created his reputation, his fortune and was content with the enjoying of it. This Bernie Greshem exuded intensity and power.

"Come in, Kate," he said as he directed her toward a chair in front of his desk and closed the door behind her. She felt as if he had been awaiting her arrival with great anticipation. It put her on edge. Why was she suddenly so important to the president of the company?

"Thank you," she said and seated herself. Greshem moved behind his desk and looked at her for a few moments before saying anything. Perhaps reassessing, she thought, or deciding if he wanted to go through with whatever this meeting was all about.

"Kate, I have something very private and personal to discuss with you. I'm not sure I should, but if at any point for whatever reason you want me to stop, I will. At that juncture you can walk out the door, and I will have to trust that you will say nothing of what you've heard to anyone." He paused. "If you are wondering why I trust you, it's because Jamie does. With that understood, if you want to hear what I have to say, we'll proceed. If not...." He gestured toward the door.

"Of course, Bernie." Her smile had given way to concern.

"I just have to be sure you'll stop me, if you feel uncomfortable with this." His look was dead serious.

"I will."

"After you hear the things I am going to tell you, you won't be able to work here. You won't have to worry about a job, but it won't be here. There is also a remote possibility, very remote, that this could create some danger for you, although I don't think that's a probability. Do you want me to go on?"

"Go on." She had no doubt that this had to do with Philip Barnessa and, ultimately, John Ryan. There was no way she would let fear keep her on the outside.

"There are going to be some major changes in the company that I want you to be aware of, and they're probably going to occur within days." He went on to tell her about Barnessa's threats to him and to Jamie. "I can't tell you everything that's going to happen because I'm not sure myself. It all depends on action and reaction, permutations and combinations. I don't know what the other side is doing, and I don't believe in their wildest imaginings they have any idea what I'm going to do."

"Bernie, I'll do whatever I can to help. I have an interest here." Greshem smiled.

"I know," he said. "And I assume it goes far beyond job security."

"I hope so." She smiled. "But it may take me awhile to find out."

"I like you, Kate; you're a survivor. I have always believed that women— some women—have a far greater capacity for survival than any man will ever have. That's one of the reasons I chose to talk to you first. I will be calling Don Hendrickson and Jamie later this morning to make them aware of what I plan to do. I must ask you to promise me that you will say nothing about any of this to John Ryan Stone until everything is out in the open and the dies have been cast."

"You have my word." She was not as calm as she sounded; in fact, she was struggling not to shake. Whatever he was going to tell her was far beyond Philip Barnessa wanting a part of the agency for John Ryan Stone.

"Good," he said. "The threat goes deeper than Philip Barnessa, Kate. He's just the messenger, the minnow who takes the catch to the bigger fish. You know what Philip is and in whose interest he works, but you may not know that Maury Friedman works for those same interests." He watched her reaction. There was a slight raising of the eyebrows, but it didn't seem to be a total surprise. That amused him. People like Friedman and Barnessa always thought they were operating so surreptitiously, yet their flaunting of power and attitude and their compulsion to live up to the profiles that Hollywood had created for them, let everyone know who they were.

"With Philip everything is up front and out in the open," he continued. "You know when to be wary; with Maury you don't. Maury is ambitious and Philip is in trouble; that makes both of them unstable and dangerous. Consequently, I have decided to take some actions that hopefully will extricate Jamie, Don Hendrickson, you and John Ryan Stone from further involvement."

"What about you?" she asked with concern.

"That will be a little iffy, but with a little bit of luck I, too, may be able to go on without too much interruption in my life." He proceeded to explain what Barnessa's people's connections were to Trayhorn International, how it had started, what it had come to and the fact that their ultimate goal was to take control of the company. He also explained his position and some of what he intended to do to protect the people he cared about.

As he went on, Kate found herself in a minor state of shock, and— survivor or not—she was afraid. It had all seemed like a game with a little spice added in, but it was far more than that.

"This isn't anything new, Kate. They and their counterparts worldwide control most of the entertainment industry. At this point they haven't made a lot of inroads into Nashville, but that will come in time. I've managed to keep their influence at Trayhorn to a minimum with distribution deals, some publishing participation and giving them a couple of people who I was pretty sure would make money but wouldn't last. They made money and were happy. That is no longer the case.

"I haven't told you everything I plan to do—that would defeat my purpose—but I have told you enough." He slid a brown manila envelope across his desk. "I want you to take this to Nashville. I cannot stress how important this envelope is. Give it to Don Hendrickson; he'll know what to do from there. He'll be expecting you. When you leave this office, leave as though you are going out on an errand. Go home; pack enough clothes for a week and go to Kennedy. Your flight is at three-thirty. The tickets will be at the United desk." He gave her another envelope. "This is four thousand dollars. That should see you through for awhile. If you need more, Don will give it to you.

"Again, I have to stress that you say nothing to anyone. It's all going to come down hard very soon; and the less anyone knows, the better off they are." He rose from his chair. "Good luck, Kate. I think you and Jamie and Don make a pretty good team. John Ryan Stone doesn't know what he has going for him."

"After what I've just heard, I'm sure he underestimates a lot."

"There's no need for him to know. It doesn't need to ever touch him or his career if all goes as planned."

"I don't know what to say, Bernie." He put his hand on her elbow and guided her toward the door.

"Nothing right now. Let's see how it all works out. Jamie tells me they've got some pretty nice places down there on Henderson Lake. Who knows, Kate, the South might be a good place to live." He was smiling, the brightness in his eyes still there.

"You be careful," she said and impulsively kissed him on the cheek. "Should I call when I get there or anything?"

"No, I'll know." He was already headed toward his desk.

There was a great insecurity at just leaving things behind and not even checking to see what she'd left, but those were Bernie Greshem's instructions. She wondered about her desk and how she'd left it. For a person who never left their apartment without the bed being made, it was an unnerving experience.

The knock on John Ryan's door didn't wake him; he had slept little. It was ten o'clock in the morning, time to complete the trip that had started in Myrtle Beach what seemed a lifetime ago. He thought about Paul Crockett's empty seat. They were leaving him behind. Let it go, Son Cochran had said, and he was trying to do that.

When he opened the door, Son was standing there. "You all right?"

"What's all right? Yeah, I guess. How soon are we pullin' out?" He flopped in an easy chair next to the window and looked out at nothing.

"Thirty or forty minutes," the bass player said, sitting on the bed. "Doesn't look like you slept in it."

"Laid down for awhile. Didn't make a production of it."

"There's something I think you need to hear."

"What's that?" John Ryan's mind flinched at the thought that something else had happened.

"Just that nobody on the face of this earth could have saved Paul."

"I think you already said that."

"I wasn't sure whether you heard it, and I'm damned sure you don't believe it. Dying was his choice, John Ryan; that's something you can't understand."

"What do you mean?"

"People that don't have an addiction can't understand. Not husbands, wives, doctors, therapists. They all mean well, but they're in la-la land and it's not their fault. We have four well-documented choices: quit, death, insanity or jail. Paul made his choice."

"Ever talk to him about it?"

"We talked, but he had pretty much made up his mind. I was waiting for it to happen."

"How the hell do you make up your mind about something like that?"

"Will. You make up your mind to exert your will or not to exert your will. If you don't then you only have three choices left, and if you're lucky, death is the one that comes first."

John Ryan was silent and then he asked, "How did you beat it?"

"I haven't. That's just it. Nobody ever does. I'm doin' okay right now, but who the hell knows? I've been sober for five years; the tiger is still sleepin' on my shoulder, and it can wake up any time. If you're askin' how I stopped drinkin' and pillin', my only honest answer could be that I don't know. Believe me, I've thought about it a lot. Some people say they have a revelation and maybe I did, or maybe I got tired of bein' controlled by somethin' I couldn't talk back to or punch out or just decided I wasn't ready to hang it up yet. I do know I got awful tired of the humiliation I saw in me. Nobody else saw it, but I did and that hurt a lot. If you're askin' me for one specific reason I quit, I don't have a pissant's clue why. I do know it had to be me and me alone with a little spiritual help, which according to some people may or may not be there, but believin' it was helped."

"It's sad," John Ryan said. "The boy could make pretty music."

"He probably thought the junk helped him do that, but it didn't. Never does. We'd better get movin'. Maybe you can sleep on the bus."

What Son said made him feel better, but it didn't take away the anger.

By the time they reached Charlotte, Remy Soileau was sitting in the lobby of the motel waiting for them. As the band straggled in, he looked them over and picked out the one he thought he might be working for.

"You Jean Rine Stone?" he asked as he walked toward the one he had chosen.

"Jean? I guess, but I don't know you," John Ryan answered. The man standing before him was thin enough to hide behind a swizzle stick. He wore jeans, a cowboy shirt with pearl snap buttons, a leather vest and well-worn boots. His black, stringy hair was well below his shoulders and there was a smile on his face.

"Remy Soileau. I'm from Des Allemands, Louisiana, me. Also Nashville and mos everywhere else but mosly Des Allemands. Don Hendrickson told me ya'll be needin' a harp player real quick and I done come on up here."

John Ryan was speechless. The man didn't look like a member of his band, didn't look like he'd know which side of a harmonica to blow in, spoke with a heavy Cajun accent and did look like the type who would spend Sunday afternoons standing around the gas pumps at the local filling station in Des Whateveritis.

"How long you been waitin'?" he asked, having no idea what else to say.

"Bout tree hours. I was in Nawlins. Got in bout tree hours ago."

"You playin' down there?"

"Naw. Been seein' a woman. Used to be my wife. She say. I never believed her, no. I was drunk." It wasn't a statement, given the present circumstances, that gave John Ryan any relief.

"Well, if Don sent you...." The man looked totally out-of-place; John Ryan couldn't imagine him fitting in. It was discouraging. "I guess you'd better check-in with the rest of the band and get settled. We're gonna be here for a few days, and I've got to check out the rehearsal arrangements. I'd say we've got a lot of work to do." He didn't intend for it to sound sarcastic, but it did.

Remy Soileau walked over to the desk to register just as Son Cochran walked through the door. John Ryan watched as they recognized each other and shook hands with smiles and small talk.

"We lucked out," Son said as he approached John Ryan.

"How?" John Ryan said incredulously.

"Remy Soileau. Wait'll you hear him."

"He can play?"

"He can play, and he'll add things Paul never thought about. Gets carried away sometimes. I once heard him break into a Cajun rendition of *The Tennessee Waltz* in the middle of *The Orange Blossom Special.*" Cochran was smiling. "Funny thing was, it worked."

"I guess we'll see," John Ryan said, unconvinced.

"What can I do?" Angelina Digirolamo asked.

"Nothin'," Barnessa answered. It was four o'clock in the afternoon, and he was still in his robe. He had tried to call Maury Friedman, but was told he was out of the office. When he asked for a number, the secretary said she had no idea where he could be reached. He also tried Bernie Greshem without success. A feeling of impending catastrophe was descending upon him, and he couldn't find anything to stop it.

"Philip...."

"Shut the fuck up. You don't know nothin'. You think you know somethin'? You don't know nothin'. You don't understand."

"Then explain it to me for God's sake. I can't understand if you don't explain it." She was pleading and that was not natural for her. It was the third time since the call that she had felt her eyes fill with tears.

"I'm bein' sent for. Giannini Tedesco is sending for me. Somebody don't just send for somebody unless somethin' big is happenin'. People who are sent for usually don't have very good prospects."

"Prospects for what?" It was also her third panic of the day.

"For tomorrow. Jesus Christ." He jumped up from the chair and ran into the bathroom. Angelina could hear him retching and she began to sob. She had never seen him like this. There was no spirit, no anger or hostility, just a frighteningly submissive despair.

When he came out of the bathroom, there was no color in his face, and his hands looked transparent, blue veins showing through the skin. She had not seen that in a person before. She tried to console him, comfort him, but he didn't want to be touched. She saw panicked struggle going on behind his eyes.

"What can we do?" she asked. He turned to her, his face sagging.

"There's nothin' we can do. You don't have to do anything. I'm the one's gotta do somethin', and there's nothin' for me to do except go."

"What's going on, Philip? What's gonna happen?" He stopped for moment and seemed to relax, just the slightest bit, a slender look of hope on his face.

"I don't know," he said as if the words were a surprise, something he hadn't thought of before. "I really don't know. Lou said it was just for dinner." His face dropped again when other thoughts drove themselves home. Giannini didn't come to Atlantic City for dinner, and the casino stuff was bullshit. Maybe it was something else. Maybe he wasn't in trouble. But then why wasn't he told ahead of time that they were coming? Every other time Tedesco came down, he was told to set up dinner and provide the broads. The old man liked two, sometimes three at a time. He and Lou had joked behind his back that at his age maybe it took that many. This time he hadn't been asked to set up dinner or provide the women, and Lou was being sent to pick him up. It was bad. Angelina had asked him something, but he couldn't remember what it was. Maybe he should call his wife. Why? He couldn't concentrate and knew that was his only chance. Survival was dependent upon thinking. Outsmarting.

"Maybe we can go somewhere, not be here." Her voice came out of the fog.

"There ain't nowhere to go. Why don't you get dressed and go somewhere."

"Philip...."

"Get the fuck outta here. I got things to do," he screamed and then immediately softened. "Go home. I'll call you tomorrow." His words caused her to break down completely.

"But you said..."

"Forget what I said. I'll work it out. Get dressed. I don't want you around when Lou gets here. I gotta shower and get ready. Don't be here when I get out." He turned and went into the bathroom, locking the door behind him.

Angelina DiGirolamo watched the door close, went into the bedroom and began dressing.

The conversation would have to be delicately and perfectly structured, telling just enough, yet not exposing every nuance of his plan. There had to be alternatives kept in reserve. Bernie Greshem had tried to anticipate all of the possible questions and responses that Don Hendrickson might come up with and, in turn, create a logical and effective response. He looked upon this telephone call as the most critical part of his whole strategy.

"Bernie. What a surprise!" Don Hendrickson said.

"I like to do that sometimes. Keeps people on their toes. How's the southern part of the empire doing?"

"You talkin' about Trayhorn or Greshem?"

"I guess both."

"Well, one's muddlin' along, and the other is sittin' on pins and needles with his fingers crossed."

"I can't complain about either one of those assessments. What about you?"

"I'm doin' all right. What can I do for you?"

"Quite a bit really, and I hope something for you." he paused. "Don, I need your confidence. Things are getting testy up here and I'm not comfortable with it."

"One guess. Barnessa."

"Yes, but also Maury and the rest of them."

"Stone have something to do with it?"

"He accelerated things, but it's been coming for a long time. They want ownership of him and have threatened me for it. Of course I won't give it, but more than that, they want control of the company."

"Tell me what's happening, Bernie."

Bernie Greshem repeated the whole story he had told Kate Belden. "The bottom-line is that I don't like to be threatened. I also see the inevitability of what's to come. As I said, I'm not surprised. I've taken some measures to protect Jamie and myself, but I'm going to need your help. I don't think there will be any risk for you from those people; however, you will have to gamble a little bit of your security."

"I'm listenin'. I have no idea what you're talkin' about, but it's beginin' to sound exciting." Bernie could hear the anticipation in his friend's voice. The man was still a wild-catter and that's what he needed.

"Have you ever wanted your own label?"

"What in God's name are you talkin' about, Bern?"

"Just what I said. Have you ever wanted your own label?"

"Doesn't everybody?" he chuckled. "Well, now that I think about it, I guess not. You know this as well as I do—new labels are a very shaky proposition. Hell, only one out of a thousand ever lasts through one release and makes their original money back, and to do that they have to have a major hit, which in itself is a fluke for a new label. Even then they usually go under or sell out to a major."

"I agree."

"So why are you askin'?"

"How much do you believe in John Ryan Stone?"

"A lot, but it may not happen overnight. I'm not sure where you're goin' with all this."

"I'll tell you and you may think I'm a damned fool, but I believe it'll work. The most essential thing is that I have your trust and confidence because you're the catalyst for what I have in mind. It could turn out very well for you and Jamie and Stone. I'm not sure how it will work out for me, but that's not the primary objective."

"You know you can trust me, Bernie. Hell, we've been together for a lot of years considering longevity in this business. I'm gettin' the feelin' that what you want to tell me is bigger than anything I can imagine, but I'll listen, and after I've listened, I'll tell you my reaction. Above all, whatever you say will be between us unless you want it otherwise." He waited with the anticipation of a poker player itching to see the next card.

Hendrickson did not interrupt him.

The president's plan was complex. As he explained its intricacies and the timing necessary to make it work, Hendrickson became apprehensive. Not for himself or Jamie, but for Bernie. He said he had covered all the contingencies, yet neglected to explain how he would escape Maury Friedman's wrath and the resources he and Tedesco had at their disposal. The prospects outlined for Jamie and himself were exciting to say the least, but there was no way to calculate the results should there be a failure at any level.

When he was finished, Greshem paused.

"Now the most critical part and the biggest favor I have to ask. Don, I want you to explain all of this to Jamie. From that point on all decisions will be left to the two of you."

"Bernie....."

"I don't see any obstacles. I have arranged for everything to move smoothly on your end, as far as I can see. I would like to have the letters I mentioned in my office within forty-eight hours. That will eliminate any conflict-of-interests, legally. Kate will be calling you as soon as she arrives. I suggest that you go over the papers I have sent with her yourself first. If they're acceptable, you and Jamie sign them, and you can take it from there. Providing you are agreeable of course."

"I wish I had more time to consider...."

"In my opinion we don't have any time. I think this is about as close as we can cut it. Don, if you're reluctant...."

Hendrickson thought for a moment. "What the hell, let's have at the big boys and see what happens. Startin' over from scratch ain't anything new for me; I been doin' it all my life."

"Thank you, Don. If you have any questions about the agreements or anything else, call me. And keep me posted."

"I will."

When he hung up the phone, Don Hendrickson had ominous feelings about everything that was going to happen in New York.

Remy Soileau was thirty minutes early for rehearsal and was surprised to find John Ryan working with Cade Wilhite on sound levels. The singer had put exhaustion aside and ignored the opportunity for a couple of hours rest before rehearsal. Depression was weighing in on him. He was afraid that if he went to sleep, it would be difficult to force himself back out of bed. It was easier to work than to think.

"E'nin', Boss," Remy said as he stepped up on the stage.

"Remy." John Ryan acknowledged him verbally but didn't stop what he was doing.

"You want to check your instrument level on that mike over there?" Cade Wilhite said to the new man.

"You de boss, Boss. Anythin' you wanna hear, Jean Rine? I can play 'mos anythin'. Yes." Stone wondered if the man's ability equaled his ego.

Carl T. Smith

"What about *Suzi Q?*" As soon as he said it, he felt badly about pulling out the old Dale Hawkins tune. It wasn't exactly on everybody's play list and was difficult to make interesting with only one instrument.

"Dat be next door, man."

"Next door?" John Ryan asked.

"Yeah. Next to my heart. Out de swamp. I taught you gone gimme sompin' tough. Tes' me out. Yes."

Remy Soileau put the instrument to his mouth and began to blow. He started with a whisper, playing it far away, letting the basic rhythm pattern bring it closer as the beat intensified. When the sound was next to him, he broke into the melody with the upper register, while maintaining the rhythm with bass notes. At times the melody became obscure and hidden, visible only to someone who knew the song well. In the middle he took a wild break that left the song behind until it found its own path and came back.

John Ryan watched Remy in awe, not just because of the sounds he was creating, but also because of what he was doing. From the moment he began to play, the man never stood still. He didn't hug the harmonica to the mike as most players do. He bent at the waist, stomped his right foot hard, swung the long hair from side to side with a freedom that embodied his own spirit. He made a propeller motion with his upper body and finally broke into something that looked like a clog dance. He had an inherent sense of his distance from the mike and blew harder to make up the difference. At the end of the number, there was applause from the back of the club. The other members of the band had come in and observed what was going on.

The performance was outstanding. Maybe too outstanding. Even after the time spent in Nashville and all the music and musicians he had studied and was familiar with, John Ryan was consistently surprised at the quality of people he had never heard of who seemed to appear out of nowhere.

The other members of the band came to the stand and gathered around the harmonica player to compliment him on what they had just heard. Mountain Red was the first to leave the group and begin noodling on his instrument. The others followed. Remy Soileau approached John Ryan.

"Dat be all right, Boss?" From most people that question might have sounded aggressive; from Remy Soileau it was merely asking for approval. John Ryan got the distinct impression that if he said 'no', the Cajun would shrug, go pack his bag and get on the next bus home. He didn't answer immediately, trying to determine what to say. Remy picked it up.

"Dat jus' be for you. Yes. I don' be doin' all dat stuff when we play for sure. No. Dat jus' to show you I can play. You tell me what you want; dat's what I do. I play like in Sunday school you want. You de boss, Boss." John

Ryan Stone smiled. Remy Soileau was going to be one hell of an addition to the band.

———•••———

After rehearsal was over, most of the band went out to get food, but John Ryan passed. He was still exhausted. It had been a tough two days since the glory of Myrtle Beach. When he opened the door to his room, it was totally dark. The drapes had been pulled and there was no light on. His first thought was that housekeeping had left it that way, but the hair prickling on his arms made him pause.

"Come in and close the door," a voice said. John Ryan hesitated, considering whether or not to close the door or get the hell out of there. "You talk to me or we take Kate Belden; it's up to you, pal. The broad's easier."

It didn't take any thinking to determine who had written this scene. John Ryan closed the door and left the lights off.

"You can turn on the lights now," the voice said. It came from the far left corner of the room. There was a chair there, but no light switch as best he could remember. It was a gamble. The army had trained him well, and he knew darkness could be an ally, especially when you didn't know what you were up against. He only sensed one other person in the room. Another gamble.

"I prefer the dark. What do you want to talk about?"

"Cute. You think I'm here to rob you? Mug you? What? You can relax. I was definitely told not to hurt you. You're the golden goose or whatever. They didn't say the same thing about Kate Belden or the Greshem kid..."

"You..."

"Shut up and listen. It's all up to you. You deal with us or the pony ride is over."

"You haven't told me who you are or what you want; how am I supposed to deal?"

"Just think of me as a man from Philadelphia. We want you, Stone, and if you don't work for us, you don't work for nobody."

"Sounds like a movie line." It was a dumb thing to say, but it gave him time to think.

"You are a wise ass, aren't you? Remember what I say. You're our messenger boy. You give the message to Greshem and make sure he tells his daddy. That's important. We're not gonna wait long, pal. It's your ass or Belden's and, if necessary, Greshem's."

John Ryan could hear him moving, getting up from the chair. As he had been taught, Stone had moved slightly after each verbal exchange. The man from Philadelphia had no idea where he was.

"I heard about the guy in your band. Could have been you. Too bad." The man said as he moved closer. "Turn on the lights."

"No." With the mention of Paul Crockett and the implication that it carried with it, John Ryan's anger overcame any fear that may have held him. As he took another step toward the door, John Ryan, in one motion, turned on the light with his left hand, balanced himself and threw a hard right into the man's stomach, pushing through it. As he bent over, his legs kicked out from under him and he felt John Ryan's boot heel in his back, threatening to snap his spine. He was pinned to the floor.

"I have no idea who you are," John Ryan said in a voice filled with rage, "but I know where you came from and who sent you. And you tell him I know. Now you're the messenger boy. And you tell him if he or anyone else ever threatens Kate Belden or Jamie Greshem again, he will have to deal with more than he ever bargained for. He won't want that. Tell him in spades, you sorry son-of-a-bitch."

He lifted his foot and the man started to get up. As he did, he made a rush for John Ryan, but his timing was off. The singer grabbed him by the collar and shoved his face into the corner of the desk. He could feel the initial resistance and then softening as the cheekbone collapsed. The man screamed in pain and fell to the floor. John Ryan lifted him to his feet and threw him out the door. In anger he had actually considered throwing him over the railing, but his better sense prevailed. He watched the man stumble, fall down, get up and move down the cement balcony. He had the stairs to manage, and if he didn't get to a hospital and get the bone in his face repaired, his head would be forever lopsided.

John Ryan sat on the bed and his whole body began to shake. What was this? Where would it end? He was supposed to be an entertainer, a songwriter, not the hero of a grade B movie. He didn't know what to do. Police would be no help. What would he say? There was time to think. It would take time for Barnessa to get the word. By that time John Ryan Stone might be out of the business, he thought. Regardless, he would say nothing to Kate or Jamie until he had time to speak with Don Hendrickson.

Lou Molinaro arrived at six o'clock, and put his arms around Philip Barnessa as he had done a thousand times before. The warmth of the greeting gave Barnessa a small relief and a minor sense of security. Nothing had changed. On the ride to Atlantic City they talked about things they had shared together over the years, asked about family and people they knew, and they laughed. Molinaro did not mention Jamaica, and Philip Barnessa asked no questions. It was the rule.

On the way Barnessa had to make two bathroom stops. Once it was excused by having had too much coffee during the day; the second time disguised by stopping at a bar to buy a bottle and get cups of crushed ice for the rest of the trip.

Giannini Tedesco had a suite of rooms at The Chalfont-Haddon Hall, an elegant turn-of-the-century hotel, regarded for years as Atlantic City's finest place to stay. The rooms were spacious for its time, and though the years had brought with them the inevitable deterioration of age, it still remained elegant.

When the two men arrived from Philadelphia, Tedesco was dressed in a navy blue silk suit, pale blue shirt and wore a green and navy striped tie. His black shoes gleamed. His clothes, tanned complexion, silver gray hair and steely eyes made him an imposing and frightening figure. Nicky Gagliano was there along with Franco Digiovanangelo. Barnessa was relieved to see that Maury Friedman wasn't with them.

"Philip," Tedesco said with a broad smile as he embraced the much larger man. "It's good to see you."

"It's good to see you, too, Giannini." The Philadelphian could not muster the same amount of enthusiasm though he tried.

The next hour was spent with drinks and small talk. Conversation roamed from the changes in the city that the casinos might bring and how long it would take for the voters to approve them to the beach house Tedesco was considering buying in either Ventnor, Margate or Longport. It was time to buy, he said, before the casinos took real estate prices out-of-sight. There were laughs and excitement at the number of hookers the new entertainment element would bring in and that evolved into a discussion of each man's preferences and whether white or black women were the best. It was a locker room, a dormitory, a fraternity house. There was no mention of business.

At eight-thirty they went to dinner at The Knife and Fork, listed for more than forty years as one of America's best restaurants. There was no reservation system and the place was always crowded; however, when Giannini Tedesco and his party arrived, their table was waiting. Orders consisted of a variety of things including soft-shell crabs, Linguini with white clam sauce and garlic, Pasta de la Puta, Osso Buco, mussels marinara and Veal Picante. There were bottles of red and white wine. It was a hearty time shared by men of power, but throughout the whole meal all Philip Barnessa could think about was getting back to his apartment in Philadelphia, his haven of safety.

After the food was gone and the table cleared, Tedesco suggested they go back to the suite, have a drink and plan the night ahead, maybe bring in some girls, find a game, whatever they decided to do. Despite Barnessa's protestations that he needed to get back to Philly, the don insisted. Without argument, he went. It was only after the second round of brandy that Tedesco brought up the real purpose of the evening.

"So Philip, how's business?" he asked. It was offhanded, as if the response was unimportant. Barnessa could feel the sudden coolness of sweat forming on his forehead.

"Good, Giannini. Good."

"How good?" The voice was serious. Philip Barnessa wanted to scream, to break and run. It was here; he resigned himself.

"We got it covered. Bernie's in line. Since our little talk, he knows what he's got to do. I've got the product in the warehouse ready to go out tomorrow or the next day. We've got a week. Trekorian will take care of the cut-outs and the Trayhorn stuff. The distributors are lined up, and they all 'decided' that buying a few useless cut-outs was worth being preferred customers on new stuff. Everything is set to go." It actually sounded pretty good as he said it. He couldn't think of a reason why Giannini would be upset. It was as good an answer as could be expected, but he had no idea what Tedesco was looking for.

"When does the product hit the shelves?"

"Saturday. That's the release date."

"You sure?" Tedesco stared at him. He could feel his shirt getting damp.

"Sure I'm sure. Why? You know somethin' I don't know?" Get aggressive, he thought. "You know somethin'? Tell me. I feel like I'm in a in...in..."

"Inquisition?" Tedesco offered.

"Yeah. An Inquisition here." It was time to be quiet, let Giannini play his hand.

The man began calmly, quietly. "Let me tell you how business is, Philip." It was quiet, but menacing. There was no longer any friendship in the voice, no camaraderie left over from dinner. Now there was only the cold, fixed look that Giannini Tedesco could use better than anyone else in the world. "Business is no good. I give you a responsibility you can't handle? You tell me you can handle it, but then you don't. What happen, Philip? You used to be good. Not the smartest, but good at what you do. Now you just fuck up everything I give you. Why, Philip? Why you do that? Huh?"

"What's goin' on here? I tol' you..." Tedesco held up his hand.

"I know what you told me. You think I'm deaf? I know what you told me and it means nothin'! You don't tell me anything," he pointed his finger at Barnessa, " cause you don't really know nothin'. You been cruisin' along hoping business will take care of itself. You believe all this movie stuff about us. Everybody's afraid and makes everything easy for us. You're wrong, Philip. Business don't take care of itself; you got to take care of business, and that takes work. We work hard. You don't do that anymore."

"Giannini...I send somebody...."

Tedesco slammed his fist on the table. "Don't interrupt me." He nodded and Franco Digiavangelo brought him a thin, brown paper bag. "You know what this is, Philip?" He held it up for the man to see. Barnessa shook his head. He wanted to answer, but his throat was full. "I'll show you." He pulled the John Ryan Stone album from the bag and held it up. Philip Barnessa's eyes bulged. He could feel his heart pounding irregularly.

"Where did you get..."

"Jamaica!" Tedesco yelled, smashing the album to the table and getting up from his seat. "We got it in Jamaica. They been selling it there for a week. How did that happen?"

"The *molenjen*. That son-of-a-bitch. I'll take care of him, Giannini, I'll...."

"You don't take care of nobody. The nigger's being taken care of. How? How did it happen? That's the question. Because you weren't taking care of business. That's how." He paused. There was no sound in the room. "So. What we gotta do? Huh? We gotta wipe these damned things out. Down there. In Jersey. You know why? Because it's fucking counterfeiting and it's been exposed. You know who that brings in? Do you?" His voice turned white with anger. "Tell me!" Barnessa couldn't speak. "The Feds, goddammit! We don't need to deal with them. You say you got Bernie Greshem on a leash? You don't got nothin'. Maury will take care of that. I want you out of it, Philip. I don't want you to do anything else. Don't go near your warehouse. Don't call Jamaica. You don't do anything until you hear from me personally. You got that?"

"Yeah, Giannini, I got it." Philip Barnessa was overwhelmed with relief. Out of it was where he wanted to be. The fuckin' hillbilly was bad news from the beginning. Nashville was the minor leagues. Never should have gotten involved. It was time to get out, get out of it all. Angelina had been truly worried about him. She was a feeling woman. He liked that. Maybe they'd get married. Tedesco's voice brought him back into the room.

"Philip," he said as he held out his arms. Barnessa stood up on wobbly legs and Tedesco embraced him. "Philip, I don't like these things. We been friends too long. You're like a son to me. I don't like to yell at my little boy, but sometimes it has to be done. Capisce?"

"Capisce." Philip Barnessa's head was pressed tight against the smaller man's.

"You go home, Philip. Forget all about tonight." Giannini Tedesco smiled, kissed him and looked him in the eye. "Except for the food, huh? And the friends?"

"Thank you, Giannini." The big Italian's eyes were filled.

"Hey, cut that out. A little mistake. It's taken care of. Hey, Philip, I never thought it was such a good idea anyway." He turned to Lou Molinaro. "Hey, Lou. Take Philip back to Philly. Philip back to Philly. That's funny." He laughed and everyone else smiled with him. "It's been a big night. I'm tired. Franco. You go with. Keep Lou company on the way back."

The three men left the hotel and went to the car. Franco drove, Barnessa sat in the passenger seat, Lou Molinaro in back. Once they were on the White Horse Pike headed toward Philadelphia, Lou produced the bottle they had bought on the way down.

The bottle was passed around, the chatter filled with humor, ego, tall tales and reminiscences. Philip Barnessa relaxed for the first time in months. Giannini Tedesco had removed all the pressure. He really was too old. It would be good to leave the New York operation behind. There were things he could do in Philadelphia. That's what he would tell Tedesco. Sort of a semi-retirement. He wouldn't get rich, but he could make enough, contribute and there wouldn't be any pressure.

Just after they passed through Hammonton, Philip Barnessa felt something cold and hard pressed to the back of his head. His bladder seemed to expand like a balloon filling with air. His breathing stopped. He couldn't get his breath or his voice. He felt like he was suffocating, and he had to fight to keep the food he had eaten from rising up through him. His heart felt as if it were pounding outside his chest. Finally, in a tearful voice, he managed to speak.

"Lou?"

"Don't, Phil."

"Lou, you don't have to do this." The world was crashing in on him. He could feel every pore and cell in his body. He had never felt life so present, yet he was sitting in the front seat of a car with a gun pressed to his head. Sitting in the front seat. That should have been a clue. Why hadn't he argued about sitting in the front seat. They didn't ask; he did it voluntarily. He made it easy for them. It was an amateur's mistake. It wouldn't have made any difference anyway. He knew that.

The car turned off the Pike just before they reached Blue Anchor.

"Lou, we been friends; we...Our wives...."

"Phil, please. Don't make it hard. This is business."

"Please, Lou..." He was crying in earnest. He never heard the sound, never saw the spray of red spume that covered the dash and the passenger-side window, and he didn't get to feel the pressure released from his bladder.

On Tuesday morning *The Philadelphia Inquirer* ran a short front-page article about an 'as-yet-unidentified' body having been found near Blue Anchor, New Jersey. The body was wrapped in black garbage bags. According to the article, it had 'all the markings' of a mob hit. A second article in the South Jersey section gave a brief account of a fire at Select Storage in the Westville Industrial Park. No cause for the blaze was found, but arson was suspected.

66 H i." The word was an emollient, soft, smooth and apologetic, that allowed John Ryan Stone's brain and body to begin working again. It was four-thirty in the morning, and he had been awake most of the night trying to reach Kate. The first call was in the afternoon, but the people at Trayhorn—even Barbara Allred—could give him no information on her whereabouts. The telephone in the apartment went unanswered. There were scattered moments of dozing between calls, but most of his time since rehearsal was spent alternating between periods of worry, anger and paranoia. Relief spread over him, but suspicion and anger made him cautious. Finally he said: "Hi yourself."

Before he could get another word out, she said: "Are you angry?"

"I don't know," he answered. "You wanna tell me why I should or shouldn't be?" The Iceman, she thought.

"Well, let me see if I can phrase this properly." John Ryan could hear the nervousness in her voice. "You probably should be, not knowing the circumstances; however, when you know the circumstances, you shouldn't be. Does that make any sense?"

"I'm not sure. Sounds kinda like Mickey-talk."

"Are you?"

"I don't know. I've been in a mild panic for the last twelve hours, but I'm not sure I should let you know that."

"Can I explain?" The voice was shaky.

"Yes."

"I love you."

"Uh-oh."

"Uh-oh what?" she asked.

"When a woman prefaces what she's going to say with 'I love you', it's usually not good. In the movies it usually means 'good-bye', a personal philosophy created by vast experience and seeing a lot of movies."

"Don't be glib, John Ryan; it's been a very strange day. The reason you haven't been able to reach me is because I'm in Nashville."

"Nashville?"

"You said you'd listen....I've just been through one of the most frantic days I've ever had. I'm sorry I didn't call, but it was impossible. Well, maybe not impossible, but difficult and I didn't. You have to trust me. I'm not sure why I'm here. Bernie sent me. Just handed me a package to give to Don; told me to pack for a week; that my tickets were at the airport. I don't know what's going on. I have a meeting with Don and Jamie in the morning, and I guess I'll find out then; but that's all I can tell you right now." She wanted to tell him more, everything she knew, which was little enough, but Bernie had been adamant.

"That doesn't ease my nerves much."

"Bernie assured me everything would be fine, just some changes in the company structure." It was the only thing she could think of to allay his fears. Even that small bending of the truth brought regret. "It won't affect the record."

"Do you think that's my main concern, Kate?"

"I don't know."

"It's not...Why didn't you call when you got to the hotel?"

"My plane was late. When Don picked me up at the airport, he had been waiting for over an hour. We stopped and had a bite to eat. I thought I might be able to find out something to tell you, but he didn't even open the package. I guess he knew what was in it. He told me I'd know everything tomorrow, not to worry. I don't know what to say, John Ryan. I tried your hotel once. The line was busy and I fell asleep. I'm sorry."

There was silence on the line. Two minds searching desperately for a direction to proceed from where they were. John Ryan didn't know what to think. Several times since that session on Hendrickson's terrace, he had felt naive and confused about the nature of the business. He thought he was getting a handle on things, but this conversation was making him feel that way again. He imagined Kate with the phone pressed to her ear, a questioning look on her face.

"It's okay," he said. "I don't understand it, but it's okay. Right now my mind is about as bent as a Bonsai tree." Kate laughed at the line and felt easier. "You're in Nashville?" he said as if he still couldn't believe it.

"And glad to be."

"Sounds like you're gettin' used to it."

"I'd like to." If he only knew, she thought. "How's the new man?" she asked, again trying to change the direction of the conversation.

"Remy Soileau. I don't know how to describe him. He's...unusual." He chuckled at the adjective. "Right out of the swamp. American Primitive with a Cajun accent. And he can play harmonica like nobody I ever heard. Kate, he knew what we were gonna do before we did it. We would start playin' a song, and within a few measures, he was right in there with us. It's uncanny."

"I'm glad....Do you trust me?"

"I guess at this point, I don't have much choice."

"I'm glad about that too," she said.

"Are you crying?"

"Not yet, but I might if I don't get off the phone."

"Call me after the meeting. Leave a message if I'm not there. Rehearsal's at eleven; should be over by four. Kate, if I don't hear from you, I'm gonna come to Nashville."

"I'll bet you would."

"Bet on it. I love you, Kate Belden," he said. And in a firm tone, "Don't ever do this to me again."

"I promise."

When he hung up the phone, John Ryan's mind was in turmoil. One step at a time, he told himself. One thing at a time.

———————

Don Hendrickson was overwhelmed by what Bernie Greshem had told him on the telephone and even more by what was in the package Kate Belden had delivered; however, he had long ago ceased to be surprised by the machinations and maneuverings he witnessed in the business. Bernie had at once presented him with the greatest opportunity and the biggest gamble he had ever faced. Although his indomitable spirit and 'truth or dare' attitude had prompted him to give the senior Greshem a positive answer, he had done some serious reconsidering since the call.

There was his financial position. Though it was strong and relatively secure, it was far from being assured in the face of disaster. What Bernie proposed made disaster a distinct possibility. There was also the inevitability of a much greater work-load, which would not sit well with Sylvia. She had stuck with him through thin, but he knew she wasn't anxious to visit that country again. He also thought about Jamie, John Ryan and Kate. From what Bernie had said, their whole future depended on this deal and he, Don Hendrickson, was the fulcrum upon which everything rested.

At nine o'clock Tuesday morning, Jamie Greshem, face flushed and with a look more than concern, walked into the vice-president's office.

"What's going on, Don? There was a message on my machine this morning from my father saying to be here at nine sharp. I don't know why he didn't call me at the apartment; from the tone of his voice, it sounded ominous."

"Just another day in the ward," Hendrickson said with a double-edged smile. He took measure of the young man who sat before him and felt like an old man getting ready to do something he needed to be twenty-something to do. "Have a seat. We've got a lot of ground to cover. Is that all he said?"

"And that I wouldn't be able to reach him for several days; he'd get in touch with me and not to worry. He's never said not to worry to me in my whole life. He sounded different."

"Okay. I'll try to explain what I know, which I am sure is not everything. Jamie, you know your father as a man better than I do, but I know him as a businessman better than you. I trust him, and you need to. I just had to say that before you hear all the weirdness I'm gonna be layin' on you. This is as new to me as it is to you. I got a call from him yesterday. I was rollin' along thinkin' everything was goin' smoothly, had my mind on a couple of other company projects when I got his call."

"You want to get to the point, Don?"

"The point. The point is that evidently—and I don't know all the details—Philip Barnessa's people have decided to take control of the company." He paused. "By whatever means are necessary."

"Trayhorn?"

"Accordin' to Bernie, Barnessa barged into his office a few days ago, threatened him and you, and demanded a piece of ownership in Stone. Havin' John Ryan could mean a lot of money, but an artist is a temporary item, a—what do you call it?" He thought for a moment. "A consumable. They'll use him and throw him away the day he stops makin' money and then sue him for all he's got saved, claiming unpaid production and promotion costs. You know the routine. The second wave will be Maury Friedman, and he'll want control of the company, he'll say, just to prevent that from happenin' or worse. John Ryan is just the free toaster at the bank."

"Good Lord, I can't believe this. So what's he going to do? Can he save it? The company is his whole life." Jamie Greshem was worried about his father, but he was also afraid for himself and his project. He was wise enough to know that he didn't have the knowledge or maybe the courage to stand up to those people. It was more than he could comprehend.

"The answer to your second question is 'no'. He thinks it's a losin' battle. Maybe it could be postponed, but sooner or later they'd get what they want or ruin it for anybody else. They take pride in that too. However, your daddy has come up with the damnedest idea I ever heard of and he's willin' to finance it. It could possibly bail us all out. In fact if it works, the music business will never have seen anything like it. Guaranteed to be another Nashville legend."

Jamie looked at Hendrickson. "What do we have to do? What's he going to do? I'm not leaving him hanging out to dry. John Ryan, the record, I'm not saying that's not important, but...."

"Hold on, podna, I don't think Bernie Greshem's gonna leave himself hangin' in the wind. I sure as hell don't know all the details legally, but Bernie didn't get where he was by makin' mistakes." Hendrickson took a deep breath. "The first thing he's gonna do is resign from the company. That's not all. You and I are going to resign too."

"Don..... What happens to...."

"John Ryan? The record? We—you and I—own it all. It's brilliant if it works."

"Explain it to me."

"As you know, Bernie has final approval on every Trayhorn contract before it's signed. He can put in, take out whatever he wants. There's a clause in a lot of contracts that is totally overlooked by anyone who doesn't deal with artist contracts on a day to day basis. It's worded very peculiarly, but what it says in essence is that the company has the right to sell an artist's contract with all its ancillary agreements to anyone they wish. It's actually a protective clause for the company in a twisted sort of way." Jamie's face was blank. "Say an artist is signed to a three-record deal, and the first one doesn't make it. Now the company could and many times does just ignore their obligation. Most new artists don't have the money or knowledge to fight them, so they just hang on hopin' that someday they'll get back in the studio. On the other hand, there are some performers who have managers who think they're smart to sue. If that happens, the company can sell the contract to a bogus company that immediately goes belly-up, relieving them of any financial responsibility. Lawyers will tell you it can't be done, but then they say that about a lot of things. Nobody, including lawyers and yours truly, understands this business."

"Good God."

"Son, there's tales I could tell you that'd make that little deal look no worse than stealin' Cheez-its at recess. That's the clause Bernie's usin'. He's sellin' John Ryan's contract and all it's ancillary rights, the Cross Country label and the product to us. He's the only one with the power to do it, and he doesn't have to have anybody else's approval.

"Which is why we have to resign. Conflict."

"That's the idea. Setting up our own company is already taken care of. We'll do our own distribution."

"This is absolutely the most bizarre idea I've ever heard. How are we going to distribute? Put 'em in the back of pick-up trucks and deliver 'em?"

"Bernie said he has a distributor all lined up."

"They're not going to let him get away with it, Don. God knows they might..."

"He knows that. Says he's got it covered. He told me not to worry, too, Jamie. I don't know what else we can do. Right now, if you're agreeable, we got some documents to sign and get back to him."

"Where?"

"He's got a post office box."

For a moment Jamie Greshem looked as if he might fall apart, but Hendrickson saw the muscles in his face tighten. He was gritting his teeth and that was a good sign as far as he was concerned. "What's goin' on in that head of yours?" he asked.

"I'm angry as hell. Why should we have to give up everything for...." Don Hendrickson held up his hand.

"Hey, just hold on, hoss. I've got to say this because in doin' what we're gonna be doin' or not doin', we got to be realistic. Above all, as far as I'm concerned, we have to be honest with each other. I won't do it under any other circumstances. I can survive—live well in fact—without this company or John Ryan Stone or any of it. I can go sit on my terrace and watch the 'purdy flars' grow. At this stage of my life my adventures don't have to be quite so thrilling or rewarding as they once did.

"You may not want to hear this, but I'm not goin' into business with somebody who hides from the truth, doesn't know the truth or denies the truth to himself. I don't know how much you been told and maybe it's not my business to tell you, but I'm gonna. We got to get started on the right foot or we don't start at all.

"Your daddy built Trayhorn from a two-bit business that wasn't much more than a recording booth like you find at an amusement park. 'Pay three dollars and make a record for your loved ones'. He took that little business, which was owned by some less-than-respectable and somewhat crooked people, and created the company that it is now. Now to do that in most any business, but particularly in a business like this one, you have to be a hustler and you have to deal with people like Barnessa and Giannini Tedesco.

"What you have to understand and accept is that Bernie knew exactly what he was doin' when he got involved with them. It was that or never realize the dream he had. Despite what the civilians might think, he didn't have an option. He also knew the day would come when they weren't satisfied to just lick the fudge off the spoon; they'd want to lick the pan and take the candy home with them. He used them; they used him. It's amazin' he's kept them out this long.

"The point is this is not somethin' he didn't expect, and from what he said to me, he's ready for it. What he does want to do is protect you and me and everybody else around him and himself at the same time. He might just be able to pull it off."

The paperwork was not complex as far as what they had to do; the creation of it, however, was a maze that even Jamie had difficulty understanding. Bernie had sent a predated resignation letter for both of them. He included an agreement forming a partnership between his son and Don Hendrickson. There was also a document turning over to that partnership a small corporation, The Cotton Corporation, he had formed in his grandmother's maiden name when he was just beginning to build Trayhorn. He had chosen that name because his great grandfather had changed his name to Cotton to avoid being recognized as Jewish—a holdover from Nazi Germany. It was a tree of ownership so intricate that it was virtually impossible to determine that Bernie Greshem was the sole proprietor.

There was also a distribution agreement with Mini-Corp Distribution, a small company Bernie had bought into with cash and an agreement to distribute Cross Country records. The last document was a copy of an Agreement of Sale between Trayhorn International and The Cotton Corporation for the contract, masters, label, product and all rights pertaining to John Ryan Stone.

Jamie Greshem's jaw dropped when he read the Agreement of Sale and saw that they were paying five hundred thousand dollars to Trayhorn International for their part of the package.

"Don, this price...."

"Bernie put up two-fifty and I'm puttin' up two-fifty. Hey, son, I've always said, 'If you're afraid of the train, you shouldn't be on the track.' I'm not afraid of this train or I wouldn't be doin' it." He handed Jamie a pen. "We've done enough talkin'. You ready to go into business?" The was a broad smile on his face.

By the time Kate Belden arrived, the two new partners had completed the signing of the documents and sent them on their way to New York.

"Well, you ready for the adventure?" Don Hendrickson asked as he greeted her.

"I'm still dizzy from the last twenty-four hours, but I'm ready to listen. I'm still basically in the dark."

Jamie gave her a hug, and they all sat down to enlighten her, go over what had transpired, decide the part each of them would play and what they had to do.

Don Hendrickson and Jamie would share the production-end duties of their new partnership whose only asset was John Ryan Stone. They would assist Kate in organizing an agency and management arm. Jamie, in cooperation with Don's personal attorney, would handle the legal aspects of the company, and the new ex-vice-president would act as president with Jamie sharing equal decision-making authority.

When everyone was in agreement as to their job descriptions, Jamie suddenly got a shocked expression on his face.

"I just had a fleeting thought," he said. "It might not be important, but it is worth mentioning. We have been sitting here talking about this company we now own, that you and my father paid a half a million dollars for, without considering the fact that we don't have one operating dollar to work with." Kate's face fell, and they both looked at the man behind the desk. His head dropped, and then he looked up with a mischievous look.

"How much ya'll got in your savin's accounts?" They looked stunned. Hendrickson laughed. "There is one little insignificant detail I forgot to mention to either of you. The Cotton Corporation has assets in excess of two million dollars. Now, as a matter of trust, the value of those assets still belong to Bernie, but legally they go with the corporation; consequently, we can, with a phone call, get a line of credit for whatever we need." He laughed again. "Damn! I wish all the problems we're gonna have were as easy to solve as that one. Come on now. Smile. We're in business. And I think we need a drink to celebrate." He went to small liquor cabinet and pulled out a bottle of bourbon.

"Isn't it a little bit early?" Jamie asked. "It's only eleven-thirty."

"Gotta be five o'clock somewhere," he answered with a grin.

"I shudder to bring this up, guys," Kate said, "but what about John Ryan? Shouldn't he be informed about all this?"

"I was gonna come to that," Hendrickson said as he poured the drinks. "Yes. He has to know, and he has to know why." His tone was serious. "I told Jamie, we have to be truthful and honest with each other. I'm not such an idealist that I believe we can or will be totally honest with everybody else, but I'll never knowingly lie to an artist or someone who is being straight with me. I hope you two will respect that policy. So now that the first

251

presidential edict is out of the way, does anyone have any idea how we can explain all this without scaring the bejesus out of him?"

"I can do it," Kate said, not knowing how she would do it. "But I think I should do it face to face. I can go to Charlotte."

"Damn! They're already asking for expense money," Don joked.

"I can cover it," Kate shot back with amusement. "The company can reimburse me."

"God, I love bein' at the bottom with so much space above me. Gives me someplace to go." He turned to Kate. "We'll be operatin' out of Jamie's apartment and my home for a few days until I can find us some office space. We're both gonna be off Trayhorn land before sundown."

"I've got to find a place to live and get my stuff shipped down," she said.

"Ain't it fun?" Hendrickson was at the top of his game, giggly with joy. "When do you want to leave for Charlotte?"

"As soon as I can get a flight; I didn't even unpack last night"

"That's good." Don Hendrickson raised his glass. "We gonna kick ass and cut grass, chillun'."

Jamie Greshem's thoughts were divided between the joy of what he was a part of and worry for his father. He wouldn't rest until he knew that the man hadn't fooled himself into thinking that he 'had it covered'.

Kate Belden was anxious about seeing John Ryan and laying this all out before him. She hoped the flight would allow her the time to put her thoughts together and determine exactly what she would say.

While Kate was arranging a flight, leaving a message at John Ryan's hotel in Charlotte, and getting to the airport, Hendrickson was waiting for a prearranged call from Bernie Greshem. It came at three-thirty. Hendrickson informed him that all had gone well in the meeting with Jamie and Kate and that he had good feelings about the whole project. Bernie was pleased at his optimism and thanked him. He also told his friend that a body identified as Philip Barnessa a.k.a. Philly B. was found in a remote area in the Pinelands near Blue Anchor, New Jersey, and that he would be out of touch until Monday.

The news about Barnessa left Hendrickson shaken, but Bernie assured him that he was safe and so were all of the others involved. It didn't assuage his concern, but it was too late to turn back.

It was only the second day of rehearsal, but John Ryan Stone knew the music was there. Remy Soileau was adding new life to pieces that had remained common with Paul Crockett, and on those numbers in which the harmonica was featured, Soileau soared. Beyond the music that came out of his instrument, his appearance, vitality and movement gave the band a different personality, one of vigor, energy and visible comradeship.

Soileau was on the stand harping by himself. As John Ryan moved toward the stand, he heard the harmonica player make the instrument talk, doing a very credible job of saying 'Good morning, John Ryan Stone'. John Ryan stopped dead and bowed his head in good-natured homage.

At rehearsal the band looked more like a group of brick layers on a lunch break than a band of professional musicians. The songs went well. Soileau, for all his untethered creativity, was a perfectionist, asking that every number be repeated until he knew what each of the other players was doing. He fit his music into it, shining when it had to shine and falling in line when it had to be a part of the whole. He knew his place.

The band rehearsed for three hours and broke an hour for lunch. John Ryan called the hotel, but there were no messages. He was having a difficult time concentrating on the music with everything else in a mysterious state of flux.

It was six o'clock by the time he got back to the hotel. Now, reading the message Kate had left for him, the angst that had possessed him the night before came back. The fact that she would be in Charlotte, in his arms, in his bed on this night lifted his spirits to unreasonable heights; that she had been sent from New York to Nashville to Charlotte for no reason that he knew, brought those same spirits back to earth.

"This is getting to be a habit," he said as she walked though the gate. "I hope you consider it a good one," she replied with a smile as he took her in his arms. He held her tightly, squeezing as if he wanted to pull her inside his body. He kissed her, oblivious to the people moving around them.

"I love you," she said.

"I'm glad, but it does seem like you're beginnin' to chase me." Kate Belden grimaced.

"Were you totally flabbergasted that I was coming?" They were moving toward the baggage area.

"Flabbergasted, surprised, scared, amazed and frightened."

"Me, too."

"Want to tell me?" He tried to sound calm.

"Yes, but first I want to have a hot bath and order dinner for two from room service." Kate knew he was confused and anxious, but the flight had not provided her with the words to explain all that was going on. "Have you eaten?"

"Would it matter?"

"No. If you're not hungry, you can pick and I'll eat."

Kate stopped in the middle of the concourse and turned to face him. "John Ryan, a lot—more than you can imagine—is going on, and I'll tell you everything I know, but not in the airport and not until we've both had a chance to calm down and put our heads back on straight."

"That might be difficult," he said, sounding perturbed.

"Don't be angry. I promise you'll know everything. Just trust me."

"You say that a lot."

"I think when you've heard everything, you'll be very happy. Okay? Can we leave it at that for an hour or so, take a time out and be happy with the surprise of being together?"

Hendrickson had made a reservation for her at the Governor's House, upscale and far removed from where the band was housed. The suite was lovely. Kate couldn't help wondering if it was the last of the high-class perks she would enjoy now that she was with a new and struggling company.

John Ryan was patient and let Kate lead the conversation throughout dinner. It wasn't until they were having brandy that she began to unravel the labyrinth of all that had occurred and was happening even as they talked. She had been right. After the shock of the resignations, the sale of his contract and the founding of a new company, he was pleased that his career was not being directed by a bunch of suits in New York. He felt even better that Philip Barnessa's people, who were more involved than he had ever suspected, were seemingly out of the picture.

Two things did bother him: the insecurity of a new company having to sustain itself with him as the only product and how Bernie Greshem would extricate himself from the problems at Trayhorn.

Kate watched as he sat silently digesting what he had been told. She wished she were inside his head, privy to the thoughts that resided there. Her foundation was no less shaken than his. He just had more to lose.

"A penny," she said.

"Lord, I wouldn't know where to begin. I guess we just changed trains. I'll have to see where this one is headed."

"It's a better train that we were riding; I'm sure of that. New York has been crazy for months, everybody walking on eggshells, no one knowing what anyone else was doing. I've felt guilty because I've tried to be positive with you when I wasn't positive myself."

"I appreciate that. It's been hard not to get discouraged. Guess that sounds pretty ungrateful considerin' all that's been happenin'. Hell, look where I was when all this started? Problem is I started projectin', dreamin' the big dream, gettin' carried along, high on gigs, bein' brought back down by the lapses and postponements; it's given me somethin' to think about. Now this...."

"You've told me you take things one step at a time...."

"I try, but I'm not really sure."

"Of what?"

"If it's really what I want or maybe if I'm too lazy to go after it, not willin' to pay the price. You'll think I'm crazy, but I still think about the old dream: just makin' a livin' writin' songs. I still think that's the best of all possible worlds." He looked at her and smiled. "Pretty romantic, huh?" Kate didn't say anything. "Does that disappoint you?"

"I was just thinking that I've never met anyone else like you in this business, someone not driven by ego or money or whatever."

"What I said doesn't mean I want to be poor. Don't give me too many virtues."

"I wouldn't love you if you had too many. Can we put all this deep thinking aside and go to bed? Shameless hussy, huh?"

"Shameless." He stood up and held out his hand.

"I'll take the glasses," she said. "You bring the bottle."

A mischievous grin formed on his lips. "Lay on, MacDuff and damned be he who cries 'Hold enough.'"

Don Hendrickson called at ten o'clock on Wednesday morning. Kate was still in bed, but John Ryan had already made coffee and ordered breakfast. After he assured his new boss that Kate had done her job in explaining how everyone's life had been turned upside down, Hendrickson dropped the Barnessa story on him.

The visit by Barnessa's man was now irrelevant. If pressure came again, it would come from a different direction far more serious than John Barnessa. There was no reason to tell Kate or anyone else. With what Kate had told him, everyone had enough to think about without that.

The news was a shock and another unfamiliar reality, another negative on what seemed to be becoming an endless list. Alone, he might have packed it all in, gone back to The Farm and picked up where he had left off or chosen another path altogether. Now, however, there was Kate. There were also Jamie, Hendrickson, Mickey, the band, Cade Wilhite and Larry Foster. Sipping his coffee, he wondered if he could carry the weight of it all. He believed he could.

As soon as Philip Barnessa's death was confirmed and the warehouse in Jersey destroyed, Maury Friedman began preparations for his takeover. It wouldn't happen overnight, but, in his mind, the outcome was assured. According to Barbara Allred, Greshem was out of town until Friday, which he considered fortunate. He wanted to set things in motion and he wanted no surprises. Bernie's absence would facilitate that.

Maury Friedman had access to every document stored in the Legal Department; however, he also knew that Greshem had a safe in his office. There was no way to guess what might be in there, if anything, but the fact that he had no access bothered him. Any breach of security in Bernie's private domain would tip his hand, and he didn't want to fuel suspicion until he faced him. His confidence rested in the fact that he had seen the contracts, that there was nothing to prevent Bernie from turning over control of what everyone seemed to think was Trayhorn's most viable product.

Barnessa had said that Bernie was already intimidated by his threats, and his sudden absence from the office for no apparent reason seemed a classic case of avoidance. It was a screwy business that so much importance could hang on the success of a hillbilly. This game would be played by 'Maury's Rules', he said to himself with anticipation of the blind side Bernie Greshem was facing when he got back.

Don Hendrickson was not afraid of starting over. Sam Phillips in Memphis and Norman Petty out in little Clovis, New Mexico, had started at the bottom with little more than debt and dreams, and they had come up with Elvis and Buddy Holly. In comparison, he was starting at the top. He had an artist worth the risk, a superior product, an organization, years of experience, knowledge and contacts—all at the highest level—and some money. And they were clean. There was nothing to be afraid of except his own failure, and in thirty-five years he had never considered that a possibility.

From the moment he agreed to be a part of Bernie Greshem's future, he had begun to form a plan of action and get it rolling. The beauty of it was he didn't need anybody's approval. The dates in Charlotte and Danville would provide a solid warm-up for the state fair in Raleigh, and, according to Bernie, the product had already been shipped under the Cotton Corporation agreement with Minicorp Distribution, a company whose well-insulated director was one Bernie Greshem. John Ryan Stone's album would be in stores by the time the band hit Danville.

At ten o'clock Thursday night the band completed their final rehearsal. It had been a grueling week, more complex and emotional than anything John Ryan could remember. The few hours with Kate had been a welcome respite, yet he had been relieved when she boarded the plane to return to Nashville. He needed time for the music and time for thought. He managed to put the organizational changes of the business end of his career aside and leave that to those who knew what they were doing. The recent revelations redefined his concept of the term 'babe in the woods'. He trusted those people, and trust—wise or unwise—allowed him latitude to confront those things he alone had to face.

His relationship with Kate was approaching necessity. She seemed to have an intuitive sense of what he needed and managed to provide the right mixture of ingredients—respect, love, sex, humor, admiration and intelligence—to keep him stable. In the last week he had come to the admission that he needed her as much as he needed the music. He also realized that the music would be easier to replace.

Bernie Greshem arrived at his office at six-thirty on Friday morning. He expected a showdown and he wanted Maury Friedman to find him waiting, not the reverse. It was to be his scenario to play out, not Friedman's or anyone else's. In the three days since he dropped out of sight, everything he needed to accomplish had been done. All the necessary documents had been legally executed and registered, and his life after Trayhorn had been arranged. He was ready for whatever Maury Friedman had to throw at him.

His office looked more like that of the senior partner in a prestigious law firm than that of a man who, on a regular basis, dealt with uneducated, long-haired rock musicians and other outrageous industry types. The office breathed power and stability. It was designed to intimidate, and he had watched it work successfully on many people over the years. He went to the bookcase, removed a small, red volume and placed it on his desk. It was a book he had used extensively as a guide in planning and corporate negotiating. He placed it so that the title faced the visitor's chair and could be easily read. *The Art of War* by Sun Tzu. The implication was evident.

At seven-fifteen there was a knock at the office door. Greshem opened it and admitted two well-dressed and stern-faced men who, after a brief conversation with him, were led to the small private apartment that adjoined the office. Bernie Greshem closed the door behind them. The last piece was in place. There was nothing left to do but wait. He didn't have long.

When the phone rang, there was no doubt in his mind who was calling.

"Good morning, Maury," he said pleasantly. There was a moment of silence before the stunned caller responded. One point for me, Bernie thought as he waited. The caller cleared his throat and tried to sound casual.

"Bernie. You're finally back. I thought I'd try early and maybe catch you."

Maury Friedman had seen his car in the parking lot and was distressed that Greshem had arrived first. "Someday you'll have to explain how you knew it was me." He chuckled uncomfortably. "Listen, several things have come up that I need your input on. Could you possibly stop by my office and give me some advice?" Play the game on your home turf, Maury thought, but at all costs get the game played.

"I'm afraid not, Maury. I'll be leaving again in an hour or so, and I have some things of my own to care of. Why don't you just bring what you'd like me to look over and come to my office. We can talk while I attend to these odds and ends. You know how things pile up when you're out." He knew it was the last thing Maury wanted to do, but he had left him no choice. Point two.

"Yes...uh...okay, Bernie. Yes, I can do that. I'll be there in a few minutes. I don't think what I have will take long. It's basically cut and dried." As soon as the words were out of his mouth, he felt stupid. If it was that simple, why did he need Greshem's input? Stupidity made him angry, and, as Jimmy Hoffa said: "When you begin to get angry, you forget to think." He had to calm down and get himself together before he went to the president's office.

Bernie was sitting at his desk having a cup of coffee and making idle notes when the knock came. It wasn't yet eight o'clock, so neither Barbara Allred nor any of the secretaries were in.

"Come in," he said, and Maury Friedman opened the door. Bernie Greshem did not rise, nor did he look up from what he was doing. He gestured toward the visitor's chair.

"Have a seat, Maury. Tell me what's on your mind."

Hit him right from the top, Maury thought. "I assume you've heard about Philip."

"Yes, I did." Unperturbed. "What do you know about it?"

"Not much. What do you think?" Maury asked. Greshem looked up at him for the first time since he'd had entered the office. He caught his eyes dead-on.

"I would imagine he got out of line or didn't produce or he in some other way offended Giannini Tedesco." Point three. He wondered if it were going to be a shutout. Friedman was clearly thrown by his statement. The don's name was never mentioned in the building and to accuse him openly was beyond belief.

"Living a little dangerously, aren't you, Bernie?" Start the probe, remind him who he's talking to.

"I don't think so, Maury. Now what did you want to see me about?" Maury Friedman stared at him. The man's stupidity was hard to fathom. He could not write it off as confidence.

"John Ryan Stone." Cut the warm-ups; get to the game.

"Maury, again I ask: What can I do for you?" Greshem was back at his notes, not looking up. Unflustered. Making his adversary feel juvenile and inferior. Don't do his work for him.

"Okay," Maury started, "you want to play it that way, that's the way we'll play it. You know why I'm here, and I know you know why I'm here. Philip came to see you a couple of weeks ago. I think he made it perfectly clear what you were expected to do. I haven't seen anything cross my desk that indicates you've administered any changes in the company's contractual agreements with Stone or your son. The album's due out in a week, I understand, and you're running out of time. We're very serious about this, Bernie. I think you remember what Philip said about the consequences. Know that they are a distinct possibility. Perhaps he should have listened to his own advice." For the first time the steely, gray eyes caught sight of the book on the desk. Friedman picked it up and put it back with disdain. "Bernie, you don't know what war is all about." He smiled.

Bernie Greshem put down the pen he was writing with and looked Friedman straight in the eyes.

"Look at me," he said. "And listen to me. I won."

"Won what?"

"The war." At the words a subtle smirk crossed Friedman's face.

"You want to explain that?"

"I'll be happy to. I'm not going to make any changes in John Ryan Stone's contract because Trayhorn no longer owns John Ryan Stone's contract. It's been sold, along with all copyrights, ancillary rights, product and the Cross Country record label." He saw Friedman getting ready to explode. "Before you say anything, Maury, there's nothing you can do about it. It's all legal. I have the authority and it's done." The color had drained from Maury Friedman's face.

"I'm going to save you some trouble, Maury, and tell you the whole story. It will save you some research, but I'm not sure you'll have time for that anyway. The whole package was sold to The Cotton Corporation, an independent production company that is—believe it or not—clean as a whistle. Also, to save you any further threats, I have resigned—legally and duly recorded—as president of Trayhorn International as have Jamie and Don Hendrickson, so in-house reprisals are no longer an option. That's about all I can tell you." Point four. "By the way, Maury, Trayhorn is yours for what it's worth. Do with it what you will." He turned his attention back to the papers on his desk.

"You're insane. You're a dead man, Bernie, so is your kid and Don Hendrickson. Tedesc..." He stopped short. His temper had overcome his caution. "It will be seen to; you can bet on it. You know the penalties. You know who you're dealing with. There's nowhere any of you can run. We'll be right behind you."

"You're wrong again." He paused and looked up. "Maury, you're having a bad day." Bernie Greshem smiled and called out. "Mr. Smith. Mr. Jones."

Maury turned as the door to the private apartment opened and the two men who had entered earlier stepped into the room.

"Maury Friedman, Mr. Smith and Mr. Jones," Greshem said as he stood up behind his desk. "The names are obviously not their own because of the nature of their work." A look of unbridled fear crossed Friedman's face and he began to shake.

"Bernie...."

"Not to worry. They're not here to do you any bodily harm. They work for the F.B.I., and their employers are very interested in hearing everything I know about Giannini Tedesco and his whole family. They want to hear about fraud, extortion, counterfeiting—yes, I know about Barnessa's deal with Hardtime Danny Steel—and about you, Maury. And I am going to tell them." Bernie held up his hand. "I know what you're thinking. 'We'll find you'. I don't think so. These men and their organization are creating an entirely new life for me. Bernie Greshem no longer exists, Maury.

"When I leave this office, you will never see me again. It's all over, and if you have any thought of harming Jamie or Don or anyone else involved with Cross Country Records or The Cotton Corporation, you'd better think twice. The F.B.I., the F.T.C., the F.C.C. and any other F you can think of will be watching like the proverbial hawk. I think the situation has reversed itself. There's nowhere you can hide. The worst of times and the worst of times, eh, Maury?" Maury was slumped in his chair not knowing who to be the most afraid of. Point Five.

Bernie pushed a file folder across his desk. "Here is the documentation of the sale and the three letters of resignation. You probably want to see them, though I doubt they'll be of any use to you." He picked up the book lying on the desk and handed it to his adversary. "You might want to read this. 'If you know your enemy and you know yourself, you will win one hundred of one hundred battles.' Know your enemy, Maury."

He walked out of the room with the two men leaving Maury Friedman alone and speechless.

66 It's over." The tone of Bernie Greshem's voice exuded a relieved finality. Don Hendrickson was sitting on the terrace of his home. It was a brilliant day. The call came earlier in the morning than he expected, but so many unexpected things had happened over the past few days he wasn't surprised.

"Do you want to tell me about it?"

The voice was businesslike. "I won't tell you the details because I can't. Suffice to say, Maury was shocked. He thought, as always, that he was in control of the situation, but he didn't expect what I laid on him. You would have enjoyed it. He has the goose for a very short time, but its egg-laying days are over. You don't have to worry about Trayhorn or any of those people, Don; they will be finished in a matter of days. Watch the *New York Times* and the trades; you'll read about it." Hendrickson wanted to say something, but he let Greshem go on.

"However, you know those people aren't done. Somebody will take their place, not at Trayhorn—the company is a dead issue or soon will be—but they will move into another company or begin one on their own. I don't have to tell you; you know how it works. Just watch your business back and keep it as clean as possible. Involving Cross Country or Cotton with their kind does not have to be the price of doing business, although the pressure will increase." He paused for a moment and then continued.

"Nashville is on the verge of breaking out, and you guys have a wide open field. I listened to Stone's album last night, all of it. He may or may not be the artist to lead it in the direction it's going, but I believe his songs will. If you don't make money with the singer, you will with his songs. After all, publishing is where the profits are.

"I've got to go now. Tell Jamie to relax and have fun. His mother and I are fine. You both have a box number and you have the emergency contact number. I can't say when either of you will hear from me, but it won't be long. Don't worry, for God's sake. I am more insulated and protected than I ever have been, believe me. And, Don, thank you."

"The mystery goes on, huh?" Hendrickson said.

"Just for a little while. You can tie up your loose ends at Trayhorn now and get to work. You and Jamie have a company to run. I'll be watching." Bernie Greshem hung up the phone.

Don Hendrickson wasn't worried; he was exhilarated. Today would be a beginning and an end. He went into the kitchen, grabbed Sylvia, gave her a hug and swung her around in a circle, lifting her feet off the floor.

"Don?" she said with a concerned laugh.

"I've got to go fight poverty, Mom. I'm off to the Crusades. Got wrongs to right and new countries to conquer. I'll call you this afternoon. Tonight we just might celebrate."

There was no guilt about leaving the company. Too much had happened over the last few months to sustain any allegiance, but there was concern about the people in the office. He didn't explain his actions to them, just told them he had resigned and that they would be contacted by the New York office shortly. He also suggested that the Nashville office of Trayhorn might be closing. In the meantime, business was to proceed as necessity required. He also wired New York advising them that the Nashville office would remain open and staffed until his replacement arrived. The wire was sent to the attention of Maury Friedman. With that last act, he left the building and Trayhorn International behind.

Walking to the new offices of Cross Country Records, just a few blocks away and out of the main traffic of Music Row, the past few days scrolled through his mind like a piece of film. He and Jamie had spent time looking for office space and come up with three rooms in a converted small house, had phones put in, gone shopping, bought inexpensive office furniture and file cabinets, installed a not-too sophisticated sound system, which Cade Wilhite would improve when the band returned to the city, and moved in what little they had. Don had one room, Jamie and Mary Louise—now the company secretary—the larger one, and Kate the other. The size of the individual offices didn't really matter; they could talk from one to the other without yelling.

By Wednesday afternoon Hendrickson was putting his own wheels on the road. The whole publicity and promotion campaign had to be handled delicately and fast because he wanted the record to enter the country market with crossover potential a forgone conclusion. He contacted everyone he knew associated with The Drake Organization to alert them of the new release. Bill Drake had made a heavy impact on the industry by formulating play-lists for radio stations who subscribed to his services. To get played on a 'Drake Station' assured play throughout most of his subscriber list, dependent upon area tastes and past histories. He also contacted Kal Rudman, whom he had known for years. Rudman wrote a column for the trades, which listed new releases that he gave a thumbs up or a thumbs down. The direction of his thumbs carried a lot of weight. Don Hendrickson was a longtime friend and the columnist loved off-the-wall picks.

By midday Thursday the ball had begun to roll. Kate Belden was back in Nashville picking up on promotion and publicity and working with Jamie on bookings beyond Raleigh. They had already made significant progress by being able to promise a record-release date and had even received some referrals from the Bubba Moultrie network. Hendrickson called in copy for ads in Charlotte, Danville and Raleigh announcing the performances and naming The Cotton Corporation as John Ryan's production company. Everyone was immersed in proprietary energy.

Kate gave a full report on John Ryan's reaction to the recent events as well as the progress of Remy Soileau's inclusion into the band. She assured them that there was nothing to worry about as far as the music was concerned and spent the rest of her day helping the two partners put some order in their workplace.

Jamie was having a difficult time dealing with the unavailability of his father even though he knew it was coming. The phone in the lavish apartment in which he was raised had been disconnected. He tried to call once after their last conversation, and when the operator spoke those words, reality hit him like a jackhammer. Don Hendrickson hoped that a report on the morning's conversation with Bernie would ease the stress the young man was feeling.

———•◦•———

Help me live this life I'm livin',
and leave the past where it belongs;
let me taste the world you're givin',
and put the promise in my songs.

The words toiled in John Ryan's head. They weren't right, but the thought was clear. Within one week he had been hit or graced with Kate's declaration of love, his realization that she had brought to life what he had been repressing in himself, Paul Crockett's death, Hendrickson's call about Philip Barnessa and the news from Nashville. It had been an emotional gauntlet. Looking at the crude beginnings of the lyric, he wasn't sure whether it was addressed to Kate or to God.

He put the guitar and pen down and stretched out on the motel room bed. His mind was not structured enough at the moment to write, yet the emotional weight within him demanded it. He had been there before—when he was trying to make up his mind to leave a saner life and move to Nashville and when Jenifer had left—but the weight this time was different. About Kate and his career, he was unable to take the one-step-at-a-time attitude.

He tried to lock down what it would be like to really succeed in the direction he was headed. It had never been a reality, more like watching a movie about someone else, guessing what would happen but not being affected if it didn't, and being able to walk out of the theater and leave it behind. Now opportunity and possibilities were staring him in the face. Everyone's future seemed to depend on him. He didn't allow himself to consider how hard they might be working for him to secure their own prospects.

Kate said she wasn't sure he wanted the life; she had no idea how close she was to the truth. He had seen Faron Young's entourage the day they met in Nashville. The people, the pace of the man, his asking where he had to go next and what time he had to be there had made John Ryan take a step backwards. The music was inside him, but the performer and the songwriter were two different people. At this moment, he thought he liked the songwriter better.

Thoughts of Faron Young asking where he was supposed to be and what time kept recurring to him. The man—no different than any other performer, he assumed—was a delivery boy, delivering a product that had been purchased, the product being himself, his body, his talent and his life. He couldn't help wondering how the music and the original impetus to create it could avoid getting lost in that kind of existence. The glory and the money could fade, but where did that leave the person? He berated himself for being too analytical and too idealistic.

It made obvious that most of his consternation was centered around the element of time, the essential question being how much time he needed for himself and his music, and how much time for Kate and for them.

None of the three sets at The Ranch House were what the band or John Ryan expected. Although Hendrickson's ads had run in the paper, the crowd was small and unresponsive. Regardless of the name, The Ranch House was more a 'singles bar' than a 'country' club. Everyone was too concerned with finding someone to spend the night with to be interested in what was going on onstage.

The music was good for a first night, stronger with the addition of Remy Soileau, but no matter what they did—including Cade Wilhite upping the volume—they weren't able to capture the crowd. There was appreciative applause; however, the night left the band and John Ryan empty and dreading the second night. There had been times—the second night in Biloxi and one in Florida—that were not satisfying, but on those occasions the music had not been good. On this night it was.

⸻

The fact that the audiences in Charlotte did not respond enthusiastically made Jamie Greshem nervous. It didn't appear to bother Hendrickson at all. 'A different kind of crowd,' he had told him. 'They didn't come to hear the music; they came to get laid. In Raleigh they're gonna come to hear the music, and John Ryan Stone is gonna blow their socks off. I got a feelin'.'

In Jamie's mind, John Ryan Stone, as a project, was not yet complete. It was all there, but the package hadn't been wrapped. All the stock was in place, the shelves filled, but the sign hadn't been lit and the doors opened for business. There needed to be one simple thing that would tie the ribbon on the package and open the doors. He looked at his watch. It was five-thirty. He picked up the phone and dialed Don Hendrickson.

"It's got to be Greshem," the sleepy voice said. "Nobody else is nervous enough to call me at what?" There was a pause while he looked at the clock. "Five-thirty in the mornin'."

"I guess you nailed me," Jamie said, chagrined.

"And what can I do for you at this ungodly hour, young fella?"

"I've been thinking...."

"I've been sleepin', but I guess if you've been thinkin', that means I have to, too."

"I'm sorry about the hour, but something's been bothering me. We've got a good artist, a good band, a good album, but I don't think it's finished yet. I don't know how to explain it. We lack something that puts us at a level to work with Faron Young at a state fair and create star credibility in the public's mind. I think we need something beyond the music to give John Ryan and the band that little push from average to exceptional."

"You're worried about 'em movin' from The Thunderbird in Danville to the big time in Raleigh? At five-thirty in the mornin'?"

"It's a pretty big jump," Jamie said.

"Not really. I hadn't planned on givin' a lecture on country music status at this hour, but it's not that big a jump. I know you wouldn't find some big rock and roll act playin' a small club, but country isn't like that. Hell, Conway Twitty was at The Thunderbird a few weeks ago. Those people know their music. They buy records and listen to the radio. They're opinionated, sometimes mean-drunk, sometimes they work and sometimes they don't, but they do listen to music, and they'll make a hero out of you if you let 'em. Don't worry about that little element that's missin', Jamie. I got it covered. Cost us a bit of money, but it's gonna be one helluva surprise. Now you get back to your worryin' and I'll get back to my sleepin'. I'll see you about nine. Okay?"

"Thanks, Don. I'm sorry I woke you."

"Hell, you expected to, didn't you? Hey, podna, I'm relaxed just knowin' you're doin' all the worryin'."

"I'll get right to it."

Everything the band felt they had lost in Charlotte came back in Danville. They took a day off and then spent three days of hard rehearsal in Charlotte before hitting the road. By the time they stepped onto the stage at The Thunderbird, John Ryan knew his assessment of the band's readiness was on the mark.

The Thunderbird was not much more than a huge Quonset hut on Route 58 just outside the city, but over six hundred people showed up to dance, yell their responses to the songs and have John Ryan Stone albums autographed. Hendrickson had made sure that Cleveland's Music Store was well supplied before the date. The radio had done the rest. It was the first time the band had seen the album in hand and even that seemed to raise enthusiasm that translated itself into the music. The excitement was back along with tight music and a spirited crowd.

In Nashville the week had passed nonstop. Kate, who was now staying with the Hendrickson's, found herself swamped with work. *Billboard* had selected *One Lonely Night* as a pick to watch. Kal Rudman gave it a good comment and suggested it as a possible crossover even though country music was seldom mentioned in his column. Suddenly Kate found herself not only handling agency with Jamie's help, but also taking orders and working with Minicorp Distribution on shipments. It was a whole new world.

Don Hendrickson was putting out feelers to manufacturers for additional pressings if they were needed. He had seen it all happen before—exciting, harried, illogical and unpredictable. He had only told Jamie Greshem that the missing element was covered; he still hadn't told him how.

J ohn Ryan Stone stood silently on the porch of the converted bunga-
low that housed Cross Country Records. There was a smile on his face
as he watched Kate Belden working the telephone. He had never seen her at
her desk before. She appeared so professional and focused that he could
imagine the intimidation the person on the other end of the line must feel.
Watching her work and knowing she was doing it in his behalf filled him
with pride.

When she hung up the phone, Kate looked up and caught him eyeing
her through the window. All of the professionalism and focus left her. A
wide grin broke across her face as she jumped from her seat and ran to the
door. He opened it and took her in his arms.

When they broke apart, Jamie and Mary Louise were standing at the
door of Jamie's office watching them.

"Don't let us interrupt," Jamie said.

"That's okay," John Ryan replied. "It's hard to capture lightnin' twice
in the same place. How are you, Jamie? Marie Louise."

"I really haven't had time to look and see," Jamie said. John Ryan and
Kate were still standing in the doorway, half in and half out. "Come on in.
Welcome to Cross Country Records, Nashville's newest independent."

"I think we got a little help," John Ryan said. Jamie Greshem's face
went serious. "Any news?"

"No. Nothing yet." He changed direction, controlling where his
thoughts were headed. "Don's out for awhile, but he wants you to be at the
bar at The King of the Road at five-thirty. Think you can make that?" Jamie
looked at his watch. "It's one now."

"What's he got in mind?"

"I have no idea. Just said for us all to be there. Said he would meet us
there and take us to dinner. I know he's got something up his sleeve. After

all, I wasn't born in a poke." He laughed and guided Mary Louise back into their office.

"Hey, when the boss speaks," John Ryan said after them. He turned to Kate. "I guess I'd better get movin'. I got about six inches of road grit to wash off before I'll be human."

"You look human to me," Kate said, "but I guess I'll find out for real later."

"Is that a promise?"

"You bet."

"Think I might be able to persuade a lady of quality such as yourself to spend the night at The Farm? I could see you to work in the mornin' if you're able."

"I was counting on it; I've already got my clothes in the car. Watch me work for twenty minutes and I'll go with you now. Look at these while you're waiting." Kate handed him the copies of *Billboard* and *Record World* that mentioned his song. "Page fifty-six in one; thirty-four in the other. I've just got to confirm a date in Wheeling, West Virginia. It's a big show."

John Ryan sat in the chair reading, still disbelieving.

After the drive to The Farm, showering together, making love, and driving back into the city, John Ryan and Kate found themselves entering the bar at The King of the Road. Hendrickson spotted them immediately and signaled them over to his table.

"Welcome home, son, it's good to have you back. He cleans up pretty good, don't you think, Kate? Ya'll sit down. I'll get us somethin' to drink." He was gone before John Ryan had time to say 'Hello'.

"Looks like a man on a mission."

"I have found since I've been a part of this new organization that Don is on a mission even when he is not on a mission," Kate said.

"Kinda guy I want on my side."

"And he is. He really believes in you. So do I for what it's worth."

"You know you did something on the way here that made me feel better than I've maybe ever felt," he said.

"What?"

"While I was driving, you put your arm on the back of my seat and rubbed the back of my neck. I don't think anyone's ever done that before."

"Then I'm glad. I'll remember."

"Please do."

Don Hendrickson came back to the table carrying three glasses filled with ice and bourbon.

"The product of good connections," he said. Before they had a chance to drink, Jamie and Mary Louise arrived. Hendrickson immediately procured two more drinks.

"To the first full gathering of our new family," Don Hendrickson said as he raised his glass. "Now we've got a big night ahead. Let's go to dinner. I'm drivin'." Jamie looked a bit somber, but was trying to join in the celebration.

"All of us?" Kate asked.

"You'll see," he said.

When they walked out of the motel, everyone except Hendrickson stopped dead in their tracks, jaws dropped, closed and dropped again. Don Hendrickson looked at their faces and smiled as if he would burst. Standing directly in front of the entrance was a gleaming silver and black bus with an airbrush painting of seven stallions coming out of a cloud of dust and the name JOHN RYAN STONE scrolled in bold black letters across it's length. It was as big as any bus John Ryan had ever seen; he was speechless. Wylie Nate was standing in the door-well laughing.

"Well, are we just gonna stand here or are we gonna look at your new toy?" Don asked.

"Helluva toy," John Ryan muttered. "Damn!" He turned to Kate. "Did you know anything about this?"

"Not a clue," she said, shaking her head and laughing.

The interior of the bus was as shocking as the vehicle itself. There was a lounge, complete with couches and a coffee table, a full kitchen and dining area, a small bunk area with four pull-down bunks and a shower, and, in the back, a master bedroom with a queen-size bed, a bath and vanity area. Everything sparkled. Music from John Ryan's album was emanating from speakers throughout the bus. It was luxurious.

"Good Lord, is this what you were talking about that cost a little money?" Jamie asked aghast.

"This is it, but don't panic; we just leased it for three months with an option to buy."

"How much?"

"Not enough to break us, but enough to get us noticed."

"I might even be willing to go on the road in this," Kate said.

"You don't have a choice," John Ryan commented. "Damn!" He had gone from one end of the bus to the other.

"Let's go to dinner, Wylie," Don said and the huge diesel began to roll. "Party time." He opened a cabinet door and a Lazy-Susan bar appeared. "I'm pourin'. John Ryan your music is as pretty as any I've ever heard, but if you don't mind, I think on this occasion we need somethin' a bit more rowdy." He slipped a new tape into the deck. "How about some Hank, Jr.?"

As the music changed pace, Hendrickson poured drinks and the talk and laughter commenced.

"By the way, Don, where are we going to dinner?" Kate asked.

"Hendrickson's by the lake," he yelled over the music.

"He was right," John Ryan said to Kate. "They sure as hell are gonna notice us."

Although it was not the largest house on the mountaintop on the island of Antigua, it ranked among the most elegant compounds of the rich; and it was, by far, the most secure. Surrounded by state-of-the-art surveillance apparatus, gated, with three former F.B.I. agents sharing round-the-clock shifts, the four bedroom mansion had a pool, a tennis court and a spectacular view of the Caribbean.

Standing on the verandah, looking out over the sea and sipping a very dry martini, Bernie Greshem anxiously awaited the agreed upon time to make his call. There was much he could say, but he would make it brief. Most of what Jamie and the others didn't know, they would be able to read in the newspapers in a few days. As a result of his depositions, Giannini Tedesco, Lou Molinaro, Franco Digiavanangelo and 'others to be named' had been arrested and charged with murder, extortion, arson, counterfeiting, racketeering and tax evasion. Maury Friedman and 'others to be named' were charged with extortion, conspiracy to commit murder, fraud, counterfeiting, racketeering and tax evasion.

That they would be out of the way if convicted and on very thin ice if they weren't was some consolation for Bernie Greshem and would hopefully ease Jamie's mind. Only Bernie knew that the vigilance could never stop because those people and counterparts who didn't even know them never forgot. It was too late to be concerned. All in all it's safer than living in New York under any conditions, he chuckled to himself as the sun dipped below the horizon leaving only a red stripe across the water.

He had arranged to call Hendrickson's house at eight o'clock. It was a difficult wait; he was anxious to talk to his son. He knew the boy was worried, but there had been no alternative. He wanted this call to assure Jamie of their safety and that they would be seeing him soon though he could not say how or where.

When the time came, he dialed a new private number at Don's house. It was a secure line installed at Bernie's instruction as part of his agreement with the government. The phone rang only three times before it was answered.

"We're all here," Hendrickson said when he picked up the phone. "How are you doin'?"

"We're fine. How's Jamie?"

"Worried, of course, but I think he'll be all right after you talk to him. You sure you all are okay?"

"Yes. Check the papers the next few days and watch the national news; I think you'll see some familiar faces."

"Really? Who?"

"All of them. I'm not sure how long any of them will be out of circulation; but, according to the F.B.I., even if they get minimums for what they're charged with, I will have lived an exceptionally full and pleasant life, and be dead and gone long before they're scheduled to get out if ever."

"Couldn't happen to a nicer group of people. Everything is goin' well here, but I'll let Jamie tell you about it."

"I'll call again the Monday after Raleigh. Same time."

"Good. Hold on."

When he called Jamie to the phone, Hendrickson didn't explain who was calling.

"Hello?"

"Jamie?"

"Dad?"

"It's good to hear that; I'm tired of Bernie."

"Where are you or shouldn't I ask? I...."

"No, you shouldn't. Not right now. I just want you to know that your mother and I are fine. We're comfortable, well-protected, and you have nothing to worry about except your business. It's all in front of you, son, and you've got a good man to guide you."

"I know, but I...."

"Just listen to me for right now. You'll be reading about what's going on with Maury and the rest of them, but try not to let it bother you. I will write you a letter very soon explaining everything I've done and will be doing, but know that we are happy, living a good, if somewhat restricted life for the moment and more safe than we ever were on Park Avenue. Trust me, Jamie."

"I do, but I have a lot of questions...."

"Not now. Tell me about Cross Country."

Jamie tried to be brief, sensing urgency though there was none. He tried to tell his father anything of importance he could think of—about the mentions in the trades, the bus, and the bookings that were beginning to come in. When he had said all he could say without asking questions, he was silent.

"It all sounds very good," his father said. "Just remember, I still have an interest, so I'll be here if you need me. Just let Don know; it's safer that way."

"I will."

"I love you, Jamie. I know that may be hard to understand after all these years, but it's the truth."

"I love you too."

"I'll call again soon. And don't worry."

Jamie felt a great weight lifted from his shoulders when he put the phone down. Bernie was a pragmatist; if there were danger, he would have said so or not called at all. He walked back into the living room with a smile on his face.

"Everybody ready to eat?" Hendrickson asked.

A State Fair in the South is a celebration. To some it is a big carnival with rides, cotton candy, greasy foods, freaks, wonders, and games of chance; to others a livestock and horse show as well as craft, pie-baking and quilting contests. Some people come only at night when the midway lights are bright or just for the fireworks displays; some come early in the morning when the chill is in the air, the dew still heavy on the brown trampled grass, and stay all day, soaking in the fair smells and atmosphere.

The biggest crowds turn out on the weekend evenings when the name entertainers come to perform. The *Raleigh News and Observer* projected a crowd of more than ten thousand people for The Faron Young Show, featuring newcomer, John Ryan Stone. The paper lay at John Ryan's feet as he sat on the bus, looking out at the people he could see milling about.

The band, as well as the producers, had insisted that John Ryan and Kate share the maiden voyage on the new vehicle. The band followed in the old bus and watched the reactions of people in the cars they passed. When they made their one stop, each of the musicians found an excuse to step aboard the bus to ask John Ryan or Kate a question. Son Cochran joked that the most common reaction he could read on the lips of the people they passed was: Who the hell is John Ryan Stone?

It was a fun trip. Kate and John Ryan easily adapted to the luxury and spent most of the time trying out all the amenities the bus offered, but the most exciting aspect of the trip was that they were together. On the road. As soon as they pulled into the fairgrounds, walked the midway, and had eaten a hot dog, Kate announced that she was going to freshen up. She was like a kid with a new toy and had to try everything out.

The bus was parked next to Faron's in back of the performance area, which was surrounded by huge banks of bleachers. As big as they looked, John Ryan could not imagine them holding ten thousand people. That number made his knees weak and his hands quiver. He wasn't sure this was going to be fun.

It was only four o'clock in the afternoon, and the only thing he had to do was go to the stage at four-thirty for a sound check. Cade Wilhite and Foster had been working with Young's roadies since early morning. It was four and a half hours until show time and John Ryan Stone didn't know what to do with himself.

"A penny," he heard Kate's voice. She was standing at the door of the bedroom. She had a towel wrapped around her and her hair was wet.

"That's not fair," he said. He got up and went to her, taking her in his arms. "For a penny or a dollar, right now, I couldn't tell you what's on my mind."

"Should I consider that an insult?"

"No. I just don't know what to think. It's here and I don't know what to do with it. I feel like we ought to go find a barn somewhere and practice one more time. I'm beginnin' to think music is tougher than farm labor."

"It is and always has been, but it's a lot more fun. She dropped the towel, smiled and turned into the bedroom. "Want to talk to me while I get dressed?"

"I'm afraid I'd miss my sound check."

"Another insult. Then why don't you go over and get that done. When you get back, maybe you can get some rest."

"You gonna wait till I get back to get dressed?"

"In your dreams, Stone."

John Ryan was surprised to find three teenaged girls and one well-worn young woman waiting outside the bus to have albums autographed. He talked to them briefly, signed the covers and headed toward the stage. No one else recognized him as he made his way through whirring generators and small utility trailers that were crowded out of sight behind the playing area. His heart was pounding.

Cade and Larry were waiting for him. It was obvious that they were as anxious as he was. Red, Cochran and Mickey were also there. The rest of the band had done their checks and gone off to enjoy the fair.

"Don and Jamie just pulled in," Cade said. "They've gone to get something to eat. Said they'd come by the bus when it was time."

"That's good but I might be asleep." Larry Foster didn't know whether to take John Ryan seriously or not. "Let's get on with it," the singer said.

People wandered into the area while they were working, listened to what they were doing and then moved on. Some sat in the bleachers and watched the whole process. As early as it was, there was already a feeling of anticipation and excitement in the air.

Kate was dressed casually in slacks and a sweater, sitting on a couch and having a drink when he got back to the bus.

"I'm glad you're back," she said. "Can I fix you a drink?"

"You could fix me about five, but then we might have a problem." He looked at his watch. "I guess it's still early enough. One." He sat down and looked at his watch again. It hadn't moved. "Jamie and Don are here; they'll be by at show time."

"Good. Would you rather rest or talk?" Kate wasn't sure how to handle the moment either.

"Why don't we do both," he said, taking his drink and leading her by the hand to the bedroom. He stretched out on his back and Kate lay on her side next to him. She brushed the hair from his face.

"Worried?" she asked.

"Not really. Nervous but not worried. Only one person has to approve of me and that's you."

"Thank you. I do, but I'm not sure at this point that would be enough. You've worked too hard."

"I've thought about that. I guess I had to grow up to find out what I didn't need. I don't think anything outside yourself can make you feel whole. Fame, sex, drugs, money. None of those can fill you up and I'm tired of runnin' on empty."

"And I do that for you?"

"You're a damn big part of it," he said. Kate leaned over and kissed him full on the mouth. There were tears in her eyes.

"You make me very happy, John Ryan Stone, but I can't imagine you're thinking about me at a time like this."

"Let me know when I don't. I sometimes get pretty wrapped up in me. I lost Jenifer a little bit at a time; she lost me the same way. We never knew. I won't let that happen again."

"It's not going to be easy. You're booked solid for three months, and the way it looks, you could have two hundred and fifty dates over the next twelve."

"Well, let's just take it as it comes and see what happens. Hell, you can be a fossil in this business in three months."

"Is that yours or somebody else's?"

"Somebody else's." He laughed and looked in her eyes. "You know I was thinking this morning, the look on your face when we make love is totally innocent, full of trust and wonder. It's different. I'd like to get that in a song someday."

"We'll have to work on it," she said with a smile. He closed his eyes, and she watched him as the alcohol began its relaxing effect.

At seven o'clock Kate laid out his clothes while he was in the shower. She chose the same outfit she had seen in Savannah: tailored jeans, the collarless ivory-colored shirt with epaulets, conch-shell belt and freshly shined boots. When she remembered how his appearance had affected her, she wondered if she was shooting herself in the foot. By seven-thirty he was dressed and waiting.

At a quarter of eight Son Cochran and Mountain Red stopped in to wish him luck. Mickey and Howie and Remy Soileau—their new companion—stopped by. Mickey and Howie were not touching the ground, and as much as he loved them, he was relieved when they left to head for the stage. Kate watched it all, glad they had come by to keep his mind busy.

At eight o'clock Faron Young stuck his head in the door. There was a broad smile on his small mouth.

"Leave somethin' for me out there, son. Do what I said. Have fun. They gonna love you. I heard that record. You got music, boy." And he was gone.

It was only a few minutes before they heard the announcer begin to warm up the crowd. Jamie Greshem and Don Hendrickson hadn't arrived. John Ryan didn't know whether to be surprised or concerned.

"Ladies and gentlemen," The announcer's voice said, "The John Ryan Stone Band." John Ryan's heart took a great leap as though it might jump out of his chest. The sound of the band beginning their intro songs doubled the pace. Just as the music began, Don Hendrickson and Jamie came on the bus.

"Well, hoss, I'm not gonna ask if you're ready cause you might answer me. Course if you ain't, you're in deep stuff." Hendrickson said with a laugh.

"There's a passel of people out there. You never saw a crowd like this and they're still comin' in, but don't let it scare you. It's beautiful. The moon is shinin' and you're gonna burn 'em up."

"Ditto," Jamie said. "I'm too nervous to talk. We might want to get started."

"Yeah. I'll be right out," John Ryan said. Jamie and Don got the message and stepped out the door. John Ryan took Kate in his arms.

"Well, I guess it's time to go out and conquer the world," he said.

She looked up into his eyes. "Suppose it doesn't want to be conquered?"

He kissed her lightly on the cheek. "I don't think that's really the most important thing."

He let her go and stepped out of the bus into a small group of people standing at the door. There was a mild reaction, but Kate didn't look. He suddenly reappeared in the door and took her in his arms, holding her so tightly that she almost lost her breath.

"Of all the things I ever do," he said, "this is for you. I love you, Kate Belden."

"Thank you," she said, tears welling in her eyes.

"Can I fall into your skin?"

She looked at him. "Think we can both fit?"

"Oh, yes. I do believe we can."

He was gone. She listened to the band through their numbers and heard the announcer's voice boom John Ryan's name at the segue into the *Ring of Fire* intro. There was a resounding roar from the crowd and she knew he was on stage. She left the bus and headed toward the performance area.

"Love is a burning thing,
And it makes a fiery ring."

'You are going to be big, John Ryan Stone,' she thought as she walked toward the stands, 'but you are right; that's not the most important thing.'